MURDER AT RAVEN'S EDGE

LOUISE MARLEY

Storm
PUBLISHING

Ebook ISBN: 978-1-80508-345-0
Paperback ISBN: 978-1-80508-347-4

Cover design: Ghost
Cover images: Shutterstock

Published by Storm Publishing.
For further information, visit:
www.stormpublishing.co

To my grandparents,
who gave me my first book of fairy tales

ONE

The village of Raven's Edge was surrounded by a dark, tangled forest. The kind of forest that evoked the wrong sort of fairy tale, where you should never stray far from the path. The trees here were ancient, gnarled and twisted, huddled together against the storm. Branches dipped to the ground with every lash of rain and the wind tore at their leaves, sending them spiralling high into the air as though it were November rather than June.

Rain fell thick and fast and hard. It hammered the roof of Ben's car and bounced off the road in front of him. Not that he could see the road. He could barely see further than the end of the car. There were no street lamps on this road, no houses and no other cars. No one else was stupid enough to be out on a night like this. He swerved around a fallen branch, crunched over another, saw a sign flash past in his headlights. It told him there were another five miles to Raven's Edge, but 'another five miles' felt like forever.

It was 1.00 am and he was desperate to get home. He'd had enough – of the vile weather, the never-ending journey, but most of all his ex-wife. He'd driven all the way to London with only enough of a break for them to fight, before he'd climbed straight back into the car and driven back. Now here he was, five miles from home without the sole reason he'd put himself through the visit in the first place – his six-year-old daughter, Sophie.

Lightning illuminated the sky, revealing a road strewn with debris. He slowed to 20mph, forcing his fingers to relax their death grip on the steering wheel. There would be other chances to see Sophie. In a month, it would be the school holidays and she'd be visiting him for two whole weeks. It would be great. They could go hiking in the forest and visit the castle at Norchester. He was making too much of this. He was lucky. It could be worse.

Really? Just *how* could it be worse? His ex-wife had cancelled this month's visit and was now threatening to take him back to court to review their custody arrangement, which would neatly take care of any future holidays. So, right at this very moment, how could his life *possibly* get any worse?

Another streak of lightning slashed the sky, revealing the miles of unbroken forest reaching down to the river, the almost horizontal rain that was threatening to turn into sleet – and the woman walking in the centre of the road.

It was one of those split-second moments that stretched out forever. He saw her terrified expression as her arms went up to protect herself. He saw her tense, awaiting the impact that would surely kill her. He hit the brakes and then he hit her.

The car went into a skid, sliding elegantly around as though on ice. He prayed the car would miss her; that she would intuitively throw herself out of harm's way, but she seemed to have frozen in shock. Then the wing caught her hip, knocking her off her feet and into the air before the darkness swallowed her whole. The forest blurred as the car spun through 180 degrees and then smashed back into a tree. The impact slammed him forward; his seatbelt jerked him back again.

Seconds passed. Ben took a deep breath and then another to reassure himself he was alive. The engine had stalled but the wiper blades slashed back and forth at speed. On the radio, Caro Emerald was singing about love and loss. The rain still ricocheted off the car, the road and the sodden lump of rags now huddled there.

Ben picked up his phone to call emergency services but the battery was dead. He'd driven to London and back without bothering to charge it. He'd driven to London and back without stopping at all, and here were the consequences: a dead phone and a dead body.

He undid his seat belt, shoved open the car door and practically fell out onto the tarmac as his legs gave way beneath him. The rain soaked through his suit in seconds. He couldn't have been more drenched if someone had upended a barrel of water over him. He did his best to disregard his shredded nerves as he walked out into the road, bent over the body and gently turned it over.

'Ahhh!' it said, and sat up.

He stepped back, his heart pounding so hard he thought it might burst right out of him. *She was alive!*

'You *hit* me!' she shrieked.

Very much alive.

'I'm sorry,' he said. 'It was an accident. You shouldn't have been—'

'*Bastard!*'

'Understandably, you're upset—'

'Upset? *Upset!* Of course I'm *upset!*'

'You were walking in the middle of the road!' Despite the rain, despite the dark, he could see her cheeks were streaked with mascara and she was shaking violently, either from cold or shock, he wasn't sure which. 'Are you in any pain?'

'What a stupid, b-bloody question! I've been hit by a car!

What do you think?' She held out her hand to him, as imperious as any duchess. 'Help me up...'

He took hold of her hand and hauled her up as she qualified that with, 'So I can punch you.'

This meant that he instinctively dropped her.

She was back on her feet in a second, aiming a furious punch in the direction of his stomach. It was easy enough to step back and avoid her, and to block the next blow she sent his way too.

Stoically, he caught hold of her flailing fist. 'Have you been drinking?'

What other reason could there be for walking in the middle of the road?

'What do you care?' she snapped back. 'You're not the police.'

'Well, um actually...'

She stared at him. '*Seriously?*'

'Seriously.'

'Perfect,' she muttered.

Any other time he might have found this exchange entertaining, but the rain was dripping off his eyelashes and the end of his nose. He was tired, miserable and thoroughly fed up.

Despite all this, he did feel sorry for her. 'Are you hurt in any way? Would you like me to take you to the hospital?'

It was a good twenty-minute drive in the opposite direction and, according to the radio, the road was now blocked by a fallen tree.

She appeared to consider this, looking him up and down, presumably trying to judge whether he was trustworthy. As she no longer appeared to be about to inflict grievous bodily harm on him, he released her.

'It's up to you,' he said.

She rubbed at her wrist, presumably to make him feel guilty. He hadn't held her *that* tightly.

'You could offer me a lift to the next village,' she said.

'You mean Calahurst?'

She shrugged. 'Whatever.'

She was soaking wet and filthy. The road back to Norchester was blocked by that tree and the road up ahead was likely to have been flooded out by one of the many tributaries that flowed into the River Hurst. They weren't going to get anywhere near Calahurst tonight. That meant being trapped in the car with her until it was cleared – it could take hours – or taking her back to his house. He could hardly leave her out in a storm like this. He wouldn't even leave his ex-wife out in a storm like this.

OK, possibly he might.

'Give me a minute,' he said. 'I need to fetch something to protect the inside of my car.' He'd bought plants for his garden the weekend before and had lined the interior of the boot with plastic to keep it clean. He could put that on the front passenger seat.

He had enough time to see her mouth the words 'Protect the *car?*' before he walked around to the rear, which was firmly wedged up against a tree.

He swore again. He hadn't realised the damage was so bad. The bumper was split; one set of lights had smashed and the boot was squashed in. The exhaust, fortunately, was on the opposite side and undamaged.

Now it hardly seemed worth worrying about a bit of mud, but when he went back to tell her the good news she'd vanished.

He looked up and down the road. She might have been a complete pain in the proverbial, but he felt responsible for her and—

Distracted by a knocking sound, barely discernible above the howling wind, he turned his head towards the car – and saw her sitting in the passenger seat.

She mouthed the words: 'What are you *doing?*'

Good question. What *was* he doing?

He got into the car and slammed the door against the storm, leaving them in a warm cocoon of silence.

'What took you so long?' she said. 'Didn't you think you were wet enough?'

Unable to trust himself to speak, he turned the key in the ignition. The car started without any trouble, although the exhaust rattled a bit. The radio sprang into life; now it was playing an old jazz classic, one of his favourites. He felt some of his tension ebb away.

'Well, this is rubbish,' she said, promptly flicking through the radio stations until his car vibrated to the thud, thud, thud of mindless dance music.

Finally, Ben thought, grinding the gears as he put the car into a three-point turn and continued his journey home. *Finally* he'd met someone he hated more than his ex-wife.

She managed less than two minutes of silence before asking, 'Where are you taking me?'

'You got into a car with a stranger and didn't think to check?'

'I don't really care,' she said, 'provided it's warm and dry.'

Good luck with *that,* he thought. 'Where were you going when I hit you?'

'I was in Calahurst for the music festival, but someone stole my bag and left me stranded. No money, no train ticket, no phone, so I thought I'd walk back to Norchester. I've got friends who live there.'

'Are you *insane?* A twenty-mile walk in the dark, during a thunderstorm—'

'I didn't *know* it was a twenty-mile walk. I didn't think it through. I was angry and then...'

He didn't think he could handle her life story right now. 'Where's home?'

'Wherever I want it to be,' was her sullen reply.

In other words, she had no intention of telling him. Fair enough.

'The road to Norchester has been blocked by a fallen tree,' he told her. 'It was on the radio. They say it won't be cleared until morning. We're heading back towards Calahurst, but I suspect the road will be blocked in this direction too. There's a small bridge straight ahead, crossing a tributary of the River Hurst. Did you walk across it earlier? Unfortunately, we've now had so much rain I think it'll definitely have flooded.'

'Whatever,' she said again, settling back in her seat and closing her eyes. 'Wake me up when we get there.'

Ben's fingers repeated their death grip around the steering wheel.

He'd rescued a damsel in distress and now it appeared he was stuck with her. What was that saying? Oh yes: no good deed goes unpunished. He didn't even know anything about her. She could be anyone, from lottery millionaire to axe murderer.

He took his eyes from the road long enough to give her a quick once over, in much the same way as she'd done to him earlier. She had long black hair (currently hanging in rats' tails over her shoulders), and brown skin. She was wearing the clothes that were practically a uniform amongst festival goers – knee-high boots, shorts, a plain white T-shirt and denim jacket. Her only jewellery appeared to be a silver charm bracelet glinting on her wrist, and she wasn't carrying a bag, although she'd explained what had happened to that...

'Stop it,' she said, opening one eye to glare at him.

He feigned innocence. 'Stop what?'

'Playing Sherlock. If you want to know who I am, ask me. Bloody police,' she muttered beneath her breath.

'You might lie.'

She laughed at that. 'I lie all the time.'

He hoped she was joking. 'I'm Ben,' he said, making an effort to be conciliatory.

'Miller.'

'No, Ben Taylor.' It was a good name to have – strong, sensible, *anonymous* – not like the one he'd been born with, *thank goodness*. There was the added bonus of knowing there were plenty of other men with the exact same name.

One should never under-estimate the merit of anonymity.

She rolled her eyes. 'No, no. I said, "I'm *Milla*." It's short for Camilla – Camilla Graham.'

Why did he have the feeling she'd made that up on the spot? Yet she had no reason to lie, unless... Oh yes, big mouth here had told her he worked for the police.

An ear-piercing shriek jolted him back to the present. The steering wheel was yanked through his fingers and violently spun to the left. He slammed his foot on the brake, but it was far too late. The car bumped over the grass verge and went straight into a ditch.

He switched the engine off, aware his hands were shaking, and rested his forehead on the steering wheel.

'If you're serious about killing yourself,' he said, with what he thought was commendable calm, 'please stop trying to involve me.'

'Excuse me? I saved your life! The road is out. Didn't you see? It's like Lake Windermere out there.'

He raised his head and looked out through the windscreen. As much as it pained him to admit it, Milla was right. Even though the rain was easing, the road ahead was completely flooded with churning brown river water.

Ben got out of the car, but this time didn't even bother to check for damage. It was obviously a write-off. Instead, he walked along the road towards the nearest house – a pretty little cottage, complete with a thatched roof and surrounded by its own garden.

'Where are you going?' she asked, running to catch up with him. Then, when she spotted the house, 'Do you know the person who lives here?'

'Yes,' he said. 'That would be me.'

'It looks like a little gingerbread house.'

It was how his daughter always described it. As his fingers closed over the top of the gate, he felt a moment of pure despair. Then, resolutely, he shoved open the gate and walked up the path, not bothering to check if Milla was still following.

Unfortunately, it appeared she was.

'Your house is really close to the river,' she said, chattering away as though near-death experiences were an everyday occurrence for her. 'What if that floods as well?'

'Then we move upstairs,' he said, and tried not to dwell on the thought that (at this rate) he was going to be severely tempted to murder her long before the water reached the front door.

TWO

Ben's house really did look as though it ought to have been made out of sweets, Milla thought, huddling beneath the little thatched porch while waiting for Ben to remember which pocket he'd left his keys in. As it turned out, he'd left them in his briefcase, in his car. This involved another walk in the wind and the rain, but he now seemed beyond caring how wet he got. He wasn't one of those people who dealt well with stress, she decided, which begged the question: how on earth had he ever become a police officer?

Yet his house was lovely and could have come straight out of a fairy tale. Without a single straight edge to it, the whole structure leaned slightly to the right. It had tiny casement windows, containing even tinier glass panes, all bubbled and flawed, and almost impossible to see through. Milla knew that because while Ben had gone off for his keys she'd bent down and tried to peer through one.

When Ben finally returned, he unlocked the door and, with an ironic bow, allowed her to go inside ahead of him. He had such a quaint, old-fashioned air about him, yet he couldn't be much older than her; certainly no more than thirty, despite the lines beneath his green eyes.

The door opened straight into the sitting room. The ceiling was low and whitewashed, and set with ubiquitous oak beams that barely cleared the top of Ben's head. The focal point should have been the cute inglenook fireplace, but the sofa and chairs were all turned towards a huge television. *So, the man did occasionally allow the twenty-first century into his life.*

As Ben came inside, a black cat sprang from the back of the sofa and walked towards the door. Ignoring him, it stood on the threshold and stared out at the storm, tail swishing.

'You don't want to go out there, buddy,' Milla said, carefully stepping over it. 'The weather is foul.'

The cat turned pale green eyes on her before moving closer to the doorstep and sniffing the air.

'Fine, don't take my word for it.'

'He's looking for my daughter,' Ben said, bending to rub the top of the cat's head. Milla felt slightly mollified that the cat ignored him too. 'I was supposed to collect her today, but her visit was... called off.'

'Meow,' the cat said, looking up.

'I know, Binx,' Ben sighed, closing the door on the storm. 'Me too.'

While Ben lit the fire, presumably for the benefit of Binx, who immediately settled down beside it, Milla took off her boots. They were full of water, so she opened the door and tipped them outside. This little house was too pretty to spoil with water and mud. Ben took the boots from her and placed them by the fire to dry. Binx moved disdainfully to one side. Milla hoped that Ben would now ask her if she wanted a cup of tea (or preferably something a whole lot stronger) because she needed something to warm her up.

Instead, he surprised her. 'You need to get out of those wet clothes.'

'*What?*'

'The bathroom's upstairs. You can use it first. If you leave your clothes on the landing, I'll put them in the washer-dryer and they'll be ready for you to wear again by morning. There are fresh towels in the cupboard and a robe hanging up on the door. I'll heat up some soup.'

She sincerely hoped her mouth hadn't dropped open.

'Will you marry me?' she said.

Instead of returning the banter, he smiled tightly and disappeared into the kitchen.

'He's an odd one,' she told the cat, who merely stared back with those strange peridot eyes.

The message was clear: play nice or find yourself right back outside in the storm.

Milla sighed and turned away to climb the crooked staircase.

In a house this small the bathroom was easy to find but she tiptoed past it to explore further. 'Tiptoe' wasn't quite the right word, due to the combination of squelchy socks and creaking floorboards, but, with the clatter of crockery from the kitchen below, hopefully Ben wouldn't guess what she was up to.

When she opened the first door, she fully expected to see some grand four-poster bed, preferably *not* already occupied by a wife or girlfriend, but the furniture inside was bland, pale oak and very modern, and there was no clutter or any evidence of sharing. It seemed Ben lived alone with his cat. There was one item of interest. On the table beside the bed was a photograph of a small child on a swing. The daughter he'd mentioned? How old was she? The photograph was too far away for Milla to see.

She closed the door and headed along to the only other one leading off the passage. This room was more interesting because it did have a four-poster bed in it, albeit a miniature one. Of dark, exquisitely carved wood, it had been created for a child with aspirations to be a princess. Each post was shaped to represent a tree trunk that expanded into branches, leaves and even tiny acorns. There were garlands of silk leaves draped around the walls, interspersed with hundreds of tiny white fairy lights. In pride of place was a bookcase as old as the house, filled with ancient volumes of fairy stories by Charles Perrault and the Brothers Grimm.

So... Ben Taylor was a divorced father with a much-beloved daughter who lived with her mother most of the time. You didn't need to be Sherlock Holmes to work that out.

The love which had gone into creating his daughter's bedroom was touching but it was bringing back memories of her own childhood that Milla would rather forget. She closed the door and returned to the bathroom, where she stripped off her wet clothes, throwing them out into the passage as she'd been instructed, before entering the shower.

Ben knew he'd made a terrible mistake.

Inviting a stranger into his house, even if she was an attractive woman, was asking for the worst kind of trouble. He'd be lucky if Milla only robbed him.

He'd deliberately left a twenty-pound note beside the telephone, hoping that she'd take that and not go rummaging through his belongings. He'd already heard her sneaking along the upstairs passage and checking out all the rooms. He tried to tell himself it was only human nature – normal curiosity about who he was and how he lived. For all she knew, he could have been a regular Bluebeard. If he'd been in her position, he might have done exactly the same thing.

Except he knew that wasn't true.

Eventually he heard her enter the bathroom and close the

door. He gave her a few extra minutes before retrieving her clothes. That was something else he hadn't properly considered. Sorting her T-shirt and shorts from her... er, more delicate clothes would make him feel like some kind of pervert.

He shoved everything into the washer-dryer and hoped for the best, as Binx sat beside him with a very judgy expression.

'What?' he asked the cat.

But Binx just stalked back into the sitting room.

＊ ＊ ＊

When Milla returned downstairs she had the idea that she and Ben would have a drink and sit around the fire talking. Every man she'd ever met liked to talk – mainly about himself. That was fine. It meant she didn't have to exert herself remembering today's fabrication of her life story. She was slightly disconcerted when he met her at the bottom of the staircase and coolly informed her he was going to bed but that she should make herself at home. He'd made up a bed on the sofa for her and there was soup waiting in the kitchen. He apologised for being antisocial but unfortunately he had to get up early for work. He said he knew she'd understand.

She didn't understand at all. In fact, she was unsure whether to be relieved or offended, or even to believe him. He was such a strange one; she hardly knew how to take him. Preferably not at all. She liked unobtainable bad boys, with dark hair and dark eyes to match their dark shrivelled hearts. With his height, blond hair and neatly trimmed beard, Ben Taylor had the look of a haughty medieval prince. He was most certainly a good boy and she didn't have the time to waste corrupting him.

Milla ate her supper with only the cat for company. She offered him the remains of the chicken soup, but he turned his back on her and went to sleep. So she switched off the light and clambered onto the rickety old sofa that was to serve as her bed. It was surprisingly comfortable. She cuddled beneath the duvet and was asleep before she even had the chance to yawn.

She awoke three hours later, just long enough to take the edge off her tiredness. The storm had passed and moonlight now glinted through the sitting-room window, creating little silvery squares on the bare floorboards. The black cat – Binx? – was asleep in front of the fire that was now little more than glowing embers. The soup bowl had been licked clean.

Milla threw back the duvet and headed to the kitchen to retrieve her clothes. Ben had chucked everything into the washer-dryer together; he wasn't as domesticated as she'd assumed. Her clothes were now so badly creased even an iron wouldn't have made a difference. Her jacket, being heavy denim, was damp in places but she could live with that. Her white T-shirt was now blue and her shorts were sadly crumpled. Her socks had shrunk but were wearable. Her knickers, being cotton, were fine, but her bra... She held it up to the light and winced.

The man obviously had *no* idea how to launder women's underwear. Her bra, not much more than a scrap of transparent lace, had been underwired. Now one wire had snapped completely in two and the other was sticking out through the fabric. He was lucky it hadn't wrecked his washing machine. She sighed and dropped it straight into the bin.

She used the phone to order a taxi. Seeing a twenty-pound note on the table beside it, she stuffed it into her jacket pocket and scribbled him an IOU.

Twenty pounds wasn't really enough but a quick look around the sitting room revealed there was no more to be had. There wasn't much of *anything* to be had, which was suspicious in itself. The cottage, the car, the huge TV, the fancy way in which he spoke – Ben Taylor certainly wasn't broke.

She headed upstairs. The steps squeaked and creaked,

exactly as they had done earlier. She had her excuses ready but when she stepped onto the landing she could hear feathery snores from the other side of his bedroom door.

He was sound asleep. He'd not drawn his curtains, so there was light enough to see him sprawled diagonally across the bed, the sheets tangled and rucked down past his waist. He was using one arm as a pillow, the other carelessly dangling over the edge of the bed. One foot stuck out from beneath the duvet, which was in the process of sliding off.

A man used to sleeping on his own.

Now, where did he keep his money? Not on him, that was for sure since he appeared to be sleeping naked.

She found his wallet on top of a chest of drawers. It contained a neat array of credit cards, which she left alone, as well as nearly a hundred pounds in cash. She took it all but then, hit by guilt, put twenty back along with the IOU she'd already written.

She had to walk back past his bed to reach the door. In sleep he appeared much younger. There was a tiny, half-moon-shaped scar on his temple, but the lines beneath his eyes were blurred and his body, now out of that staid, old-man suit, was promising – long, lean and elegantly muscled, his white skin even paler by moonlight.

She felt a flicker of desire and firmly squashed it, settling instead for kissing her finger and pressing it lightly to his forehead.

'Goodbye, Ben.'

It was a stupid thing to do. He stirred, shifting amongst the bedsheets, mumbling something she couldn't quite hear. Quickly she stepped back and out through the door, closing it softly behind her.

When she reached the bottom of the stairs, she caught a blur of movement through the little casement window. The taxi had arrived and was parked outside. The roads must be clear. She unbolted the front door and slipped out, running down the garden path before the taxi driver had a chance to sound his horn and wake her sleeping prince.

THREE

Detective Sergeant Harriet March lived in what had once been the servants' quarters of a five-hundred-year-old, half-timbered house on the high street in Raven's Edge. Now it was a busy florist called Foxglove & Hemlock, specialising in lavish arrangements for films, fashion shoots and weddings, which meant Harriet often had to battle her way through lush displays of flowers, often taller than she was, just to enter and exit her apartment.

The scent and aesthetic *was* lovely though.

Today, the rooms on the ground floor were filled with buckets of dark red roses, burgundy anemones and magenta sweet peas, with lots and lots of purple foliage already arranged on antique wrought-iron stands. Harriet breathed in hard to slide between them.

'Let me guess,' she said to Amelia Locke, the head florist. 'Vampire movie?'

'Close,' Amelia replied, 'but if this was for a film shoot they'd have to be fake or end up wilting under the lights. No, these are for a wedding this evening at Norchester Castle. An I-can't-tell-you-his-name-because-then-I'd-have-to-kill-you   rock star has decided to go the whole Bram Stoker. Apparently there'll be bats, dry ice and his-and-hers coffins.'

Harriet pulled a face. 'Really? Oh well, your flowers will look lovely!'

'They certainly will – if I can get the *cotinus* to stay put. Gabriel!' she yelled to her partner. 'I'm going to need another frog!'

Presumably a 'frog' was a florist's term and not an actual amphibian, because that would be a wedding to remember.

Harriet stepped out onto the high street, still picking rose petals from her hair. She was already late for work, so she made sure she kept her head down as she walked past Anya's: Raven's Edge, the fashion boutique next door, in case her mother spotted her.

Anya March had never understood why Harriet had wanted to become a police detective like her father – 'It got him *killed*, sweetie. My darling George played the hero one too many times and I don't want that for you. Why don't you come and work for me? You have a good eye. You'd be fabulous!'

Harriet loved fashion, it was true. She'd definitely inherited *that* gene from her mother, but she loved being a police officer more. Helping victims, solving crimes, ensuring the perpetrators didn't literally get away with murder...

What use for anyone was a talent for colour-coordinating accessories?

Her next stop was The Crooked Broomstick, one of three coffee shops in Raven's Edge, but the closest one to the police station. There was no queue – unsurprisingly, because most of the clientele were her colleagues and they'd already be at the morning briefing.

She was so late...

But still, priorities.

'Hi, Misha,' she grinned up at the tall blond barista that she'd crushed on since high school. 'Could I have a cappuccino to go, please, with double sprinkles, and do you have any of those white chocolate and raspberry cookies? Because I'll take two.'

'Straight from the oven.' Misha dropped two into a brown paper bag that had a broomstick logo on one side.

At least he wasn't one of those judgy people who'd say, '*Cookies*? For *breakfast*?'

She handed over her reusable mug (pink, with *The Queen of Everything* written along one side in gold) and he slid it beneath the machine, which began to hiss and splutter.

'I hear you've been unfaithful?' he said.

Was that a lame joke? Because, really, she expected better from him.

'The Witch's Brew?' he added. 'Kat's place? I hear you've been going there for lunch?'

'You'd make a better detective than some of the guys I work with.'

'I have spies *everywhere*...'

She rolled her eyes. 'A cookie for breakfast is one thing but even I can't eat cake for lunch. You start selling muffins filled with bacon and cheese, and I'll be right back. Promise.'

He considered this. 'Actually, that's not a bad idea.'

'Excellent. I'll take ten per cent commission on the profits.'

'No.'

'Five?'

'You can have the first one for free.'

'Done,' Harriet said. 'Now hand over my cappuccino or I'll arrest you for obstruction.'

He laughed and sprinkled her cappuccino with a generous helping of chocolate shavings, using a stencil in the shape of a witch's hat, snapped the lid on her cup and slid it across the counter along with the bag of cookies. Harriet handed over the exact change in a neat pile of coins.

'Have a nice day,' he said, sweeping the cash into his palm and dropping it into the till.

He sounded as though he meant it. Was that a good sign?

Yes, a sign that he wanted her to come back and buy more cookies, because he'd already turned to the elderly woman behind her and said, 'Hello, gorgeous. What can I get you?'

The woman chuckled. 'Oh, Misha! You're such a dreadful flirt!'

Harried sighed and scooped up the coffee, dropping the cookies into her bag. Hopefully she'd get to eat a few crumbs before lunch.

The police station was not as old as the other buildings in Raven's Edge and had once been the courthouse. It had two storeys and was built in pale stone, with a sagging tiled roof rather than thatch. The front entrance was meant for public use only, but Harriet ignored that and sprinted through the door, giving the receptionist a thumbs-up when he buzzed her through to the offices at the back.

'That's the very last time, March!' he called after her. 'You'll get me the sack!'

'Cross my heart,' she said, but if anyone was likely to get the sack it would be her. Ben was off this week, or she'd never have risked being late, which meant *she* was in charge.

It was like a punch to the chest so see Ben's boss, the suave DCI Doug Cameron, giving the morning briefing. Although he and Ben had both been fast-tracked through the ranks and were tall and bearded, that was where the similarities ended. Cameron's black wiry hair was cropped close to his head, his beard was a sculpted work of art and he always dressed immaculately, usually in Ozwald Boateng. But as chief inspectors rarely left their office, *he* didn't have to worry about ripping the trouser knees out while rugby-tackling a villain to the ground, which was what had happened to the last good-quality suit Harriet had worn to work.

Fortunately, Cameron didn't appear to have spotted her, so she ducked down and slid into a seat at the back, next to DC Sam King, who she'd known since they'd started school together at the age of five.

'What have I missed?' she asked, taking out the cookie bag and doing her best not to rustle.

'A couple of things. Jewellery robbery from Vanders in Port Rell.' Sam shoved a print-out at her. 'A necklace from their heritage collection. Eighteen oval, cushion-shaped rubies, surrounded by diamonds, set in silver and yellow gold, worth more than both our annual salaries combined. Personally, I think it's very odd that the thieves stopped with one necklace when they had the whole shop to choose from.'

'They could have chosen smaller pieces, easier to dispose of without needing to break them up?'

'Exactly.'

'Stolen to order then. Is that why the DCI is honouring us with his presence?'

'You've certainly picked the worst possible day to be late. Although I don't think he's noticed...'

'DCI Cameron notices everything.' Harriet took out one of the cookies and snapped off a chunk. 'I'll see him after the briefing and make my apologies.'

'Good luck with that.' Sam held out his hand.

Harriet sighed but dropped the chunk of cookie into his palm. 'What was the other thing?'

'They've found a body at King's Rest.'

'The Grim House?' Every kid who'd grown up in Raven's Edge had heard of the sinister burnt-out mansion in the middle of the woods. It was practically a rite of passage to spend the night there.

'Lydia Cavill was the first officer on the scene,' Sam said. 'The CSIs are working there now.'

'DI Cavill?' Harriet frowned. 'What about us? What about *Ben*? King's Rest is on our patch, not Calahurst's.'

Not that 'patches' would matter once HQ got around to setting up their new Murder Investigation Team.

'DI Taylor is on leave,' Sam reminded her. 'He drove to London yesterday to collect Sophie.'

'Actually,' DC Asheem Chopra interrupted from Sam's other side, 'DI Taylor is back in Raven's Edge. I was helping Traffic put out "Road Closed" signs last night – half the team couldn't get in, due to the storm – and DI Taylor's car is currently parked in the ditch outside his cottage. He's had a bad smash, front and back.'

'Oh no! Do you think Sophie's OK?'

'We'd have soon heard if either of them had been hurt,' Sam reassured her.

'Good point.' Harriet put a chunk of cookie into her mouth and, when Sam held out his hand, absent-mindedly gave him another chunk too. 'I'll phone him later. Although... If we're super-quick, and get Ben to King's Rest, he'll be named investigating officer, not Lydia.'

'You know it doesn't work like that,' Sam said. 'If Lydia Cavill is there, DCI Cameron has already assigned her the case.'

'He could change his mind?'

'Not him.' Ash held out his hand.

Without thinking, Harriet gave him the remaining chunk of cookie. 'Maybe if I explained the advantages?'

'I'd like to see you try!'

'You're on,' she said.

'How do you propose to do that?' Sam enquired, as the meeting finished and everyone began gathering up their belongings.

Harriet held up the bag with the second cookie, and grinned.

'Seriously? I've never seen the DCI eat junk food. He's more a "my-body-is-a-temple" person.'

'Ah, but these cookies are to *die* for—'

'DS March!' the DCI barked, making the three of them jump. 'My office, *now!*'

* * *

Something woke Ben up. He lay on his stomach, disorientated, and then he remembered the events of the night before and groaned. What had he been thinking, allowing a strange woman to spend the night in his house? He was lucky not to have been murdered in his bed. She'd probably robbed him blind. If so, he only had himself to blame. He had the strangest feeling he could smell the scent of her though, which was unlikely. She'd showered using his toiletries. If she was going to smell of anything, it would be him.

And that was plain disturbing.

He rolled over and switched on the bedside light. The bedroom was empty and his wallet was where he'd left it. He was almost disappointed. So she hadn't come sneaking into his room in the middle of the night, looking for money, comfort or sex. Why should he be surprised? He'd given her no cause to think he was attracted to her and presumably she'd felt it wasn't worth her effort to make him change his mind. His ego took a hit at that, but he shoved the duvet aside and got up anyway.

He knew Milla was gone as soon as he opened his bedroom door. The whole vibe of the house felt different. He didn't bother to check; merely headed for the bathroom to shower and then dressed in his usual suit and tie before heading downstairs. He had nothing else to do. He might as well go into work.

Milla hadn't remade the sofa bed. The sitting room was in chaos, with the duvet and sheets left on the floor where they'd fallen. She'd not had any breakfast. Or if she had, she'd managed to eat it without using any utensils or crockery. And she'd left her soup bowl, which Binx had licked clean, on the floor beside the fire.

Ben picked it up. 'Really, Binx? You know you're not allowed to have cream.'

The cat, as usual, ignored him.

Ben sighed and put the bowl on the table. The money he'd left beside the telephone had gone. He wasn't surprised but a little disappointed. She hadn't even left him a note. The telephone was set at an angle, so presumably she'd called for a taxi. He straightened it automatically and then remembered the feeling that she'd been in his room. He slid his wallet from his pocket. Sure enough, it was completely devoid of cash.

He supposed he should be grateful she'd left him his credit cards.

Driving his car into a ditch, even under mitigating circumstances, turned out to be a nightmare of bureaucracy. It took him most of the morning to sort out the insurance, recovery and a replacement vehicle. His day was further improved by someone hammering on his door fit to wake the dead.

Standing on the doorstep was a short blonde wearing a pale-grey trouser suit and glittery pink wellingtons.

'Detective Sergeant March,' he sighed. 'What can I do for you?'

She grinned up at him. 'You really ought to be careful who you say that to. Can I assume from the car you've parked in your ditch that you're having a particularly bad day?'

'Something like that.' Over the top of her head, he saw a tow truck had drawn up outside his house and two mechanics were now arguing about the best way to drag out the car. There was a lot of arm-waving going on. He ducked back into the cottage before they decided to solicit his opinion, muttering, 'Come on in,' to DS March, almost as an afterthought.

Harriet March entered the house with indecent haste, possibly because he rarely invited any of his team home. At least she paused long enough to take off her boots before prowling around his sitting room, picking up photos, stroking ornaments and generally having a good snoop.

'I thought you were planning on taking the week off to see Sophie?' she said.

'My plans changed.' He headed into the kitchen, partly to switch on the kettle and offer refreshments, but mostly to get away from her chatter. Unfortunately, she followed him. 'How did you know I was home?'

'I saw the tow truck,' she said. 'Your car looks bad. Was anyone hurt? How did it happen?'

'I had a rather eventful evening.'

'Yes,' she said. 'So you did.'

It took a moment for him to work out why she was smirking, until he saw Milla's discarded bra half hanging out of the bin. He knocked it back in with his foot.

'It's not what you think—'

'None of my business,' she said cheerfully. 'I'm here because when I told the boss about' – she broke off to thumb in the direction of the breakdown truck – 'he told me to come and pick you up.'

'Very kind of him.' Also, suspicious. Why did Detective Chief Inspector Cameron feel the need to go to all this trouble on his behalf? 'However, I've arranged a hire car and it should be here sometime after lunch.'

'You can't wait that long, a job's come up. Because we thought you were out of the county, it was passed to Detective Inspector Cavill over at Calahurst. Now the boss knows you're back, he wants you to take it. You need to get over there right away. DI Cavill won't give it up without a fight; you know how ruthless she is. It's the kind of job that can get a person promoted to insp— I mean, *chief* inspector.'

Now it was his turn to grin. 'Are you sure this offer of a lift is entirely altruistic on your part?'

Harriet fixed him with a look. 'DCI Cameron specifically told me to tell you to get your arse over there and stake your claim.'

'Specifically?'

'OK, maybe he didn't mention your arse.'

Why was he prevaricating? He was only prolonging the inevitable.

'I'll get my coat.' After all, it wasn't as though he had anything better to do.

Harriet looked pointedly at the leather shoes he'd spent a good chunk of the last hour polishing. 'You're going to need boots.'

FOUR

'You're going to need boots' could mean anything from a pig farm to a well-rotted corpse. Ben chucked his Hunters into the back of Harriet's sports car without comment and got into the passenger seat beside her.

Over the course of the morning the neighbouring river had subsided considerably. He could see both the road and the bridge, although council engineers were now swarming all over it and a familiar red 'Road Closed' sign had been placed right outside his front gate.

They travelled through the forest towards Norchester and then took the turning to Raven's Edge. After about ten minutes Harriet slowed down, turned left and then stopped, parking her car at the end of a line of emergency vehicles. The road ahead was blocked by a pair of massive gates. Where the hell were they?

'From here we walk,' she said, getting out.

Ben paused only long enough to thrust his feet into his Hunters and stride after her.

The gates stretching across the road were of decorative wrought iron but sturdy, despite the rust and peeling black paint. Beside the gate was a house in miniature, boarded up but in good repair – a lodge, he realised, meaning these were the gates to some old mansion. This was nothing out of the ordinary. The King's Forest District was full of big old houses, built in Georgian or Victorian times and then abandoned when they became too expensive to run. Sometimes they were transformed into retirement flats or, more often, demolished to make way for new housing estates.

A uniformed officer was standing directly in front of the gates. They'd been locked with a rusted chain and padlock, but now stood ajar with the chain hanging loose. Ben flashed his warrant card and the officer stood aside to let them pass.

'What is this place?' Ben asked Harriet, once they were on the other side.

'Don't you know?'

'I'm not local,' he said. This wasn't strictly true but the fewer people who knew his past, the better.

'I forgot you came from the Met,' she said. 'It seems like you've been here forever.'

Hopefully she meant that as a compliment.

As they walked further into the estate, the condition of the road deteriorated significantly. Presumably this was why all vehicles had to be left on the other side of the gates. Whole branches, even the occasional tree, had collapsed onto the road and lay where they'd fallen. The undergrowth encroached so badly that after a few hundred metres all they had to walk on was a narrow asphalt strip, and that was mostly buried beneath rotting vegetation.

'The official name of the place is King's Rest,' Harriet told him, 'but everyone around here calls it the Grim House, as in, the Brothers Grimm.'

Something stirred in Ben's memory. 'It's haunted, isn't it?'

'If you believe in that kind of thing.'

'Do you believe in that kind of thing?'

'It's a really old house and the family who used to live here died. Of course there are going to be stories about it.'

Now he was intrigued. 'What kind of stories?'

'The made-up kind! People come here seeking cheap thrills. It attracts all kinds of weirdos.'

'There doesn't appear to be any security.'

'The current owner gave up trying to keep it secure about ten years ago. Now everyone walks all over the estate and thinks they have a perfect right to do so. The house is derelict and unsafe but that doesn't stop anyone. It got worse after it was featured on one of those ghost-hunting TV shows a few months back. Now it's considered a rite of passage for the local kids to spend the night here.'

It wasn't hard to predict how that had panned out. 'Let me guess, last night one of them found a real live dead body?'

'Their story is that they were sheltering from the storm when they stumbled upon the victim.'

'Are they suspects?'

'Not really, the crime scene is too stylised for that.'

Even more interesting. '*Stylised?*'

'You'll see,' was all the reply he got.

'OK, tell me about the people who lived here. The ones who died. The ones who are supposed to haunt the place.'

She gave him a sideways look, presumably trying to work out if he was teasing her. 'The house is seventeenth century, something like that. It's been rebuilt and remodelled, and sold and resold, and then in the 1980s it was bought by a publisher called Henry Graham.'

'Graham & Sons?'

'You've heard of them?'

'I owned one of their bumper collections of fairy stories when I was a child. Sophie has it now.'

'When Henry retired, the company was passed to his sons Patrick and Dermot, and then it all started to go a bit *Macbeth*.

First Henry died in mysterious circumstances and then the two brothers fell out while battling for control of the company. Patrick wanted to continue publishing children's books, Dermot wanted to move into other media. For a while no one was sure whether the company would be split in two or just implode, and then...' Harriet paused, staring up at the trees now looming over them.

As though on cue, the sun went behind a cloud and the atmosphere subtly changed, becoming sombre, even sinister.

'Yes?' he prompted, slightly irritated.

Harriet pointed to the trees. 'This happened.'

What was he supposed to be looking at? The drive had petered out, becoming more earth than tarmac, indivisible from the undergrowth and woodland that surrounded them.

'What?'

Harriet muttered beneath her breath, grabbed at the sleeve of his suit and yanked him sideways.

'What the—'

And then he saw it.

The trunks of the trees were not brown, they were grey. Except they were not trees at all but slabs of crumbling stone, arranged into some kind of overgrown folly. No, this was far too big to be a mere folly. He followed the line of stones beyond the trees, refocused, and realised he was standing almost directly in front of the blackened shell of a Palladian mansion, now as one with the forest.

'What the hell happened here?'

'Patrick Graham. It was his daughter's birthday. He threw a huge party – bouncy castles, magicians, live music, the lot, then had a spectacular row with his wife and kicked everyone out. The next we knew, the house had burned down and his family were dead – that is, everyone except him. He protested his innocence, paid for the best legal team available, but the jury found him guilty and he was given a life sentence.'

'Oh my...'

Harriet ducked beneath a branch and took a short cut through the undergrowth towards the house. Someone had spray-painted bold swirls of vines and flowers around the columns of the front portico. Slightly surreal, but certainly an improvement on the sinister, smoke-damaged stone.

The door might have been secure sometime in the past, but the lock was now smashed and the door hung open at an angle. The entrance hall beyond was remarkably whole. The floor had been decorated in traditional Georgian style, with black and white stone tiles; only a dozen or so were missing, although many were cracked. The walls, once painted pale blue, had been scrawled over with graffiti but not quite so expertly as the audacious designs outside. Leaves and rubbish were strewn across the floor and the pitiful skeletons of birds that had become trapped. Creepiest of all were the ancestral portraits still hanging on the walls, defaced by vandals and blackened by smoke, but still seeming to watch their every move.

A couple of his own team were sullenly signing everyone in and dishing out disposable forensic overalls.

'You're too late, sir,' one said. 'DI Cavill's beaten you to it.'

He didn't deign to reply but followed Harriet up the wide and surprisingly robust staircase. It opened onto a gallery overlooking the hall, with two passages leading away, one east and one west. The passage leading into the east wing had been boarded up but most of the planks had already been deliberately broken.

'You don't want to go that way,' Harriet told him, as he attempted to peer through the large gap. 'That wing was where the fire started. It's not structurally safe.'

There was very little natural light, and the burned and blackened walls didn't help, but Ben could see a distinct trail of footprints stretching away through the dirt and dust. Harriet was becoming twitchy though, so he turned away and followed her into the west wing.

'All the rooms on this floor are bedrooms,' Harriet said, her voice echoing along the cavernous corridors as they passed room after abandoned room. 'The fire started in the east wing, in the master bedroom, and quickly spread. There were no smoke alarms or sprinklers. The flames devoured everything they touched. Fortunately, the cook's teenage daughter called treble nine, else the damage would have been worse. The east wing's a shell. This central section suffered smoke damage but the west wing, where we're heading now, survived intact.'

Ben paused to admire the intricate plasterwork decorating the ceiling of one of the bedrooms. 'Why was it never rebuilt?'

'Dermot Graham didn't want possession and neither did anyone else. There's been talk of turning the place into a hotel or apartments, but it's too far gone to be financially viable.'

His gut twisted. He'd already glimpsed discarded toys in the corridor of the abandoned east wing. 'How many people died?'

'Patrick's wife Rosemary and three of their four children.'

'That's awful.'

Harriet stopped then, looking back, almost as though she were sizing him up. 'We're here.' She dropped her voice to a whisper. 'This is the crime scene. Now remember, sir, you have as much right to be here as DI Cavill. More right, because this is your patch. DCI Cameron is already on your case, so don't let her boss you around.'

Just what kind of an opinion did they have of him? 'I don't let *anyone* boss me—'

'Yeah, right, whatever,' said Harriet, and shoved him towards the open door.

Eighteen years the house had been abandoned and yet the furniture remained. Old, dark furniture, more in keeping with the house's Jacobean origins than the structure that stood here now. The room was cold and damp but the floor had been recently swept, in stark contrast to the rest of the house. Most curious of all, candles covered every available surface, the thick, heavy kind usually found in churches, now guttered to pools of hardened wax.

'Stylised', Harriet had called it. As usual, she was right.

The victim was lying on a four-poster bed, perhaps even older than the house. The wooden posts had been scratched and hacked at by vandals; the hangings were of faded crimson velvet and thickly coated with dirt and dust.

DI Cavill was standing just inside the room, in deep conversation with someone.

When she saw him, she nodded an icily polite acknowledgement. 'Ben.'

'Lydia,' he returned, equally politely.

The bed itself had been draped with red brocade from a more recent era, and adorned with wilting petals, mosses and leaves. It was almost too easy. The victim lay on her back with her arms crossed, clutching a beautiful leather-bound book to her chest. Given the location and the setting, Ben had a horrible feeling he knew exactly which book. Because although the woman looked as though she'd been laid out for a funeral, she was wearing a luscious evening gown of gold silk, the strapless bodice encrusted with a mass of sequins, pearls and little golden beads.

A beautiful woman, not dead but sleeping. The allegory was clear.

'I've seen that dress before,' he said.

DI Cavill was distracted from her conversation. 'Unlikely,' she said. 'It's vintage Dior, worth thousands. It belongs in a museum.'

That would have put him neatly in his place, except he *had* seen the dress before. He was sure of it. If only he could remember where.

'Do we know her name?'

DI Cavill chose to ignore him and for a moment no one else seemed inclined to answer.

Then one of her DCs took pity on him. 'Camilla Graham.'

It was like being punched in the gut. '*Milla?*'

'We found her bag. It didn't contain much – make-up, a pay-as-you-go phone, a small amount of cash and three credit cards in the name of Camilla Graham.'

'That's impossible...'

He pushed his way into the room until he stood directly beside the bed, staring down at the face of the woman who lay there.

In death, she was beautiful. Her thick, black hair splayed out across the pillow and reached down to her waist. He could see her South Asian ancestry revealed in her brown skin and delicate features, but her eyes were closed so he couldn't see their colour. She wore no jewellery.

She didn't look dead, merely sleeping. She didn't look as though she'd been caught in a thunderstorm, hit by a car and spent the night sleeping on his couch either. *This* woman had come straight from a beauty salon; he could see that in her immaculately styled hair, in her subtle make-up and her flaw-less manicure. And he knew that because—

'This isn't Camilla Graham.'

The reaction wasn't quite what he'd anticipated. There was some nervous laughter, DI Cavill didn't even glance up, and Harriet rolled her eyes.

'We all know *that*,' she said, pulling him away from the bed. 'Honestly, sir! Weren't you listening to a word I said? Eighteen years ago, big fire, mother and children killed. Remember?' Without giving him pause to answer, she turned him in the direction of the bed, forcing him to look upon the body once more. 'So I ask you, does that look like an eighteen-year-old corpse to you?'

FIVE

The woman calling herself Camilla Graham was sitting in a quaint little pub in the shade of Norchester Cathedral, completely unaware she was supposed to be dead.

The pub had once been a coaching inn and was the kind of place that was always going to be popular with tourists. Milla had chosen it for that very reason – lots of potential witnesses if her plan went horribly wrong. She had found a shadowy corner to lurk in, right at the very back, with an excellent view of the door. Now all she had to do was wait.

She'd bought a new phone less than an hour ago, linked it to her old account and scrolled through a day's worth of messages. They were from the same person and they said exactly the same thing:

> Where are you?

Without bothering to explain the disaster that had been yesterday, Milla had fired back a response, telling the sender to be patient and that all was going according to plan. Then she switched the phone off. She didn't need someone checking up on her every few minutes. She knew the man she'd arranged to meet here today would show. He wouldn't be able to resist it.

She was taking a risk meeting in this particular pub because her apartment was directly opposite, but she was running out of time. Last night's storm had caused chaos on the roads in and out of the city but the taxi she'd ordered to collect her from Ben's cottage had somehow found a way through and she'd arrived back at her apartment shortly after 7.00 am. There was no point in reporting her bag stolen. Anything she'd lost could be replaced and her credit cards had been blocked some time ago. Anyone attempting to use them would get a very nasty surprise.

So here she was: £10 poorer after ordering a tuna melt and a diet cola. At 1.00 pm the pub grew busy but by two it was quiet again as the tourists returned to the sightseeing trail. She ordered a flat white and sat back, happy to people-watch.

Five minutes past the agreed time, the Managing Director of Graham Media, Mal Graham, strolled into the pub as though he owned it. As his mega-rich father was famous for gobbling up entire corporations before most people had eaten breakfast, perhaps he already did. She was only surprised he'd agreed to meet her himself, in person and alone, rather than send a whole army of lawyers. It was encouraging but hardly made her feel any safer.

There again, she hadn't felt truly safe for years.

She watched Mal walk inside and glance casually around, and wondered whether she should rise to greet him or wait to see if he recognised her first.

It had been eighteen years since she'd last seen him, which would make him around twenty-six now. He was tall and lean, with brown skin, and black hair worn too long for a business-man. Instead of a suit, or even something smart-but-casual, his T-shirt was faded and his jeans nondescript to the point of boring. Nothing special, nothing worn to deliberately catch the eye, yet every woman in the pub snapped to attention. Sunglasses hid his eyes but as he walked into the gloom of the pub he took them off, shoved them carelessly into his pocket and saw her in an instant.

How did he *do* that?

It was too late to hide and fairly pointless too. There was nowhere to go unless she wanted to make a very unsubtle dash to the rest room. She tried not to appear as though she'd been attempting to blend into the decor and took a sip of her stone-cold coffee. It tasted disgusting and it was difficult to keep her expression bland, even more so when he dropped into the seat beside her when there were two others he could have chosen.

'Hello, Milla,' he said. He didn't bother to introduce himself, presumably because he expected her to know who he was on sight. 'May I call you that? Assuming that it *is* your real name?'

She attempted a careless shrug, aware he wasn't fooled for an instant. 'It's what everyone calls me. My real name's Camilla.'

His mouth curved mockingly. 'Truthfully?'

When had she ever been truthful? 'Why would I lie?'

'Why indeed? I'd have known you anywhere but I suppose that's the idea?'

More than he could guess. She'd worked hard on her writing career and for the past year had contributed a review column to one of the UK's bestselling music magazines. There were photos of her all over the internet. Camilla Graham did not legally exist but neither did Milla Graham. Mal might have known her anywhere but he hadn't recognised *her*, of that she was certain.

His easy smile faded as he leaned forward, resting his arms on the table. She noted the expensive watch on his slim wrist, his brown skin dusted with dark hair, and then she looked up into his eyes. They were an extraordinary contrast to his skin and far too beautiful for a man: silvery grey, with darker rings around the edge of the irises.

It was like looking into a mirror.

'Who the hell *are* you?' He spoke so softly, so politely, that at first his words didn't register.

'You know who I am. You were the one who contacted me.'

'You say you're Camilla Graham, and no doubt you have the documents to prove it or you wouldn't be sitting here, but who are you really? You're not my little sister because she's been dead for years.'

All said with a chilling lack of emotion. She'd succeeded in obtaining his complete attention and had to remind herself that this was what she wanted.

It didn't prevent that little shiver of apprehension.

'My name is Milla Graham,' she said, the name tripping easily off her tongue, as it always did. 'Yes, I do have the documentation to prove it and, as you can see, I'm very much alive.' She produced what she hoped was a convincing frown. 'Why is my identity so important to you? You asked for this meeting. I assumed you wanted to offer me a job at one of your magazines? If that's not the case, I'll go.'

'You'll stay, because you assumed no such thing.'

It wasn't as though she had a choice. Instead of sitting opposite her as she'd expected him to do, he'd picked the chair beside her. This meant he was effectively blocking her in, which was a rather massive fail on her part. She could make a fuss and demand to be let out, but she remained where she was, to see how this would play out.

'You grew up with foster parents?' he said, in an abrupt change of subject.

While he'd grown up as the pampered prince of a publishing dynasty. Their lives could hardly have been more different.

'Do you know who your real parents were?'

Did he intend to be deliberately insulting? 'I have a birth certificate.'

'Are the blanks filled in?'

Apparently he did.

'Yes,' she said. 'These are very intrusive questions. Why do I need to prove who I am?' She picked up her coffee, in what she hoped was a casual way, and took another sip. It hadn't grown any warmer. She'd never let him guess that though. 'What's it to you?'

'For some months you've been deliberately implying you're part of my family, yet none of us have heard of you. I think we're entitled to be suspicious, both of you and your motivation.'

'I can't help the name I was born with,' she began flippantly – and then saw his expression darken and thought better of it. 'Graham is a very common name. Who knows, maybe we're related a few generations back?'

He raised an eyebrow at that.

'Trust me,' she said, meeting his penetrating gaze straight on. 'I don't want anything from you or your family.'

'Oh, you want something,' he said. 'I just haven't worked out what that is yet.'

'*You* contacted *me*—'

'And *you* dangled yourself in front of me like a big juicy worm. If you'd wanted anonymity you'd never have called yourself Camilla Graham. Stop the prevarication and tell me what it is that you want.'

He assumed he had the upper hand. If she hadn't had an ulterior motive, she would have walked out there and then. Hell, she wouldn't even be here. He intimidated her. He knew that, and *that's* why he was smiling.

But he didn't know her true identity, so for the moment she was safe.

'I don't want anything,' she told him. 'I'd be quite happy to walk out of here and never see you again.'

He merely looked at her.

'You'll need to move your chair though,' she added. 'You're blocking me in.'

He grinned at that. 'I'm foiling your attempt at a grand exit?'

'Unfortunately, yes.'

'We seem to have got off on the wrong foot,' he said, 'and for that I apologise.'

He pushed his seat back from the table. Did that mean he was going to let her leave?

He reached into the back pocket of his jeans and withdrew his wallet. Taking out a business card, he laid it on the table in front of her.

'Come for dinner tonight,' he said, surprising her yet again. He pointed to the card. 'That's the address of my family's home: Hartfell. It's not far from here, beyond a little village called Raven's Edge. My family is in residence, you'll be perfectly safe.'

Milla wasn't sure what to say; this was beyond her wildest expectations. So she kept quiet.

He seemed to take her silence for suspicion.

'If you have any doubt about your safety,' he said, 'please feel free to bring a friend with you. Or even your lawyer. I promise, we don't bite.' He placed a fifty-pound note on top of the card. 'For today's expenses. Do you have transport? Would you like me to send a car for you?'

Allow him to find out where she lived? She didn't think so!

'I have my own car.'

'You'll be there?'

Go alone to the home of a man she'd only just met, purely to solve an eighteen-year-old murder? It would be either incredibly smart or incredibly stupid. She rather thought the latter, especially since this would be the second time in the space of two days she'd done the exact same thing.

'I'll be there,' she said cheerfully. 'Wouldn't miss it.'

And that, finally, was the truth.

'I look forward to speaking with you again,' he said. 'It's entirely up to you how you wish to introduce yourself to my family, but I would suggest calling yourself Camilla Graham might be overplaying it.'

'OK, call me Milla Perrault.'

If she'd thought he wouldn't catch the reference, she was wrong.

'Why not?' he said. 'I suppose one fairy story is as good as another.'

He left, so she ordered herself another coffee and a slab of cake to give him enough time to leave the vicinity. When she finally emerged onto the little cobblestone street, blinking in the bright sunlight, there was no sign of him. To be absolutely certain, she walked around the block before performing her favourite trick – walking through the door of a boutique and straight out the fire exit at the back, ignoring the outraged shouts from the staff.

Now she was back in the same street she had started out from.

Her apartment was opposite the pub and over an art gallery. It had its own entrance, but the first clue that all was not well was when the door fell open as soon as she touched it. She let it swing back against the wall and regarded the staircase in front of her. It led up to a little landing and her apartment door, which was ajar.

Maybe she hadn't locked up properly?

Yeah, right.

She took a vial of perfume out of her satchel (sweeter smelling than mace and, more importantly, legal) and carried on up the stairs. The kind of mood she was in, if there was a burglar in her apartment, he would soon be extremely sorry.

She didn't even get halfway up before she heard such a terrible crash that it caused the staircase to vibrate beneath her feet. What the hell was going on?

She took the last few steps two at a time, held the perfume in front of her with her finger on the atomiser, and kicked open the door.

Her sitting room was wrecked. The furniture was over-turned and broken, even the TV lay smashed on the floor. Everything came with the apartment, so she wasn't too bothered – apart from knowing she'd have to clear up the mess afterwards.

Right in the very centre of this chaos, two white men were apparently trying to kill each other using a mix of street fighting and martial arts. Part of her would be quite happy to see them succeed, because it would save her doing it, but the more sensible part of her was wondering who they were. The younger, dishevelled-looking man who appeared to be winning she'd never seen in her life, but the other one...

'Ben?'

He glanced up at the sound of her voice – and in that split second of distraction the other man got in a beautiful sucker punch. Ben's head whipped around from the impact, his eyes rolled back and he was unconscious before he even hit the ground.

The other man touched his forehead in a mock salute. 'Thanks, babe,' he said, before stepping over Ben's body and walking out through the open door.

Malcolm Patrick Fergal Graham may have been eight years old, but he wasn't stupid. He knew the only time adults bought him presents was when they wanted something from his wealthy father. His sweet-natured mother fell for it every time, but his father's expression only turned more cynical, if that were even possible. Malcolm never understood why he didn't tell the lot of them to get stuffed.

At least today it was Camilla's birthday party, so most of the attention was on her. It was easy for him to sneak off to the kitchen and try to trade all the junk he'd been given for one of those bottles of champagne. But the cook had laughed and patted him on the head, and the next thing he knew he was being dragged off to his room by his Uncle Dermot.

He'd thought he was well and truly busted but, before the door had been slammed in his face, Uncle Dermot had grinned and tossed a gift bag in his direction with the words 'Happy un-birthday, Mal.'

The bag contained the latest Artemis Fowl – a book so new it wasn't in the shops. It had even been signed by the author.

He bloody loved his Uncle Dermot.

SIX

One hour earlier

Harriet watched Ben walk away from the murder scene and into the corridor. He was rubbing that scar on his forehead. Did he suffer from migraines? Because this really wasn't a convenient time for him to have one.

Ignoring the murmurs and whispers from the officers behind her, she took a strip of paracetamol from her bag and followed him. He was leaning against the grubby wall outside; not something she'd recommend while wearing the kind of grey suit that would show every dust mark.

'It's not her,' he was saying, half to himself, as though to convince himself. Realising Harriet had followed, he repeated it more firmly. 'That was *not* Camilla Graham.'

'And you're sure of that because...?'

'I spent last night with her.'

Fabulous.

Harriet held out the paracetamol while wondering on her best approach, tact not really being her forte.

Maybe request a transfer to the new MIT before he took her career down with his own?

'Thank you.' He took the paracetamol, popping two tablets out of the blister pack and handing it back, swallowing the pills straight down before she could offer him a bottle of water. Now he was massaging his eye socket, beneath his left brow. 'If that poor woman isn't Camilla Graham, who is she?'

Was that a rhetorical question?

'She has Milla's – *Camilla's* – bag and ID,' he added, so Harriet was glad she hadn't spoken. 'Is it a case of mistaken identity or does the murderer want us to believe the victim is Camilla?'

Two Camilla Grahams? In the same village – *three* if they counted the child who'd died so long ago. What were the odds?

'But—' she began, feeling she should at least *try* to get him back on track.

'Humour me, Harriet. Let's assume, for the moment, there are two people with the name "Camilla Graham". The one who died as a child and the one I met last night.'

She remembered the bra half hanging out of the bin in his kitchen and began to get a really bad feeling. How much did she know about DI Ben Taylor after all? She'd only worked with him for five months.

'That would be one hell of a coincidence...'

'I don't believe in coincidences,' he said.

That was one thing they could agree on.

'Missing persons,' he said abruptly, raising his head. 'I'm an idiot. Call DC Lawrence, ask her to check the missing persons report, with particular attention to any woman meeting the description of the deceased, who went missing within the last twenty-four hours, even those which haven't been officially recorded yet – *especially* those.'

'OK...' It couldn't hurt. She took out her phone and then

hesitated. She could still hear the other officers talking in the bedroom, not troubling to speak quietly.

'*What was he doing here? It's not his case.*'

'*I don't know what the boss was thinking.*'

'*It's embarrassing. He's so far out of his depth.*'

'Harriet?' Ben said. 'If I worried about what other people thought of me, I'd never get out of bed in the morning.'

But it was *her* fault they'd barged into another officer's case. If she hadn't made that suggestion to DCI Cameron, who seemed to like Ben, despite... everything.

'Let's walk back to the car while you make the call,' Ben suggested.

Translation: do your job.

Harriet called the station. It didn't even take a full minute for DC Dakota Lawrence to link the victim with a young woman who'd been reported missing from the music festival the night before. The officers at Calahurst Police Station had recorded the details, but an official case hadn't been created because the woman in question hadn't been missing for long enough.

'Amita Kaal,' Harriet told Ben, putting her phone back in her bag. 'She had a jewellery stall at the festival and one of her co-workers reported her missing last night. She could have gone off with a guy she met, she could have just sloped off home after the rain hit, which was why Calahurst didn't take her disappearance seriously, but her friend insisted that it was completely out of character, to the extent that Amita's brother is already flying home from wherever he is at the moment. They're a very close family, apparently.'

'Were' a voice said in Harriet's head. They *were* a close family.

Jewellery stall...

Could it be connected to the robbery at Vanders?

Unlikely. As Sam had said, Vanders sold pieces worth a

year's salary (or more!) and the Kaal family were targeting the festival crowd.

She and Ben shed their protective clothing as they walked through the hall and began the long trek back to those huge double gates at the end of the drive.

'We now know who the victim was,' Ben said, stepping over a fallen branch. 'We need to work out why she came here and how she arrived. If she'd walked this way last night she'd have been soaked. Perhaps she met someone she already knew, who convinced her it would be a good idea, or bait in the form of a big contract?'

Would Ben have been able to connect the dots so quickly if he hadn't met the 'other' Camilla Graham last night and known immediately the victim wasn't her? Why did Amita have Camilla's stolen bag? And as for that peculiar crime scene, with all those candles and flowers, like something out of a film... *None* of it made any sense!

'I can hear your brain ticking over from here,' Ben said. 'Out with it. What's your theory?'

'I don't have a theory.' Not one that she could share with him anyway. 'I was thinking about the crime scene. The candles, the flowers, that amazing dress. Dakota said that when Amita went missing she was wearing a blue dress with pink roses on it. So why put her in a ballgown? Why go to so much trouble?'

'Because she was soaked from the storm?'

'And the murderer just happened to have a vintage ball-gown to hand?'

'When we discover the answer to that, we'll have a motive and be one step closer to catching the murderer.'

He made it sound so simple. Usually, they'd begin looking at the victim's family, their friends, their life – but if Amita had been mistaken for this other Camilla, then she was the woman they'd need to research.

The only thing Harriet knew about Camilla was that she was possibly sleeping with Ben...

It was not a great start.

Harriet watched him nod a friendly greeting to the officer guarding the gate and be completely blanked in response. The officer was from Calahurst Police Station. Another of Lydia's team? How long would it be before Lydia realised her team had misidentified the victim? If Amita hadn't had friends and family to fight for her, would Lydia have ever realised her mistake? It was a sobering thought.

One thing was for certain, both Harriet and Lydia appeared to have seriously under-estimated the dull, unobtrusive, and supposedly boring Detective Inspector Taylor.

* * *

Ben had always liked Detective Inspector Lydia Cavill. She was a good detective; quick-witted and determined. He'd considered inviting her out for dinner once but thankfully had never got around to it, because he appeared to have seriously under-estimated that determination and now he was on the wrong side of it.

'Raven's Edge is my patch,' he said. Why did she make him feel like a child trying to wear down a parent? 'This is *my* case.'

'You weren't available,' Lydia replied. 'It came to me.'

'I'm here now. I'm taking it back.'

Lydia looked as though she'd have liked to say something along the lines of 'Over my dead body' but was far too professional. She glanced to their boss to support her, only to realise the Detective Chief Inspector wasn't paying either one of them the slightest attention.

DCI Cameron frowned at the slim cardboard file lying open on the desk in front of him. 'Is *this* all you've got?'

Lydia was clutching a cardboard file of her own, along with

a hefty hardback book. She dug into the file and brought out a sheaf of colour photographs, which she proceeded to place in a line across DCI Cameron's desk.

'Our victim was a twenty-four-year-old woman who worked as a journalist for a music magazine,' she said. 'She spent the weekend at the Calahurst festival. Early this morning, a group of teenagers found her body at King's Rest – an abandoned mansion in the woods, south of Raven's Edge.'

'Ah, the notorious Grim House. *Ghoulies and ghosties, and long-leggedy beasties.*' Originally from Lewisham, with a Scottish father and a Jamaican mother, today the DCI's Celtic genes appeared to be winning out. 'With that history, I suppose it was only a matter of time before someone got creative.'

'Coincidentally our victim shares her name with six-year-old Camilla Graham, who died along with the other members of her family when the house caught fire eighteen years ago.'

'I don't believe in coincidences,' Cameron said flatly. 'Now tell me the worst of it.'

'The victim was laid out on a four-poster bed in what was once a guest bedroom.' Lydia leaned over the desk, tapping her finger along each of the glossy photographs she'd placed in front of him. 'The bed, so far as we can tell, is original. The elaborate quilt she's lying upon is not. We're attempting to trace the supplier.'

From Ben's viewpoint, the photographs were upside down and he had to tilt his head to view them. It was easy to recognise the scene from this morning. The way the young woman had been dressed in that beautiful gold gown, and the way she'd been laid on a bed of flower petals as though asleep, the photographs looked more like a shoot for an upmarket fashion magazine than a crime scene.

'Our victim is wearing a vintage Dior evening gown,' Lydia was saying. 'It's made of silk and the bodice has been decorated with simulated pearls, rhinestones and beads. This particular gown was originally created in 1964 for Brianna O'Flaherty, an Irish heiress who became Brianna Graham on her marriage. She's Camilla Graham's grandmother.'

Another connection, Ben realised uneasily, but Lydia was still talking. It appeared there was more.

'Brianna's husband, Henry Graham, founded a publishing company in 1970 using her inheritance. At first they specialised in children's books, particularly classic fairy tales. In 2000 they republished the collection in a series of limited anniversary editions, with all-new illustrations.'

Lydia dropped the heavy, leather-bound book she'd been clutching right on top of the pile of photographs. It hit the desk with a thump, causing the photographs to flutter along the blotter. Brightly coloured post-it notes had been used to mark various pages, and Lydia opened the book at one of them.

'This is a copy of the book the victim was found with.'

'Damn,' Cameron said when he saw the page Lydia had marked.

'You will note that the colour plate for the story of *Sleeping Beauty* shows the titular character wearing the same Dior gown.'

Inside his head, Ben was going through his collection of Anglo-Saxon curses. *How* many times had he read and re-read that story out loud to Sophie? It was one of her favourites. She'd even drawn a picture of herself wearing the same dress. Before the book had belonged to Sophie it had been his, a gift from his grandparents that he'd read over and over again. And *still* he'd failed to recognise the dress.

Cameron leaned over the book, examining the illustration more closely. 'I really hate murderers with imagination, even if it does make them easier to catch. They usually trip up over their own cleverness – but not before some other poor soul has paid the price.' He closed the book, careful to keep the paper markers in place, and set it to one side before gathering up the photographs and tucking them neatly into the cardboard folder. 'What do *you* have for me, Benedict?'

It appeared Cameron wasn't expecting much; he didn't even pay Ben the courtesy of looking at him.

'DS March and I came to the same conclusions as DI Cavill,' Ben said. 'Except the victim's name is Amita Kaal and she has no connection to the Graham family at all.'

Now he had their attention.

'We already have ID,' Lydia pointed out, somewhat coldly. 'The woman's name is Camilla Graham.'

'You identified a victim from the contents of her bag? Don't you have any other corroboration?'

For Lydia, this was surprisingly sloppy.

'We're doing our best to contact next-of-kin, but apparently the addresses Camilla used to apply for her credit cards belong to other people.'

He wouldn't have been surprised if the credit cards had belonged to other people too, but he kept that thought to himself.

'The victim's name is Amita,' he repeated. 'She's from Southampton. My team have already made initial contact with her relatives. She was working on one of the jewellery stalls at the festival. It's a family business. Her sister designs the jewellery and her brother controls the financial side. Amita is part of the sales team and travels around all the festivals selling stock and taking commissions. I have no idea how Camilla's bag came to be in her possession but I have arranged for Amita's brother to formally identify her body. He was out of the country but is flying back today. We've already taken a statement from one of the other women working on the stall.'

He had the satisfaction of seeing Lydia's superior expression falter. 'Are you certain of this?'

Ben slid his own cardboard file onto Cameron's desk, right on top of the book of fairy tales. 'The victim is part of a close family, who reported her disappearance the moment they realised she'd gone. There is a superficial resemblance to the music journalist you mentioned – the original owner of the bag found in Amita's possession – but it is definitely not the same woman. Camilla Graham is younger than Amita – in her early twenties, I'd say. The photographs on her bio show she has a lighter skin tone and eyes that are a distinctive pale grey.'

'Coloured contact lenses,' Lydia said, a little too promptly.

'I shall be sure to ask when I interview her.'

Again he'd disconcerted her. 'You've found her? Alive?'

He had no intention of admitting the truth, so prevaricated with 'I contacted the magazine she works for. She submitted a review of the music festival early this morning. They've also given me her address.' He then realised the submission didn't necessarily mean she was still alive. Anyone could hit 'send' on an email.

And he really wished he hadn't had that thought.

It was clear Lydia was keen to continue their argument but Cameron denied her the opportunity. 'Do we know how Camilla's bag came to be in Amita's possession?'

'No, but according to a woman Amita worked with, she had a conversation with a man interested in commissioning a considerable amount of stock for a shop he said he owned. However, her family are adamant that she would never have gone to any kind of business meeting without her brother.'

There was one last remaining photograph on the desk. Cameron picked it up, staring down at the Sleeping Beauty on her bed of flowers.

'How did she die?'

'We suspect some kind of poison,' Lydia said, 'but it's all conjecture until the post-mortem.'

'Anything likely found at the scene?'

'No.'

'Murder then,' Cameron sighed, 'as if we were in any doubt.

King's Rest is in Raven's Edge so this will be your case, Ben. Send all requests for extra funding through the usual channel and I'm sure Lydia will help with manpower, should you need it.' He handed both files back to Ben.

Lydia inclined her head, gracious in defeat. 'I'm only too happy to help in any way I can.'

Ben wasn't fooled for an instant.

SEVEN

'Who is this Camilla person anyway?' Harriet wanted to know as they drove around Norchester in her open-top sports car.

'Aside from a complete pain in the arse?' Ben said. 'Very lucky she's not dead.'

They had arrived mid-afternoon to find the streets packed with tourists and nowhere to park. Now Harriet was lapping the cathedral for the third time.

'I might have to do something illegal,' she grumbled. 'Bloody tourists.'

'Not here,' Ben told her. The street where Milla lived was one of the narrower, medieval alleyways that twisted out from around the cathedral. If Harriet left her car here she'd block the entire street, drawing attention. 'Find somewhere less busy and meet me on foot. If desperate, use the police station.'

'I thought our visit was a secret?'

'Not at all. We're just not telling anyone.'

Especially Lydia. Technically, Norchester was her patch.

Harriet pulled onto the side of the road, ignoring the 'no waiting' yellow lines. 'Where am I meeting you?'

He looked down the narrow cobbled street, squinting

against the sunlight filtering between the buildings. 'The one over the art gallery, halfway down, opposite the pub.'

Harriet probably said something like 'See you soon,' but it was drowned out by the blare of horns as she blithely pulled back onto the main road, straight in front of a delivery truck.

It transpired that Milla lived in a surprisingly nice part of the city, not at all what he'd been expecting. There were little tea shops and boutiques in addition to the art gallery. Even the coaching inn would have been at home in a Dickens adaptation. How could she afford to live in a place like this? Unless, of course, she'd conned her way into it?

Not for the first time, he was grateful his initial confrontation with Milla was not going to be witnessed by Harriet. It was not likely to go well.

Milla's apartment had its own access to the left of the gallery. There was no name on the intercom but the door was already swinging open so he had no compunction about walking straight in and up the narrow stairs. At the top was an open window with a beautiful view across the city rooftops, and another door that had also been left ajar. Slightly more cautiously this time, he pushed it open.

On the other side was an attractive sitting room beneath sloping eaves, with an open-plan kitchen in one corner. Opposite from where he stood were three more doors, presumably two bedrooms and a bathroom, although they must have been incredibly tiny. What interested Ben the most, however, was the scruffily dressed man currently opening and thoroughly checking every single drawer and cupboard.

'Hello there,' Ben said. 'May I help you?'

The man, who had his back to the door, tensed and then slowly turned around, as though he had every right to be there. 'Maybe you can,' he replied, limping towards him.

Ben got ready to duck in whichever direction required it.

He didn't have long to wait. The first punch came as soon as the other man was within striking distance.

Ben was a black belt in taekwondo and if the intruder had stuck to that, or even the street fighting he'd started out with, it might have been easier to take him down. But he switched from one to the other and back again, and it required all Ben's concentration to calculate exactly what kind of blow was coming next and block it. He was aware of the apartment being trashed around them, which would alert anyone in the gallery below. Then he remembered Harriet, who could walk through that door at any moment. Knowing Harriet, she wouldn't think twice about coming to his rescue – and could get badly hurt.

He had just come to the opinion that it would be better to let the man leave, when he heard a voice that chilled him.

'*Ben?*'

Milla was standing in the doorway, holding what appeared to be pepper spray.

As he opened his mouth to tell her to run, something slammed into his jaw with the force of a speeding train.

And that was the last thing he remembered.

Milla regarded Ben's unconscious body helplessly. Was he dead? He looked dead. His skin was even whiter than when she'd seen it last but now he had a cut over one eyebrow and it was bleeding profusely. If there was one thing she remembered from her rather erratic attendance at school, it was that a corpse wouldn't bleed so much.

Every instinct told her to run. So why was she still standing here, willing him to wake up, even if it was only to yell at her for running out on him? What was he even *doing* here? Did he want his £100 back? He hadn't seemed the type to miss it. How had he known where to find her? Oh yes, he was a police officer, which meant she now had a trashed apartment with an unconscious cop in it. Terrific.

She prodded him with her toe. He didn't move.

She leant over him. 'Are you going to wake up or do I need to fetch a bucket of water?'

There was no response. His eyelids didn't even flicker.

'Bucket of water it is then,' she said.

She found a small bowl in one of the kitchen cupboards and filled it with cold water, then grabbed a clean tea towel from one of the drawers. At least, she assumed it was clean. She'd never used the kitchen in all the time she'd lived here.

When she returned she half-hoped he'd gone, but no, he was right where she'd left him: flat on his back on her sitting-room floor. She knelt beside him, dipped the cloth into the cold water and began cleaning the blood from his face. She could hardly let him bleed out on the carpet. She'd lose her deposit for a start.

She was careful to steer clear of the cut itself. It had stopped bleeding and she didn't want it to start again. It might need stitches; it would certainly leave a scar to match the tiny one he already had on his temple. She ignored the flutter of guilt in her stomach. It wasn't as though she'd asked him to come to her rescue. There was no way this was her fault. Not at all.

Even though it was.

She slapped his shoulder. 'What were you *thinking*? You could have been killed. And for what? A hundred pounds? You're *insane*.' She leaned closer. 'Can you hear me, Ben? I said you were insane.'

He grabbed her wrist. '*Yes!* I hear you. The whole street can hear you! *Please* shut up. My head is killing me.'

She wrenched her hand away and dropped the cloth back into the bowl. It slopped bloody water all over the carpet but by now she was past caring about carpets and deposits. She didn't have to help him. He had no right to be here. She should kick him out and—

She noticed the skin over the left side of his jaw was red and swollen.

'Is your jaw broken too?'

'It's fine.' He moved it experimentally. 'I've had worse.'

Gentle Ben, a brawler?

'When?' she derided. 'Twenty years ago in the school playground?' At least the colour was returning to his cheeks, leaving him one shade up from recently deceased. She lightly traced his skin with her fingertips, drawing back when she saw him wince. 'What's giving you the most pain?'

He opened his eyes and glared at her. 'Do you really need me to answer that?'

Hurt, she went on the attack. 'What were you thinking, tackling a burglar on your own? And what about the state of my apartment?'

'You're welcome.' He sat up, wincing again.

'I'm not insured. I'll have to pay for the damage.' She could hear the whining note in her voice and wondered what was wrong with her. She wasn't going to be paying for any damage; she'd do a moonlight flit like she always did. She didn't care about the apartment. The whole building could collapse into a sinkhole for all she cared.

'Send the bill to me,' he said. 'I'll pay.'

Now it was her turn to glare at him. 'Don't be stupid. Why would you do that?'

'Right now I'll agree to anything if you'd shut up or at least speak quietly. *Can* you speak quietly? Or is everything maximum volume and maximum drama with you?'

It wasn't too late to tip that water over his head and she wanted to, she really wanted to.

'I didn't ask you to come here and save me. I don't need

saving; never have, never will. I don't need a hero in my life so—'

'Good, because I have no intention of being one. Now, why was that man ransacking your apartment?'

'*Ransacking?*' She sat back on her heels. What was he talking about? Ransacking would imply searching, stealing...

He waved his hand at the devastation surrounding them. 'I didn't do this by myself.'

'I don't have anything worth stealing...' She'd never cared for collecting possessions. They slowed her down, held her back.

Brought back memories.

Instinctively her fingers went to her bracelet, the one which hadn't left her wrist for eighteen years.

'Why else was he here?' Ben asked.

He was watching her closely. *Police*, she reminded herself, resting her hands back in her lap.

'I might have left the door open...' Even she knew that lie was pathetic. Her mind slid from theory to theory. She didn't have anything worth stealing, anyone could see that. An opportunist would walk straight out when he realised how little she had – maybe leaving a donation on his way. If the scruffy looking stranger hadn't wanted cash or something to sell, the only other thing worth stealing from this apartment was information. Information on her. And who would want that?

Oh no...

'Milla? I can't help you if you don't talk to me.'

She affected a shrug. 'I don't know why he was here. Like I said, I must have left the door open. He was a chancer.'

It wasn't usually this difficult to lie. Unable to maintain eye contact, she took another look around the apartment. She'd miss the place, it was a nice neighbourhood. Realistically, there was nothing here for her and it had never been a home.

No place ever felt like home.

She stood up but so did he.

'Milla?'

Why was she still here? There was nothing she'd be sorry to lose. A few clothes, a few inexpensive toiletries; everything could be replaced. All that she owned was kept packed up in the back of her car, as always, for just such an occasion. Except her laptop and that was in her satchel.

Her gaze dipped towards the floor. Her satchel had fallen on its side, the contents spilling out beneath the upturned sofa.

Ben reached down to pick it up for her, but she beat him to it, snatching it up and shoving her belongings back inside. Her sudden movement seemed to take him by surprise because when she dashed towards the door he didn't try to stop her.

Or perhaps he was too clever to try something so blatant?

She glanced back at him standing there, swaying slightly.

'Milla, don't do this,' he said, quite calmly. 'I can't help you if you run.'

She had two choices. Stay or make a grand exit on that ever-reliable line 'You can't help me, no one can.'

But his comment about everything being maximum drama still stung.

So she simply left.

* * *

Norchester was a quaint medieval city, enclosed by a high stone wall and guarded over by its own castle. It had been built on the site of a Roman fort, so the streets were still set out in the original grid pattern and easy to navigate.

Harriet knew better than to park in the local police station. She'd visited before and knew the barrier would only lift for a swipe of her warrant card – and the last thing she wanted was to advertise the fact that she and Ben had been here. But it was the height of the tourist season and there were no parking spaces to be had. In desperation, hoping she and Ben could be back before her car was clamped, she used the cathedral car park, then jogged back to Camilla's apartment. The door was wide open and a crowd had gathered outside.

What on earth was going on?

'I've called the police,' said a rather grumpy-looking woman standing outside the art gallery.

They'd soon have company then.

'Good for you,' Harriet said, stepping into the entrance hall and coming face-to-face with a tiny, furious brunette. Her like- ness to the murdered woman was remarkable, so Harriet felt fairly confident in saying, 'Camilla Graham?'

For a split second it appeared everything was going to end amicably, then Camilla gave her a surprisingly hard shove and sprinted off down the alley.

Harriet picked herself up and dusted off her suit. Now what?

'Harriet?'

She tipped her head back. Ben was leaning over the bannister at the top of the stairs, looking as though he'd been in a boxing match. Had Camilla done that to him?

'Do you want me to give chase?'

He nodded wearily. 'Yes, please.'

'I'm on it!'

She slung her bag across her body and sprinted after Camilla, who was easy to spot amongst the pastel-clad tourists in her heavy denim jacket and shorts. Unfortunately, she glanced back and spotted Harriet closing in.

Camilla moved fast though, ducking and weaving amongst the crowds, exactly as though she'd done this before. Many times. She even tried the in-the-front-door-out-the-back routine, followed by losing her jacket and gaining a red baseball cap, but the next switch Harriet missed, which was how she ended up grabbing Camilla and spinning her against a wall, only to discover she was holding an increasingly irate teenage boy wearing an identical baseball cap.

'Sorry!' Harriet stepped back, holding up her hands. 'Mistaken identity!'

The boy glared at her, his fists still clenched. 'You're lucky I don't call the cops.'

An 'I *am* the cops' quip would not go well, so Harriet returned to the apartment.

There was still a crowd outside, but she ignored that and ran up the stairs.

Ben was alone inside the apartment, leaning over with his hands on his thighs as though he were about to be sick. She slid a waste-paper basket in his direction.

'I left you alone for five minutes,' she grumbled. 'What happened?'

She could hear sirens, growing louder.

What was wrong with him? Why didn't he answer?

'Sir? Are you OK? You look terrible.'

At this he straightened, raising an eyebrow.

'Well, you do.'

'We don't have much time. I need you to check this place over as quickly as possible.'

The sitting room was completely wrecked. It could take forever.

'Did Camilla do this? Did she attack you?'

'No, I walked in on a break-in, but instead of stealing something, I think he left something behind. I need you to find it.'

'What am I looking for?'

'Something illegal is my guess. I suspect he was trying to set her up.' He stepped forward, as though to help, then slumped back against the wall.

That didn't bode well. 'Are you sure you're OK?'

'I'm *fine*.'

'But—'

'You'll need to check the really obvious places first.'

Obvious? That made no sense.

'But—'

'Just do it, Harriet!'

As he appeared to be in a lot of pain, she bit hard on the retort about to come out of her mouth and began opening cupboards.

'Fingerprints, Harriet!'

She tore off a section of kitchen towel, wiping clean what she'd already touched, also obliterating any evidence left by Camilla. Didn't this make her an accessory? Still, the quicker she did this, the quicker they could leave.

She checked each kitchen drawer, then the cupboards, then the jars on the side labelled 'Tea', 'Coffee' and 'Sugar', swilling the contents around with her finger. Something glittered at the bottom of the jar marked 'Sugar'. She hooked it out and gasped.

It was a gold necklace, with huge red stones surrounded by diamonds. The kind of thing a duchess would wear.

She shook off the sugar and held it up. 'There was a robbery at Vanders jewellery store in Port Rell yesterday. A necklace matching this description was the only item that was taken.'

'The only item? Then that'll be it.'

The sirens outside became unbearably loud and then abruptly ceased. Harriet heard voices drifting up from the street, including one very familiar one.

'Quick, give it to me.' Ben held out his hand.

She dropped it into his palm and he stuffed it into his jacket pocket, just as they heard footsteps on the stairs.

'Now forget you ever saw it.'

'*What?*'

'Trust me, Harriet.'

Trust him? Up until this moment she would have trusted him with her life. But now?

'One last thing,' he said. 'Do you see that book beneath the sofa? I need you to put it in your bag and pretend it's yours.'

Harriet regarded the hardback book that lay partially open beneath the overturned sofa. 'Why?'

'It's important.'

'I'm not sure it'll fit.'

'Please, Harriet!'

She cursed beneath her breath but barely had time to grope beneath the sofa, drag out the book and stuff it into her bag, as several uniformed officers crowded into the tiny apartment, followed by Detective Inspector Cavill. The book was so large the zip of her bag wouldn't close properly. Harriet had to tuck the bag beneath her arm to hide it properly.

Lydia Cavill entered the apartment in time to see Harriet scramble guiltily to her feet while Ben was still leaning against the wall for support.

Lydia's eyes narrowed suspiciously. 'What have you two been up to? We've had multiple reports of a disturbance.'

'Nothing much,' Ben shrugged. 'We happened to be passing and heard a commotion. There was a break-in, as you can see. Sadly, the man responsible got away despite our best efforts, but it was good of you to respond to the call... and so many of you...'

Lydia surveyed Ben's battered face with her usual lack of emotion and gave him the kind of look suggesting that if he hadn't just crawled out from beneath a rock, then he really ought to think about crawling back under one.

'The last time I checked, this was *my* patch,' she said.

She *had* to get that in.

'Quite right,' Ben said, pushing away from the wall. 'I'll leave you to get on with it. Come along, DS March.'

Harriet held her breath, waiting for him to lose his balance or keel over, but he managed to reach the top of the stairs without mishap, although his fingertips turned white as he gripped onto the bannister.

'I'll need a statement,' Lydia said, but made no attempt to stop them.

'Absolutely,' Ben said. 'It will be on your desk first thing tomorrow.'

'And Ben?'

'Yes, Lydia?'

This time the tiniest smile quirked her lips. 'You might want to reconsider field work.'

It was way past his bedtime and the house was eerily silent. Malcolm couldn't even hear the babies crying.

Camilla's birthday party must have finished hours ago but if the stupid nanny was too drunk to order him to bed, he fully intended to stay awake all night, even if he had to listen to her and his father snogging in her room next door.

He forced his drooping eyelids open and took a hefty swig of the hot chocolate she'd left for him, but he'd been so engrossed in his new book it had gone cold and tasted disgusting.

He spat it out and wondered if there was any alcohol left in the kitchen.

Maybe one more chapter first...

EIGHT

Milla did not consider herself a journalist, investigative or otherwise. She wrote reviews and occasionally did interviews. Mainly when her editor couldn't find anyone else willing to spend their weekends in a muddy windswept field, chatting up zonked-out musicians no one else had ever heard of. But she was delighted with the amount of information she'd managed to dig up on the notoriously secretive Graham family. They guarded their privacy fiercely (ironic for a family who'd consolidated a fortune invading the privacy of others) and they had the wealth to do it.

The Hartfell estate appeared to be where they resided when not in London. It included the large chunk of forest that encircled the village of Raven's Edge. When Milla turned her car into the drive she found it blocked by massive black gates topped with barbed wire. Two security cameras also stood sentry. *How welcoming*, she thought, leaning out of her car to jab the button on the intercom.

'Hi,' she said, aware of the cameras panning around to check her out. 'I'm Milla Perrault.' The intercom remained silent but eventually there was a soft 'click' and the gates slowly parted.

The house was about a mile from the main gate. It was a modern building (all symmetrical cubes of stone, slate and obsidian glass) and located in the centre of a man-made lake with only an elegant footbridge connecting the house to the mainland. Yet as Milla got out of her car and approached the front door it remained resolutely shut. There was no knocker or bell. She banged on it with her fist and waited, forcing patience. The sun was low on the horizon but it warmed the pale stone wall of the house and the heat reflected back at her. Sweat begin to trickle down her back.

Why had no one opened the door? They knew she was here.

It was tempting to vent her frustration by giving the door a hefty kick but she gave it one last try, rapping sharply on the door before walking away across the bridge.

'My apologies, miss. I didn't hear you.'

She turned slowly, levelling her gaze at the house and the man standing inside the open door. Was he the butler? He was white, with grey hair cut short and thinning on top, but he wasn't wearing any kind of a uniform, not even a suit. She forced a friendly smile and walked back over the bridge, her Doc Martens thud, thud, thudding like one of the Billy Goats Gruff.

On the other side of the door was a cool, spacious hall, minimalist in furniture and decor. Bland, boring and nothing to indicate the personality of the owner.

Presumably that was the point.

'What a lovely home,' she said. 'It's so light and airy and modern.'

'Thank you, miss. You're very kind.'

From his dry tone, she should probably dial it down.

'Why did they build it on a lake?'

'Why not?' he replied smoothly. 'If you would follow me, Miss Perrault? Mr Mal Graham is aware of your arrival and will be with you directly. Would you like an aperitif?'

She must have regarded him blankly because he added, 'A drink?'

'Something non-alcoholic would be great.'

She'd kill for something stronger.

'Home-made lemonade?'

Bleugh.

'That would be lovely,' she said.

Was it the light in here or did his eyes just twinkle?

And why did she get the feeling he could see straight through her?

He led her through the hall and opened a door on the left, opposite a wide central staircase. 'If you would like to wait in here?'

She wandered in, looking around with interest. There'd been very few interior photographs of Hartfell to be found online and she'd not seen this room before.

'A library?'

'Graham Media are first and foremost a publisher.'

His dry tone was back. She seemed to be creating quite an impression.

'Did they publish all these books?'

'No, this is Mr Dermot Graham's personal collection.'

'That's some collection!'

There must have been thousands here. Had he read them all? Had anyone?

'Indeed,' the butler said. 'Someone will be along with your drink shortly,' and then she was left alone.

More fool him.

She walked over to examine the books. Some were old and

(by the way they were locked away behind glass) some must have been valuable. There were all the classics. Her fingers stroked over her favourites, R.L. Stevenson and Mark Twain, including *Treasure Island* and *The Prince and the Pauper*. Fairy stories were conspicuous by their absence but this was perhaps not unexpected. According to her research, no children lived here.

The sunlight sparkling on the lake lured her through the French windows and onto an attractive wooden walkway that jutted out over the water and appeared to surround the house. The gardens were entirely on the other side of the lake, stretching down to the sea in elegant terraces of topiary and water features, without a flower to be seen. Milla turned her back on the view, leaning against the balustrade to survey the house. Most peculiar of all were the floor-to-ceiling glass windows, with no curtains or blinds.

She hardly noticed the man strolling along the walkway towards her until he was practically at her side. At first she assumed he was Mal. They were both tall and lean, but this man was a good twenty years older. His black hair had thick streaks of grey and his features were gaunt. The first prickle of fear danced into her awareness when she realised this could only be Dermot Graham, head of the family.

And the man she suspected of murdering her mother.

She tried to remember her pre-rehearsed speech but one glance into those intimidating grey eyes and 'Hello, I'm Milla' was all she could manage.

'The woman Mal met in a pub and invited home for dinner?'

Said like that, it was hard not to cringe. 'Does he often do that?'

'My son meets any amount of women in pubs and clubs; he spends most of his time there. You, however, are the first one he has brought home to meet his family. He was struck by your likeness to his late sister and believes you might be a relative.'

There it was, right out in the open. Milla waited for the inevitable interrogation, where he would demand to know who she was and why she was here, and how much it would take for her to leave and never come back.

She had her story all planned out and had done so for months. Any question he thought of, she'd created the perfect response. When he didn't say any more she had to prompt him.

'Odd, isn't it? That I look so much like her?'

Dermot shrugged, leaning back against the balustrade. 'In his youth, my Uncle Fergal was a dead ringer for Robert Redford. If anyone wanted to goad him, all they had to do was whistle "Raindrops Keep Falling on My Head" and off he went, fists flying, making a complete show of himself. What do you think of my house?'

'Your... house?' she repeated, completely thrown.

And there it was: the brief glimmer of a smile. 'Too modern for you? It's not to everyone's taste.'

Thoroughly unnerved, she struggled to get the right words out and in the right order. It was some kind of test, it had to be. Why else would they be discussing architecture instead of murder?

'I think your house is beautiful,' she lied, 'but why are there are no curtains or blinds?'

'How astute of you to notice. Most people don't.'

Until they wanted to close them?

'What about privacy?' she asked.

He indicated the lake and gardens surrounding them. 'There's no one to see.'

Wasn't that the truth? To the front of the house was the sea but behind was only forest, with the glimpse of a stone folly just visible over the trees.

And no one to hear you scream, said a helpful voice-over inside her head.

'I'm teasing,' he said. 'The glass turns opaque at the touch of a button.'

All these months of planning and rehearsing what to say to the man who'd ruined her life, and she couldn't think of anything more to talk about than curtains? And what of him? Surely he only had to take one look at her to know exactly who she was and why she was here?

Her fingers automatically touched her bracelet, tugging at each charm in turn, in the way she always did when she was nervous.

'Pretty,' he said, his gaze following the movement, 'and very unusual.'

'Isn't it?' She held out her wrist to show him. 'It was a gift from my father.' Had he recognised it? Apparently not, for he barely glanced at it, his attention drawn back to the house and to the man who had strolled out onto the deck. Mal Graham: stunning in a formal open-necked shirt and dark trousers.

'Dad, you're terrifying the poor woman,' he said. 'And you wonder why I never bring anyone home.'

Milla felt seriously underdressed in her jeans, T-shirt and Docs.

Mal was carrying two glasses, one of wine and one of lemonade. He handed the lemonade to her. 'From Hodges,' he said.

She regarded the wine enviously. Why had she asked for lemonade? What had she been *thinking*?

'Miss Graham is tougher than she looks,' Dermot said, effectively chilling her.

'My name is Milla *Perrault*.'

Dermot merely smiled. 'Enjoy your meal. Unfortunately I have to go out – an unexpected request to meet with the local authorities – but I did want to meet you before I left. And Mal?'

A wry smile lifted the corner of his mouth. 'Be sure to introduce
Milla to your grandmother.'

That sense of unease, already squirming in Milla's stomach,
turned abruptly to stone.

What on earth did he mean by that?

Outwardly Mal's grandmother was a typical little old lady,
although at about five foot ten she wasn't remotely little. Her
long white hair, which might once have been strawberry blonde,
was worn coiled around her head like a warrior princess. She
wore minimal make-up, which did nothing to hide her freckles
and, unlike many women with her wealth, she had evidently
spurned the current fashion to nip and tuck the instant a
wrinkle or blemish appeared. Her eyes, unlike her son and
grandson, were of a bright, cornflower blue – and they were
currently fixed beadily on Milla, who shifted nervously from
one booted foot to the other.

'How did you meet Mal?' was the start of the lady's
inquisition.

'At the pub—'

'One of the local ones, here in Raven's Edge?'

'No, Norchester.'

'Oh, you live in Norchester?'

'Yes – I mean, no. I mean, I used to, but—'

'You met by pure chance?'

One accomplished liar tied up in knots.

'Mal contacted me and we agreed to meet for lunch,' Milla
continued valiantly. 'I'm a journalist—'

'How interesting! Which newspaper?'

'I visit gigs and festivals, and interview musicians. I've been
published in all the major magazines.'

Brianna switched her attention to her grandson, who was

enjoying the entertainment immensely. 'I didn't realise you were such a huge fan of music, Mal?'

'I saw Milla's photo online,' Mal said. 'I was struck by the family likeness, so of course I had to meet her.'

'Quite,' was his grandmother's dry retort. 'But if you're planning on getting busy beneath the sheets, you might want a DNA test to check she's not family. You know full well your grandfather has bastards all over the country. Are you all right, my dear?'

This last remark was directed at Milla who, thinking the attention was finally off her, had made the mistake of fortifying herself with a gulp of lemonade. If she hadn't swallowed abruptly, she'd have sputtered it right out across the stone floor. Sadly, that also meant she choked.

Mal, hardly stirring himself, reached out and walloped her on the back.

Brianna lifted one subtly pencilled eyebrow.

'I'm fine,' Milla croaked, eyes watering. 'Really.'

'I know it's only lemonade, but you shouldn't knock it back so. It's hardly becoming for a young lady.' Then, in the same abrupt switch of conversation her son had performed earlier, 'If you *are* a bastard, I should warn you, there's no money. It's all tied up. My father didn't trust the Grahams an inch and neither should you. Liars, cheats and scoundrels, the lot of them,' she added cheerfully.

While Milla was wondering what she should reply to *that*, Brianna patted her arm and moved away, saying, 'Lovely to meet you, my dear.'

Mal was grinning. 'What do you think of Granny Brianna?'

'She's adorable.'

He laughed. 'I think she likes you.'

'Liars, cheats and scoundrels?'

'It's a family joke. The Grahams were Border Reivers, bandits, if you like, along the Scottish borders back in Tudor times. Although the O'Flahertys weren't much better – they were Irish pirates. Are you *sure* you want to claim kinship with our family?'

Milla swiped his glass of wine right out of his hand and knocked it back in one greedy, desperate gulp. 'I think I'm going to fit right in.'

NINE

Ben and Harriet returned in silence to Raven's Edge Police Station. CID was on the first floor and by the time Ben had reached his office almost everyone in the station had seen his bruised and battered face. Harriet had produced a clean tissue from the bottom of her bag which he held against the cut on his forehead, but his white shirt was already liberally splashed with blood. He looked as though he'd been in a road accident. The mumbles of consternation followed him all the way up the stairs.

'I'm fine!' he growled at the third person to enquire after his health, aware Harriet would be rolling her eyes behind his back. As she'd had to stop the car twice on the journey back from Norchester to allow him to throw up, she knew perfectly well he wasn't fine. Something she emphasised by slamming the wastepaper basket onto his desk, right beneath his nose, the moment he sat down.

'I'm *fine*,' he repeated tersely, removing the bin and placing it back on the floor.

She hovered.

'Are there any other points you wish to make, Detective Sergeant March?'

'I can't believe you made me do that,' she began, her voice low and furious. She must have been building up a head of steam ever since she got into the car. 'Interfering with a crime scene, removing evidence, *destroying* evidence. Goodness knows how many laws and regulations I've broken for you. And you don't seem to give a damn, or want to talk about it, or discuss it...'

Ben leaned forward wearily, resting his elbows on the desk and his head in his hands. 'Please, Harriet. Keep your voice down.'

Her response to that was to wrench open her bag and slap a packet of paracetamol onto the desk.

He had meant that he didn't want anyone overhearing their conversation, but by now Harriet was beyond furious.

'I was going to offer to help you go through all these files,' she told him, 'but you know, I think I've just remembered I have something better to do – like salvage my career!' She dragged Milla's book out of her bag and dropped it onto his desk with a hefty thump. 'Here, happy reading!' She tripped over a cardboard box on her way out but still managed to slam the door behind her.

He waited for the reverberations to stop echoing around his head and then opened his eyes. The door to his office had a small glass panel that he sometimes kept covered with a blind. Thanks to Harriet's dramatic exit, the blind had snapped up and he could now see a host of enquiring faces turned towards him.

Growing up as part of the most notorious family in the county, he was used to people talking about him at a very early age. It didn't mean he liked it. He got up, strode across to the door and yanked the blind back down, even though everyone in the outside office had immediately turned around and pretended they hadn't noticed.

On the way back to his desk, he tripped over the same cardboard box as Harriet. What idiot had left that there? He crouched down to take a better look. On the side was stamped 'Archives'. Beside it were five more exactly the same. *What the—*

He got up and wrenched the door back open. 'What's this junk cluttering up my office?'

'They're the files about the Grim House case,' Sam said. 'You said you wanted them directly.'

Ben shoved his fingers through his hair, partly to stop it sticking to the cut on his forehead, partly to calm his filthy mood. 'I didn't mean that I wanted the *original* documents sent over, only the digitalised files.'

'There are no digitalised files,' Sam said. 'We didn't have computers back then. The archivist told me they're slowly digitalising everything, but this case is closed and it wasn't considered worth it.'

Until now.

At least no one had shredded it. Ben closed the door with slightly more care and surveyed the boxes. There were six of them in all, carefully numbered and labelled with a crime reference number. They had little cardboard lids for easy access and handles for transportation. He suspected there were more of them, buried in the depths of the archives, but he didn't feel much like adding to his workload right now. He lifted the lid from the first box, hoping that someone might have at least catalogued the evidence, and that the most important stuff, the most *relevant* stuff, would be in this one, along with some kind of index. Or was that too much to ask?

He was in luck. There *was* an index, running to several sheets of neatly typed paper stapled together and plonked on top. The files beneath were the most important ones – witness statements and reports from the Fire Investigation Unit, the coroner and the inquest. He picked up the entire box, dropped it onto his desk and settled down to read.

The Investigating Officer at the time had been a newly promoted Detective Inspector Paul de Havilland. The Grim House murders (as the press called them) had taken place at the height of summer after an extravagant birthday party for the Grahams' only daughter, Camilla. The 999 call had been made by the cook's teenage daughter at around 11.00 pm. By the time the emergency services had arrived, the fire had taken hold.

At first it was assumed it had all been a terrible accident but then, as the investigation progressed, Patrick Graham had been arrested and charged with the murder of his wife Rosemary, and their three children: Camilla, George and Henry. The cause of the children's death had been given as smoke inhalation, although there was also evidence that all three had been given a strong sedative. Ben had read dozens of autopsy reports in his ten-year career but he always found it particularly difficult when the victims were children. He forced himself to read right to the very end of each one, before closing the file and setting it aside. Those poor children. It was gut-wrenching. He remembered the toys he'd seen, still strewn around the upper floor of the house. And then he remembered something else, something Harriet had said.

'Patrick and Rosemary Graham had four children.'

What had happened to the other one?

He began taking the other files out of the box and stacking them on his desk, but soon realised the light was fading. How long had he been sitting here, reading in the twilight?

Leaving the box on his desk, he got up and opened his door. The CID office was deserted. Everyone had gone home. Except...

There was a movement by the door as Sam reappeared.

'Oh good, you're still here. Sir.'

Why did everyone only remember the 'sir' as an afterthought?

'Yes?' he said, somewhat caustically.

'Dermot Graham's turned up. Do you want me to put him in the interview room? He's come on his own – that is, he's not lawyered up.'

Give him strength...

'Lawyered up? Really?'

'I mean, Mr Graham has attended for interview voluntarily and without legal representation. Er, sir.'

'Remarkably efficient of him. Did we ask him to come in?'

'We did, sir. He's the legal owner of the Grim – I mean, King's Rest. Well, it's held in trust and he's one of the trustees.'

Ben glanced at his watch. It was almost 8.oo pm. Not unreasonably late but strange that a man as successful (and therefore, presumably, as busy) as Dermot Graham had agreed to turn up so quickly.

Strange and incredibly suspicious.

Perhaps he'd been a police officer too long.

'Is DS March still here?' he asked Sam.

'No, sir. She finished her shift some time ago. She's gone home.'

Lucky Harriet.

'In that case, please escort Mr Graham to the interview room and we'll see what he has to say for himself.'

'Will do.'

'Oh, and Sam?'

'Yes, boss?'

'You'd better have this before I forget and it ends up at the dry cleaners.' Ben pulled the ruby and diamond necklace from his pocket amidst a shower of sugar granules, and casually dropped it into Sam's hand.

Sam gasped and held the necklace up to the light. 'Isn't this...?'

'Yes, it is.'

'But how—?'

'Anonymous tip-off. Found it in a jar of sugar. What are the chances, eh?'

'Slim,' muttered Sam, shaking off the sugar, but thankfully saying no more on the subject.

Dermot Graham was not what Ben had expected. He'd seen photographs of the man in the press, usually of the long-distance, rather grainy type. Dermot Graham, apparently, valued his privacy. Ben had expected someone older, flashier, but the man waiting was only in his early fifties, if that.

Dermot didn't bother to turn around as the interview room door opened but continued to stare out through the tiny window and across the station car park towards the dark, gloomy forest beyond. Instead of a suit, he was dressed casually but conservatively in dark trousers and shirt, both of which emphasised his pallor.

He didn't even turn his head when Sam placed a tray of refreshments on the table, but merely said, 'This is a very old building. Is it seventeenth century, or earlier?'

Who cared?

'I'm not sure,' Ben said.

'I was surprised to find you weren't somewhere more modern.'

Why? Ben knew from the reports he'd read that Dermot had been a regular visitor to the station, following his brother's arrest all those years ago. If it had been anyone else, he'd have thought the man was nervous. Dissembling, perhaps?

'I think the most modern building in Raven's Edge is the church hall,' Ben said, 'and that's two hundred years old.'

'Quite,' was Dermot's dry response.

Finally, he turned away from the window.

His eyes were the strangest colour Ben had ever seen, like tarnished silver. Unusual, yet at the same time frighteningly familiar.

Milla...

Had she been telling the truth?

'Would you like coffee, Mr Graham?' Sam asked, thankfully jumping into the silence.

Dermot regarded the tray of coffee and biscuits with polite disinterest, before sitting in one of the chairs grouped around the central table. It was the chair Ben had earmarked for himself, but it seemed petty to say so. Had it been deliberate? Ben didn't care. He merely plonked himself in the seat opposite as Sam left, closing the door behind him.

Ben had changed his shirt and washed the blood from his face, sticking a small, unobtrusive plaster over the cut on his forehead. He couldn't do much about the bruise on his jaw, which ached when he talked. He hadn't attempted to eat or drink anything, and he wasn't about to start now. Despite his hunger, he pushed the tray to the other end of the table, before glancing up to find Dermot staring at him.

'Is it painful?' the other man enquired.

It was pointless pretending not to know what Dermot was talking about. 'Not as bad as it looks.'

'Car accident?'

OK, just how bad *did* it look?

'A run-in with a burglar.' And that was all he intended to say on the matter.

'Poor you,' Dermot said.

'Thank you for coming in so promptly,' Ben said.

Dermot inclined his head.

'You've been told of the events that occurred early this morning at one of the properties you own, King's Rest?'

'I was sorry to hear a young woman had died. Do you know how it happened?'

Presumably in case someone sued.

'We can't divulge that information due to the nature of the ongoing investigation. We wanted you to be aware of the event and we'll keep you informed of any developments.' He could have been reading from a probationer's manual.

'My trip here was pointless?'

'Not at all,' Ben said, although privately he agreed with him. While it was encouraging that Dermot was happy enough to turn up as requested, it was too early in their investigation to quiz him about past events in the remote chance that they were connected. He had to read up on the case first. If he did begin talking about the night that fire destroyed King's Rest, Dermot would realise Ben believed the two events *were* connected. Again, not something he wanted the outside world to begin speculating about. It was unlikely Dermot would want those past events brought back into the public eye, but his company did own several newspapers.

'The victim's name was Amita Kaal, does that mean anything to you?' Ben opened the file as he spoke and slid out a photograph of Amita. The photo showed her at a family celebration and she was wearing traditional salwar kameez.

There was a split-second pause before Dermot took the photograph. If Ben hadn't been watching for any kind of reaction, he might have missed it.

Interesting...

'I don't know her at all,' Dermot said, too abruptly. 'I'm sorry, I can't help you. What a terrible tragedy for her family.' He handed the photograph back, as though he couldn't wait to be rid of it. A guilty conscience? One of Amita's co-workers said she'd been seen talking to an older man. Could that have been Dermot? Ben made a mental note to send someone round to show the woman Dermot's picture.

'How about this one,' Ben said, taking out a photograph of Milla in jeans and T-shirt that he'd downloaded from the internet. There was no mistaking her South Asian ancestry nor her resemblance to the murdered woman.

This time Dermot smiled. 'Ah yes, I know Milla.'

Not the reaction he'd expected.

'You do? How?'

'Milla is a friend of my son and also a distant relative.'

'How distant?' asked Ben.

'I'm not certain. I could look into it further, if you think that would help?'

Shouldn't that have been his line?

Ben tucked the photograph back into the file. 'I don't suppose you have any idea where Milla is now?'

'Oh yes,' said Dermot. 'She's currently having dinner with my mother.'

The girl lay in bed and fumed.

Sent to her room during a party? How fair was that?

Sure, she'd heard the shouting and the screaming and the fighting. It was hardly anything new. She'd heard the voices in the nanny's room too, even with the pillow over her head.

Whispering.

Promising.

Lying.

Until all became silent.

Too silent...

In the next bed her cousin had fallen asleep in her Alice in Wonderland *costume.*

The girl gave her a shake, gently at first.

'Wake up!' she demanded, shaking harder.

But the other girl's eyes remained closed.

TEN

Dinner with the Graham family was a surreal experience.

Milla knew they were wealthy and that there'd be staff waiting on them, although she hadn't realised there would be quite so many other guests, most of whom seemed to work for the various family businesses. They ranged from publishing directors to newspaper editors, as well as their husbands and wives, and even included the local vicar. Maybe being asked to dinner wasn't such a big deal after all?

There were twenty-three of them altogether; presumably Dermot would have made twenty-four. It was only when Milla, bored with all the publishing talk, took to counting heads that she realised even his place-setting was missing. How odd, to invite all these people to dinner and then not bother to show up.

The dining room had been created for entertaining. It overlooked the lake and the topiary: darkly sinister chess pieces standing sentry throughout the garden. The walls had been painted a smoky grey, the table they were seated around was opaque glass, the place settings were slate and the chairs had been upholstered in the softest black leather. Apparently, Dermot had a favourite colour and was determined to stick to it.

Milla had assumed the most important guests would be sitting at either end of the table, but it didn't take her long to work out they were the ones grouped around the middle while she, along with the other lesser guests, were banished to the ends. It was tempting to stir things up a bit, but she decided to behave in the hope she might learn something. This proved to be optimistic.

By 11.00 pm most of the guests had departed, leaving only a few milling around the reception rooms. Dermot had not returned. Brianna was playing the piano in the main salon and leading a sing-along, although slightly off-key. The remaining guests had drunk enough alcohol to cautiously join in. Mal had disappeared.

Now would be a good opportunity to explore. If caught, she could pretend she was looking for him. The best room to head for would be Dermot's study, because she might never have another opportunity, but that would be reckless even for her. It was one thing to be caught sneaking about public rooms, quite another to be found in Dermot's private office.

Milla swooped up a wine glass (not her own, but who cared) and headed out into the corridor. There was no sign of the butler – Hodges? She walked confidently towards the front of the house, remembering the location of the library from her earlier visit, but when she went inside and switched on the light, a voice said,

'Thanks.'

She almost screamed and dropped her glass.

Mal was reclining in a huge leather seat by the garden window. There was a half-drunk glass of whisky in his hand, which would have shown remarkable restraint except the rest of the bottle was right there on the desk beside him.

'Why are you sitting here in the dark?' she grumbled, checking the bare floor for any wine spills. There was only the tiniest splash and she was able to rub that into the flagstone with the toe of her boot. 'You frightened me half to death.'

'My house,' he countered. 'Why shouldn't I sit in the dark?'

'Because it's weird.'

'The dark and the quiet help me to think. Does that satisfy your curiosity? Why are *you* here?'

She went for whiney. 'I was looking for you. You left me on my own. I don't know anyone. No one will talk to me.'

None of which impressed him. 'You know my grandmother.'

At least Milla didn't have to fake the grimace. 'She's *singing.*'

He grinned. 'And you, a music lover.'

'I wanted to explore.' The best fibs usually held a little bit of truth. 'This is some house. It's so light and airy and... and...' How did it go? 'So... *modern.*'

Fortunately, copious amounts of alcohol appeared to have muddled Mal's thought processes. 'I suppose I could give you the guided tour,' he said, although he didn't move or even put down his glass. 'The house is certainly something.'

The way he spoke, it didn't sound like much of a compliment.

'Something' was definitely the right word. Milla recalled those fairy stories of the evil Snow Queen and her ice palace. Dermot's home was exactly like that ice palace except, instead of ice, everything had been created from the same sinister, dark glass.

She forced a suitably inane smile to her lips. 'And you have such a *lot* of books!'

'That's why it's called a library.'

OK, she'd asked for that.

She watched him raise the whisky glass to his mouth and drain the contents before pouring himself another. How drunk was he? And why would he choose to drink alone in the dark, instead of joining in the fun in the salon? She could hardly ask; she barely knew him. She feigned interest in the nearest book-shelf instead, which turned out to be a mistake; it was filled with books on twentieth-century engineering. Terrific...

'The fiction is on this side,' he said, thumbing over his head to the extensive shelving behind him.

'Thank you.' She turned, walking the entire length of the library with her Docs clomping over the stone floor, going silent every time she hit a rug. She was well aware he was watching her.

A-ha, twentieth-century *fiction*. Hardbacks, first editions – Dermot Graham certainly liked books. It was a pity she hadn't heard of any of the authors...

'What is it you like to read?' he said, after she'd been pretending to study the spines of the books for a good couple of minutes, her head tilted awkwardly sideways.

'Pretty much anything,' she said, catching herself telling the truth again. Not that she'd had much opportunity to read lately. All her spare time had been taken up researching his family, mostly online. Not that she was going to admit to *that*.

'Have you read...' He mentioned one of last year's best-sellers.

'Oh, yes,' she said, even though she'd only read about that online too.

Luckily he took another swig of his drink and turned his attention back to the garden. She tried not to feel piqued that he was uninterested in her, and took the opportunity to study him more closely. He was wearing the same black trousers and white shirt he'd worn at dinner, although the shirt was now unbut-toned several notches. With his unfashionably long black hair and melancholy air, he looked ridiculously romantic, like the hero from a Gothic novel.

Or possibly the villain.

Now it was her turn to grin.

'What's the joke?'

She cursed her elementary mistake; he'd seen her reflection in the glass.

'I was thinking what lovely books you have,' she said.

That beautiful upper lip curled into a sneer. 'Are you really this obsessed with literature or are you too polite to admit to thoughts along the lines of "poor little rich boy, drinking his life away"?'

'I hadn't got *quite* that far,' she confessed, although she would hardly call him 'little' or a 'boy' either – he must be practically thirty. She had felt a moment's jealousy though for the fabulous life he must have led, surrounded by wealth and opportunities – everything he took for granted, everything that must have fallen right into his lap – and which she'd had to fight for.

The Prince and the Pauper indeed.

'Have you found a book yet?'

'No, I...' *Wasn't actually looking for one.*

He turned his attention back to his drink. Milla turned to leave but was distracted by a huge oil painting above the door. She had completely missed it when she'd come in.

Her breath hitched.

'Is that...' She took a few steps towards it and then stopped.

'Henry Graham senior,' Mal said. 'My grandfather – and a right evil bastard.' He took another swig of his drink, only to find the glass was empty. 'Damn,' he said, turning the glass upside down and shaking it.

'Did you know him?' she asked, even though she knew what his answer would be.

'Not really, thank goodness. He died when I was seven.'

Milla moved closer. The portrait was of a wealthy, successful man in his late fifties. In the background was a library – but not this one, although she recognised some of the books. They were the lavishly illustrated volumes which

Graham & Sons had been famous for; the classic fairy stories so conspicuously absent from the library she now stood in.

Henry Graham had the same black hair and darkly brooding air as his son and grandson. He also had the same extraordinary eyes, fractured silver that was every shade of grey. But the most shocking thing of all?

'He looks like me,' she said. 'Except he's white, obviously.'

'Why so surprised? Aren't you one of the bastards? Or are you going to change your story yet again?'

He still hadn't recognised her?

'I was always given the impression my parents were married.'

'You have the Graham eyes.' He didn't bother to hide his derision.

'Would you like them back?'

He laughed at that, but when she thought it was safe to relax, he said 'OK, let's go back, way back to the very beginning. *Who* are *you?*'

'Camilla Rosemary Graham.'

Any remnants of humour disappeared in an instant. 'That is not possible.'

'Why? *Why* is it so hard for you to believe?'

He deliberately dropped his glass, not even blinking as it shattered into a million tiny fragments, scattering like diamonds across the dark stone floor. 'Because she's dead.'

Milla determinedly didn't jump. 'Are you sure?'

For a moment he was silent, and then, 'Do you seriously think I'm going to fall for this returned-from-the-dead scam?'

'I'm your sister—'

'*Don't* push me.'

'I'm *Milla*.'

'And there you go. We never called her Milla. She was always *Camilla*.'

'Why won't you believe—'

'Because Camilla is *dead.*'

It was slipping away from her.

'I was there, the night of the fire. I remember everything. *You* were there and together we—'

'Camilla is dead,' he repeated flatly.

'No, you're wrong, you see—'

Mal wasn't listening. 'Can you imagine? Of course you can't. You come here with your lies and your tricks, and you've never stopped to consider what it was really like, to lose your entire family in one night.'

He kicked out at the table. The bottle wobbled but didn't topple over. Milla had to force herself not to reach out and steady it.

'I'm sorry,' she said. 'I didn't mean—'

'I couldn't have helped them. It came out at the inquest that we'd been drugged. My father said they didn't suffer and I want to believe that, I *have* to, but somehow I can't...' He held up his hands and showed her his palms. 'I was eight years old and I thought I could put out the flames with my bare hands.'

Milla's stomach turned over. Unlike the rest of his skin, which was a perfectly smooth brown, his palms were creased with faded scars. She took one hand in hers, gently tracing the palms with her fingertips, hardly able to believe what she saw.

For a moment he let her...

And then abruptly snatched his hand away. 'Now you're disturbing me...'

She held out her own hands, palms up.

He stared, silent and incredulous, at the scars identical to his own. Then he looked up into her face.

'*Kiran?*'

ELEVEN

By the time Ben had finished the interview with Dermot Graham and written up his notes, the CID office was in darkness and everyone but the night shift had gone home. When had it become normal for him to work so late? Deciding he could review his report tomorrow (when it would probably make more sense), he phoned for a taxi and then scooped up the box from the archives as he walked out of the door, remembering to chuck Milla's book in on top.

When the taxi drew up outside his cottage less than ten minutes later, he could see his own car was no longer parked in the ditch, although there was plenty of evidence where it had been. The hawthorn hedge now had a huge chunk missing out of it and there were bits of foliage strewn across the road, along with two thick skid marks gouged out of the grass verge.

He paid the driver with one of the twenty-pound notes he'd got from Raven's Edge's one and only cashpoint and told him to keep the change. The taxi driver muttered something beneath his breath, which sounded very much like 'cheapskate', before using Ben's driveway to turn around and head back to Raven's Edge, leaving Ben alone in the dark.

The cottage, which he'd inherited from his grandmother less than twelve months previously, was located in a very rural part of the King's Forest District. There were no street lamps and, as he'd been out for most of the day, there were no lights on inside either. Despite its pretty, fairy-tale appearance, the cottage now seemed so unwelcoming he was reminded how much he hated coming home to a house that was empty except for the cat. No dinner would be waiting for him; there'd be no one to nag him for being late, or to worry about his bruised and battered face.

He kicked the gate open. Why was he being so maudlin? He lived alone. So what? It had been a year since his divorce. He should have got used to it by now. He strode on up the path, hearing the gate clang shut behind him. One wife, ex or otherwise, was enough for anyone. He was happy on his own. He didn't need another woman to muck up his life. He was quite capable of doing that on his own.

Divorce was possibly the only thing he and his ex had ever agreed on. Neither of them wanted Sophie to grow up thinking their toxic relationship was in any way normal. But he couldn't go on like this: working all day and into the night, counting down the days until Sophie's visits. It wasn't living, it was – he grimaced at the cliché – existing.

An image of Lydia popped into his head. When he'd first transferred from the Met he'd been attracted by her cool, professional demeanour – now he knew he'd had a lucky escape. She was too controlling, too superior, too... too *cold*. The only other woman he met on a regular basis was Harriet – cute and funny, when she wasn't bossing him about, but hardly his type – and she undoubtedly felt the same way about him.

It was depressing to realise that in the last six months Lydia and Harriet were practically the only two women he'd spoken to. But if he never did anything other than work, eat and sleep, how the hell was he ever going to meet anyone who wasn't a work colleague?

Or a suspect.

Oh no...

He leant forward, resting his forehead against the cool wood of his front door.

No, no, no. He definitely didn't want *Milla*. She was a liar and a thief – and a 'person of interest' so far as the police were concerned. Hell, it was unlikely her name even was 'Milla'. That woman wouldn't recognise the truth if it bit her on the arse. She was so transparently a con artist and a scammer and... and...

And as attractive as hell.

Damn.

He lifted his head away from the door, tempted to bang it right back again. Hard. It was the only way to knock some sense in. He was *not* attracted to Milla. Obviously his body had decided it needed a woman and wasn't planning on being picky about which one.

But not Milla. He was better than that. He could never be serious about anyone he wouldn't want to introduce to his daughter, and there was no way Milla was ever going to meet Sophie. His libido would have to wait.

He tucked the box from the archives under one arm to unlock the door before going inside. With no fire burning in the little inglenook fireplace, the sitting room felt cold and bleak. Even switching on the overhead light didn't make much difference. He hooked his phone into the speaker system. Paloma Faith's last album began to fill the room. Better... but even then he was reminded of the way Milla had changed the radio station in the car when he'd been playing classic jazz.

He dropped the box onto the table beside the door. Binx was there in a flash, the tip of his tail quivering with excitement. Binx had a thing for boxes, preferably empty.

'Sorry I'm late,' he told the cat. 'Did you wonder where I was?'

'Meow,' Binx said, with a distinct lack of interest, and went back to sniffing at the box.

The automatic cat feeder must have dispensed food on cue or Binx would be making more of a fuss.

Ben sighed. Even his cat hadn't missed him.

The light on the answering machine was blinking but instead of the man from the local garage he heard the voice of his ex-wife apologising for their argument. It was enough of an event for him to sit down and play it for a second time. Caroline *apologising* and, better still...

'Would you like Sophie next weekend?' he heard her ask in her usual abrupt way. 'No need to come here, I'll bring her to you. I'm heading your way to a conference at Norchester General. I can drop her off and you can return her on Sunday evening. I'm sorry you can't have her for the whole week but she's due back at school on Monday. I hope that's OK? Call me.'

In other words she wanted an unpaid babysitter, but he didn't care. He'd be able to see Sophie again and for that he'd put up with any amount of hassle.

Aware he was being petty, he didn't return Caroline's call right away, deciding to let her stew. Instead, he went into the kitchen in search of supper but both fridge and cupboard were empty. He'd had no food delivery booked because he thought he'd be spending this week away and he'd shared his last tin of soup with Milla.

Binx, ever hopeful, appeared by his feet.

Ben bent to rub his head. 'At least one of us got fed, eh boy?'

He checked his watch. If he moved quickly, he had enough time to order a delivery from Pizza at Cosimo's before they closed. His jaw still hurt like hell but he was starving.

He took a beer from the fridge and returned to the sitting room to call the restaurant, retrieving his wallet from his jacket while he waited for them to answer the phone. They were closing up but, after a bit of banter, Cosimo agreed to drop something off on his way home. It was only when Ben took his credit card from his wallet that he realised it had been put back in the wrong slot.

Milla, *again*.

He paid for the meal and tried to slip the credit card back into its usual place but instead it stuck. There appeared to be something already wedged inside. He held his wallet up to the light, poked around and found a screwed up twenty-pound note and a tiny scrap of paper he recognised as having been torn from the notepad he kept beside his telephone. It said,

IOU £100
Sorry!!!
Milla x

He stared at it in disbelief. Since when did thieves leave IOUs? At the bottom she'd even scrawled out an email address. It wasn't a phone number, and he could probably have found the email address himself from the magazine she wrote for, but the intention to pay back the money was there. So, still a liar but possibly not a thief?

Right beside him was the box he'd brought back from the station. He leaned forward and flipped off the lid. There was Milla's book on top. It was one of the classic books of fairy tales published by Graham & Sons over a quarter of a century ago. He'd recognised the distinctive dust jacket the moment he'd seen it fallen beneath Milla's sofa. Had she realised she'd lost it yet? Now he had her email address, he could let her know he had it.

He quashed that thought. *Suspect*, he reminded himself, picking up the book.

It was *Alice's Adventures in Wonderland*. He flipped it

open. Inside, written neatly on the flyleaf – far too neatly for a child – it said,

Kiran McKenzie

Except someone had scribbled that out with a pink gel pen and replaced it with,

Milla Graham

Kiran McKenzie? Why did that name seem familiar? The answer was on the next page.

Alice's Adventures in Wonderland
By Lewis Carroll

Illustrations by Rosemary McKenzie

It took seconds to do a search on his phone:

Rosemary McKenzie: British artist primarily known for her illustrations of the Graham & Sons Classic Fairy Tale Collection... Daughter of Alastair McKenzie, Scottish journalist and broadcaster...

And, further down:

Married Patrick Fergal Graham, formerly CEO of Graham & Sons (now Graham Media).

Kiran McKenzie was presumably a relation of Rosemary's. A sister or niece, or even a daughter from an earlier relationship? Or could Kiran and Milla be the same person?

He picked up the book again, flipping through it, paying

particular attention to the beautifully drawn illustrations. They were of a traditional style, similar to Rackham and Dulac but with a modern edge. Alice, despite wearing authentically Victorian clothes, was most definitely of mixed race, with light brown skin and long black hair, tied back in a thick, shiny plait.

Ben traced his fingers over the illustration of Alice talking with the Cheshire Cat, and admired the vivid colours of the fantasy forest surrounding them. Alice looked exactly how he could imagine Milla might have done as a child. Was it her? Had Rosemary used a real-life model? This book certainly seemed to prove Milla's connection to the Graham family but how, exactly? He double-checked the publication date. The model was possibly too young to be Camilla, which left the mysterious Kiran McKenzie.

Milla, Camilla or Kiran?

He was beginning to feel as though he'd fallen down a rabbit hole of his own.

There was something he was supposed to be doing, Malcolm was sure of it. He tried opening his eyes, but it was as though someone had superglued them shut. He groped his face just to check – who knew what trick Camilla would think up next – and prised one eyelid open.

It turned out he'd fallen asleep at his desk, right on top of his new book, and now it was digging painfully into his cheek.

He pushed it aside, sleepily watching as it slid across the desk and over the edge, hitting the floor with a soft 'clunk'. Was it damaged?

But thinking required effort, so he closed his eyes and went back to sleep.

TWELVE

The door to the library had opened without either Milla or Mal being aware of it.

'You,' Dermot said, pointing a finger in Milla's direction. 'My study. Now.'

'Hey, Dad,' Mal said, in that lazy drawl she was beginning to find so irritating. 'You'll never guess who this is.'

'Your cousin Kiran? Yes, I know. *Study*,' he repeated, glaring at her.

To be left alone with him? No chance.

'I'm sure whatever you want to say to me, can be said in front of Mal,' she told him.

'I would suggest otherwise.'

What did *that* mean? She glanced towards Mal but he shrugged.

'You might as well get it over with,' he said.

How very supportive of him.

As much as she wanted Mal to be the friend she remembered from her childhood, he had changed so dramatically he was almost another person. Was 'her' Mal in there somewhere? She was beginning to doubt it.

She left Mal contemplating his whisky bottle and followed Dermot into the study, aware that from the way her Docs were clomping across the stone floor he'd guess her foul mood. Right now she didn't care, closing the door sharply to reiterate the point. Dermot didn't react. She should have slammed it harder. Or, with hindsight, not closed it at all.

There were no carpets here either, only the ubiquitous flagstones. The walls were painted in the same smoky grey as the dining room. There were chairs and another long glass table (presumably for meetings) but no filing cabinets or bookcases. There were no photographs or paintings to relieve the starkness of the walls; absolutely nothing personal. Didn't Dermot realise this was just as much of a statement?

'So you're Kiran,' he said, surveying her from the top of her head down to the worn boots on her feet. 'I'm sure we must have met prior to today but forgive me if I don't recall the occasion.'

'Me neither,' she said cheerfully.

I remember you perfectly well, you cold-hearted bastard.

'You were very young when your aunt Rosemary died,' he said. 'It's a shame we lost touch.'

She was equally sure it was deliberate but kept that to herself. He was a strange one. It wouldn't do to antagonise him. If she was ever going to find out the truth about the way Rosemary had died, she needed to be right here in this house. For that, she needed this man on her side because it was becoming increasingly clear she couldn't rely on Mal.

'I don't suppose you remember our other house?' Dermot was saying. 'The big old manor, outside Raven's Edge? Did you ever visit with your grandmother?'

Was he serious? She, Mal and Kiran had grown up together, running all over that house and the acres of surrounding gardens and woodland. He must know that? Why was he pretending otherwise? But she nodded slowly, wary of what she should admit to, wary of what he was likely to ask her next.

'That house is now derelict,' he said. 'No one has lived there since the fire and no renovations or repairs have been undertaken. Vandals have left their mark and the locals have roamed all over the estate – and haven't taken kindly to our attempts to keep it protected with fencing and security patrols. The inhabitants of Raven's Edge seem to believe King's Rest is as much theirs as it is ours. We've tried to sell the manor house on numerous occasions but understandably no one wants to buy it, and we can't demolish it either, due to the terms of the trust set up by my maternal grandfather to protect my mother's inheritance.'

'Trust?' It was the first time she'd heard mention of any trust. As far as she knew, control of the various companies had defaulted to Dermot when his elder brother Patrick had been imprisoned.

'Demolishing the house would reduce its worth, even when the value of the land is taken into consideration. By the terms of the trust, we're not allowed to do anything that would reduce the value of an asset. My maternal grandfather had little faith in my father's ability to manage money.'

What did any of this have to do with her? 'I'm not after your money.'

'I would feel less concerned if you were. As it is, your return to Raven's Edge after all these years has me worried. Why are you here, Kiran McKenzie? If not for my money?'

Despite the distance between them, Milla instinctively took a step back. Dermot Graham was very tall and, despite his age and pallor, he appeared fit, healthy and strong. He didn't have to try to be intimidating. He just was.

Yet he appeared to be paying her very little attention at all, staring out of the window, even though there was nothing to look at but the room reflected right back at him. Milla, remembering what had happened in the library with Mal, was careful to keep her expression neutral.

But took another step back to be on the safe side.

The door is right behind me. Any trouble, and all I have to do is turn and run and—

'A body has been found,' he said. 'That is why I wasn't at dinner. I was giving a statement to the police.'

Whatever she had been expecting, it wasn't that. 'A... a body?'

'A woman of your age, who looked like you, who apparently had the same name as you. She was found in one of the bedrooms at King's Rest.'

A shiver ran through her, of pure ice.

'Some teenagers found her during the storm last night. She'd not been dead for long and the bed she was lying on had been decorated with flowers and leaves. If that wasn't enough of a coincidence to link her with our family, she was wearing an evening gown which once belonged to my mother. The detective inspector I spoke to didn't tell me any of this. I received the information from an alternative source.'

She didn't bother to ask who. She was far too interested in the fact that, 'The woman looked like... *me*?'

'Does someone want you dead?'

It was an innocent enough question – until those grey eyes met hers. This time she looked into them – *really* looked into them – and felt their chill all the way down to her toes. *This* time she didn't hesitate.

She bolted.

He hardly had to take two strides to grab her arm and haul her back.

'If I'd wanted you dead,' he said, 'you'd be dead. With the minimum amount of fuss and effort.' He shoved her in the direction of the nearest chair. As the back of her legs hit the soft leather seat, she overbalanced right into it.

She glanced towards the door. Even if she made it through, there was still the main door and a huge garden to get lost in before she even got to the main gate. She wondered if her car was where she'd left it. Somehow she doubted it. She looked back at him. He raised one black eyebrow, giving every indication that he knew exactly what she was thinking the moment she'd thought it. And also, something else...

'What are you not telling me?' she demanded.

'That detective friend of yours has identified the dead woman as Amita Kaal.'

It was as though the walls darkened and surged in on her. 'Amita!' Her fingers tightened over the arms of the chair, but Dermot was there in front of her, ready to shove her back down again should she even consider getting out of it. 'Oh no! *No!*'

'Calm yourself!' He loomed over her, his face inches from hers. 'Have you had recent contact with Amita? Have you any idea why she was here in Raven's Edge? Did she come here with you?'

'I saw her at the music festival in Calahurst. She had a stall; her family make jewellery, she travels to all the—'

'Did you talk to her?'

'I tried but... she wouldn't talk to me.'

'Your bag, with your purse, phone and all your ID, was found in her possession.'

'*What?*'

'You didn't give it to her for safekeeping?'

'Why would I do that? She wasn't my friend. She hated me. She'd have just as likely chucked it into a ditch!'

'You have no idea how your bag came to be in her possession?'

'I thought it had been stolen.'

'Where were you when you realised it had gone?'

'In the bar,' she admitted ruefully. 'My bag kept sliding off my shoulder so I put it on the bar beside me, right where I could see it, not tangled beneath my feet where anyone could pinch it. I had a bit of banter with the barman and then someone shoved into me, spilling my drink, and the next moment it had gone.'

'Classic diversion.'

'Yes, I *know*,' she said. 'I can't believe I fell for it either. But it couldn't have been Amita. She wasn't like that. She was a lovely woman. Who—' she broke off, realising what she was about to admit to.

'Hated you.'

'Ah... Yes.'

'May I ask why?'

'I... er, slept with her fiancé. Well, not so much *slept* as in... er, the other thing.'

For a moment he stared at her. 'You did this, yet she was your friend?'

'It wasn't my proudest moment. I was trying to prove a point. You see—'

He held up his hand. 'Spare me the gruesome details. You were sent to live with Amita's family when your grandmother died. You were about ten, I believe?'

She frowned. 'How did you even *know*—'

'You're Rosemary's niece; of course I kept track of you.'

'Not terribly hard! The Kaals threw me out when I was sixteen. It would have been nice to have had a fairy godfather turn up in my life at that point.' She refrained from adding 'Even you.'

'I assume they had good reason?'

'I assume you can work it out!'

'The unfaithful fiancé.'

'He was a pig. He was only interested in her family's money. She was well rid of him.'

'They thought otherwise and you found yourself out on the street?'

'Not *literally* on the street. I had friends. Friends with spare rooms and sofas. I had to leave college, but I got a job and an apartment of my own. I did all right.'

'Yes,' he said. 'So you did.' For one horrible moment, she wondered if he *had* kept track of her all these years and known *exactly* how she'd spent them. 'I've told the police you're here,' he added. 'They seem quite anxious to talk to you.'

Damn.

'I'm sorry to have dragged your family into this,' she said politely. 'I'll leave right away.'

He paused long enough to cause her concern her bluff hadn't worked.

'No,' he said. 'You'll stay here. The grounds are enclosed with CCTV and security personnel. There is nowhere safer. No one can access the estate without my staff knowing about it.'

Or leave.

A couple of hours ago this offer would have been beyond her wildest hopes. Live in a luxurious mansion completely free of charge? Brilliant! But if there was one thing she truly hated, it was being outsmarted.

'That is *so* kind of you,' she said, beaming up at him. 'Thank you very much.'

'Welcome to the family,' he said.

Milla was left wondering if she had even fooled him for a second.

While Dermot phoned his housekeeper to arrange for one of the guest bedrooms to be made ready for her, Milla volunteered to return to the salon. She'd give him this one. Let him think he'd won. She could scope the premises, check the exit routes and maybe snoop around a bit more. She hadn't got beyond the ground floor, now she had the perfect excuse to go upstairs.

Welcome to the family? The bastard had *no* idea...

Once alone in the hall, her bravado evaporated. A

woman had been found dead at King's Rest – her cousin *Amita* had been found dead – right now, right at the very moment Milla had reappeared in Raven's Edge and made herself known to the Graham family. There was no way it could be coincidence. But why *now*? *Was* it really her fault?

Completely.

Poor Amita. She'd been happy to go through her life, doing as other people wanted, obeying her family in everything, including who to love and who to marry. She would have been an easy mark for a conman, for a murderer...

Milla cursed again, a particularly foul word that would have had Grandma McKenzie reaching for the soap if she'd heard her, only to realise this time she was not alone. The shadows around the staircase had shifted and, although at first she dismissed it, the next time there was no mistaking it. Someone was watching her.

Mal? But why would he want to spy?

She kept perfectly still.

Dermot was speaking on the phone, although not loudly enough for her to hear what he was saying. Milla let her head rest back against the study door. Anyone watching would assume she was eavesdropping. From the other end of the corridor there was the faintest glimmer of light. She felt a flicker of triumph.

Got you!

There was another glint, stronger this time, and then the sound of high heels tapping across stone. Milla froze. It was a woman who stepped into the light, walking confidently towards her, not stopping until she had well and truly invaded Milla's personal space.

Even after eighteen years, the woman was as coldly beautiful as Milla remembered, with her pale blonde hair and eyes the colour of sea glass. It was her jacket which had given her away, part of a black trouser suit with silver buttons that glinted and sparkled in the overhead light.

'Hello, Lydia,' Milla said, determined not to show fear, even though the woman towered over her, even though any number of bad memories were crowding into her head and screaming at her to run.

But the witch only smiled.

THIRTEEN

'You finally came back,' Lydia said.

'Yes,' Milla said.

'For money?'

'Why else?'

'You tell me. You're the one who's left a trail of destruction all around the county: the music festival, the apartment you rented in Norchester – although they've never received any rent – not to mention a rampage through one of the city's more exclusive boutiques. Busy little thing, aren't you?'

Milla shivered. How did she *know* all that? 'I do my best.'

Lydia's face tightened and Milla was wondering if this new calm demeanour was about to crack when the door behind her opened.

'Hello, Lydia,' Dermot said. 'Were you working late again?'

'Something like that,' Lydia said. 'Sorry.'

'I see you've met our new guest. Kiran was Rosemary's niece.'

Lydia inclined her head.

'Lydia was the daughter of our previous cook,' Dermot told

Milla, 'and your babysitter. I suppose you were too young to remember?'

Witch. Evil, cruel, black-hearted—

'Although now she's the detective inspector in charge of Calahurst CID.'

Oh *no*. Another one!

Lydia didn't even bother to glance in her direction. 'Dermot, if I might have a word?'

'Of course, my dear.' Dermot indicated Lydia should precede him into the study, before adding, 'Goodnight, Kiran,' to ensure she knew she was being dismissed.

It was like being six years old again. It was tempting to stick her tongue out.

The study door closed, not quite in her face, but pretty much as good as. She moved nearer, eager to hear the argument she hoped was about to erupt, when a hand lightly tapped at her shoulder. She spun around, instinctively getting ready to punch, and found an unrepentant Brianna Graham.

'People who listen at doors never hear any good about themselves. Surely you know that darling?'

'I never hear much good about myself anyway,' Milla retorted. She'd intended it as a joke but realised it hadn't come out that way when she saw Brianna's blue gaze soften.

'I understand you'll be staying with us for a while? I've arranged for a lovely room to be prepared for you. Green, with delicious cream furnishings – one my son hasn't managed to get his hands on yet. Come along with me and I'll show you. You'll love it.'

Although desperate to drink in every detail of the grandmother she hardly remembered, Milla forced herself to casually glance past Brianna towards the back of the house, where she hoped a rescuer would appear at any moment. Right now, she'd even be glad to see Mal.

'What about your guests?'

'Pish. They can entertain themselves. I'd be a poor judge of character otherwise.'

'I wouldn't want to put you to any trouble. Dermot has already called the housekeeper.'

'Dermot might expect his staff to work both day and night but I certainly don't. Mrs Briars is long gone to her cosy little cottage on the other side of the village. I'll take you to your room myself.'

Brianna said this as though it was a huge honour but Milla inwardly cringed. What had she done or said to attract such close attention from Dermot's mother?

'Please, don't go to any trouble. Just give me the directions and—'

'Humour me, Kiran. I'm sure you're longing to explore the place and put it down to being lost, but the rest of us would like to go to sleep without worrying about you walking through a glass window or falling off a balcony. And yes, before you ask, it has happened. My son might adore this house but the rest of us merely tolerate it. Now, it's been a few years since I had someone to spoil. I'm quite looking forward to it.'

Better to nip *that* in the bud right away.

'I'm not planning on staying long.'

'Whatever you feel is best,' Brianna said breezily, taking hold of her arm and bustling her towards the staircase before Milla realised what was happening. 'Perhaps you'll change your mind when you know us better?'

Brianna didn't make it sound optional.

Milla recognised the same tone Dermot had used earlier – and Mal before him. That sunnily pleasant voice that implied they agreed wholeheartedly with the other person, yet all the while intending to do the opposite. She should know. She did the exact same thing herself.

Seeing echoes of herself in these people, who were *strangers*, was disconcerting.

At the top of the staircase was a corridor stretching in both directions. Brianna walked to the door at the far end and opened it. She moved disconcertingly fast for someone who must be in their seventies. Milla followed her into the guest room. As Brianna had said, everything was decorated in green and cream and there was actually a carpet on the floor. Like the rest of the house, one wall was complete glass from floor to ceiling, overlooking a wide balcony with recliners and a little fountain bubbling between an arrangement of large, rounded stones.

'Isn't it lovely?' Brianna said. 'Very reminiscent of woodland glades, spring mornings and a fresh new day. I'm very pleased with it. What do you think?'

'It's beautiful,' Milla said, and it was, although she could hardly say anything different.

'All our guest bedrooms overlook the forest and if you stand on tiptoe, you might be able to see the church spire in the village.' Brianna indicated the panel of buttons on the wall. 'Another of my son's quirks. He loves technology, as I'm sure you've noticed. See? There's a button for everything, quite clearly labelled. You're smart. I'm sure you'll work it out.'

'I'm sure I will.' It was like being swept along by a river.

'There's a small refrigerator and a coffee machine. If there's anything else you require, press the call button and one of the staff will help you. There's usually someone on call morning or night. My son insisted on it, ever since—' She broke off and started again, smiling brightly to cover her slip. Too brightly. 'I hope you sleep well, Kiran. I'll see you in the morning. You've had such a terrible time. At least you're among family now.'

Before she had the chance to go into reverse, Brianna leaned down, kissed her cheek and left while Milla was still in shock.

She waited until she heard Brianna's heels tapping down the stairs, then locked the door and wedged a chair beneath the handle. It wouldn't keep out anyone who was determined to get in, but she'd sleep a whole lot better. Was the room bugged? She had a quick check and found nothing. That didn't mean they weren't there, just extremely well-hidden. Or maybe she'd watched too many movies?

She bounced on the bed; it seemed comfortable enough. She switched on the TV, flicked through the channels and then left it on, one decibel below deafening – before picking up the remote and turning it down, telling herself not to be childish. She went to investigate the large ensuite bathroom, which had a full complement of expensive toiletries, and then turned on the taps to run herself a bath.

She didn't feel quite so gleeful when she entered the walk-in wardrobe and found her clothes already hanging up, along with her possessions stacked neatly in one corner. Someone had cleared out her car while she'd been blithely working her way through that five-course dinner. What if she wanted to make a quick getaway? She'd be forced to leave everything she owned behind. Unless she found out where they'd stored her car and repacked it?

She sniffed at the dress hanging nearest to her. They'd even had her clothes laundered! And then, when she returned to the bedroom, she found the T-shirt she habitually slept in had been folded and arranged on the pillow like some fancy hotel – bloody *hell*!

Throwing the T-shirt across the room, she marched into the bathroom and stripped off her clothes, allowing them to fall in a crumpled heap before lowering herself into the bath. Belatedly she remembered the large window, presumably exposing her assets to the outside world, but, as Dermot had said, it was unlikely there'd be anyone loitering about the forest at this time of night.

Lying back against the bath, Milla closed her eyes. She needed to calm down and get a grip. She was twenty-four years old. Far too old for tantrums. She was exactly where she wanted to be – inside the house of her enemy, in an ideal position to discover what had happened to Rosemary all those years ago. Dermot, Mal, Brianna, Lydia – even the butler – one of them knew the truth; she just had to wait for that one mistake that would reveal the killer.

After suffering the tiny shower at her apartment this bath was *bliss*, she had to give them that. It was huge too, plenty of room to stretch out and plenty enough room for two. She remembered Ben sprawled across his bed and smiled, and then hurriedly thought of something else.

Amita. Poor, poor Amita. Had she really stolen Milla's bag? Why? They had run across each other before at these festivals. Milla always smiled and tried to be polite. Amita always ignored her. It had become a ritual, which was why she found it so hard to believe Amita would do something so petty, so *spiteful*, as to steal her bag. But what was the alternative? Had someone stolen the bag deliberately, to make it look as though Amita was her? Who were they attempting to deceive? The murderer? Or the police?

As for the shock of seeing Lydia again! Grandma McKenzie had been strict but fair, certainly nothing compared to the teenage Lydia, who delighted in reporting any misdemeanours back to Rosemary and Patrick. She had been an evil bitch, dishing out sweets and treats to Mal, yet deliberately ignoring Camilla and Kiran.

Milla let herself sink further beneath the scented bubbles and wondered why. Jealousy? The Grahams were rich, whereas Lydia had come from an ordinary family in the village. But that didn't explain why she'd favoured Mal. He'd been a handsome lad but only eight years old, whereas Lydia would have been around seventeen or eighteen. It made no sense.

Milla sighed, opening her eyes. The position of the bath meant she looked straight through the window. Or she would have done, had it not been past midnight. The view must be stunning during the day, right across the garden to the forest.

The bathroom lighting was dim, which meant she could see the faint glow of the street lights around Norchester. Closer were a sprinkling of tiny white lights from the village of Raven's Edge. The Hartfell estate enclosed it completely. What a thing to own so much land – an entire village – like medieval lords.

One of the little white lights moved.

There *was* someone out there!

Her first impulse was to duck right down into the water, and she did – sending it surging up and splashing over the sides. Then she realised she was being an idiot. The sides of the bath were high and she'd filled it right to the top with water and frothy bubbles. No one could see anything, unless they'd been watching when she'd got in.

With the reflections caused by the overhead lighting, it was hard to distinguish one tiny light from the dozen or so in the village. She pushed herself up, keeping one arm covering her breasts, even if it was a little too late for modesty.

There! She saw the light again – moving, flickering, as it disappeared between the trees and out of sight. For one very long moment it vanished completely, before reappearing higher up. She remembered what Brianna had said, about being able to see the church spire if one stood on tiptoe, but it seemed too close to be the village.

She yawned widely. Maybe there was some other building in the grounds? Over the next couple of days she'd make a point of finding out what it was. Right now she had more important things to do and one of those was getting a good night's sleep. She grabbed a towel, wrapped it around herself and then, when she was sure she was decently covered, she got out of the bath, dripping water everywhere.

There would be no more inadvertent strip shows tonight.

The girl tiptoed along the corridor. It was so quiet she could hear each floorboard creak. If everyone had gone to bed, why were all the lights on? She glanced back nervously, remembering every ghost story Malcolm had ever told her, and moved just that little bit quicker.

The first bedroom she entered belonged to the twins. They had a bed each but had cuddled up together and were sound asleep. She closed the door and moved on to Malcolm's room. He was lying on the floor, still dressed, snoring gently.

The girl dropped to her knees and shook him. She pulled his long hair and then she punched him. Nothing had any effect. So she left him.

There was one last family room, right at the very end of the corridor. The door was shut but there was a strip of light showing beneath it. Should she knock? What if she got into trouble?

She quietly opened the door, just the tiniest crack, and saw a woman lying on a bed of flowers, surrounded by candles. She wore a long scarlet gown, like the princess in a fairy tale, and looked so beautiful that at first the girl didn't notice the man standing on the other side of the bed.

The man who was leaning over the woman and whispering.

The man who was holding a knife.

Then the man noticed her.

FOURTEEN

Milla awoke late, showered, and dressed practically in jeans, T-shirt and her favourite Docs. It was raining steadily but she couldn't resist pulling back the sliding doors and stepping out onto the balcony. If the weather had been fine, she would have seen all the way to the village. With the rain and low-swirling mist, she could barely make out the boundaries of the garden. She'd better leave that exploration for another time.

Downstairs the house was deserted, with only Hodges on duty in the hall. He looked up and smiled as she clomped down the staircase, but it was a strange smile. Friendly? No, that wasn't right. Fake-friendly? No... Satisfied? Yes, but how did *that* make sense? Maybe her default paranoia was kicking in but paranoia had always kept her out of trouble in the past.

Hodges opened the nearest door with the air of a children's entertainer producing a rabbit from a hat. 'Breakfast, Miss McKenzie?'

Well, look at that. An entire room dedicated to breakfast. How the other half lived.

Something must have shown on her face because his brow immediately furrowed. 'Miss McKenzie?'

'Thank you, Mr Hodges,' she said.

Miss this, Mr that; had she fallen into a Jane Austen movie or did rich people really talk like this? All the time?

Apparently she wasn't convincing enough because his eyes were about to disappear beneath that frown.

Once more with feeling?

'That would be splendid,' she said.

Decorated in shades of cream and brown, the breakfast room was certainly more welcoming than the dining room. The array of food arranged on hot plates along the sideboard was also impressive, although there was a peculiar arrangement of dead leaves in the centre of the breakfast table that did look very 'Dermot'. That man definitely had a Dark Side obsession going on. Fortunately, she was distracted by the buffet before she could come right out and say so.

How long had it been since she'd eaten? Last night? It seemed like forever.

'Wow, Mr Hodges,' she said, summoning up due reverence. 'This is truly amazing.'

Pleasure immediately lit his face. 'Enjoy!'

She caught the door before he could close it. 'Mr Hodges? I want to go out and I'm going to need my car.' He'd been friendly, on the surface anyway, so how to say this without sounding insulting? 'Is it where I left it?'

'I'll arrange for your car to be brought to the front entrance, Miss McKenzie.'

He was smiling at her again, in that very unnerving way, as though she were some kind of celebrity that had deigned to appear in his presence, but at least it didn't appear that she was a prisoner – always good to know!

She piled her plate with eggs, sausages, and bacon, almost before the door had swung shut. Well, there was always the chance Dermot might change his mind and kick her out by lunch-time.

When finished (the pancakes were particularly scrummy) she grabbed a handful of fruit from a cut-glass bowl and dropped them into her satchel. It was tempting to shove the fancy bowl in there too but the bulge in her bag was already embarrassingly noticeable. How observant was Hodges? He was already on the other side of the door when she opened it. Didn't the man have anything better to do?

'Might we expect you back for luncheon, Miss McKenzie?'

Had she time-warped into the 1930s and not noticed?

'I should think so, Mr Hodges.'

And afterwards, maybe she could squeeze in tea with the Vicar.

As she attempted to sidle around him, his attention snagged on the bulge in her bag.

Damn.

'One thing, Miss McKenzie?'

She got her excuses ready but, instead of hooking her satchel from her shoulder and checking it for the family silver, he took a small bottle of mineral water from the sideboard inside the breakfast room and handed it to her.

'It's very humid today, despite the rain. Better keep hydrated.'

She didn't know whether to hug him or burst into tears. Why did he have to be so *nice*? Did Brianna and Hodges truly believe she was Kiran? It would explain their strange behaviour. They seemed genuinely delighted she was here. Staying detached was going to be increasingly difficult – and she really needed to squash down on that instinct to roll over like an overeager puppy every time someone showed her a kindness.

Hodges opened the front door with another flourish, but she ignored both his cheery goodbye and little wave, and set off across the little bridge.

It was almost a shock to see her car parked in the same place she'd left it, albeit a whole lot cleaner and with a strange man standing beside it. He was smiling too. This was getting beyond surreal.

'We've filled her up for you, Miss McKenzie,' he said.

Did *everyone* know who she was?

'And topped up the oil and water. You've got a nasty bit of rust around the wheel arches, did you know?'

'Yes. And the rear reflector has a big crack in it and my windscreen wipers only work on Tuesdays. What of it?'

His broad smile dimmed. 'When you bring her back, we can sort that out for you.'

Bloody hell!

This was probably the part where she should thank him profusely, but her charm had bailed out and she was pretty sure she was glaring at him distrustfully because he almost threw her key at her as though he thought that if he stepped any closer she might punch him.

The key, warm against her palm, was her spare. She closed her fingers around it. It usually lived in a magnetic box tucked under the wheel arch, so she put it back and got into the car. He'd valeted the interior and hung one of those smelly cardboard trees from the rear-view mirror. That went out the window before she'd even driven halfway to the gate. Where did Dermot *find* these people?

King's Rest was ten minutes' drive away, although she could have taken a stroll through the forest and arrived at roughly the same time. Were the police still hanging around? Rather than chance it, she parked in a layby and walked the last few metres. Sure enough, there was a solitary patrol car parked outside and an officer in uniform guarding the gate.

Only the one? It was almost insulting.

Also guarding the gate was a Victorian lodge, half-hidden amongst the lush summer foliage, unloved and unlived in. No one had thought to place a guard outside that.

Amateurs.

Sliding over the waist-high surrounding wall took very little effort. Likewise, her leisurely stroll around the side of the house and her silent-but-speedy shimmy over the higher wall at the back. There was no time to admire the view. She dropped softly into last year's dead leaves, landing on her feet.

She was in.

If the police officer heard rustling amongst the foliage, he didn't deign to turn his head.

She stepped out from the shelter of the trees and onto what had once been a private road. Despite the potholes, it was giving off less of a *Sleeping Beauty* vibe than the last time she'd visited. Someone had even removed the oak tree that had crashed down during last summer's storms.

The closer she drew to the house, the darker the sky became – as if the house knew she was coming. *Keep out. Stay away. Turn around right now or Bad Things Will Happen.*

Right on cue, there was a distant rumble of thunder and the rain began to fall in earnest. Big, fat drops slapping the tarmac and stinging her bare arms. She was soaked by the time she reached the hit-and-miss shelter of the manor's crumbling porch. The main door had been hanging from its hinges on her last visit, like a drunk making a last-ditch effort to grab a lamp post before hitting the pavement; now it was securely boarded up. She thumped her fist against the wood, hearing the dull thuds echo through the hall on the other side. *Very* securely boarded up.

This had *not* been part of her plan.

She turned her back on the door and surveyed the wilderness that had once been an elegant garden. She'd roamed all over the grounds as a child. The garden was overgrown, but she remembered every way in and out of the house, from the fancy portico to the rather grimmer coal chute into the cellar. Hopefully it wouldn't come to that.

She stepped back into the rain (the best she could say about it was that at least it was warm) and followed what was very nearly a path beneath a stone archway and onto what had once been a grand terrace. This was where the adults had gathered on the night of the party; waiters with trays of champagne circling amongst all those animal masks and sumptuous dresses, the ethereal 'Aquarium' from *Le Carnaval des Animaux* pouring through the open windows and into the garden.

Another fallen tree had left a huge hole in the terrace, along with a tangle of exposed roots. The paving slabs surrounding it were upturned or broken, or missing completely. Yet the whirling ghosts in her head danced right over them.

Milla shivered. When had it turned so cold?

It was so hard to keep going when all she wanted to do was turn around and head home – but where was home anyway?

Stepping around the fallen tree, she passed the dining room, with its huge bay window (also boarded up), and headed in the direction of the kitchen – the oldest part of the house. Here the windows were too high and too narrow for her to climb through, and the door squatting between them had been sealed with more panels of chipboard.

But this chipboard was old and had begun rotting at the corners.

She turned sideways to slam a kick at the weakest point. The wood splintered. A few more kicks and she could pull one panel off completely, tossing it behind her.

And people always asked why she wore boots in summer.

The house was darker than the forest. The fire that had destroyed the east wing had not reached the servants' hall, but the walls here were still black with soot and vandals had left their own (less pretty) graffiti. Since her last visit the cupboard doors had been torn off and scattered around the floor, and the oven door was hanging at an angle – maybe too well-made to yank off completely?

It was a small oven for a house this size, barely enough room for a child to hide.

Hide? In an oven?

Someone had read too many stories about witches and gingerbread houses.

She bent to peer inside... then jerked back as another memory hit.

'Don't come out, whatever happens! Promise me!'

Where had *that* come from?

She closed her eyes, concentrating on the fractured images. A boy with long hair and an anxious smile, brightly-coloured sweets, a man in an over-sized hat – *'Come here, my little White Rabbit...'*

What did it all mean?

Dermot had said Amita's body had been found in one of the bedrooms but the first one Milla checked was empty. Although untouched by the fire, the furniture and fittings had been stripped out and there was nothing left, not even the fireplace. Yet she could almost see an elderly Indian lady sitting beside the fire, beckoning her closer.

Had Grandma McKenzie once been a guest?

Why couldn't she *remember*?

The next bedroom had also been stripped, although a small doll lay abandoned on the windowsill. She picked it up. Had it been hers? She doubted it, and allowed the doll to fall through her fingers. It hit the floor the same time as she heard a distant crash.

Thunder?

Or did she have company?

She'd have thought that boarded-up front door would keep out a marauding army.

Unless someone had followed her around to the back?

She really was going to have to stop spooking herself. It was only a *house*. No demons, no ghosts; only mice and rats and birds, and other woodland creatures seeking shelter from the storm; *Snow White* not *Amityville Horror*.

The echo of her footsteps bounced off every wall. If the corridor had ever had a carpet, it was long gone. Paint peeled from the walls, plaster flaked from the ceiling... Was this why nothing was familiar?

At the end was the room where Amita must have been found. Furnished with a bed so huge it couldn't have been moved, each of its four posts had deep grooves carved with random initials and obscenities. If the bed had ever had hangings or a mattress there was no evidence of them now. Fragments of dead leaves and flowers lay scattered on the floor, splashes of colour against the dusty boards. Strangest of all were the pools of hardened wax dotting the wooden floor. That did tug at her memory. Before it could form into a distinct image, another crash shook the floor.

What the *hell* was that?

Had a door or window been left open?

No, because everything was boarded up and the sound was too regular to be something slamming in the wind. It was too constant, as though marking time.

One, one thousand; two, one thousand; three, one thousand...

Pounding. *Beating.*

Like a heart?

If someone wanted to spook her, they were going the right way about it.

Well, they'd have to try harder. First rule of a scam? Don't try to cheat the con artist.

She retraced her steps to the top of the stairs. The sound was coming from the boarded-up east wing. She almost rolled her eyes. Of course it was.

Resting her palms on the boards that blocked the passageway, she peered through the gap.

The banging stopped.

It had done its job. It had caught her attention. Now she should turn right around and leave by the quickest route.

And let this clown win?

She waited, allowing her eyes to adjust to the gloom. At first she could hear nothing except the rain beating against the roof but slowly, very slowly, she became aware of a soft fluttering sound, like wings – or someone whispering?

They were good – she'd give them that – but really? *Ghosts?* That was how they wanted to play it?

The whispering and scratching grew louder.

Now they really were pushing it.

She aimed her heel at the weakest point of the board and kicked until she had a section big enough to walk through – but failed to duck low enough and her hair caught, yanking her head back.

'Ow!'

The whispering stopped abruptly.

She shouted along the dark corridor. 'Not so brave now are you?'

Was that *laughter?*

Impatient to move on, she pulled her hair free and lost a good chunk of it in the process. Whatever. It wasn't as though she didn't have a head full of the stuff.

So... this was the notorious east wing?

The first thing to hit was the smell. The sweet scent of decay pervaded the entire house but here it was the absolute worst. The sinister black soot was everywhere, coating the walls in a thick powdery crust. Floorboards creaked and squeaked with every movement – she was unlikely to be sneaking up on anyone but that was their plan, wasn't it? To coax her into a trap?

Of slightly more concern was the sensation that the rotting floorboards were buckling beneath her weight.

She took a step closer to the wall.

That same sixth sense warned caution as she was about to step into the twins' old room. It turned out to have no floor and no roof, only a hole straight into the billiard room. And it was a dizzyingly long way down, thanks to those high ceilings.

Milla retreated into the corridor, feeling slightly sick, then realised she was outside the room that she had once shared with her cousin. She took an eager step forward – then froze.

Whenever she remembered her old life, it was always about her family and the fun they'd had, but here was the reality. The beds, the wardrobe, the toy chest, even the doll house that had been a perfect miniature of King's Rest, had been completely destroyed. It made her want to cry for the family she'd lost, for the girl she'd once been. The girl who believed in fairy tales.

She almost didn't recognise the mass of twisted metal in the corner as the mirror her mother had designed for her, but the flowers and leaves that had curled around the frame were still there, even if the glass was long gone.

Instead of the wall behind, she saw a young girl, twirling around, her full skirt swinging out around her.

'Do I look pretty? Do I look like a princess?'

'You look beautiful,' Nanny had said, before turning and looking directly at her. 'As for you, Little Miss Awkward, what would you like to be? If you won't wear the Alice dress, how about being a cute little White Rabbit?' She waved the bunny ears she held in her hand. 'I can paint your face too, if you like?'

'No thanks.' Milla had snatched a top hat from the heap of costumes on the bed. 'I'm going to be the Hatter.'

'Uh uh,' Nanny had said, trying to take it from her. 'Your Uncle Dermot has his eye on that.'

'It's mine!'

'It's mine,' Milla repeated, her echo drowned out by thunder.

A streak of light lit the room and, for a split second, the silhouette of a man stark against the broken window.

Had that been... *real*? Had she actually seen—

The lightning struck again. The shadow turned its head and she screamed, instinctively stepping back – too quickly, too forcefully.

There was a horrendous crack. The floor shuddered and vanished from beneath her feet, and then she was falling through a snowstorm of plaster flakes.

She landed on her back on a hard surface, the breath knocked out of her, cracking her head so badly all she could see were stars.

As she lay there, struggling to reclaim her breath, she heard a laugh.

They'd set their trap and she'd fallen right into it – literally.

It was too painful to sit up, so she rolled onto her side – and promptly fell off the dining table she'd apparently landed on.

After exhausting every swearword she knew, in both English and Punjabi, she shoved herself up. At least she hadn't broken anything (despite her very best efforts) but it was going to be a long, painful walk back to her car.

Yeah, right. She grabbed a chair from the neat row of six, closed her eyes and smashed the centuries-old window, before kicking out the boards on the other side.

So sue me, Dermot.

It was only when she was safely on the other side that she realised (1) she'd cut herself on the broken glass, (2) it had finally stopped raining, and (3) there was a very familiar man standing directly in front of her, staring incredulously.

'*Milla?*' Ben said. 'What the *hell* are you *doing*?'

'Leaving,' huffed Milla and, as he didn't look as though he was about to move any time soon, she shoved him out of her way and stalked off without a backward glance.

FIFTEEN

Knocked off balance, Ben attempted to recover by stepping back – only to tumble into the hole left by the fallen tree. It was barely a metre deep, but he used the overhanging roots to haul himself out, ignoring Harriet's outstretched hand.

'Don't say a word,' he warned her.

She didn't bother to hide her smirk though. 'Shall I dash off in hot pursuit or would you prefer to do that yourself, sir?'

'There's no point. I believe I know where she's going.' He attempted to brush the mud and leaves from his suit but only made it worse.

Thankfully, Harriet's attention was on the ruined house. 'What do you think she was doing in there? She's a little old to be on a ghost hunt.'

'Milla is trying to convince anyone stupid enough to listen that she's Camilla Graham back from the dead.'

Harriet frowned. 'But we have a body, an autopsy, a death certificate. Camilla Graham couldn't be any deader.'

The thought that Milla had mental health issues had already occurred to Ben. 'I did wonder if it was a scam designed to part Dermot Graham from his money. She's so blatant about it though.'

'A double bluff?'

'I'm more concerned about her connection to Amita Kaal.'

'We really need to interview her.'

'We really need to catch her first but the woman never stays still long enough.'

'I did offer!'

'You did, and thank you, but let's concentrate on one thing at a time, eh?'

Harriet didn't bother to reply to this but went over to the bay window and stuck her head through the broken pane.

'It's the dining room,' she announced. 'Or rather, it used to be.'

'Be careful—'

Too late. Harriet had clambered through the window with no trouble at all, despite her elegant trouser suit.

'It's totally wrecked,' her voice echoed back to him. 'There's rubble all over the floor and a great big hole in the ceiling. Was that there before? I can't remember.'

Ben sighed. Feeling exactly as though he were only days from drawing an old-age pension, he carefully checked the window frame for remaining glass and then followed her. He felt his jacket catch and then rip on a shard of glass.

Harriet turned at the sound. 'You should have waited. I could have opened the door for you.'

'I am quite capable of climbing through a window.'

She grinned. 'You do it all the time?'

He was tempted to point out that his height meant it was a tight squeeze but remained silent, aware his dignity hung by a thread.

'This place is in a right state,' Harriet was saying, turning away. 'What do you think Milla was hoping to find? There's nothing worth nicking.'

'No idea, but I can guess how the hole came to be in the ceiling.' He pointed to the clean patch on the dining table. It was recognisably human-shaped, as though Milla had been playing at snow angels in the dust.

'She fell from all the way up there? Bloody hell!'

'Bloody lucky.' Ben picked his way through the pile of debris that had once been the ceiling and carried on into the main hall, where he took the stairs two at a time while Harriet hurried to keep up with him, the clomp of her wellingtons echoing around them.

By his reckoning, the dining room was in the east wing and, from what he remembered of the plans, directly beneath Camilla Graham's bedroom. It *was* lucky Milla had survived a fall from that distance without any apparent injury, but what bothered him most was how she had known which bedroom had been Camilla's in the first place.

The coincidences were piling up.

When Ben reached the top of the stairs, he turned his attention to the blocked-up passageway into the east wing, which was blocked no longer. In fact, there was a Milla-sized hole in one side and a chunk of hair dangling from a rusty nail. He pulled it free and held it up to the light. The strand was long, silky and black; it definitely belonged to Milla. He let it drift to the floor and out of sight as Harriet arrived on the landing beside him, not remotely out of breath.

She rummaged in her bag and brought out a small Maglite torch, which she flicked on and shone through the gap. 'Ugh,' she said, wrinkling her nose. 'It's disgusting.'

He had to agree with her. Even after all this time the house still smelled strongly of burnt wood and plastic, and possibly other substances he didn't care to identify.

'Do we really have to go in there?' she said.

'No, it's not safe. Milla's already fallen through and she's a tiny little thing—' He broke off, realising Harriet was regarding him speculatively. 'I thought I saw footprints when we were here yesterday,' he said to distract her, but when Harriet moved the torch to check it out, he realised what he'd said was true.

Harriet squinted into the darkness. 'Are they hers? Do you think she's been here before?'

He sincerely hoped not. 'Impossible to tell just from scuff marks in the dust.'

'I suppose we could get CSIs up here to check them out?'

'Yes.' He could hardly say 'no'.

'They'll totally love us for that.'

'It might not be safe.'

'*Might?*' Harriet said. 'It's got "death trap" written all over it.'

Before he realised she'd offered him a get-out clause, Harriet had taken out her phone, all ready to call up Headquarters. Fortunately it rang before she could do so.

'Yes, this is DS March,' she said. 'Really? OK, good thinking! I'll tell him. We'll be there in ten.'

'Tell me what?' Ben enquired, as she dropped the phone back into her bag.

'Amita's brother, Ravinder Kaal? He went to Norchester mortuary to formally identify her body, and Sam asked him to come to Raven's Edge to give a statement.'

'Kaal agreed?'

'Yes, he absolutely insisted, which Sam found surprising.'

Far better Kaal came to Raven's Edge than Lydia got her hands on him.

He clapped Harriet on the shoulder. 'Let's go.'

'Good. I hate this house.'

Ben agreed with her. He didn't believe in ghosts or that houses could be 'evil', but there was definitely *something* about this place. It had certainly earned its sobriquet of the Grim House.

They left the way they'd entered, out through the dining-room window and across the terrace. Ben knew the house was empty, yet he still couldn't shake the feeling they were being watched. As they went down the steps towards the drive he cast one last look back through the trees, half-expecting to see Milla.

But no one was there.

* * *

Ravi Kaal looked like a man who would rather be anywhere other than Raven's Edge Police Station. Harriet could hardly blame him. His sister had been murdered, he'd had to identify her body, and presumably he was in the midst of arranging her funeral. She could only wonder why he'd agreed to come here at all. He could have given a statement to the officer who'd accompanied him to the mortuary. Someone could have visited him at his house. But no, Ravi had insisted on coming to Raven's Edge with his solicitor. She didn't have to be a police detective to work out something was up.

Harriet learned exactly what that was barely two minutes after she'd entered the interview room, introduced herself and Ben, and started the recording.

'Kiran did it, didn't she?' Ravi announced. 'She's always been jealous of my sister. First she steals her fiancé and then this. That woman is pure evil. Have you caught her yet? I know exactly where she'll be – hiding out with her rich relatives and laughing at us, thinking she's got away with it.'

He didn't endear himself to Harriet by directing his comments to Ben, presumably because he was the senior officer, but they'd already discussed the interview in the car on the way here. Harriet was to ask the questions, so that Ben could concentrate on Ravi's reactions. He wouldn't have to try very hard. The whole station could probably hear the fury in Ravi's voice.

She was also grateful that she now had more than a passing

familiarity with the Graham family tree or she wouldn't have had a clue about who Ravi was talking about.

'I'm sorry for your loss,' she said, while assessing the best way to handle this. She'd expected a grieving brother, but Ravi's craving for vengeance was coming off him in waves. Was Ben still happy for her to proceed? She glanced in his direction and received a cursory nod in return.

OK, focus...

Ravi was a handsome man in his early thirties, with a slightly darker skin tone than Milla's. His hair was short and neatly styled, with only a nod to current fashion. His suit was elegant and expensive, although she didn't recognise the brand, and his beautifully manicured hands were currently tapping impatiently on the table. He clearly thought the police were idiots and would have no compunction in telling them so if they didn't tell *him* what he wanted to hear – and that was that Milla (Kiran?) had murdered his sister.

Harriet was half-inclined to agree with him, but where was her motive?

It transpired that Ravi knew the basics. Amita had been found at the Grahams' ruined manor house with Milla's bag and her ID. Harriet knew that if she tried to prevaricate, with any mention of coincidences, Ravi was likely to explode.

So she opened the rather too slim file of information they had collated on Milla/Kiran, slid out her photograph and held it out to Ravi. 'Can you identify this woman?'

Ravi glanced at the photograph and then back at Harriet. 'We all know who that is. Stop wasting my time.'

Would he have spoken to Ben like that?

'Formally, for the record?'

Ravi sighed extravagantly. 'Kiran McKenzie.'

She glanced down at her notes. Ben had already briefed her on his theory that Milla was Rosemary's niece, Kiran, so that was one mystery solved at least.

She still required formal confirmation though. 'How is Kiran related to you?'

For a moment Ravi glowered at them, and then the solicitor leaned forwards and whispered something in his ear. Ravi nodded and seemed to relax slightly, although he clearly wasn't happy.

'My grandfather's sister, Parminder Kaal, married Kiran's grandfather, Alastair McKenzie. He was a journalist, quite well-known back in the 1980s. They had two children. Robert went into the army. I have no idea what happened to him. We lost touch. The McKenzies always thought themselves above us. It was no great loss. Their daughter, Rosemary, was a famous artist. She married Patrick Graham. He killed her, about twenty years ago, in that very house where... where Amita was found.'

'So Kiran is Robert's daughter?'

Ravi shrugged. 'My Aunt Parminder swore Kiran was Robert's child, but we didn't even know he was married. I always suspected she was Rosemary's, from a previous relationship.'

There was Kiran's motivation for turning up in Raven's Edge: she wanted to find out more about Rosemary. Harriet could understand that, but why the elaborate charade with her name? Why would she go to so much trouble to create a fake identity for herself, when it was so easy to prove she was lying?

Unless she wanted to bait someone? The Graham family? *Dermot* Graham? He was the one with all the power.

'When did you last see Mil— I mean, Kiran, Mr Kaal?'

'Eight years ago, when we threw her out.'

That surprised her. 'Kiran was living with you?'

'Yes. Her grandmother died, my parents felt sorry for her and said she could come and live with us. She would have been about ten...' Ravi trailed off, glancing towards his solicitor, who imperceptibly nodded.

Read between the lines was something Ben always said, and

she could see him shifting in his seat with the effort of keeping quiet. She hid a smile.

'Your parents regretted it?' she asked Ravi.

'Kiran was a child; of course they didn't regret it. But later...' He sighed. 'My great-aunt had not been in the best health. Kiran had been left to run wild. She had no discipline. She told lies; small ones at first. She wouldn't answer to her name; she wanted to be called "Milla". My mother humoured her. It was a mistake. The lies got bigger. She told people her name was Camilla Graham, that she was Rosemary's dead daughter. My mother kept making excuses for her. She said we had to be kind, that Kiran had lost all those close to her and it was her way of dealing with it.'

That made sense. 'You didn't agree?'

'It was disrespectful and because she wasn't corrected it got worse. Kiran got into trouble at school and then refused to go anymore. She told everyone her father was rich, that she didn't need to get a job, that studying and exams were pointless. Then she stole a large sum of money and disappeared.'

'How large?' Ben interrupted.

Ravi told him.

'Did she leave an IOU?'

Ravi frowned. 'Yes, she did. How did you know?'

Harriet kept quiet. Where was this going?

'In other words, she borrowed the money rather than stole it?' Ben said.

He almost sounded triumphant. What did he know that she didn't?

'An amount that large?' Ravi's voice dripped scorn. 'She would never have been able to pay it back!'

Good point. Harriet glanced back at Ben, but he seemed content to remain silent.

So she was the one to ask, 'What did your parents do about that?'

'They contacted the police. But when the police brought Kiran back, my parents refused to press charges. They said she was family; that she had problems, that we must make allowances for her.'

'Then what happened?'

'Instead of sending Kiran back to school, my parents allowed her to stay at home. She had a way with words, they said. Why not put them to use? She could learn marketing or PR and help with the business.'

'And did she?'

'What do you think?' Ravi's voice was scathing. 'While we were all involved with the arrangements for Amita's wedding, Kiran stole her fiancé from under her nose and ran off with him to London! My parents *had* to throw her out after that. They had no choice. Amita's heart was broken.'

Poor Amita. While accepting that Ravi was biased, Kiran was coming across as a deeply unpleasant character. There were two sides to every story, but deliberately setting out to steal someone's fiancé? There was no excuse for that!

'Did Kiran ever make contact with you again?' Harriet asked him.

'No.'

It wasn't surprising. 'Did she try to contact Amita?'

'She tried. The relationship with Amita's fiancé lasted a matter of days. He came crawling back but Kiran didn't. After a few more years she resurfaced. Amita began seeing her at all these music festivals. Kiran tried to approach her on several occasions but Amita wouldn't have anything to do with her.'

Time to wrap it up.

'Amita was found with Kiran's bag in her possession. Do you have any idea why?'

'Are you sure it's Kiran's bag?'

'It has all her ID inside it.'

Ravi smirked. 'Kiran's ID? Or ID she's forged or stolen from someone else?'

Another good point, to which there was no answer. Ravi really didn't have one good word to say about Kiran. Harriet wondered if Ravi and Amita had felt neglected and jealous of the attention their parents had devoted to their cousin.

'Well?' Ravi asked, breaking in on her ruminations. 'Have you arrested her yet?'

Harriet replied without thinking. 'She's not a suspect.'

It was hardly audible, but beside her Ben sighed.

Ravi muttered something to the solicitor in Punjabi. The solicitor replied and shrugged.

Before she could stop him, Ravi snatched up the photograph of Kiran and waved it in front of her. 'This woman killed my sister. All her life, she's been jealous of what my sister had. You *will* arrest her.'

'We can't arrest her, unless we have proof that she's actually broken the law.'

'Or that you *suspect* she's broken the law,' the solicitor said helpfully.

'Exactly,' Ravi nodded. 'I have told you all that she is.' He flicked at the photograph with his finger, knocking it onto the floor. 'You will do your duty and arrest her, and charge her with my sister's murder, or I will tell every journalist I can find how you and your colleagues are not doing your job.'

Fabulous.

'But we're not sure Kiran is involved in your sister's death—'

'You need proof? I can give you proof. Take my statement right now. Kiran McKenzie has lied, she has stolen...'

Wearily, Harriet retrieved the photograph before Ravi decided to grind it into the floor to further ram home his point.

Although he was in full rant now. '...She has no sense of loyalty, of honour, of family...' Beside him, the solicitor nodded sagely. 'These are the things that matter above all. *Family.*

Everything we did for Kiran and this was how she repaid us? She stole the man Amita loved. Just because she could; just for the fun of it. It broke my poor sister's heart. And now because of this, Kiran has no family. She is dead to us.'

'Do you know where Kiran is now, Mr Kaal?' Ben interrupted. 'We think she may be in danger —'

'Do you think I'd *care* if something happened to her? Without friends, without family you are *nothing*. Kiran never understood this. *Never.*'

Harriet had the idea Kiran probably understood only too well, but there was no point in arguing with Ravi.

Instead, she glanced at Ben, who nodded, so she tucked Kiran's photograph back into the file and politely terminated the interview.

Malcolm opened his eyes, wondering what had woken him.

His sister?

There was no sign of her now.

He was lying flat on his back, staring up at the plaster rose on his bedroom ceiling, which seemed to be slowly spinning around. As he watched he felt queasier and queasier, and only just managed to roll onto his side before he was horribly and hideously sick. When he'd finished, he didn't feel any less nauseous, but he certainly felt more awake.

He sat up and took a deep breath, which proved to be another mistake; this time he threw up until he had absolutely nothing left to be sick with.

As he waited for his strength to return and (more importantly) for everything to stop spinning, he realised again how quiet it was.

He shared a house with two warring parents, three boisterous siblings and numerous domestic staff. It had never, ever been this quiet, not even in the middle of the night.

What on earth was going on?

SIXTEEN

By the time Milla returned to her room at Hartfell she felt as though she'd been run over by a truck. She stripped off her dusty clothes, left them piled on the floor and got straight back into the bath, hardly waiting for it to fill first.

Oh, that felt so good...

Closing her eyes, she sank into the bubbles. Apart from the whole living-with-her-enemy thing, she could certainly get used to the luxury of baths three times a day.

She dozed until the water cooled. When she got out, she wrapped a towel around herself and headed into the walk-in wardrobe. Her clothes from yesterday had not magically reappeared, so she dressed in jeans (which someone had taken the trouble to iron with neat little creases down the front), a black vest and an emerald-green crocheted sweater. First though, she took time to examine all her scratches and bruises in one of the full-length mirrors. She actually *did* look as though she'd been run over by a truck. She also had a sore spot on top of her head from when she'd caught her hair on the wooden boards but, thankfully, no bald spot.

Drying her hair, she re-did her plait and pulled her sweater over her head as she wandered into the bedroom. Only to find someone already there, leaning against the door.

'You do love baths,' Mal said.

Her fingers tightened around the hem of her sweater. 'Spying on me?'

He thumbed towards the wall. 'I'm next door. I hear the bath fill up, the bath drain, the hairdryer, lots of door slamming, a delicious but far too brief period of silence before *more* door slamming, the bath filling up, the bath draining—'

'OK,' Milla held her hand up, 'I get the idea. What I don't understand is why you felt the need to come into my room to whinge about it without at least knocking first?'

He shrugged. 'I knocked.'

'Incredibly quietly.'

Mal didn't even attempt to look sorry. 'I came to invite you to lunch in the village,' he said. 'Just you and me.'

It sounded tempting but after the morning she'd had, would she be up to a cross-examination?

'Are you planning on interrogating me about my motivation for turning up on your doorstep after eighteen years?' she asked him.

'You can count on it.'

She sighed theatrically. 'I thought we were past all that?'

'I could dangle you over the balcony by your ankles but wouldn't lunch be more civilised?'

Milla thought of the large, purple-red bruises already developing on her posterior.

'Almost familial,' she agreed, scooping up her wallet and phone as she stepped past him and out into the corridor.

And smirking because she'd got the last word.

The village of Raven's Edge probably hadn't changed in over five hundred years, Milla thought, as Mal drove them down the high street. The cottages on either side huddled tightly together, as though to create distance between themselves and the forest. The pavements heaved with tourists, some with backpacks and maps, but most were struggling with brightly coloured bags from the many gift shops and tea shops, all of which shared a common theme.

Practically Magic had an enticing display of crystal balls and candles. Foxglove & Hemlock was a florist on the ground floor of a beautiful old manor house. The Secret Grimoire might be a bookstore, Milla wasn't entirely sure. It was terribly dark inside but there *were* a lot of books. They'd already passed a teashop called The Witch's Brew, in a cottage almost entirely covered by Virginia creeper, giving it the appearance that it had not so much been built as grown organically, and that the forest would quite like it back.

Spellbound offered a free tealeaf reading with every cuppa. The Crooked Broomstick was, as the name suggested, a tiny, twisted, one-room cottage, with a bent broomstick over the door, and a queue that reached all the way to the post box, which someone had covered with a knitted topper of a raven.

'This is a very odd place,' Milla said, unable to remain tactfully silent any longer. 'It's almost as though an entire industry has been built around the village... being... being...'

'Strange?' grinned Mal. 'You're not far wrong. When the railways came to the King's Forest District, bringing the very first tourists, our Victorian forefathers needed a unique selling point to compete with their neighbours. Calahurst has a river and a marina. Port Rell has a pretty harbour and a beach. Norchester has a medieval castle and some bits of Roman wall. So our ancestors combed through the parish records and found stories about a trouble-making witch, a vengeful highwayman and ghostly Cavaliers still fighting the English Civil War, which they embellished and turned into fact. They even changed the name of the village, from Buckley to Raven's Edge.'

'Very clever.'

'And very lucrative.'

He parked his silver Audi outside the church and they continued on foot over a humpback bridge, where the last building sat hunched against the forest. It was an ancient coaching inn, all whitewash and blackened beams, the ropes of wisteria around the windows appearing to be the only thing keeping it upright. The inn was also the only building in the village without a witchy name; the sign above the door proclaimed it to be The Drop.

Was this a play on words? The last drop of alcohol before leaving the village? As they crossed the crumbling stone arch, more hump than bridge, Milla saw the dizzying descent into a gorge below. At the very bottom was a river, swollen from the recent storms, crashing noisily away into the forest.

She shivered. That was a *very* long way down.

Mal had already crossed the bridge and was waiting impatiently in a pretty courtyard filled with hanging baskets and troughs of flowers. As she caught him up, she pointed to the sign swinging gently in the breeze above the door. It depicted a black-haired woman with a raven on her shoulder.

She pointed it out. 'I'm assuming there is some quaint, ye olde kind of story behind that too?'

'That's our famous witch, Magik Meg,' he said, 'also known as the Raven Queen. Three hundred years ago, the villagers chucked her off the bridge and they've been reaping the financial rewards ever since.'

'I hope she survived to put a nasty spell on them?'

'Allegedly, she turned into a hundred ravens and now haunts the village and surrounding forest.'

'Good for her.'

'Would you like to eat inside or outside?' Mal asked, pausing with one hand on the door.

The sky was overcast, although it was no longer raining.

Milla would have suggested sitting outside to ensure a quick getaway, but she had nothing to fear from Mal, did she? The courtyard was already busy with customers. If she and Mal were going to start talking about unsavoury family history, it might be better to do it in private.

'Inside,' she said.

He held the door open with a mock bow. 'After you.'

The inn was sturdier than it appeared from the outside, with low beams and lattice windows, and large open fires. Small bunches of flowers and herbs had been hung from the beams to dry, and a small square of plaster had been removed from one wall to reveal the wattle and daub beneath.

'Parts date from the fifteenth century,' Mal said, and he'd obviously been here many times before, because he knew all the places to duck so that he didn't knock his head. 'It was built by the local bishop and used to provide accommodation for pilgrims. Queen Elizabeth I stayed at least twice, and complained bitterly about the damp – presumably from the river below.'

'How do you *know* all this?'

Mal shrugged. 'Everyone who lives here does.'

They were shown to a table overlooking the gorge.

Milla skipped a starter and ordered wild mushroom risotto, with an apple crumble and cinnamon custard for pudding. To her surprise, Mal asked for the same. She was also surprised when he asked for a jug of water rather than anything alcoholic.

The food arrived promptly, and Mal entertained her by telling more stories about the village.

'A hundred and fifty years ago, an Oxford professor arrived in the village, convinced there were fairies living in the woods.'

'You're making this up. *Fairies? Really?*'

'It's the honest truth! Professor Wainwright went into the forest with all his camera equipment and was never seen again.'

'The *fairies* got him?'

Mal shrugged. 'Or perhaps the ghosts of the Cavalier soldiers?'

'Or the witch? Maybe she turned him into a raven? Has anyone counted them recently? Maybe there are now a hundred and one?'

He laughed, raising his glass of water in a toast. 'Now you're catching on.'

They were getting along far too well. It was time to ruffle some feathers.

'Have your family always owned the village?'

'Why would you think we own the village?' The chill was back in his voice. 'Because we're rich?'

'Do you, or don't you?'

'Of course not! This is the twenty-first century, not the Middle Ages.'

'A simple "no" would have sufficed.'

'For you? I doubt it.' He downed his glass of water.

She bet he regretted not ordering something stronger. 'Listen to us,' she said, 'arguing like brother and sister.'

'Don't start,' he warned her. 'Just don't.'

'I thought you were going to interrogate me? I was looking forward to it.'

'No point. If I let you jabber on for long enough, you're bound to trip over one of your lies.'

'Don't count on it.'

'Then let's have a truce,' he said. 'I'll ask you one question, which you'll answer truthfully, and in return you can ask one question of me.'

It sounded fair enough. What was the catch?

'How will you know if I'm telling the truth?'

He merely looked at her.

She shrugged. 'OK, do your worst.'

Instead, he surprised her.

'What was Grandma McKenzie like? I only have the

vaguest memory of her. After my mother died, I never saw her again.'

'She wasn't at *all* like Brianna.' Milla couldn't imagine Parminder McKenzie leading a sing-song around a piano. 'She was very strict, very traditional, always dressed in salwar kameez...'

'Really? My mother never wore traditional Indian clothes. I've often wondered if it was deliberate – to hide her Indian heritage, to try to blend in with Patrick's snooty white friends.'

Milla was about to admit to never wearing them either when she stopped, realising what she'd been about to say. Her grandmother had been very traditional, yet she'd allowed Milla the freedom to wear whatever she liked – and Milla had wanted to wear jeans and T-shirts to fit in with her school friends. Fitting in had been important to her in those days. Had her mother been like that too?

Something must have shown in her expression because Mal unexpectedly took hold of her hand and squeezed it. 'I'm sorry. I didn't mean to bring back painful memories.'

Unnerved by his unexpected kindness, she eased her hand from his grip. 'What else did you want to know? Grandma McKenzie died when I was ten, so I don't remember a lot about her.'

'Do you have a photograph?'

'Not with me. Don't you have any of your own?'

'I don't know whether you've noticed but my dad's not big on family photographs.'

Or family anything, Milla thought, remembering that strange, soulless house.

'My turn,' she said. Mal might be willing to 'play nice' but she certainly wasn't. 'Why do you call Dermot "Dad"? He's not your dad, he's your uncle.'

Mal sighed. 'Feel free to come right to the point.'

'Well?'

'As my real father tried to kill me, I feel I'm entitled to withdraw his right to be called Daddy.'

'Are you sure Patrick was guilty? I mean, he denied everything at his trial. He said he was set up.'

Mal's pale eyes remained completely emotionless. 'To state the obvious: he would, wouldn't he?'

'You're not in touch with him?'

'What the hell for?'

'Patrick is still your father,' Milla said, 'whatever you think he did.'

'Have you not been paying attention? Patrick Graham is an evil, twisted psychopath who murdered his wife and children without thought or remorse. If I ever think of him, which I don't, it's only to wish him dead.'

'He's still your *father* —'

'Say that word *one more time* and it'll be you that's dropped off that bridge.'

He didn't appear to be kidding.

'Point taken,' she said.

'*Finally!*'

'It's just—' She broke off, catching him glowering over the top of his glass. 'I suppose the reason I'm having trouble getting my head around it, is that I never had a family of my own. A real family, a proper family. I always had the idea they stick together, no matter what.'

'Through murder, manslaughter and infanticide? An interesting theory. Not one I'm willing to discuss, as I believe I've mentioned already. Several times. Let's change the subject. *Please?*'

She sat back in her chair and regarded him thoughtfully. 'You know, you sound just like him.'

'Who?'

'Dermot.'

'Hardly surprising. He brought me up.'

'You didn't used to talk like that.'

'The last time we met, I believe I would have been around eight or nine years old. I'm surprised I looked up from my books long enough to hold any kind of a conversation.'

'You did.'

Now it was his turn to appear unnerved. 'You appear to remember those days better than I.'

'Not as well as I'd like. There are whole chunks I can't remember.'

'There are whole chunks I can't forget.'

'Do you want to?'

'What do you think?'

They were silent for a moment and then,

'I think I've lost my appetite,' Milla said.

Mal beckoned the waitress over, paid the bill and they left.

Instead of returning to the car, he took hold of her arm and steered her through the lych-gate into the churchyard.

'Where are you taking me?' she asked, even though it was obvious.

'Have you ever seen your aunt's grave?'

'Rosemary has a grave?'

'Why are you surprised?'

'Sikhs don't have monuments to their dead and they're cremated, not buried.'

Mal shot her a sideways glance. 'I didn't think my mother followed any particular religion?'

She was my *mother too.*

Milla was reminded of the life Mal had experienced, while she'd been dumped on the Kaals. It hadn't been their fault. They'd tried to be kind but she'd been grieving for her grandmother and flung into a world she'd been unfamiliar with. Instead of making any attempt to adapt, she'd done her best to stir up trouble in the hope she'd be returned to her 'real' family. Maybe Amita would have been happy in her arranged marriage. Maybe Amita's fiancé would have remained faithful, if Milla hadn't deliberately seduced him to prove she could.

Saying she'd only wanted the best for Amita was no excuse. She should never have interfered. No wonder the Kaals had kicked her out and refused to have anything to do with her. She had well and truly deserved it. She had taken every kindness they had shown her and flung it right back in their faces, like the ungrateful cow she was.

Rosemary Graham's grave was with the newer ones at the front of the churchyard. There were four identical black headstones with nothing much more than the names of Rosemary and each of the three children who had died.

As Milla drew closer, she spotted fresh flowers on each grave. Pretty summer posies tied with ribbon. Provided by the florist in the village? Although she couldn't see Dermot picking his way through the long grass and the tombstones in his fancy shoes.

'Brianna comes here every week,' Mal said. 'A friend of hers, Mrs Lancaster, grows the flowers in her garden.'

Milla regarded the headstones miserably. If she'd known Rosemary was buried here, would she have come or would she have found it too painful? And why *hadn't* she known? According to Dermot, she hadn't even been here for the funeral. Had it been a deliberate act on the part of her grandmother to keep her away from the Grahams?

She had thought it would be a simple matter to come here and prove Dermot had killed her mother. Instead, she was uncovering more unanswered questions.

Did any of it matter after all this time? Rosemary was dead. Finding out the truth about what had happened the night of the fire was not going to bring her back or restore Milla to what she considered to be her rightful place in the life that had been taken away from her.

Did she even want it anymore? Mal didn't appear happy, for all his wealth.

She sighed, hardly realising she'd done so, until Mal took hold of her hand and squeezed it.

'Forget all this,' he said. 'Let's go home.'

SEVENTEEN

Ben followed Harriet out of the interview room and found Ash Chopra outside the door, obviously keen to tell him some bad news.

He sighed. 'What's happened now?'

'DCI Cameron's upstairs. He's requested an update on your progress.'

Couldn't he catch just one lucky break?

'I've put him in your office with coffee and a plate of visitors' biscuits,' Ash said.

Because that, of course, would make all the difference.

It wouldn't be fair to take his foul mood out on Ash, so Ben muttered his thanks and headed upstairs to the CID office, while Harriet made herself scarce. He couldn't blame her.

The CID office was empty (most of his team were out on enquiries) and the blind on his window had been drawn down, but he was damned if he was going to knock on his own door. He turned the handle (with possibly more force than was necessary) and entered.

DCI Cameron had made himself comfortable in the chair behind Ben's desk, his long brown fingers tapping idly at his laptop, the plate of visitors' biscuits untouched beside it. He wasn't that much older than Ben, and both had experienced a similar fast-tracked promotion through the ranks, although Ben had stalled at Inspector. He was immaculately dressed, as usual, in what was probably a designer suit, but Ben didn't know enough about that kind of thing to be sure.

Harriet would have known.

The collection of boxes from the archives were lined up on the other side of Ben's office, still covered in a faint layer of dust, evidence he hadn't even opened them. Worse still, he caught a distinctive sickly-sweet scent of violets wafting towards him as he closed the door.

'Hello, Ben.' Lydia's legs were elegantly crossed at the knee and the hem of her black trouser suit had slithered up to offer a glimpse of slender ankle.

'Hello, Lydia.' Whatever else he could have added to that would only sound like sarcasm, so he directed his attention to the man sitting behind his desk. 'Hello, sir. Is everything all right?'

'You tell me. I understand you've been interviewing Ravinder Kaal. What did he have to say for himself?'

Ben relayed the conversation they'd had with Ravi, keeping to the facts and omitting Ravi's personal opinions about Milla. Belatedly, he realised he should have brought a chair in from the outside office. Standing gave him a distinct disadvantage, but it was too late to do anything now. He leaned against the bookcase instead.

'Ravinder Kaal seems certain this Kiran woman has something to do with his sister's murder?' DCI Cameron said.

Ben still couldn't get used to the idea that Milla's real name was Kiran. 'Yes.'

'What do you think?'

'I don't think she's the person we're looking for.'

Lydia raised an eyebrow.

'Although there are far too many coincidences,' he conceded.

'You do feel Kiran McKenzie is involved in some way?' Cameron persisted.

Ben didn't want to say it but, 'Yes.'

Beside him, Lydia shifted in her seat and, as he glanced down, he was surprised to catch an expression of satisfaction flit across her usually impassive face. Lydia seriously thought Milla was capable of murder? Is that why they were here? To pressurise him into making an arrest? The public might like to see this kind of violent crime wrapped up quickly, but it wouldn't give a good impression if they arrested Milla, only to release her later through lack of evidence. And so far he had nothing – unless you counted credit card fraud. He supposed he could arrest her for that but what would it serve the investigation?

He kept silent.

'We have new information,' Cameron said, with a glance towards Lydia. 'Perhaps Lydia had better explain. It was her investigation which raised the issue.'

Ben's cynicism increased. How far from 'her investigation' to 'her case'? Was this a sign Cameron intended to replace him?

'There's something you need to know.' Lydia leant down to pick up an A4 envelope leaning against the side of her chair. She checked the contents, hesitated and then passed the envelope across to Ben. 'Perhaps it's better if you see for yourself.'

Ben took the envelope, careful to keep his expression neutral. The envelope was of plain manila, hadn't been sealed and had been addressed to Lydia at her office in Calahurst. It had been sent from a company called Kieran Drake Investigations and their return address was in Port Rell. He flipped the envelope open. Inside was a thick piece of cardboard protecting a selection of large colour photographs. Well aware he was being stitched up in some way, Ben slid the photographs out.

He didn't even need to flip through them; the one on top was enough to send him reeling.

It was a photograph of Milla – laughing, smiling, her long black hair blowing around her face rather than being tied neatly back in the thick plait he was used to seeing. She was wearing cropped jeans and a T-shirt, nothing special, and she wore no make-up either. She looked happy. She looked *stunning*.

She was standing on a beach with a long stretch of golden sand behind her, but the coastline was not one he recognised; it certainly wasn't Port Rell or anywhere local. He turned his attention to the other person in the photograph – and felt his mouth drop open.

'Oh, no...' It wasn't *possible*! 'Is this...'

He didn't need to complete the sentence. Lydia was there before him, delighted to be the one to put the boot in.

'Yes,' she said. 'It is.'

And everything he thought he knew about the woman calling herself Milla Graham turned right on its head.

She opened her mouth to scream but the man was already beckoning her forward.

'Come here my little White Rabbit. Don't be afraid.'

She stayed exactly where she was. His voice sounded familiar, but his face was painted with thick make-up and he wore a big green hat with a ticket tucked into it.

'Don't you recognise me, my darling?'

Still she wasn't sure. 'Uncle Dermot?'

He dropped to one knee and opened his arms. 'Come and give me a big kiss.'

She took a step backwards, bumping into someone standing directly behind her.

Malcolm was finally awake.

'Run,' he said, his warm breath tickling her ear. 'Run little rabbit. Run as fast as you can. Go down the stairs and out of the house and into the woods. And don't stop for anything. Not even me.'

EIGHTEEN

Mal drove home at high speed, hardly waiting for the gate to open fully before shooting through it. Milla, who prided herself on having nerves of steel, closed her eyes and tensed, awaiting the inevitable collision. When there was none, not even the ear-shattering squeal of metal upon metal, she opened them, only to find him regarding her with a definite smirk: a tantalising glimpse of the old Mal. There again: the only time she ever saw any kind of spark was when she provoked him.

By the time the car drew up beside the little bridge over the lake she felt distinctly sick and was only too eager to jump out. She moved too soon. Mal barely waited long enough for her to exit the car before driving straight off again – without even saying goodbye, the *bastard*. She'd hardly got started on her interrogation. OK, reliving the night your family died was always going to be painful, but the fire had taken place almost twenty years ago. It was as if he blamed himself, but he'd been eight years old; what could he have done to prevent it?

Spending the last eighteen years living with the Prince of Darkness probably hadn't helped to cultivate a cheery demeanour. Milla stared up at Dermot's opulent glass palace and sighed. In the gloom of an overcast sky, all that opaque glass and granite made the place appear quite Gothic. It was depressing just looking at it.

Speaking of Gothic...

She looked towards the forest and the strange stone folly half hidden by the trees, remembering the lights she'd seen and how they had appeared to move upwards. Had someone been inside?

There was one way to find out.

Dermot's glass palace was set on a lake in a huge garden so formal it could have been Elizabethan – ironic for someone addicted to new and shiny. Milla assumed the quickest route to the folly was through this garden. Fifteen minutes later, standing nose-to-nose with a towering hedge so neatly clipped it could have been made of stone she had to admit she was wrong. What was it with Dermot and security? What was he so afraid of? Why not go the whole hog with armed guards and search-lights and watchtowers?

Was that the purpose of the tower in the woods?

The leaves of the hedge were thin and needle-like. Was it yew? She didn't know enough about plants to be sure. And wasn't yew poisonous? It would certainly fit in with everything else she knew about Dermot.

She found a place where the branches grew more thinly and forced her way through. The hedge fought back, snagging on her sweater and scratching her skin, and when she fell through to the other side she landed on her hands and knees in the middle of a deserted lane. There were clear tracks in the mud beside her, evidence a four-wheeled vehicle had recently passed by, as well as the imprint of a man's boot. She might be alone now but apparently that could change at any moment.

She hitched the strap of her satchel over her head and across her body, and ran through the wasteland beyond, past ruined outbuildings and an abandoned tractor, not slowing down until the trees had closed safely around her.

Thanks to the wet summer the forest was lushly verdant, with shoulder-height ferns and brambles spiralling out to rip at her clothes and hair. The trees here were ancient, with great hollowed trunks and gnarled branches, and the path she followed was so overgrown with nettles it was hardly there at all.

Fifteen minutes later, it petered out at an unexpected outcrop of rock.

Something stirred in her memory.

Children playing games of tag, hiding amongst the trees and scrambling over rocks.

She tipped her head back.

High above, almost hidden by the mist and eternal twilight of the forest, was the tower.

Scrambling over rocks...

She stepped off the path, forcing a route through the undergrowth until she stood directly beneath the cliff. A deep fissure had split the rock in two and large stones had been set across the gap, creating rough steps that must be centuries old. There was no handrail, nothing to grab hold of if one fell. And it would be a very long way to fall. But give up now? Not a chance!

The steps were slippery with moss and wet from the rain. The fissure was so narrow in places even Milla had to turn sideways to pass. When she reached the top there was the tower, so decrepit the ivy crawling over it seemed to be the only thing holding it together. There was no door, only a large window high above her head. A proper, mullion window, the kind found in medieval houses. No glass remained, only a pair of wooden shutters apparently tacked on as an afterthought, now hanging brokenly on rusted hinges.

It could have come straight out of a fairy tale.

'Rapunzel, Rapunzel, let down your golden hair...'

How silent the forest had become. No birdsong; even the leaves were still.

She shook off a sense of unease. Did birds even sing in the rain?

Walking around the tower, she went right to the very edge of the cliff and the dizzying drop below but still couldn't find a way to enter. She surveyed it again, wondering if there was some kind of secret door opened by a hidden mechanism, or even with 'Open sesame' – it was that kind of place.

'I'm missing something.'

The tower was too old to be a Victorian folly. It was also a missed opportunity, if there was no way to get inside. From what she knew of her family, they were not the kind of people to miss opportunities.

There *was* a door, she just couldn't see it.

Because it was hidden in plain sight?

The ivy was remarkably lush for a plant growing out of barren rock, almost as though it had been cultivated...

Sure enough, as she began to pull away the tangled strands they parted like a thick green curtain, revealing a plain wooden door.

The door was old and rotten with no key in the lock and only a huge iron ring serving as a handle. She took hold of it in both hands, forcing it to turn.

The door swung inward, revealing a circular room with damp walls. It looked sinister and smelt terrible, and it was empty apart from a central staircase of rusting wrought iron that creaked and groaned as soon as she put her weight on it. She climbed it anyway, up through a hole in the ceiling and into the room above.

Despite the rot, despite the decay, it was like stepping into a little hobbit house with quaintly rounded furniture built to fit the gently curving wall. But it was the series of pen and ink drawings that caught her attention, arranged around the wall to tell a story. The frames were broken and the glass was dusty with spidery cracks, but she immediately recognised the story of Rapunzel and her tower. And in the corner of every drawing was a familiar, spiky signature:

R McKenzie

They were her mother's drawings; neglected, discarded, and utterly forgotten.

Beside the window was a tilted table with a little stool set beside it and for a split second Milla thought she saw Rosemary sitting there, staring out over the trees, lost in her own magical world.

'Draw me, Mummy! Draw me!'

'Of course, my darling. Who would you like to be?'

'Alice!'

She had clapped her hands. She may have even jumped up and down.

'Please may I be Alice?'

Rosemary had fastened a fresh sheet of paper to her desk with silver clamps.

'I think you would make an excellent Alice.'

Milla's heart wrenched. Was this how it had begun? A quick sketch and a themed birthday party? If she had chosen a different fairy tale, would her life have turned out differently too?

A torn shred of paper remained caught beneath one of the clamps and she retrieved it carefully, hoping for some kind of clue. But the paper was blank on both sides, brittle and bleached yellow from the sun. She tried to handle it gently but the paper crumbled, falling between her fingers like confetti.

She could have cried.

She remembered this tower differently – as a place of

laughter and magic. Why had it been left to fall into such a depressing ruin?

There was no glass remaining in the window; nothing to stop the wind and rain from blowing into the room. She rubbed at her arms, wishing she'd chosen to wear something warmer, and saw furry streaks of dust appear on her sleeves – and distinct clean patches on the table where her fingers had touched.

How long since anyone had been here? Eighteen years?

Half-hidden by the ivy snaking through the window were more of Rosemary's illustrations, more disturbing versions of the classics. Little Red Riding Hood, pursued through the forest by a malevolent wolf. An elderly Rapunzel, watching another prince fall to his death from her tower. Except Rapunzel's skin had been shaded brown and her long hair was black and streaked with grey, rather than stereotypical blonde.

Was this how Rosemary saw her own life? Hounded, imprisoned... deserted? But by whom? Her husband? Her family? Her *children*? Is that why she'd worked from this tower in the middle of nowhere? Was this her way of escaping from her life – from the drudgery of domesticity – or from something more sinister?

There were other pictures, half hidden beneath dusty glass, but Milla no longer wanted to see them. She'd hoped for an insight into her mother's world but this wasn't what she'd expected – or even, if she was being honest, what she wanted to know. Her mother, despite seeming to have everything, had been desperately unhappy.

Without looking back, Milla climbed the staircase to what she hoped would be the last room, only to find a small door instead. It wasn't locked and opened onto a narrow walkway that led around a pitched roof. From here she could see the forest stretched out below, as well as the creepy blackened ruin of King's Rest – far too close for comfort. She'd walked further through the forest than she'd thought. She was practically in Raven's Edge.

She felt the rain dampen her skin but ignored it, walking in a complete circle until the little door was once more in front of her.

Or should have been.

She had a brief impression of someone blocking her way. A man: blond, slender and very tall.

She screamed, instinctively stepping back, but on such a narrow path there was nowhere to go.

The back of her legs hit the low surrounding wall, knocking her off balance. Instinctively she threw out her hands, hoping to grab onto something, *anything*. Her fingernails scraped uselessly over the slippery wet stone and then...

And then she fell.

NINETEEN

He lunged forward, grabbing her sweater, clenching the fabric into his fist. As he yanked her back, Milla heard the wool rip. When her feet slid over the wet flagstones, and there was nothing beneath her but air, he wrapped his other arm around her and hauled her back onto the roof.

Milla buried her face into the warmth of his sweater and, perhaps for the first time in her entire life, felt safe.

'Thanks, Dad.'

The only sound was the pattering of the rain against the flagstones and her breathing, gradually slowing to a normal pace.

Then his other arm came around her, hugging her hard.

'I thought I'd lost you,' he muttered, somewhat gruffly. 'I gave you a fright. I'm so sorry, my darling. You could have been killed. I didn't realise you remembered this place.'

She could hear his heart pounding beneath her cheek, despite the double layer of vest and sweater.

'I saw the roof above the trees,' she told him. 'I was curious.'

'Curiosity killed the cat,' he said.

As Brianna might have said: *Quite.* Lately her life seemed to be one long near-death experience. And if one counted what had happened to poor Amita...

She shivered. Had the air grown cooler?

Patrick Graham moved his hands to her shoulders, holding her away so he could look her up and down. 'Are you sure you're all right? Not hurt in any way?'

She shook her head, happy to gaze upon the man who until very recently had been nothing more than a memory and a grainy photo from a newspaper clipping.

He looked like Brianna. They were both tall and slender with freckly skin and thick hair that was an equal mix of blond, auburn and grey. Patrick's hairline was receding (he was in his fifties, after all) but he'd made no effort to disguise it. His hair was confidently brushed back from his forehead in a style he probably hadn't changed for thirty years. The only likeness to Milla was in his eyes: they were the exact same shade of grey. They even had the darker ring around the outside edge; it was uncanny.

'Are you cold?' he persisted. 'That sweater of yours is all holes. No wonder you're shivering.'

'I'm fine, really,' she said, pleased by his evident concern. How long had it been since anyone had cared about her? 'It's supposed to look like this. It's crocheted.'

Patrick stuck his finger in and out through one of the holes. 'It hardly meets its job description. Look at you, soaking wet and shivering. Back inside, right now!' Keeping his arm around her shoulder, he leaned past to hold the door open.

Milla went down the staircase first, the rusted metal shrieking its protest, and stepped back into that disturbing sitting room. It hadn't improved in her absence. Despite the large window, open to the elements, there was a definite scent of mould and mildew that she hadn't noticed before. It was vile and she couldn't wait to leave.

Patrick, however, had other ideas, spinning around on his

heel and intently surveying the place before announcing, 'What a bloody mess!'

'Why didn't you tell me you were here in Raven's Edge?' she asked him. 'If I'd known, I'd have come right over.'

'How would I have reached you? For all we know, the police are monitoring your calls.'

Monitoring her calls? 'I don't think I'm that interesting.'

But he'd wandered off to the window, hitching one hip onto the sill before leaning out through the gap where the glass should have been. She held her breath as he checked first in one direction and then the other, the damp drizzle creating a delicate sheen on his blond hair and misting his sweater. What was he looking for?

Before she could ask, he'd ducked his head back inside and was directing all his attention towards her. 'Never under-estimate the police, darling. That's probably what they'd like you to think.'

She supposed if she'd spent fifteen years in prison for a crime she hadn't committed, she'd be more than a little bit paranoid too.

'You ought to get yourself a burner,' he added. 'It would make communication easier.'

The slang sounded odd spoken in his refined accent. It was hard to keep a straight face. 'Sure, Dad. I'll get right on it.' Because of course she had money to waste on disposable phones.

'Although by now they're probably following you.'

Seriously?

'I'm on private property! So what if the police know I'm here? I've done nothing wrong. Hartfell House has a high wall around it, electronic gates and cameras. Your brother is completely obsessed with security, as I'm sure you already know.'

He grinned then, an unexpectedly wicked smile, reminding

her immediately of Mal. 'Ah... Well, I'm the one they want to keep out!'

She didn't ask why. She knew why.

'How did you get in?' she asked instead.

'Straight through the front gate.'

She frowned. 'You walked... Oh, King's Rest.' Dermot had told her he'd long since given up trying to keep the old house secure because the locals apparently walked all over the grounds. Still, it was a bit of an epic fail on his part not to have any kind of boundary between the two estates. It also rendered the security guards pointless.

'The two estates back onto each other,' Patrick was patiently explaining, even though she'd worked this out already. 'I don't think anyone knows where the official boundary is, or even if one exists.'

While Milla didn't doubt everything Patrick said was correct, she found it hard to believe Dermot wouldn't know exactly what was transpiring on any land he owned. He truly was that kind of obsessive control freak.

'Maybe you shouldn't have come here,' she said. 'If Dermot finds out—'

'He won't.'

Patrick was confident enough but Milla couldn't shake off that feeling of unease.

Time to change the subject.

'How did you know I was here?'

'I was on the roof and I saw your approach.'

She remembered the footprints she'd seen on the muddy lane. 'What if someone had been following me?'

'I would have stayed hidden.'

'Thanks a lot!'

He laughed, jumping up from his seat to give her a hug. 'Sorry, darling, you know I can't risk being found. I'm not supposed to enter the village, let alone the estate. If Dermot discovers I've been here, he's legally within his rights to cut off my access to the trust fund.'

She didn't bother to hide the hurt in her voice. 'And your trust fund means more to you than me?'

'You know that's not true,' – his voice was now soft, cajoling – 'but life can be very difficult for those without income. It would be impossible to find any kind of paid employment with my illustrious past.'

Still smarting from this latest revelation, she wondered if he'd even tried. Surely there were all kinds of organisations willing to help an ex-con find employment? Why didn't he do that – and tell Dermot to shove his money? This was the man Patrick suspected of killing his family after all.

But she had the idea Patrick (as much as she loved him) was unwilling to take on the kind of job these organisations offered.

The double tragedy of losing his beloved family and the years spent in prison might have made him appear older than his years, but that was the only apparent change. His nails were neatly buffed and manicured, and his clothes were expensive. Patrick Graham had never known what it was like to be truly poor and he obviously had no intention of starting now.

'Were you here last night?' she said. 'I thought I saw a light, quite late.'

'Yes, I drove down from Somerset. Charlotte's spending a couple of nights at her mother's, so she won't notice if I'm home or not. I saw the news about Amita and thought I'd better check the old place over, see if I could find anything the police might have missed.'

'Did you?'

'No, but perhaps there wasn't anything to find.'

The little flicker of hope that had risen within her died.

'I was surprised to find this tower still here,' he added. 'Although my dear brother has left it to crumble into dust. I'm surprised he would want to be reminded of...' Patrick broke off, regarding her apprehensively.

She certainly wasn't going to let that go. 'Reminded of what?'

For a moment it appeared he wasn't going to answer and then, reluctantly, 'Your mother.'

'I don't understand what you're getting at?'

'This was where your mother worked.'

It *had* been a proper memory.

'I thought I remembered her sitting beside the window.' Even now she could almost see Rosemary perched upon the stool, wearing her favourite jeans and T-shirt, gazing wistfully out of the window.

'Draw me, Mummy! Draw me!'

'Your mother would come here to work while you and Malcolm played in the woods below, sometimes with Nanny, sometimes on your own. You had become rather good at evading poor Nanny.'

He spoke as though the nanny had been an elderly woman, but Milla had a vague memory of someone young and blonde. As she was having trouble remembering, it was perhaps a clue that yes, they had been very good at losing Nanny.

'This tower was built the same time as the house,' Patrick was saying. 'When I married your mother she fell in love with it, so I arranged for it to be restored as my wedding gift to her. After you and your brothers were born, she would work here whenever she felt the need for peace and quiet. She believed these woods were magical and they appear in her work, time and time again. She was often inspired by places and the people she met walking around the village. My darling girl was always so popular... Everyone loved her...'

His voice cracked and he turned his head, staring out through the broken window instead. Milla wanted to put her arms around him, but as she took a step closer she saw his fists were clenched and she hesitated. Their relationship was very new. She didn't want to overstep any boundary.

Patrick heard the floorboards creak and turned his head, his expression still grim. 'How are you getting on?'

'I've made contact with Mal and he asked me to dinner. When Dermot found out who I was, he invited me to stay.'

'He did?' Patrick seemed surprised. 'He believes you're Camilla?'

She winced. 'Unfortunately, Dermot thinks I'm Kiran.' It was hard to keep the resentment out of her voice. 'They all do.'

'But they *have* to believe you're Camilla or it's not going to work.'

'I *know,* but it doesn't help that Mal still remembers the night of the fire and is convinced his sister is dead. You never warned me about that!'

'Malcolm should have recognised you. You'll have to work harder.'

Harder?

'I told Mal everything I remembered from the night of the fire. I even showed him the scars on my hands and he *still* refuses to believe I'm Camilla. I don't see what more I can do.'

'DNA test?'

'It won't work unless one of the family agrees to be tested with me!'

'I can't do it,' Patrick said. 'If Dermot finds out we're working together...' He shuddered. 'My brother is not a man you want to cross, trust me. No, it's better if I don't reveal I'm behind this until the matter is resolved and I can be proved innocent.'

Milla regarded him despairingly. It was easy for him to say! He wasn't the one forced to live with the enemy.

'I guess that leaves Mal and Brianna,' she said. 'Although I'd have thought Dermot would have been dead keen to have my DNA tested, if only to prove I'm *not* Camilla.'

Patrick smiled wryly. 'You're failing to consider that if you can irrefutably prove you are Camilla Graham, you would automatically gain a seat on the board of Graham Media and he'll lose a sizable chunk of control. My mother always votes whichever way she's told but one of these days Malcolm will rebel against Dermot, I'm sure of it. And if you're added to the mix... No, having you turn up out of the blue must be his worst nightmare. No wonder he refuses to believe who you are.'

Despite Patrick's casual words, Milla was chilled. 'Do you think my life is in danger?'

'Well, yes – but I thought you understood that?'

'I hadn't fully considered it until...'

Amita.

'If you want to back out, I understand perfectly,' he said. 'It's not your problem.'

He looked so noble she wanted to cry. 'You're family, of course it's my problem. We just need to decide on a strategy. I have access to Dermot's house, I could even gain access to his study, but what kind of proof am I looking for? The fire took place eighteen years ago. He's hardly the type to leave a "Dear Diary" confession lying around.'

'Simple. You find the weapon.'

'What weapon?' Surely he didn't mean—

'The knife Dermot used to murder your mother. It wasn't any old knife, you know. It was a Victorian letter opener; silver, decorated with little rubies. He kept it. He must have done, for it was never found afterwards, despite an exhaustive search.'

The shadows around them seemed to grow darker.

Milla had done her research. She knew Rosemary had died from a single stab wound to her heart. The newspapers at the time had positively relished the story. The Queen of Hearts who had died from a 'broken' heart. But no one had provided a description of the knife.

When Milla remembered her mother, it was as she had

been when alive. She hadn't dwelt on the horrible way Rosemary had died. The idea of actually touching the murder weapon made Milla feel quite sick.

'I don't think I can do that,' she said.

'I know it's difficult for you but...' Patrick broke off, gazing around at the ruin which had once been Rosemary's sanctuary. 'They used to meet here, you know?'

She saw the pain in his expression and everything fell into place.

Rosemary and *Dermot*?

'Dermot was completely obsessed by her.' Patrick's voice was desolate. 'He stalked her, coldly and methodically. You know what he's like; you've met him. He has no empathy, he's almost inhuman. He decided he wanted her; not because he loved her, but because she belonged to me. He needed another prize to display in that glass house of his.'

'Mum loved you, I know she did,' – but Milla's heart sank as she saw him put his head in his hands – 'What?' she demanded. 'What did you do?'

'Stupidly, *stupidly*... I was a little too affectionate with Nanny—'

'Oh *no*.' She loved her father dearly, but *sometimes*...

'Dermot found out,' he said. 'Even then he had spies everywhere. He knows everything that happens. You can't keep anything secret from him. So... Ah, well... you can guess the rest. You don't need hear the pathetic details.'

'Dermot told Mum,' Milla said flatly.

'I made a mistake,' Patrick said, 'Rosemary knew that. She forgave me but Dermot was putting pressure on her. She felt trapped by this obsession he had for her. He frightened her. She knew once she told him the truth – that she could never love him – it would break him. But in the end she didn't have to say anything. Once Dermot saw us altogether as a family at your birthday party – so happy, so very, very happy – he knew the truth.'

'Oh no,' Milla said again, knowing exactly where this was going.

'The house was full of people – hundreds of people. Family, guests, children, staff. It didn't stop him. He went completely berserk. In my entire life I had never seen him act that way. He was always so controlled – controlling really, like Grandpa O'Flaherty. I tried to manage the fall-out the best I could. I sent the guests home. We couldn't let the children see him like that. I threatened to call the police if he didn't leave immediately. I should have done anyway but I was trying to avoid a scandal. Dermot merely waited until dark and then he came back. He found your mother alone in our bedroom and killed her. Then he set fire to the house. It took only minutes to spread.

'I had been working in my study. By the time I realised what was happening, it was too late. The house was an inferno. I found you and Malcolm playing in the kitchen and got you to safety. When I returned, Dermot was waiting for me in the hall, still in his fancy-dress costume. He didn't care about the fire, all he wanted was to kill me. He knocked me out and by the time I regained consciousness, he'd told his own version of the story. I woke up handcuffed to a gurney in the back of an ambulance, guarded by an armed police officer. The knife had gone and there were a hundred potential witnesses willing to testify that I'd chucked everyone out of the party in a rage. Who do you think they were going to believe?'

'Why would Dermot want to keep the knife? Surely the logical thing would have been to destroy it?'

'A sane man would have done so but we're not talking about a sane man, are we? I think Dermot must have kept the knife as some kind of trophy. A last link to the woman he loved. Short of getting him to confess, finding that knife is going to be the only way to clear me.'

'Does it make any difference now? You're out of prison.'

'I already have one child who believes I'm a murderer. I can't have Sasha growing up believing the same.' His eyes softened and he reached out to stroke her cheek. 'If only you could meet your little sister. She is the very image of you. She even has your smile.'

Milla was silent for a moment and then, 'Where is this knife?'

'I haven't a clue.'

'That's extremely helpful!'

'I know, my darling, I know! Sorry to land all this on you but I really need to return home. I try not to stay away overnight. I don't want Charlotte to become suspicious and it's only a matter of time before one of the local plod turns up on my doorstep wanting an interview. Far better they find me in Somerset than here.'

Back on her own again, while he lavished his attention on his new baby daughter? It was hard not to feel bitter.

Milla followed Patrick down the spiral staircase to the ground floor and out through the little wooden door, waiting patiently as he arranged the ivy to hide it again.

'Why don't you lock it?' she asked, trying not to fidget.

'I have no idea where the key is. Rosemary kept it. I assume it was lost after her death.'

The rain had finally stopped, although the path between the fissure in the rock was just as treacherous. It took all of Milla's concentration to stay upright. Patrick fared less well, his footsteps gradually receding behind her. When she reached the bottom she glanced back to check he was OK.

But he was nowhere to be seen.

Malcolm stared at the man in the Hatter's costume and didn't recognise him at all. Even though he knew exactly who he was.

'What have you done to my mum?' He ached to run to her but knew it was hopeless. His mother's scarlet gown hid the blood but her grey eyes were open and sightless.

The Hatter glanced carelessly towards the bed. 'She's sleeping,' he said. 'Awaiting true love's kiss.' And he laughed, his long white fingers tightening around the hilt of the knife.

Malcolm was hypnotised. 'Who *are* you?' he asked, hearing the note of desperation in his voice.

'The question should really be "Who *are* you?" don't you think?'

'I'm Malcolm.' He heard the break of despair in his voice. 'You know that.'

'Ah, but have you guessed the riddle yet?' In two steps the Hatter had closed the gap between them, threading his fingers through Malcolm's long hair and yanking back his head.

Malcolm felt the blade press against his throat, and a sharp sting as it nicked his skin.

'Call the girl back.'

'No.' Malcolm closed his eyes.

'Call the girl back or you'll be next.'

'No,' Malcolm repeated, tensing, wondering if death would hurt.

Instead, the Hatter shoved him to the floor. 'Then run and save her, you ungrateful child, but I'll be close behind you.'

TWENTY

Ben couldn't take his eyes from the photograph. Yet the more he stared at it, the more he learnt. From the landmarks visible in the background – the wide expanse of sand and the Grand Pier – he recognised Weston-super-Mare, a popular tourist destination on the west coast. As Milla's appearance hadn't noticeably changed, the photo must have been taken fairly recently. She was even wearing the same denim jacket from when they'd first met. By the way Patrick Graham had his arm around her shoulders – and by the way she was looking up at him with absolute adoration – he could only conclude Patrick was her father after all. Or at least, Milla was convinced he was.

So who had they buried in the churchyard? Kiran McKenzie? And why hadn't anyone realised there'd been a mix-up? The girls would have been cousins, possibly half-sisters. Had they been that much alike? Kiran had been a whole year older – a noticeable difference at that age.

Unless this photo was another part of an elaborate hoax?

In which case, who was the scammer and who was the intended victim?

And where the hell did Amita Kaal fit in?

'How is this even possible?'

He hadn't realised he'd spoken aloud until Lydia replied, 'Patrick Graham was released from prison three years ago.'

He should have known that. *Why* hadn't he known that? It would have been easy enough to find out. One phone call; it was probably mentioned somewhere in those boxes of files – the files he hadn't had time to read.

Damn.

Lydia had stitched him up very effectively. He'd been so busy obsessing over Milla and her motivation for coming to Raven's Edge, he hadn't seen it coming, hadn't even *suspected*. He was so used to working as part of a team, it hadn't occurred to him to check over his shoulder for a knife in his back. If he'd been left alone, he'd have made the connection between Milla and Patrick by himself.

When? his conscience derided. After someone else had been found dead? He was deluding himself.

Damn.

The two of them were still awaiting his reaction.

'Three years.' Ben could hardly get the words out. 'He's been out for three years? That would mean he'd only served, what? Fifteen years? The man murdered his entire family!'

'He was only convicted of the murder of his wife,' Lydia said. 'The judge dismissed the other deaths as misadventure. Apparently, the nanny had been in the habit of adding a seda-tive to the children's hot chocolate every night, to ensure they slept while she had an affair with Patrick. If she'd survived the fire, she might have been the one facing multiple manslaughter charges.' Lydia looked pointedly at the surrounding boxes. 'Haven't you done *any* research into King's Rest and the Graham family? Surely you must have worked out the two cases are connected?'

She'd overplayed her hand and Ben had the satisfaction of seeing DCI Cameron wince.

He ignored the dig and asked calmly, 'Where is Patrick Graham now?'

'Living with a pretty new wife and baby daughter on a secluded country estate in Somerset.'

Happily ever after, presumably.

'Has anyone been to visit him, taken statements or checked his whereabouts on the night in question?'

Lydia raised one slim eyebrow. 'Isn't that *your* job?'

Before Ben could utter a pithy comeback – which would have been what, exactly? – DCI Cameron interrupted, tired of his two team leaders sniping at each other. 'My office has already made contact with Avon & Somerset. Clearly you'll need to interview Patrick Graham yourself but at the moment we have to be careful our visit doesn't look like harassment. Although Patrick no longer has any connection to Graham Media, he does have access to a substantial trust fund and therefore excellent legal counsel. In short, he might be our most obvious suspect, but we don't want to antagonise him unless we have to.'

'Not until we have something concrete,' agreed Lydia.

We? Ben gritted his teeth.

'While we wait for Avon & Somerset to make initial inquiries,' DCI Cameron said, 'you need to find that woman.' He waved his hand in the direction of the photograph. 'Camilla, Kiran, whatever she's calling herself today – and bring her in for questioning. Arrest her if you have to, at least it will keep her out of our way. There must be something on her: theft, credit card fraud, whatever. We need to wrap this up as quickly as possible, and certainly before the press get going on it. If you need extra manpower, Lydia will help you out. Eh, Lydia?'

'I'd be delighted,' was her smooth reply.

The implication being that if Ben didn't get his act together, he'd lose the case anyway, which might ultimately do his career more harm than if he royally messed it up.

And in the meantime, Lydia would be patiently waiting for him to do just that.

TWENTY-ONE

Milla waited for her father to descend the path. When he didn't appear, she started up again – and after three steps stopped and cursed herself for being an idiot. Patrick had lived most of his life on this estate, he was hardly likely to be lost. If he'd slipped, or become stuck, she would have heard about it. His disappearance was deliberate. He'd gone where he had no intention of being followed, even by her.

She understood. Really she did. After everything he'd been through, obviously he'd have issues with trust – even with his own family.

Especially with his own family.

But he could have said goodbye.

She took her time walking back through the woods, taking the lane around the outside of the garden to the front of Hartfell House. Hodges opened the door before she'd crossed the bridge over the lake, and Brianna was in the hall, pulling on a pair of very proper white gloves.

'My dear Kiran,' she said, quite cheerfully. 'You look as though you've been dragged through a hedge backwards.'

At least someone was pleased to see her. 'Forwards, actually.'

Brianna plucked a twig from Milla's hair and handed it to her. 'I'm going for tea with Gloria Lancaster, a very dear friend. You'll have the house to yourself.'

Excellent! She'd start with Dermot's study.

'*Please* stay out of trouble.'

Did Brianna know *every* devious thought that crossed her mind?

'Tea will be served at four in the garden room,' Brianna added. 'I won't be here, but I suppose Mal might have returned by then, so you'll have someone to chat to over tea and scones. Won't that be lovely?'

Chat? *Mal?*

Still, tea and scones sounded good.

'Are you certain you'll be all right on your own?' Brianna asked.

'Absolutely.'

To Milla's astonishment, Brianna bent down and kissed her on the cheek. 'Be good,' she said, as though Milla were four instead of twenty-four, and then she left, leaving Hodges and Milla regarding each other with equal awkwardness.

There was a brief moment when Milla thought he might repeat Brianna's words.

Instead, he said, 'I'll be in the kitchen if you require anything,' and disappeared down the corridor, leaving Milla alone in the hall with the door to Dermot's study directly behind her.

Oh, yes!

Hardly able to believe her luck, she turned the handle and the door opened immediately. It was far too easy, but she was hardly going to complain. She slipped through, closing the door behind her, and leant back against it to survey the room.

She remembered from her last visit how sparsely furnished

the study was, with only the long glass conference table in the centre and a more traditional desk by the window. There was an uninspiring view of the garden and the sea in the distance. It was not the prettiest stretch of coastline but a rather bleak stretch of rocks and mud. No wonder Dermot had set up his office with his back to it.

She made straight for the desk and circled around it, unable to resist sitting in Dermot's chair. This was his view every day and it was as bleak as the view from the window. There were no personal effects and his desk was empty, without even a paper-clip in sight. He left so little of himself imprinted on the house it was almost as though he didn't live here at all.

She ran her fingers over the polished wood. The last time she'd seen him, he'd been working on a laptop. Wherever he was now, he must have taken it with him. No doubt he had all sorts of secrets stashed away on that, but not the kind she was searching for.

No matter what Patrick thought, she seriously doubted Dermot would have kept the knife he'd used to murder her mother. He was cool, calm and methodical. If he'd murdered someone, he would do so quickly, efficiently and without emotion, and leave no evidence or witnesses.

'If I'd wanted you dead, you'd be dead. With the minimum amount of fuss and effort.'

OK, so she might be wasting her time, but it was unlikely she'd get the chance to search Dermot's office again. Who knew what secrets could be lurking in those desk drawers? They were locked but took seconds to pick. The top one contained nothing more exciting than stationery, most of it new and still inside its packaging. The next drawer held a selection of cardboard files. These were far more interesting. She pulled them out and dropped them onto the desk.

At first glance the files, like the stationery, appeared pristine. They'd never been used; they weren't even labelled. But about halfway down she found one with her father's name printed on one side. Eagerly she flipped it open. The file was big and fat and held a mass of reports about her father's arrest and subsequent trial, along with copies of various legal documents. Another file beneath, also labelled with Patrick's name, held a sheaf of correspondence between him and Dermot – or rather, Dermot's solicitor. The most recent advised Patrick to keep well clear of all properties owned by Graham Media or face the consequences – legal and financial.

As her father had already told her about this, she set these papers aside and continued to flick through the file until she came across some letters sent from Patrick while he'd been in prison. They sounded increasingly desperate. If Dermot had ever replied, either personally or through a solicitor, there was no evidence of it here.

The last letter, right at the bottom, was dated six months ago and had a photograph clipped to it. A baby girl, if the pink shawl she was wrapped in was anything to go by. Milla separated the photo from the letter and idly flipped it over. On the back her father had written:

> *Camilla Rosemary Graham*
> *Congratulations, you're an uncle!*

Milla froze.

What the—

The photo was recent and the baby had distinctly pink skin. Her hair, not that there was very much of it, was a coppery blonde. Basically, she wasn't Milla, even though they apparently shared the same name.

Milla placed the photo back inside the file but couldn't stop staring at it. She knew her father had married again and she knew he had a baby daughter. He'd told her the very first time they'd met. He'd always been completely honest with her. But he'd also told her his wife was called Charlotte and that his daughter's name was Sasha.

Why would he lie? To spare her feelings? Because he was worried about how she'd react? Damn right he should worry! To give another child *her* name, as though she were expendable, *disposable*.

Camilla Rosemary Graham.

What right did this baby have to those names? They were *hers*, she'd fought hard to reclaim them, and she wasn't done fighting yet.

'You *bastard*!' She swept the paperwork back into the desk drawer and then wondered why she'd bothered. Dermot had meant for her to find this. Everyone was out, his study door was unlocked, yet there was nothing for her to find except these files, locked into a desk a child could have broken into.

A child.

She yanked the drawer back open and retrieved the photo of Sasha – Milla refused to think of her as being called anything else – and stuffed it into the back pocket of her jeans.

'OK, let's see what else you wanted me to find.'

She dropped the files back onto the desk and pulled out the letter accompanying the photo. It said,

Dermot,
Here she is. My darling daughter.
I've called her Camilla, after the child you stole from me.

So there was Patrick's motivation, explained in his own hand. Calling one child after a deceased one she could almost understand, but this was defiant point-scoring between two brothers who hated each other.

Why did they have to involve *her*?

Realising the card was crumpled from being clenched in her fist, she dropped it back into the file and closed it, moving it aside to check the next one in the drawer. It was labelled 'Kiran McKenzie'.

Of course it was.

'Milla,' she muttered, teeth gritted. 'I'm *Milla!*'

There were more photos inside but this time they were of her, going right back to her childhood, along with school reports and copies of certificates – prizes she'd won for writing; she'd not bothered to take any exams. Some were official school photos but the others, dating from when she was a teenager, weren't posed. She hadn't even been aware they'd been taken. There were invoices too, for the services of a private detective, dating from the month she'd run away with Amita's fiancé right up until this week. There were no specific details – under 'Services', the invoice merely said 'As discussed' – but the dates roughly corresponded to the photographs.

It was chilling to know that while she'd been blithely getting on with her life someone had been watching her – almost constantly. This private detective must have been following her for years and yet she'd not noticed a thing. No wonder Dermot recognised her the moment they met. He already knew everything there was to know about her: he'd had the reports. Why had he never contacted her before?

Because she hadn't been a threat.

Patrick was right. There was no way Dermot would agree to any of his family taking a DNA test to prove her identity. He didn't *need* proof. He knew exactly who she was. That's why he'd left these files for her to find. He wanted to warn her off.

She tore the top invoice from the file, roughly folded it into four and shoved it into her pocket next to Sasha's photo. Then she swept the paperwork across the desk, letting it fall back into the drawer. Although she was tempted to leave it spread over his desk. Or shredded into tiny pieces. Or big pieces, scattered all round his office. Or—

She wasn't sure how she knew someone else had come into

the room. He'd made no noise; she hadn't even heard the door open. She just looked up and there he was, leaning against the door, in exactly the same way she'd done herself moments before.

Milla didn't bother to explain what she was doing. It was perfectly obvious what she was doing. So she waited for the recriminations to fall, glaring at him, daring him to speak first.

Mal merely sighed. 'Did you find what you were looking for?'

Malcolm was astonished to find himself still alive and, for the most part, unharmed, although he couldn't help his fingers creeping up to touch his throat just to check. They came away with the tiniest smear of blood.

The girl was safe as long as the Hatter couldn't find her – but where did that leave him? He didn't want to die either!

He had a second to make a decision.

If he'd had longer, he would have chosen differently.

Keeping his attention fixed on the Hatter's eyes, he gave the nearest table a hefty kick. Over it went, showering sparks and molten wax. Within seconds, the flames had licked up the drapes and set the bed ablaze.

The Hatter cursed, crashing backwards, away from the blaze.

This time Malcolm didn't hesitate.

This time he had no one to save but himself.

So he did.

TWENTY-TWO

How could Mal sound so calm? Anyone else would have been furious but he'd learned from the best. Dermot Graham would never let emotion rule him. Outwardly Mal appeared as coolly remote as ever, but he hadn't removed his sunglasses and his arms were folded as he leant back against the door, as though to create a barrier between them. He'd withdrawn into himself. Milla had lost him; possibly forever.

'Sadly there wasn't a lot to find out,' she said, and wasn't that the truth? A man whose business depended on sharing the secrets of others was unlikely to relinquish his own.

He almost smiled at that. 'Next time try asking and save yourself the hassle.'

Ask him about the knife their father was convinced lay hidden somewhere in this house? She'd certainly get a reaction to that, but not one she really wanted to experience.

Mal, it seemed, was still waiting for her answer. But what to tell him? The truth? A lie? Would it matter either way? He no longer trusted her, that much was obvious.

'Luckily Dermot thought ahead and left this for me to find.' She threw the file with her name on it across the conference table, hoping it would slide all the way to the end and he'd have to step forward to catch it. It didn't, but he didn't move either.

He could have been a mannequin standing there in his black indie rock-star clothes and sunglasses. Blank, emotionless, expressionless. A perfect copy of the hero he emulated.

'I had to work for it,' she said. 'But, you know, nothing too taxing.'

His gaze dipped towards the file with careless disinterest. 'I guess I knew you better than any of us. I didn't believe you'd have the nerve.'

'Dermot already knew who I was. He's had regular reports sent to him since I was six years old. He's had people following me, photographing me, all without my knowledge. He could have made contact at any time yet he chose not to. Why was that?'

'Why should he? You were never his responsibility. You're Patrick's niece, not his.'

She'd save that argument for another time. 'Then why go to the bother of stalking me?'

'That's the way he is. He knew you'd show up one day and wanted to be prepared. He left the file to let you know he was on to you.'

She'd worked that out for herself. 'He could have told me. He doesn't strike me as the kind of man who'd be bothered by confrontation.'

'He's not.'

'Will you tell him anyway?'

Mal shrugged. 'He'll know. He knows everything.'

'How can you live with someone so controlling?'

'He doesn't control me.'

There was no way she could let that go. 'You live in his house, he pays for everything and you work for him. If you can call it "work", seeing as you don't appear to do very much but go to the pub.'

'I do enough.' He seemed amused. 'It's the family business. I certainly need to know how to run it.'

'Why would you even want to? Wouldn't it be more fun to do something different?'

The blank look was back. 'Like what?'

'I don't know. What are you passionate about? I don't believe for one minute that it's publishing.' She knew he was about to say something glib, something that would sound exactly like Dermot, and she really couldn't bear it. 'You had everything.' It was hard to hide the bitterness in her voice. 'Wealth, opportunities by the bucket load. You could have done anything, been anything—'

He would have spoken but she held up her hand. '*Don't*. Don't give me that whole "You don't know me" speech. I *know* you far better than you think. You were going to be an author, don't you remember? You thought up all those elaborate stories, drew the characters, wrote everything down in little notebooks. What happened to them? What happened to *you*, Mal?'

She shoved back the chair, leaving the files where they were – some in the drawer, some sprawled across the desk. As something crackled beneath her foot, she realised a couple had even fallen to the floor.

'I'm going,' she told him. 'Give me time to pack up and I promise you'll never have to see me again.' But when she reached the door he didn't move out of her way.

'You're giving up?' he said. 'Just like that?'

'On the whole happy family reunion thing? I never even *wanted* it. I only came here because—'

'Because of what?' His voice was soft, dangerous. 'Why did you agree to come here, Kiran? Why were you so eager to meet us? Did you think we'd pay you off to get rid of you? Is that what it was? Money? You go on about it often enough: wealth, opportunities...'

He mimicked her Hampshire accent rather too well. She'd forgotten he had that ability.

'I don't care about your money!' OK, not *strictly* true. 'I wanted to learn more about my family and find out why they sent me away.' And pretended she no longer existed. 'I can see I've been incredibly stupid. I'll stop wasting your time and give you what you want. Me, gone. Out of your life for good. No more awkward questions about things you can't remember, that you don't want to remember, that you have no *intention* of remembering, because you'd rather live your life like your bloody Uncle Dermot: deeply frozen and completely removed from reality.'

'Where will you go?'

'Do you even care?' She hadn't thought that far ahead, as usual. There was no way she could return to her apartment. Ben and the intruder had trashed it *and* she owed rent she never meant to pay, mainly because she couldn't. She'd have to blag somewhere else to live. In the meantime, she had her car.

At least, she *hoped* she still had her car. With any luck it would magically appear out front when she requested it, like last time. Unless Mal decided he didn't want her to leave. Surely he'd be pleased to see the back of her?

She coolly looked him up and down, even though he was a good foot and a half taller than her. 'Excuse me?' she said. 'You're in my way. Unless you'd rather I stayed here forever? I never did get around to asking you about—'

That worked a treat. Mal slid his phone from his pocket and dialled the housekeeper, asking for her to arrange for Milla's belongings to be packed up and brought down to her car as soon as possible.

How terribly efficient of him.

And how terribly hurtful he should be so keen to see her go.

'Thank you,' she said, as he finished the call and dropped the phone back into his pocket.

'Do you need money?'

Ah, the quickest, speediest way to get rid of Milla Graham. Chuck money at her.

It was a stupid question anyway. She always needed money. She'd only felt disinclined to ask for it because she didn't want Mal to think the worst of her.

Too late for that, thanks to Dermot.

This was the second time Dermot had outsmarted her. He'd known she'd be unable to resist the chance to snoop if left on her own. She doubted he even used this office. So the question she should be asking was: if she was being manipulated, what result had Dermot been aiming for?

The photo of Sasha had been planted to create a breach between Milla and her father, implying Dermot knew she was in contact with him or was intending to be at the first opportunity. Divide and conquer was a maxim that went right back to Caesar. If she really wanted to get one over on him, should she stay or should she go?

He would expect her to leave. He wanted her to leave. If she did, she'd lose her chance to search for the murder weapon, but it was becoming increasingly obvious she'd never find out anything he didn't want her to know. If he had murdered Rosemary, on the extremely unlikely chance he'd kept the knife, it wouldn't be hidden here. It would be someplace completely random: buried beneath one of the trees in the forest or at King's Rest, or even Rosemary's Tower.

How *did* one go about solving an old murder? When it came down to it, she was only a journalist, and not an investigative one. Her specialities were interviewing musicians and reviewing gigs and festivals. What did she know about reading crime scenes and collecting evidence? For that she'd need...

A detective.

TWENTY-THREE

That night Ben took all the archive boxes home – and this time he was careful to read their contents. He fell asleep sometime around dawn, waking with a raging headache and still slumped on the sofa with the files scattered around him. He showered and changed but skipped breakfast before heading into work.

He gave the morning briefing, updated everyone on the fact that Patrick had been released from prison three years ago and was in contact with Milla Graham, aka Kiran McKenzie. He could almost hear everyone collectively move her up to Suspect Number One in their heads, but what would be her motive? Presumably the same as Patrick's – revenge on Dermot Graham. But Patrick had an alibi – he'd been in Somerset with his wife. And Milla? She'd been with Ben.

And that didn't look good for either of them.

He sent a request to Traffic to keep a look-out for Milla's car – she had to leave the safety of Dermot's estate sometime – and assigned two admin staff to go through the boxes from the archives and index everything.

Now, was it worth driving to Somerset to interview Patrick

Graham? Or could he get away with requesting a local officer do it for him?

Of course he couldn't. What the hell was he thinking?

He was thinking he didn't want to go to bloody Somerset.

As he sat in his office, with his head in his hands, trying to focus on the statements taken from those witnesses who remembered seeing Amita at the Calahurst Festival, a mug of black coffee slid silently across the desk and into his line of vision, closely followed by a packet of paracetamol.

There was no need to look up. Who else would it be?

'Thank you, Harriet.'

He popped the pills from their packet and tossed them into his mouth, knocking them back with a hefty slug of coffee. It was mouth-blisteringly hot but felt so good he decided he didn't care. Harriet showed no sign of leaving, so he raised his head.

She was on the other side of the desk, looking decidedly boot-faced.

'You think she's innocent, don't you?' she said.

No need to ask to whom she was referring.

'Everyone is innocent until proven guilty, Harriet. You know that.'

'Yes, well some people are more innocent than others.'

'True.'

She loitered.

'Can I help you with anything, Harriet?'

'You wanted to be notified if information came in on a white Ford Fiesta registered to Kiran McKenzie?'

'You know I did.'

'We've had a report that it's turned up in the car park at Port Rell. Shall I send someone to check it out?'

Did she mean someone other than him?

Was she *deliberately* baiting him?

'No,' he said. 'That won't be necessary.'

'What do you think she's doing there?'

'I have no idea.' It seemed unlikely Traffic were checking tourist car parks. They'd left that kind of thing to the council traffic wardens, years ago. So why had Milla's car suddenly turned up in Port Rell?

And why did someone feel it warranted reporting to the police?

'How did the information come in?'

'An anonymous phone call,' Harriet said.

Nothing new. They usually were.

'Was the person who called it in male or female?'

'Female. The caller thought the car seemed suspicious.'

A car left in a free car park, in a major tourist spot, even overnight? It wasn't remotely suspicious.

Unless someone knew he was looking for that particular car.

'Was the caller's number recorded?'

'Yes and I had it checked out for you.' Harriet produced a printed sheet from the file she carried and held it out to him. 'It was a pay-as-you-go phone,' she added, before he'd even had chance to take it from her. 'It was bought a few days back from a high-street store in Norchester and linked to an existing account in the name of Jeanne-Marie Beaumont.'

'Jeanne-Marie Beaumont?' He stared at the sheet in disbelief.

Milla Graham, your lies are showing...

'Would you like me to send someone over to check it out?'

Yes, Harriet was definitely calling his bluff.

'No need.' He folded the sheet and slipped it into his pocket. 'I'm heading in that direction myself, so you can leave it with me.'

'You're going out?' Her eyes narrowed. 'Do you want me to come too?'

'No, I'm off to meet an informant.'

It wasn't strictly a lie...

He picked up the pile of witness statements and pressed them into her hands. 'I'll be back in a couple of hours. You're in charge.'

'*Me?* But—'

'See you later!' As he headed out the door, he half-expected her to scuttle after him, but after only a moment's pause he heard his office door click shut. He risked a look behind him. Harriet was already settling into his chair and reading the first statement with her feet up on his desk.

With any luck, wading through that lot might take her mind off where he'd gone and what he was doing.

And with whom.

By the time Ben arrived in Port Rell it was gone 10.00 am and the area around the quaint little harbour was packed. He wasn't worried that Milla's car would no longer be here, because he knew she'd been the one to call the station. And he knew that because Jeanne-Marie Leprince de Beaumont was the name of the author responsible for the adaptation of *Beauty and the Beast* into the well-known fairy tale.

If there was one thing Ben hated it was being manipulated – something his ex-wife was an expert in. Part of him wanted to leave Milla to stew. And she *would* stew. It was the height of summer and in contrast to the last few days the sky was blue, the sun glinted off the sea and the temperature was climbing steadily through the twenties. As much as he'd like to haul her into the station for questioning, he had the idea he'd learn far more if he manipulated her right back. So here he was.

At least, that's what he told himself.

At first glance Milla's car appeared empty but, as he drew closer, he saw her slumped back in the driver's seat, sound asleep.

Or was she faking?

His shadow fell across her face. Her features appeared completely relaxed in sleep; her eyelids didn't even flicker. If she was acting, it was an impressive performance. He was tempted to bang on the window to force a response but then he had a better idea.

He placed his hand on the door handle, pressing his thumb against the catch until it clicked. Still there was no reaction, not even as he opened the door wide enough to slide his arm inside. He could hear her breathing, slowly and gently, echoing around the car. He was inches from her body, certainly close enough to glimpse the flickering movement beneath her eyelids as she dreamed. Of what?

Probably not him.

He reached for the key and tugged it free. The movement sent the other keys on the ring jangling together. He froze but Milla merely sighed, a long drawn-out breath he felt warm against his cheek as she snuggled further into the seat.

He withdrew from the car, closing the door and pushing against it with his hip until he heard a soft click. Then he assumed a suitably blank expression and rapped hard on the window.

Sleeping Beauty awoke, abruptly and inelegantly, shoving herself upright and rubbing her hands across her face, apparently confused as to where she was and what she was doing. All of which came back the moment she glanced up and saw him.

He couldn't resist it. He raised his hand in a cheery wave.

Milla made a move to wind down the window, before remembering she needed to switch on the ignition. She swiped her hand in the direction of where the keys should be – and missed.

He didn't need to be able to lip-read to recognise her string of curses.

He knocked on the window again, helpfully holding up the keys and letting them dangle, tantalisingly, from his fingers.

She was out of that car in less than a second.

'Give them to me! Now!'

He'd forgotten how loud she could be.

She was such a tiny little thing it was far too easy to hold the keys out of her reach, but it was hardly professional behaviour, so he dropped them into his pocket and hoped he didn't appear too smug.

'You can have them back,' he told her, 'but first we need to talk – either in one of the cafés or back at the station. The coffee at the station isn't great but it's your choice.'

He watched her whirl away from him, still cursing loudly, and assumed she was about to run out on him. He got ready to grab her by the scruff of the neck. Instead, she hauled her satchel from the car and slung it over her shoulder, narrowly missing smacking him with it.

'Lock it then,' she demanded in her usual regal way, before striding off across the car park.

While he thought it highly unlikely anyone would bother to steal such a wreck, he did as she asked before following her. As one of his strides measured almost three of hers, it didn't take long to catch up.

'Any café in particular?' she enquired frostily, flipping her thumb at the quaint little Georgian buildings crowded around the harbour.

'Your choice.'

He thought she would pick the tourist trap that was The Smuggler's Inn. Instead, she marched into the bakery and ordered a flat white and a chocolate croissant, leaving him to pay. As his jaw still ached, Ben gave the bacon sandwiches a miss (despite his grumbling stomach) and ordered another black coffee.

Milla had chosen to sit in a corner at the back, which surprised him. She would certainly find it hard to make a quick getaway from there. As the table was close to the door that led into the kitchen (and presumably the rear exit), maybe he shouldn't under-estimate her.

It didn't take long for the barista to fulfil the order. He scooped up the tray, manoeuvring between the closely placed tables to where Milla waited, her pretty face drawn into an impressively dark scowl. It seemed that she hated to be thwarted. He slid the tray onto the table before sitting down, watching her seize the croissant and bite into it hungrily. His stomach rumbled again.

He gave her a few moments and then, 'Time to pay for the coffee, love. It has to be worth your name at least.'

She rolled her eyes. 'Milla!'

OK, he deserved that. 'Your *real* name?'

She took another bite of croissant, her white teeth tearing defiantly at the pastry, but when she'd finished chewing, 'Camilla Rosemary Graham.'

'I already have a Camilla Rosemary Graham buried in the churchyard at Raven's Edge. I also have a death certificate, and an autopsy, and a coroner's report. Everything I could possibly need to prove a person is legally dead.' He looked right into her silvery eyes, daring her to lie to his face. 'If you *are* Camilla Graham, who is the girl in the grave?'

She didn't even blink. 'My cousin, Kiran McKenzie.'

'Any proof of that? Or did you just wake up one morning and decide you wanted to be someone else?'

'I'm fully prepared to take a DNA test.'

Of course she was.

'That would only prove whether you were related to the other person tested, not your identity.'

'Test Kiran.'

'Were you and Kiran similar in appearance?'

'Superficially, I suppose... Kiran was a year older and taller.'

'Do you have any photographs of her?'

'No. My Uncle Ravi might, or perhaps Brianna Graham, but I can't see how anyone could have mixed us up.'

Couldn't she?

'Unless it was deliberate?' he said.

Malcolm heard the howl of fury echo after him as he sprinted down the corridor, almost tripping over the girl sitting on top of the staircase.

'I want my mum!' she wailed, rubbing at her face and smearing her White Rabbit make-up. 'Where's my mum? Where is she?'

He didn't have time to offer comfort. He bent down and grabbed her hand, yanking her to her feet.

'Run!' he said again, quite prepared to drag her down the stairs if necessary.

Obediently she stumbled after him, down into the deserted hall.

Where was everybody?

The main entrance was locked so he retraced his steps, heading down the service corridor and into the kitchen. When he tried opening the opposite door, which led through the various staff rooms and out to the delivery yard, it was locked too. The windows were high (only the uppermost glass panels were designed to open) and the only other door was the one they had come through.

They were trapped.

TWENTY-FOUR

'I hadn't thought of that,' Milla said.

Sure she hadn't.

She was relaxing now, Ben noticed. Confident he was swallowing her story wholesale, her fingers curled around her coffee mug as she smiled happily up at him. Anyone watching might think they were in some kind of relationship.

Great.

She raised the mug to her lips. The overhead light caught on the bracelet she wore: a chain with eight silver charms dangling from it: a heart, a key, a fairy toadstool with a tiny caterpillar on top...

How peculiar.

A little teapot, a pocket watch, a potion bottle...

Drink me.

He felt himself freeze; had to forcibly look away before it became obvious, counting the seconds in his head before he could risk taking another look.

A hand of playing cards, a top hat ...

Why had he never noticed it before?

Alice.

He met her gaze; watched her smile back at him.

Had she really no idea? Or was this all part of her increasingly dangerous game?

'How long have you known you were... Camilla?' he said.

'My entire life. One minute I had a name, a family, a home. The next, I was supposed to be someone else. Maybe someone else would have accepted being told they were Kiran, Kiran, Kiran all day long, but not me.'

No, definitely not her. Ben remembered the scribbled-out name in her copy of *Alice's Adventures in Wonderland*. She was annoying enough now; as a child she must have been a nightmare. Yet he still wanted to...

He forced himself to concentrate. 'You were raised by your grandmother. How did she react when you told her you were Camilla?'

'After several incidents where I received a sharp slap on the legs, I learned to keep my mouth shut.'

'And after Mrs McKenzie died?'

'Have you been checking up on me, Detective Inspector?'

'I have a murder to solve and right now you're helping me. The moment I find you're a hindrance is the moment you find yourself arrested for obstruction. I believe my colleague DI Cavill has a few things she'd like to talk to you about too, starting with several counts of fraud.'

Her fingers tightened on the mug.

Not as blasé as she pretended?

'As interesting as I find your life story,' he said, 'I need to find the person who killed Amita.'

'Of course.'

He wasn't fooled for a moment. Oh, she wasn't completely callous. She appeared to care about her cousin and was genuinely upset Amita had been killed. But right now all Milla cared about was Milla – and whatever, or *whomever*, had brought her to Raven's Edge.

'Everyone knew I'd survived a fire where my cousins died,' she told him. 'They assumed it was some kind of PTSD or survivor's guilt. I'd say my name was Milla and they'd pat me on the head and call me Kiran. When I moved in with the Kaals they arranged for me to see a whole series of doctors and I spent the next few years receiving counselling. One doctor even contacted Dermot Graham, thinking a meeting with him and Mal would help. Dermot fired off a solicitor's letter telling them not to contact him again.'

She took a slug of coffee and then put the cup so firmly back in the saucer it rattled. 'The doctors said there was nothing they could do. The Kaals got fed up with me. Everyone got fed up with me. In the end they ignored me.'

The one thing guaranteed to infuriate her.

She must have guessed what he was thinking, because she smiled a wry little smile that didn't quite reach her eyes.

'The ignoring was more effective than the counselling. I'm not sure how long it took me to realise my life had changed forever. When I told my grandmother I wanted to go home, she told me I was already home. When I asked for my parents, she told me they were dead. Years later, when I was living with the Kaals, I overheard them talking about Dermot, saying what a disgrace it was that he wouldn't contribute to my keep – when he was so rich, when he was *family* – and how sad that I'd never meet my cousin Mal.

'I thought they meant I'd never see Mal because he was dead, not because Dermot had refused to let us meet. It wasn't until I saw Mal's photo online I realised he was alive. This is why I came to Raven's Edge – to find out what really happened on the night of that fire.'

Ben waited for her to continue, to mention making contact with Patrick, but the silence stretched out.

'It didn't occur to you that your grandmother might have deliberately concealed your existence?'

'Why would she do that?'

'In case Patrick decided to finish the job he'd started?'

'Why would he want to kill me? I'm his daughter.'

Wrong answer, he thought grimly.

'Are you aware Patrick Graham has been released from prison? He served fifteen years and has been out for three.'

She turned her attention to the croissant; playing with it, breaking it up into tiny flakes, causing the silver charms to dance on her wrist.

'Yes, I know,' she said, not sounding nearly so defiant. 'He married again and has a baby daughter named Camilla, after me.'

Who gave a baby the same name as a sibling?

'You're in contact with him?'

She shot him such a look of disgust that if he hadn't seen the photographic evidence he might have believed her. 'Are you kidding? As he tried to kill me, I feel I'm entitled to withdraw his right to be called Daddy.'

The words sounded awkward. Not rehearsed, just not the kind of phrasing she'd normally use.

'You believe Patrick was guilty?'

'Yes.'

'His defence at the trial was that he'd been set up by a third party.' Ben watched carefully for a reaction. 'He even implicated his brother Dermot.'

Milla shrugged. 'To state the obvious: he would, wouldn't he?'

He gave her one last chance to tell the truth. 'You've not made contact with Patrick at all?'

'What for?'

'Because he's your father?'

'Haven't you been listening?'

Either she didn't completely trust him, which was understandable, or there was something else going on. Were Patrick and Milla working together? To what result? The downfall of Dermot? The scenario made him feel uneasy. He didn't believe Milla had anything to do with Amita's death, but he didn't believe her to be wholly innocent either. He should take her into custody, on any charge, it hardly mattered. At least it would keep her safe from harm and out of the influence of Patrick Graham.

He tried another tack. 'Why have you turned up in Raven's Edge now, after all these years?'

'I told you, I wanted to find out how my mother died.'

'It was a very famous case. The details were widely reported. There was no need to visit. Any search engine would bring up everything you ever wanted to know.'

'The internet! Ha! Like that's always accurate.'

'OK, take it directly from the official police report. Patrick Graham murdered his wife on the night of their daughter's sixth birthday party and then set light to their house.'

'I remember it differently.'

She *remembered* it?

'Tell me your version.'

'It was late in the evening and the house was deserted. The guests and staff had gone home. Kiran and my baby brothers were so sound asleep I couldn't wake them. I went into my parents' bedroom and saw a man leaning over my mother. She was dead and he was holding a knife. He was dressed as the Mad Hatter from *Alice's Adventures in Wonderland*.'

So this was why Milla believed Patrick was innocent – she was relying on a six-year-old's memory.

He felt so sorry for her. She was obviously desperate to be reunited with her remaining family, to be a part of *any* family, she refused to believe Patrick Graham was a murderer, no matter what lies she was telling now. It was tragic.

How should he play this? If he admitted he knew she was in

touch with her father, she would instantly deny it and he would lose her trust.

He prevaricated. 'What happened immediately after the fire?'

'I remember walking through the woods. Grandma McKenzie was holding tightly to my hand. I was crying, but she took no notice of me because she was crying too.'

'You're sure that was the night of the fire?'

'I remember the smell of smoke and my hands hurt.'

She held one out to him, her palm raised, and he felt his stomach drop. The skin was scarred. Whatever the cause, it must have been incredibly painful.

'Did anyone ever interview your grandmother about what happened that night? Did the police call on her or did anyone else who was investigating the fire get in touch? Did anyone ever speak to you?'

Even as he asked, he knew what the answer was going to be.

'No.'

'The man you saw leaning over your mother, you would swear it wasn't Patrick?'

'Yes.'

'How can you be certain?'

'Do you think I wouldn't recognise my own father? Besides, he was wearing the wrong costume.'

'Costume?'

'My mother was the Queen of Hearts,' Milla was saying. 'She was wearing a beautiful long red gown. Dior, I think it was. My grandmother, Brianna Graham, has quite a collection of them. It's famous.'

A vintage Dior gown… What six-year-old would remember that? She had been coached. But by whom?

'My father was the King. He wore a red Tommy Nutter suit that had once belonged to my grandfather, with a black T-shirt underneath. Mal was supposed to have been a playing card, all in black with one of those sandwich boards over his head. but he refused to dress up.'

Ben couldn't blame him. He tried to recall if there had been photographs from the party in the files he'd been reading, or in any of the newspapers, some other way she would have known all these details.

He tried to keep her talking. 'And you were Alice?'

'I was *supposed* to have been Alice; I made a huge fuss about being Alice. But when the costume arrived it was so girly I decided I'd rather be the Hatter. I'd already seen the hat you see. It was gorgeous; an emerald top hat with a black satin band around it, but Nanny said it was part of Dermot's costume and would be too big for me.'

Subtle as a brick but he was starting to see the answer to one mystery.

'I assume Kiran was Alice?' It explained how the identities of the two girls could have become confused, although a little too neatly.

She nodded. 'I was the White Rabbit instead.'

He was going to need photographs of both girls, particularly if he had to request a warrant for DNA testing. The Grahams were unlikely to cooperate willingly. Not to mention he'd need good reason to disinter Camilla's/Kiran's grave to confirm exactly who was buried there. But did he really need to? Now, more than ever, he was convinced she was spinning him a story.

'Here's my problem,' he said, because he had the feeling Milla was beginning to believe he was her own private detective. 'My job is to find out who killed Amita Kaal. Was she killed because she was mistaken for—'

He broke off, realising Milla was no longer listening. She had picked up her satchel from the floor and was preparing to leave.

'Am I boring you?' he enquired sardonically.

'I've really enjoyed our chat,' she said, amicably enough, but he noticed she was keeping her head lowered, as though to avoid being seen. 'But now I've got to be going.'

Seriously?

His attention was drawn to the large mirror hung on the wall directly behind her, reflecting everything happening behind him. No one new had entered the bakery but standing directly outside was a very familiar blonde in a white blouse and black trouser suit – glaringly out of place amongst the tourists in their skimpy summer clothes. She was talking with two officers from Calahurst CID, one of whom he recognised as her sergeant.

What the hell was Lydia doing in Port Rell?

More importantly, how did Milla know who she was?

As Milla squeezed past his chair he held out one of his business cards. 'Call me,' he said.

Milla merely laughed. 'Call *me*,' she told him, backing through a door marked 'private'.

He remembered his story just in time. 'I don't know your number.'

'You didn't trace the call?' She shook her head in mock pity. 'Big mistake!'

The door swung shut and she was gone.

Ben checked the mirror again. Lydia, still arguing with her team, had now entered the bakery. He took his phone from his pocket, dialled his landline and began a scintillating conversation with his answer phone.

The scrape of wood against the floor told him Lydia had pulled out the chair recently vacated by Milla and was now sitting in it, regarding him suspiciously.

'Hello Lydia,' he said, terminating the call. 'What can I do for you?'

She glanced across at her sergeant, who was now questioning the barista, and said, 'Why are you here? I wouldn't have thought you had time to drink coffee.'

'I was meeting with an informant.'

'Where is he?'

'She.' There was no point in lying. 'I think you frightened her off.'

Lydia's sergeant came to stand beside the table. 'She was here,' he said, and glared at Ben. 'Talking to *him*.'

Lydia's eyes were shards of green ice. 'You were talking with Kiran McKenzie? Why the hell didn't you arrest her?'

'What for?'

She shook her head in mock disbelief. 'Fraud, theft, possibly accessory to murder...' Then, when he didn't respond, 'What *did* you talk about?'

He was heartily tired of playing nice. Of her constantly belittling him, undermining him in front of the boss, and having to continuously check his back. No wonder he couldn't get to grips with the case; he was too busy playing politics.

'What do you think?' he snapped back. What was it to Lydia anyway?

'Why didn't you bring McKenzie in?'

'I thought she would be more likely to open up in an informal setting.'

'Did she?'

'If I'd had another few minutes, maybe. Now we'll never know.'

There was a commotion from behind that door marked 'private' and he tensed, something which did not go unnoticed by Lydia.

'Let's see if I can assist you with that,' she said, but when the door opened it was only to admit another of her team, hurrying to get away from the irate kitchen staff.

'Sorry,' the officer told Lydia, somewhat breathlessly. 'She didn't come this way.'

Lydia glared at the barista. 'Is there access upstairs?'

The barista visibly cringed. 'N... no. It's kept locked during the day.'

The kitchen staff were made of sterner stuff. 'If you're going to start disturbing my customers,' said the one who appeared to be in charge, 'you'll need a warrant.'

The sergeant seemed inclined to argue but Lydia held up her hand to silence him.

'What a complete waste of time.'

'I'm sorry you feel that way.' Somehow Ben was able to keep his expression neutral. 'Would you like a cappuccino?' He paused. It was no good, he really couldn't resist it. 'Perhaps a cupcake?'

The look she sent him was chilling. 'Some of us have work to do, Benedict.'

As she swept out, he could almost see permafrost form in her wake.

TWENTY-FIVE

Milla watched Lydia Cavill and her flying monkeys exit the bakery. They didn't look back and they didn't look up – thankfully, or they would have seen her spying on them from this upstairs window. Fortunately, Lydia was too busy fuming; Milla could see that in the rigid way she held her shoulders and in the way everyone in her path moved hurriedly out of it. There was no sign of Ben. Either he was having another coffee or, more likely, he was waiting for her to reappear.

He'd have a long wait.

Milla allowed herself to relax back against the wall. She was safe – for the moment.

She'd taken refuge in the apartment above the bakery. A large bribe to the woman who lived here, the same one who ran the kitchen downstairs, had taken care of that early this morning when she'd checked the place out – another reason she'd fallen asleep in her car. But she couldn't linger. The money she'd handed over hadn't been enough for an indefinite stay, but she'd done what she'd set out to achieve. Lydia was unlikely to return, and Ben was well and truly hooked, dangling on her line until she needed him again.

She turned away, crossing into the room opposite where another large window overlooked a pretty little courtyard at the back. She sat on the sill, shoved the window open and swung her legs over the side. From here it was a short, easy drop onto the flat roof of the kitchen and then not much more to the courtyard below. There were tables here, where customers could sit outside and enjoy the sunshine. Her unusual exit caused a bit of a stir, but this was England and no one dared confront her. She kept her head down and carried on walking.

Now for part two of today's itinerary. She tugged the invoice she'd taken from Dermot's study out of her satchel and carefully unfolded it. Kieran Drake Investigations were based somewhere in Port Rell. All she needed to do was shame him into telling her why Dermot had hired him. If he wouldn't agree to talk to her, she'd set her personal detective on him. As she grinned at that thought, she turned the corner into the alley leading to the harbour – and walked straight into a familiar grey suit.

'Oh, *bother...*'

'You're not going to get far without these,' Ben said, dangling her keys two inches from her nose.

Actually, she'd get as far as she liked without her keys – she had a duplicate permanently stashed in a little magnetic storage box beneath her car – but she wasn't about to tell him that.

She swiped them from his grasp. 'Thanks.'

He made no effort to hold onto them (a fact she should have found suspicious if she'd only stopped to think about it) and she was about to congratulate herself on how clever she'd been when he snatched the invoice straight out of her other hand.

She made a grab for it and missed.

'What's this?' he asked, holding it well out of her reach.

She swung a punch, only to have him curl his fingers into the neckline of her T-shirt and hold her at arm's length. She couldn't get close enough to hurt him and she couldn't get away without tearing or losing her T-shirt. While she wouldn't normally be averse to streaking through Port Rell in her underwear, this morning she hadn't bothered with a bra, which showed a distinct lack of foresight on her part.

'Give it back!'

'*Kieran Drake Investigations?* You've hired a *detective?*'

He looked so annoyed that at any other time she might have laughed. 'Yes, what of it?'

'Is he expensive?'

What did that have to do with anything? 'Payment on results, results guaranteed, that kind of thing.'

'"Services as discussed"? What kind of services?'

'Surveillance.' Why had she said that? It was far too close to the truth.

'This is from three days ago.'

'Yes.' She stopped struggling, hoping he'd relax his grip on her. As soon as he did, she would be off.

'Kieran Drake?' he repeated, almost to himself. 'Why does that name seem familiar?'

She said nothing, patiently watching as he examined the invoice, turning it over for any kind of clue, *willing* him to let her go.

And he did.

Only to grab her upper arm instead.

Was she *ever* going to be free of him?

'We're in luck,' he said, smiling in a way she really didn't like. 'His office is only a few doors down. Let's pay him a visit.'

'Let's not.' She attempted to pull away, but he only held her tighter.

'Why? Have you been less than honest with me, Milla? I'm shocked.'

He didn't look remotely shocked.

'OK,' she admitted. 'Maybe it wasn't me paying for the surveillance.'

One dark-blond eyebrow raised a fraction.

'Maybe I was the one under surveillance.'

'Who, may I enquire, was paying for these services?'

'Dermot Graham.'

Ben was so surprised he let her go. '*What?*'

Now she had the perfect chance to escape she felt strangely reluctant to run. Ben was desperate to solve Amita's murder; she was equally desperate to see Dermot pay for what he'd done to her family. The words 'two birds' and 'one stone' dropped into her consciousness with an unmissable clunk.

'Dermot Graham has been paying Kieran Drake to keep tabs on me since I was six years old. He has a file on me with photographs and everything. If I can prove who I am, I'm entitled to claim a large chunk of his company. Every member of the Graham family has an equal share in the business. It's part of the terms and conditions of a trust set up by my grandfather.'

For a moment he stared at her. Then, 'Why the hell didn't you tell me this earlier?'

She was tempted to retort, 'You didn't ask!' but one glance at his expression and she gave an all-encompassing shrug instead.

He wasn't impressed. He shoved the invoice into his pocket, barked, 'Come with me,' and strode off down the alley without even bothering to check if she was following.

She was, although she had to jog to keep up.

'Where are we going?'

'Guess,' was his brusque reply but he didn't stop until he'd reached one of the designer boutiques at the other end of the harbour, close to where she'd left her car.

Why had they stopped here? She stared up at the storefront. Anya's: Port Rell sold clothes for middle-aged, middle-class women – not her thing at all.

'Why—' she began, but he reached past her to open a door

set to one side. A door that led to an apartment upstairs. 'I don't understand?'

'After you,' he said, with a mock bow.

Milla saw the brass plate beside the door.

Kieran Drake Investigations

* * *

As Port Rell was part of his patch, Ben already had a vague notion of who Kieran Drake was. He knew the man had once been a detective sergeant at the same station where Ben worked now, and that he'd been shot in the leg while on duty. Ben had never had reason to contact him before and assumed the man operated within the law. The business appeared to be successful for at the top of the staircase was a small reception area where the paint was fresh and the carpet was new, and there was even a receptionist: the ultra-respectable middle-aged lady now regarding them doubtfully.

'May I—' she began, before Ben took out his ID card and held it up.

'Kieran Drake?'

'Yes, he's in today. Do you have an—'

'Is anyone with him?'

She shook her head. 'No, but—'

'Excellent. We'll see ourselves in.'

'You can't just—'

'It's no trouble.' Ben opened the door labelled 'Kieran Drake' and shoved Milla through in front of him.

The first surprise was Drake was slightly younger than himself. At least, Ben assumed the man sitting behind the desk was Drake, because the scruffy jeans and sludge-green T-shirt didn't exactly go with the sleek, hi-tech office. Drake was also very tall, albeit with an under-nourished look, and his shaggy dark hair and sharp bone structure all contributed to give him the look of an evil elf king.

The second surprise, however—

'*You!*' exclaimed Milla.

Right about the same time Drake muttered, '*Damn!*'

Kieran Drake was the man who'd knocked him out in Milla's apartment.

Before Milla could launch herself across the room, which she showed every sign of doing, Ben grabbed a fistful of her T-shirt and held her back. Drake, to his credit, didn't flinch.

'I'm so sorry, Mr Drake,' he heard the receptionist say behind him, 'I couldn't stop them and—'

'No problem,' Drake said, waving her away.

'You—' Milla repeated, struggling to free herself.

Suspecting what was going to come next, Ben pushed her into the nearest chair. 'Behave,' he muttered, followed by, 'Let's start again,' to Drake. 'I'm DI Ben Taylor and this is Milla Graham.'

'Taylor?' Drake frowned. 'You're a *police* officer? That's a turn up. I thought...'

Yes, Ben knew very well what Drake had thought but would rather he didn't come right out and say it in front of Milla. The resemblance he shared with his notorious cousin always had the power to disconcert those who didn't know him. It was one of the reasons he'd moved away from the area to join the Met – to leave his past (and his infamous family) behind him.

'How the hell did you even find me?' Drake muttered.

'Your name is on the door?' Milla said.

'Although this helped.' Ben placed the invoice onto the desk.

'Ah.' Drake glanced down. 'My old man always said never to put anything in writing but that's kind of hard to explain to the Inland Revenue.'

'I can imagine.'

Drake reached out with one finger and turned the invoice around, sliding it closer towards him.

Stalling for time, in other words – time which Ben had no intention of giving him.

'You've had Milla under surveillance,' he said. 'Why?'

'It's what I do.'

'What others pay you to do.'

'All within the law.'

'You gained access to her apartment, that's hardly within the law.'

Drake remained silent.

'And planted a stolen necklace?' Ben prompted.

Beside him, Milla rose out of her chair. 'He wha—'

Ben had to shove her back down again, which meant he missed the reaction on Drake's part, if there had been any at all.

'Is this an official visit?' Drake enquired, sounding bored.

'Official', meaning did he have a warrant? For a warrant he'd need evidence. Right now he had neither and, as Drake was a former police detective and current private detective, he already knew that.

'Let's call it "unofficial", shall we?'

There was only the slightest pause. 'If I'm to be honest with you, you need to return the favour.'

'Naturally.' *Over his dead body.*

'Your name's not Taylor. I recognised you as soon as you walked through the door.'

That was taking the conversation in a direction Ben really didn't want to go. He didn't even need to look at her to know Milla had stiffened.

'It's the name I go by,' he said.

'I understand the need for distance. You're in the Force; I know how this works. But we're not here to talk about the old days.' Drake casually swiped up the invoice. Before Ben could stop him, he dropped it into a small plastic box on the floor beside the desk. 'Are we?'

The box made an ominous crunching sound, swallowing the invoice whole.

A shredder.

Hostility was coming off Milla in waves. Ben placed his hand on her shoulder to keep her firmly in her seat and waited for Drake's next move.

Drake relaxed back into his chair, lifting his feet and clonking them onto the corner of his desk. He was wearing red Chucks, so old they were coming apart at the seams.

'I'm not going to tell you who hired me,' Drake said. 'If you already know, I don't care. Whatever. I'm not going to confirm it. I'm too fond of my skin to risk it naming names. I have a good business relationship with your cousin, the kind of relationship I don't want to jeopardise, so I'm happy to give you this one favour. You understand?'

Reluctantly Ben nodded. Did he have a choice?

'Here's what I'm happy to share. *This,*' – Drake thumbed towards the shredder – 'was way before my time. Our mutual acquaintance hired my father about eighteen years ago, paying a retainer to perform regular surveillance tasks. All above board, all perfectly legal.'

'He was stalking me!' Milla threw in. 'How can that be legal?'

Drake didn't even look in her direction. 'Public places, love.'

'I was a child!'

'My father always operated within the law. *I* always operate within the law. Is that clear?'

'But—'

'*Do* you wish me to continue?'

Ben dug his fingers into her shoulder. 'I think Miss Graham is merely curious as to why you were in her apartment?'

'That I can't help you with.'

'Why not?' Milla demanded.

Drake shrugged. 'Because I have no idea what you're talking about.'

'You were there! The two of you were fighting!'

'Wasn't me.'

'You have a black eye!'

'Occupational hazard when you're paid to catch out unfaithful spouses.'

'You're *lying*!'

'Am I?' Drake smiled lazily. 'Go ahead, prove it.'

Milla glared at Ben. Any minute now she was going to accuse him of not doing his job.

Sure enough, 'There must have been fingerprints?'

Now it was Ben's turn to shrug. 'You think this guy is going to be leaving fingerprints?'

Drake's smile turned into a smirk.

'But—'

As Ben couldn't shut her up, he had to speak over her. 'Mr Drake, can you confirm you're working for only one person in this particular case?'

The smirk disappeared in an instant. 'Why?'

'One of your photographs has been passed onto a third party.'

Drake was silent for a moment, then, 'His prerogative.'

Lydia must have received the photo of Milla and Patrick from Dermot. Apparently, Ben wasn't the only one working with a potential suspect.

'Thank you,' he told Drake, getting to his feet and preparing to leave. 'You've been most helpful.'

Perhaps surprised it had been that simple, Drake said, 'So we're good?'

'For the moment – and provided you continue to operate within the law.'

'Of course.'

They both knew he was lying.

Milla, as usual, was determined to have the last word. 'If I catch you sneaking—'

Ben slipped his hand beneath her arm and lifted her effortlessly to her feet. 'Come along, Miss Graham. We have the information we came for. Let's leave the man in peace.'

Drake's final comment followed them out into reception. 'Be sure to tell your cousin how helpful I've been.'

'Who's this "cousin"?' Milla demanded, once they were back at street level. 'The Chief Constable?'

Ben winced. 'Not someone you'd want to meet.'

She could take that comment in any way she liked.

He walked her back to her car. It was almost midday. The streets were crowded with tourists. In contrast to the last few days, the heat shimmered above the cobblestones.

After watching Milla unlock her car and throw her satchel onto the front seat, Ben handed her his business card.

'I've got your number,' he said. 'Now you have mine. If you get into any kind of trouble, anything at all, give me a call. My advice to you is to drive as far away from here as possible. *Don't* contact the Graham family again. Do you understand? *Any* of the Graham family. They are not your friends.'

At this she actually rolled her eyes. 'I've worked that out for myself.'

Unfortunately, he knew by now that whatever she said to his face, she would as likely go ahead and do the exact opposite.

'I mean it, Milla. This obsession of yours has to end now. One woman has already died.'

'I can *help* you!'

'You're interfering with my investigation.'

'Who led you to Drake?'

'He had nothing to do with Amita's death.'

'You don't know that—'

'If he did, I can hardly discuss an ongoing case with you.

Give me the space to do my job, Milla. I'm not your pet detective.' When she opened her mouth to argue again, he added snappily, 'This isn't all about *you*.'

She stared at him, her expression unexpectedly serious, but he knew she wouldn't be able to remain silent for long. Sure enough,

'But what if it is?'

As the bedroom behind him burned merrily, the Hatter stepped into the corridor. He could leave now and allow the flames to do his work for him. Clean, quick, all problems taken care of, all evidence incinerated.

Yet the children had seen him.

He knew from the past how the smallest thing could wreak havoc on the most carefully laid plan. The inattention to the tiniest detail could so often be overlooked.

He had no intention of being caught out on a detail.

Would the children escape to tell their tale? Perhaps. Would they be believed? Perhaps not. They were very young.

He couldn't take that chance.

As he moved forward something crunched underfoot. He lifted his shoe. A brightly coloured sweet was embedded in the sole. There was another one, lurid green, lying a few metres ahead on the carpet. Beyond that, twins of cherry-red. It was a veritable trail, leading him past the children's bedrooms and into the gallery at the top of the staircase. From here, he could see a sweet on almost every other step going down into the entrance hall.

The Hatter smiled.

Breadcrumbs...

TWENTY-SIX

Milla had no intention of leaving and she knew Ben knew that too. How long could she poke around Raven's Edge without him catching up with her – and what exactly would he do if he did? What *could* he do? Arrest her, maybe, but for what? Although remembering the speed at which she'd abandoned her last apartment, the lost credit cards that had been fraudulently obtained and the money she'd 'borrowed', she had a nasty feeling he'd be spoilt for choice.

She liked Ben; he seemed genuinely kind-hearted and honest, but he had also got her sussed a little too quickly. He was not the easily manipulated detective she'd hoped for.

It might be safer to keep under his radar for a few days.

What should she do now? She needed somewhere to stay but the wad of cash Mal had given her would quickly run out if she booked into a hotel room or even a B&B. She was no longer welcome at Hartfell and she had no friends...

Whoopee doo. Another night sleeping in her car.

First, provisions.

The signpost to Calahurst flashed past and she slowed, remembering there was a grocery store opposite the war memorial. The road dipped, taking her through the one-way system, past the marina with its forest of yacht masts, and back up the hill. Luckily, she was able to find a parking place directly outside the grocery store. Too late, she noticed it was on the corner of the road leading to the police station but she took a baseball cap from her glove compartment and jammed it on her head. Her plait still hung down her back – there was too much of it to tuck out of sight. Unless anyone was actively seeking her, she should pass unnoticed amongst the tourists, and there were plenty of them wandering up and down the high street. The King's Forest District, with its whitewashed, timber-framed thatched cottages, was very popular with sightseers.

Once inside the store she picked up a basket and threw in a warm pasty for her lunch, along with some fruit and bottled water. There was a queue at the checkout so, as she waited, she read her way through the headlines on the newspaper stand and tried not to fidget. Patience had never been her strong point. The national newspapers were pre-occupied with a political scandal but the local ones still led on the story of Amita's death: *Sleeping Beauty Murder at Grim House.*

Sleeping? Did that mean Amita was alive?

She stepped out of the queue to snatch up *The Calahurst Echo*, dropping her basket and flipping through the pages to find the story. It soon became clear Amita really was dead – murdered, exactly in the way Dermot had told her. 'Sleeping Beauty' referenced the way Amita had been found, inferring her death was linked to the old murders, even though the police denied any connection. And they were a bunch of idiots, Milla thought, dropping the newspaper into her basket and scooping it up again. Couldn't they see it was too big a coincidence to ignore?

She forced her way back into the front of the queue, ignoring the sarcasm from those waiting in line. *Had* Amita been murdered by the same person who'd killed Rosemary or was it the work of a sick copycat? Had Amita been killed because someone had mistaken her for Milla? Or was Amita's death a message that Milla would be next?

Or was Milla doing as Ben had already suggested? Selfishly making this all about her?

She fiddled with her bracelet, running her finger beneath the chain and tugging on each silver charm in turn; the rounded toadstool, the pocket watch, the little top hat... It reminded her of the man she thought she'd seen at King's Rest. She could almost see him come into focus in front of her, like a ghost from eighteen years past.

'Come here my little White Rabbit... Don't be afraid...'

As the hard edge of the charm dug into her finger, the Hatter's clown-like make-up and emerald frockcoat faded into someone younger, balder, chubbier, but still dressed in green.

'Can I *help* you?' the cashier said, and by his scowl she realised it was her turn to pay and had been for some time.

'The Mad Hatter...'

Behind her someone laughed. 'More like Tweedledee!'

The cashier glowered. 'Ma'am?'

She quickly dumped her basket on the counter. 'Sorry, I was miles away.'

He didn't even deign to reply, merely passed each item over the scanner before packing them into a green carrier bag. He rolled the newspaper up and wedged it down the side, leaving the top part (with Amita's photograph) sticking out.

Milla paid with the last of the cash she'd 'borrowed' from Ben and hurried back to her car, dumping the carrier bag in the boot with the rest of her stuff. It promptly flopped sideways and spilled out the contents. The newspaper unfurled, landing face up. There was Amita's face, regarding her reproachfully once again.

Milla scowled back. 'If you hadn't stolen my bag, Amita Kaal, *you'd* still be alive!' She slammed the boot and stomped back onto the pavement, rubbing at her eyes with the back of her hand. She wasn't crying, she *wasn't*. She refused to—

'Ouff!'

For the second time that day she slammed straight into a body.

'Look where you're going, you stupid kid!'

Milla lifted her cap, apology ready, but the woman she'd collided with had already shoved her aside and was heading into the store.

Lydia?

Immaculate black trouser suit and high heels; the woman certainly looked like Lydia and the police station was only a block or so away. Two men in suits were leaning against a black BMW parked behind her own car. It was the same BMW she'd seen Lydia get into back in Port Rell. What were the chances?

Somehow Milla managed to keep calm, walking unhurriedly towards her own car, fumbling in her pocket for her keys...

Only to drop them into the gutter.

Damn, damn, damn!

She dropped onto her hands and knees, peering beneath the car. At least her keys appeared well within reach, but she'd have to lie flat on the filthy pavement to have any chance of retrieving them and—

'Are you OK?'

The unexpected voice made her almost bang her head on the underside of the car. One of Lydia's flying monkeys had apparently decided to offer his help.

'I'm fine, thank you,' she replied politely, careful to keep her face turned away. 'I dropped my keys but I can reach them, no problem.'

Please. Go. Away.

For one horrible moment she thought he would crouch

down beside her but perhaps the thought of spoiling his suit put him off. 'OK, but give us a shout if you have trouble.'

Trouble? She was always in trouble! Milla flattened herself on the pavement and thrust her arm beneath the car. Goodness knows what kind of filth she was lying in. Seriously, had she ever had such a terrible day?

'What *is* he doing?' Lydia's voice drifted down to her.

'He dropped his keys.'

He? Milla's fingers curled tightly around her keys. First she'd been mistaken for a child, and now they thought she was a *boy*? She wasn't that skinny! OK, so her plait had swung over her shoulder and maybe, *maybe,* from the back, in T-shirt, jeans and baseball cap she *did* look like a boy. Shouldn't she be grateful? Because if Lydia realised who she was, she'd be bundled into the back of that BMW so fast—

The flying monkey reappeared in her line of vision. '*Sure* you don't need any help, mate?'

Oh, bloody hell!

She stuck her arm out and waved the keys. 'Found 'em!'

'Never mind *him*,' Lydia said, 'something's come up. I'm going to need the car. You can go back to the office.'

To Milla's amazement, neither man queried the order. They just left.

Careful to keep her back towards Lydia and her plait out of sight, Milla got up. But when she fitted her key in the lock she realised the other woman wasn't paying her any attention but talking into her phone.

'Dermot?'

That one name left Milla completely unable to turn her key.

'How are you?' Lydia's voice was silky smooth. 'I'm afraid she got away. No, I don't know where she's gone.' Her tone sharpened. 'Obviously I have people searching for her. Do you think I don't know how to do my job?'

Dermot was looking for her? Milla would have thought he'd have been glad to see the back of her. Hadn't that been his plan when he'd left those files for her to find or had she read him completely wrong?

'I have more bad news,' Lydia said. 'The detective inspector at Raven's Edge has developed an obsession with her. Well, you should worry. He's an Elliott. Yes, Drew's cousin. Meaning he has even more dubious contacts with the underworld than you.'

What did that mean? Wasn't Ben one of the good guys?

'You want me to come over?' she heard Lydia say. 'No, it's perfectly all right. Where are you? Rose Cottage? In that case, it's no trouble at all; I'm less than fifteen minutes' away.'

As though watching a montage inside her head, Milla remembered the strangely sterile decor of Hartfell House. The monotone colours, the tinted glass, the deliberate choice of impersonal over personal.

Dermot Graham owned another house.

Sure he did. He was a billionaire. He probably owned a hundred.

Lydia was on her way there, right now.

If Milla was quick, she'd be able to follow.

What if Lydia spotted her?

But it was such a great opportunity!

Think!

She could hide in the boot of Lydia's car?

And become trapped? Not a great idea, especially with her... issues.

OK, *not* the boot.

Maybe the back seat?

Trying to appear ultra-casual, Milla squeezed between the cars and stepped out onto the road. There was traffic, but it wasn't constant. Lydia, occupied with her phone, hadn't even noticed she'd moved.

The BMW had tinted windows but there was a crate of files

wedged on one of the back seats and, tossed carelessly into the footwell, what looked like some kind of black plastic sheeting or tarpaulin. Milla tested the door handle, easing the door open, tensing for an alarm, just as Lydia dropped her phone into her jacket pocket and turned around.

Milla dropped into a crouch.

There went another missed opportunity.

'Excuse me, are you local? Could you tell me the way to—'

As the car door failed to open, Milla slowly raised her head, peering through the car windows to the pavement beyond, ready to jerk back down again if Lydia was looking in this direction. But she'd been stopped by a couple of tourists holding a map and was obviously torn between telling them to go away and reminding herself she was supposedly a servant of the public. Duty apparently won. With a patently insincere smile, Lydia bent her head over the map.

It was now or never. Milla pulled open the car door, snatched up one corner of the tarpaulin and dived beneath it. Barely had it settled around her than the door on the other side opened.

And closed.

Beneath the tarpaulin Milla tensed, expecting Lydia to yank it off her at any moment. Instead, the engine started and the car moved off, jerking her back against the rear seat. She tried bracing herself but it proved impossible, particularly as Lydia then went into a rather sloppy three-point turn. With every move the tarpaulin cracked, crackled and crunched. How could Lydia not fail to hear it? There was no way she was going to remain undetected.

Had she just made the worst mistake ever?

Even for her?

TWENTY-SEVEN

The car stopped. The engine died.

Wherever they were, they'd arrived.

Milla remained motionless, stretched out beneath the tarpaulin, waiting for whatever would happen next. Sweat trickled down the back of her neck. What was Lydia *doing*? Why hadn't she got out? With every breath Milla took, the tarpaulin rustled. She tried holding her breath instead but she could hardly keep *that* up for ever.

The car vibrated to the slam of the door and she breathed out in a whoosh. The tarpaulin blew up into a little peak and then fluttered down, plastering against her lips. It was probably a bit late now to be worrying about how clean it was.

If she listened very hard she could hear muffled footsteps outside the car and a kind of scrunching sound. Gravel? Shingle? Were they at the beach or parked on someone's drive? She couldn't imagine Lydia relaxing enough to walk barefoot along a beach, or even taking off her beloved high heels.

Were the footsteps moving away from the car? Milla held her breath again. They certainly seemed quieter. Someone spoke in a deep, male voice and she shivered.

Dermot?

Whoever it was, Lydia replied and then...

And then there was silence.

Was it safe to get out? And how could she do that without being seen? In the adrenaline-fueled excitement of getting one over on Lydia, she had thrown herself into this without thinking it through.

She took a chance, pinching a section of tarpaulin between her fingers and inching it down from her face.

Lydia was no longer in the driver's seat.

Milla sat up, the tarpaulin crackling and rustling all the way.

Lydia had parked directly in front of a five-bar gate. Leading back into the forest was a deeply rutted farm track. Apparently, they were still somewhere within the forest.

Milla wriggled out from beneath the tarpaulin, not caring she'd left it in a messy heap. There was no way she planned to repeat the experience with a return journey.

On the other side of the gate was a pretty little stone cottage, complete with thatched roof and white window shutters. It was entirely surrounded by a quintessential English rose garden: all lush foliage and overblown blooms, from the darkest, most decadent crimson, to pale virginal white. There were even roses climbing around the hobbit-sized door and more fat blossoms surrounding the windows.

Who lived here?

Other than Snow White and Rose Red?

It was easy enough to creep up to the cottage without being detected. She found an open window and was preparing to pull herself up and over the sill when someone slapped their hand over her mouth and yanked her down into a flower bed.

'What the *hell* do you think you're doing?'

Ben.

Again.

Milla elbowed him in the ribs and he released her, cursing.

'Shh!' She jabbed a finger up at the window. 'They'll hear you!'

'*What* are you *doing?*'

'Your job.' She dusted the soil from her clothes and stood up. 'Seeing as you went to all this effort to stalk me, you can make yourself useful and give me a boost up. I'm not sure I can reach the window.'

He made a pantomime of a face palm. 'Tell me you're not serious!'

'Sheesh, how did *you* ever get to be Inspector? You have absolutely zero initiative.' She hooked her foot into the trellis, pulling herself up and over the windowsill.

A lifetime of climbing into places she had no business to be ensured she landed on the floorboards with barely a creak. The cottage might be old, but it was well-cared for: light and airy and simply decorated. She spun on her heel, drinking everything in. All the furniture was wood, centuries old and polished into a warm honey-brown; everything else was pristine white – walls, voile curtains fluttering in the breeze, even the hand-knotted rag rug beside the bed.

There was a definite 'clomp' as Ben fell into the room beside her but he was either too stunned by his surroundings or by what he'd done to launch into another rant, thank goodness. It had never occurred to her he might follow her into the house. Wasn't that against some kind of police code? She really shouldn't keep underestimating him.

The door leading to the rest of the cottage was closed, although Milla could hear a distant hum of conversation. If she wanted to know what was so urgent that Dermot and Lydia had to discuss it immediately, and in person rather than over the phone, she would need to open it. But not right now. Right now she wanted to explore this potential treasure trove of clues and dig out anything that might help her understand Dermot's personality and what had happened to turn him into a psychopath.

And discover if he really had been stupid enough to keep a hold of that knife.

She turned to the nearest chest of drawers and began tugging out each drawer, as quickly and quietly as possible. Ben raised his eyes heavenwards, as though pleading for divine intervention, but at least he didn't try to stop her. Maybe he thought she'd make a fuss. He'd be right. This was a fabulous opportunity and she intended to make the most of it.

The first shock was that the narrow drawers at the top contained jewellery, all neatly arranged and in what appeared to be its original boxes. The second shock was the jewellery clearly belonged to a woman. Dermot's wife? Milla had thought he was divorced. Maybe a girlfriend? Where had she got the idea he was having sex with Lydia?

There was an image she didn't want in her head.

Slightly less carefully, Milla pulled out the remaining drawers and found women's clothing, neatly folded and smelling sweetly of lavender. Definitely *not* Dermot's bedroom. Did that mean it wasn't his house either?

She was crouching down to check the final drawer when a hand clamped onto her shoulder. It was Ben. She'd almost forgotten he was there. He held out a silver-framed photograph, but as she took it he whipped out a white handkerchief and began wiping everything she'd touched, presumably to obliterate fingerprints. He caught her smirking and did another eye roll, pointing towards the photograph.

She glanced down, expecting a glossy shot of Dermot and his ex at some glamorous media event, and instead saw a faded print of five children standing on a jetty.

Her fingers smoothed over the glass, as though she could reach through and touch the past. She *remembered* this day; she even remembered the photograph being taken.

Seven-year-old Mal was standing at one side, his too-long hair tied back into a stubby ponytail, as he proudly held up a large silvery fish. Kiran was beside him, aged about six, cringing away because she didn't want fish scales on her pretty new frock. Camilla was partly behind, one hand on each of their shoulders and laughing delightedly, as though the day had been the most fun ever. And the twins were at the front, barely two years old, clutching a red plastic bucket between them, uncertain whether to smile for the camera or make a run for it.

The twins... She hardly remembered them, hardly ever thought of them, not in the way she did the others.

The photo blurred and she blinked quickly, almost missing the sixth person partially out of shot. A stunningly beautiful woman in a white floral summer dress, not looking at the camera but at the children. Her children.

'*Mum?*'

The room seemed to close in on her as, one by one, every clue she'd missed demanded recognition. The white counterpane on the bed with its Indian-style embroidery; the silver brushes on the dressing table, each one inscribed 'RM'; the photographs, *so many photographs*, covering every surface. How could she have not seen them? Babies, toddlers, children... All with the same black hair, the same brown skin and the same silver-grey eyes.

'This isn't Dermot's house, it was my *mother's*.' Milla held up the photograph. 'There's a jetty and a little boathouse down by the river. We used to go for trips. Swimming, fishing, or just for fun... How could I have forgotten?'

Ben glanced back through the window but there was nothing to see but the mass of roses filling the garden.

'I remember when this photo was taken,' she said. 'We'd been on the boat, right out to sea. Mal caught a fish, a sea bass. He was so proud. I fell in, one of the twins lost a bucket and poor Kiran was sick. So, so sick! We could have done with the extra bucket!'

Ben held out his hand for the photograph, but she shook her head, clutching it to her chest.

'You can't have it. You're *not* having it!'

She reached past him to pick up another photograph but Ben slapped her hand away. Gently the first time; the second time it hurt.

'Ow!' She glared at him, hardly bothering to lower her voice. 'What's your *problem?*'

'We shouldn't be here.' He glanced warily at the bedroom door. 'You'd be arrested while I'd be...' He broke off, grimacing.

Fired.

'OK, OK, no touching.' But she wasn't letting go of the photo in her hand; she was taking that with her.

She'd save that argument for later.

Her mother's nightstand held only the basics. A lamp, a cubed box of tissues and an interior design magazine dated eighteen years ago. The dressing table held more photographs as well as silver-backed brushes, a sprinkling of stud earrings in a little glass dish, and a bottle of perfume. Ben caught hold of her hand before she could press the atomiser, but she recognised the brand. It was the one her mother had worn.

'None of my mother's drawings are here,' she said, remembering the tower in the woods. 'Or any of the books she illustrated.'

'This is her bedroom. Do you keep your work in your bedroom?'

It was a good point, even though Milla felt there was more to it than that. It was almost as though Rosemary had deliberately wanted to distance herself from... what? Her other life?

There was another door set in the opposite wall. Glancing at Ben, who merely shrugged, Milla used the edge of her T-shirt to open it and found a walk-in wardrobe stuffed full of clothes, from summer dresses to salwar kameez. Even though each item had been immaculately packed into a garment bag, there was still a lingering trace of the perfume her mother had loved so much.

Milla had to wait until she'd gained control of her voice before speaking. 'Everything my mother owned is still here. It's like... like a time capsule.'

Or a shrine.

What was it Patrick had said?

'Dermot was completely obsessed.'

He hadn't exaggerated.

Ben pushed past her, unzipping the nearest gown and tugging down the neck to reveal the label. She caught a glimpse of one word, *Dior*, before he yanked the zip up, grabbed her hand and tried to pull her in the direction of the open window.

'We have to leave,' he said, as she resisted. 'Now.'

'What have you found?' Milla made a grab for the gown but Ben was already tucking it into line with the others. 'Is that a clue?'

'A great big bloody clue. Do as you're told and let's get out of here. Why on earth I allowed you—'

'You believe me? You believe Dermot murdered my mother?'

'I don't know what to—'

'How can it be possible for one young woman to elude you so completely?' Dermot spoke from the other side of the door, as clearly as though he were in the room with them.

For one horrifying second they stared at each other, before Ben shoved her into the wardrobe, pulling the door shut behind him, immediately plunging them into darkness.

Milla felt her breath hitch. It was such a tiny space.

So stuffy.

So hard to breathe...

Ben's fingers curled around her upper arms, guiding her

backwards, and she stumbled over something – a shoe? – before he hauled her up again.

'Wait,' she tried to say, feeling the familiar rising panic. The darkness closing in on her, pressing against her chest until she could no longer catch her breath. 'I can't—'

'*Later!*'

She heard the chink of metal scraping metal, followed by a 'swoosh'.

'You don't understand!'

'Stand behind here.' Ben pushed her between the garment hangers until she felt the chill of a wall against her back, and then he released her.

The dresses fell back into place, surrounding her. Suddenly she was alone, enclosed in warm, muffled darkness. She couldn't see the chink of light between the wardrobe doors and she couldn't hear anything except the quickening of her own breath.

'Ben?' she whispered. Then louder, '*Ben?* Where are you? Don't leave me!'

'I'm still here. Don't worry, you'll be fine. Provided we keep quiet they'll never find us, even if they open the door.'

'But—'

'Just don't come out, whatever happens. Promise me.'

The wardrobe vanished and she was surrounded by smoke and flames. Burning... something was *burning*. And the terrible smell of it was all around, choking her.

She couldn't breathe.

She couldn't *breathe!*

Milla opened her mouth and screamed.

Malcolm opened cupboard doors, one after the other, but they were so full of junk there was not enough room left to hide. In desperation he opened the oven, yanked out the shelving and shoved the girl inside.

'Don't come out, whatever happens,' he told her. 'Promise me!'

The girl nodded silently, her little face streaked with tears.

He closed the oven door, draping a tea towel over the handle so she couldn't be seen through the glass, and had just enough time to grab a frying pan as the kitchen door crashed open.

TWENTY-EIGHT

Ben, standing beside Milla inside the wardrobe and straining to hear if anyone had come into the bedroom, heard her take a deep breath. The kind of breath that came right before a scream.

No, she wouldn't. She couldn't. Not here. Not now.

Oh, *damn*.

He slapped his hand over her mouth, inadvertently knocking her head back against the wall with a soft clunk. What was *wrong* with her? Did she *want* to be caught? He felt her fists slam into his chest as she struggled to get away from him, heard the vintage gowns surrounding them chink violently on the rail, and he was almost tempted to knock her out in much the same way as Drake had done to him. But he couldn't do it. He could never hit a woman, not even to save himself.

But he had to do something.

He wrapped his arm around her, yanking her body against his, pinning her arms so tightly she could no longer fight. The gowns slowly stopped their crazy dance and once again everything became silent, silent enough to hear her jerky little breaths.

It didn't stop her struggling though, and he could feel her heart pounding against him. A panic attack? She always seemed so confident. Did she suffer from claustrophobia? Why hadn't she mentioned it? Although to be fair, he'd shoved her in here without giving her much of a chance to say anything.

'You're perfectly safe,' he hissed. 'But you have to be quiet... *please*?'

She was struggling to get her breath but if he took his hand from her mouth would she scream? Or should he wait for her to hyperventilate her way into unconsciousness – and inadvertently kill her? She was so slight, almost the size of a child; she'd be so easy to crush.

A child...

If she were Sophie, panicking about the confined space, or the dark, or whatever it was that had sent her into meltdown, what would he say to calm her? He'd distract her, perhaps tell her a story. Yet what might soothe a child of six would hardly work on a woman in her twenties.

Would it?

It couldn't hurt to try.

He set the tone of his voice low, less easily overheard. 'Did you ever play hide and seek as a child? Climb inside a wardrobe and imagine yourself in Narnia?'

Her hands, frantically pushing against his chest, stilled. Perhaps twenty-somethings and six-year-olds weren't that different after all.

'Pretend these gowns are big old fur coats' – he hoped he was remembering the right story – 'and there are pine needles brushing against your skin.'

Her breathing began to slow to a more normal rate so he relaxed his grip, hoping it might lessen her feeling of being trapped.

'Instead of floorboards, you're standing on powdery snow. And it's cold, oh so cold...'

Slowly, carefully, he took his hand away from her mouth. He'd been pressing so hard his fingers had frozen into position and he flexed them, preparing to clamp them right back again if she so much as squeaked.

'Milla? Are you OK?'

For a moment, nothing.

And then, the merest whisper in the darkness, 'I'm sorry. I panicked.'

'Are you claustrophobic?'

There was a distinct pause before she said, 'Yes.'

A six-year-old would have seen through that lie too.

Annoyed she didn't trust him, he released her and forced the garment bags aside, intending to ensure the bedroom was empty before opening the wardrobe door. From the rustling and chinking behind him, Milla was also shoving her way between the gowns but, as he felt her try to push past him, he grabbed her again. The woman had no patience at all.

'Wait,' he said. 'Let me.'

The door opened on a hollow click but the bedroom was empty and voices were no longer echoing from the passage outside. They had been incredibly lucky.

He allowed her to exit first and, unsurprisingly, she ran straight across to the window, swinging her legs over the sill and sliding down into the flower bed below – rather too expertly. Surprisingly, she took the time to glance back and check he was following.

'Run,' he told her, leaning against the sill. 'Into the garden, as fast as you can. If I don't follow, make your way to the police station and ask for Harriet March. Tell her everything.'

'But—'

'For once in your life, do as you're told!'

To his amazement, she obeyed.

After watching to see she made it, he yanked out his phone and began taking photos. Of the room, of the pictures on the dresser and, most importantly, of the inside of the wardrobe with all those vintage gowns, especially the one with the Dior label. None of the photos would make permissible evidence but at least he had something to back up an increasingly implausible theory. He returned everything to the way it had been and wiped down as much as possible in the seconds remaining before vaulting out of the window.

Milla was not where he had told her to be. No surprise there. As though on a death wish, she'd decided to follow a low hedge around to the front of the house and was now kneeling on the lawn behind it, intently watching the front door where Dermot and Lydia were arguing.

Keeping his head down, Ben joined Milla behind the hedge. 'Time to go,' he said.

Unfortunately, she'd now recovered her equilibrium.

'It'd be safer to wait until Dermot's back inside the house.'

He gritted his teeth. After all they'd been through, she was *arguing* with him?

'It'd be safer to go now, while we know where they are and that they can't see us.'

'I want to hear what they're saying.'

'Who cares? We have all the evidence we need to obtain a search warrant and have him arrested.'

That got her attention. 'Evidence?'

'You think I'm going to discuss that now, here, with you?'

Even to himself he sounded pompous.

Milla merely rolled her eyes. 'Off you go then, Detective Inspector *Taylor*. I'm not stopping you.'

He really didn't like the way she'd emphasised his surname but there wasn't time for that conversation and, as much as he'd like to abandon her here, he'd rather ensure she left the property – and preferably the county too. He sat on the grass – it was far too late to be worrying about stains on his suit – and prepared to wait her out.

It was mid-afternoon, a deliciously warm summer's day, and in this beautiful garden he could forget how close he was sailing to disaster (and how excessively hot he was in this stupid suit), close his eyes and listen to the bees moving from bloom to bloom.

And the stridency of Lydia's voice, carrying across from the house.

'I'm doing my best to bring her in but officially it's not my case and not my jurisdiction,' she was grumbling.

He almost groaned aloud. Was Lydia *still* obsessing about Milla? Despite the circumstances, he felt his lips twitch. While Lydia fretted, here they were within spitting distance.

Dermot was more softly spoken, so much harder to hear. Ben didn't catch what he said next, only Lydia's reply.

'Well, Doug Cameron's determined to stick with him.'

Now they were discussing him? That woman really needed to get a life.

'I promise, as soon as I find Kiran McKenzie, I'll haul her in so fast her feet won't touch the ground.'

'Would you like to know where Kiran is?' Dermot said smoothly. 'Right now?'

Ben's eyes jerked open. *That* he'd heard.

Beside him, Milla tensed.

'What do you know?' Lydia demanded. 'Tell me.'

'My mechanic installed a tracker on her car.'

'Why the hell didn't you say so?'

'It hardly seemed relevant.' Apparently Dermot found Lydia's ire amusing. '*You* had everything under control.'

'If you have any information regarding the location of Kiran McKenzie, I suggest you tell me now.'

'Or what?' Dermot taunted her.

Ben glanced across at Milla, really hoping she wasn't about to do something stupid. Or, more to the point, that she hadn't already done something stupid.

'You're the one who wanted her found,' Lydia said.

'I do.'

'Then we need to work together.'

Dermot sighed. 'Isn't that what we're doing?'

As Lydia didn't reply, Ben twisted himself around and found a gap in the hedge through which he could observe without being seen in return. Lydia and Dermot were standing by the steps leading into the cottage. Dermot had taken out his phone and was staring at it, perhaps waiting for something to load. Sure enough, after only a few more seconds he gave a short laugh and turned the phone around for Lydia to see.

'What?' She took the phone from him, angling the screen away from the sunlight. 'I don't understand. What does this mean?'

'It's a map of Calahurst,' Dermot said. 'Don't you recognise it? There's the church and the war memorial, and the police station.'

Ben looked quickly at Milla, saw her increasingly shocked face and began to get a really bad feeling. 'Where did you leave your car, Milla?'

'I—'

Lydia's voice cut across her. 'This would mean Kiran's car is parked—'

'Practically outside Calahurst Police Station,' Dermot said, not bothering to hide his amusement. 'That would be the police station where you're based, wouldn't it, Lydia?'

Ben didn't catch her reply, only heard the cursing and the scrunch of heels across the shingle driveway. Dermot, shaking his head, headed back into the cottage and closed the door.

'I think it's time we left,' Ben said, when all had fallen quiet.

For once Milla agreed with him. 'I need to get my car.'

'That's impossible. Forget it.'

Her grey eyes turned distinctly flinty. 'My entire *life* is in that car.'

'There's no way for you to get there before Lydia. You have to abandon it.'

Milla was looking at him as though she thought him an idiot. 'I'm not joking. Every single thing I own is packed up into that car. I can't abandon it and I *won't*!'

'Lydia is already in her car, heading there right now, and we're a good ten minutes' walk from mine. It's not physically possible to get there in time.'

'It *must* be!'

'I'm sorry—'

'No, you're not. You don't understand at all. I can't sit here and let her take everything from me! Not that sly witch. She is *not* going to get one over on me. I won't let it happen. I *won't*!'

'There's not much I can do. Calahurst isn't even my jurisdiction—'

Milla had already scrambled up and was running towards the gate, evidently not caring whether Dermot saw her or not.

Ben knew he should let her leave. Equally he knew he wouldn't. He was the fool who had 'save the girl' hardwired into his brain.

He chased after her, catching up on the other side of the gate. Lydia's car had gone, leaving clear skid marks where she'd left in a hurry. There was no way of arriving in Calahurst before her.

Not unless she'd been in so much of a hurry to catch Milla she hadn't called it into the station first.

He pulled out his phone and dialled Harriet. She answered on the second ring and her voice was as clear as though she were standing next to him. A little *too* clear.

'Where *are* you? I've been calling and calling. I even went to your house but there was no reply and your hired car's not there. Everyone is looking for you, including DCI Cameron, and I'm tired of making excuses. You need to get back here pronto.'

He switched the phone from speaker and, holding it gingerly to his ear, waited for Harriet to pause for breath.

She didn't.

'Harriet?' he said calmly. Then, when that didn't work, slightly louder. 'Harriet!'

Silence, followed by a sulky, 'What?'

'There's a white Ford Escort parked in the vicinity of Calahurst Police Station—'

'Grocery store,' interrupted Milla. 'It's outside the grocery store.'

'Outside the grocery store,' he amended. 'If you have time, I need for it to be towed to the vehicle pound as evidence. In the meantime, most urgently, before anything else, I need you to head over there right now, seize the entire contents and meet me back at my house. And Harriet, this is very important – you can log the car onto the system, but the contents have to stay off the record – for the moment.'

'You're asking me to *perjure* myself?'

He wanted to say, 'Just this once' but had the horrible feeling it wouldn't *be* just this once. He paused, realising how incredibly unfair it was to ask Harriet to do this.

He did so anyway. 'Yes.'

'It's *her* car isn't it?'

Milla was waving her hands, trying to get his attention. He turned his back on her, but she caught his arm, forcing him to look at her. 'You don't need to break into the car,' she said. 'There's a magnetic box hidden on the wheel arch with a spare key inside.'

Ben relayed the information before adding, 'Harriet? Lydia is on her way too, so you'll need to act now.'

'Damn you,' Harriet said, and the line went dead.

Ben returned the phone to his pocket.

Milla was regarding him hopefully. 'Well?'

'Harriet says she's right on it.'

TWENTY-NINE

Harriet slammed her phone down on her desk and screamed.

Seven people jumped. Seven pairs of eyes turned in her direction.

The DCI's office door flew open. 'What the *hell* was that?'

'Mouse,' Sam said, without hesitation. He pointed beneath his desk. 'Right there.'

'Well sort it out!' the DCI snapped, heading back into his office. 'Humanely!'

Sam sat back and grinned at Harriet. 'DI Taylor, I assume?'

'Apparently I have to go and seize a car.' She picked up her phone to check she hadn't broken it. 'Right now, as though I don't have anything else to do.'

Sam opened his mouth as though to remind her that seizing vehicles wasn't in her job description, but after one glance at her face, said instead, 'How can I help?'

'You can drive while I'll fill in the paperwork.'

Was she really going to do this?

Did she have a choice?

Aware she had an attentive audience, she forced a note of calm to her voice.

'Dakota, please could you contact the towing company and send them to the grocery store in Calahurst?' Harriet scribbled the details of Kiran's car onto a pad, tore off the sheet and handed it over. 'This is the vehicle I need them to seize. Tell them it's super-urgent.'

Sam peered over her shoulder. 'Isn't that Kiran McKenzie's car? If you want to seize it, you need a reason.'

'Really? Because I thought I'd just make something up.'

Sam and Dakota stared at her in horrified silence.

'That was a joke,' she sighed. 'Let me think. It's not stolen,' – although she wouldn't put it past Kiran – 'It hasn't been involved in an accident. I wonder if it's parked illegally?'

Sam rolled his eyes. 'Maybe start with something that's easier to check? Does Kiran have a driving licence?'

'I'm on it.' Dakota turned to her keyboard and rattled off the details. 'I've found a licence for a Kiran Parminder McKenzie, with an address in Norchester. Wasn't "Parminder" the name of her grandmother?'

'Sounds like you've found her,' Sam said. 'Now check for insurance, tax and MOT.'

'She has insurance for a white Ford Fiesta and the registration number matches...'

'Damn,' Harriet muttered.

'The MOT is valid,' Dakota added, 'but her tax ran out last week. The poor girl has a lot going on. I expect she forgot.'

'I've told you before about thinking the best of people,' Harriet said. 'Stop it.'

Dakota meekly dipped her head. 'Sorry.'

Harriet slung her bag over her shoulder 'Let's go,' she said to Sam.

'Good luck!' Dakota called, as they left the office.

'Give us a ten-minute head start, then tell the DCI where we've gone. Big it up. Make it sound as though there's a load of evidence just waiting to be had. We don't want Lydia phoning him and throwing a strop.'

Sam stopped so suddenly she almost walked into the back of him. 'Lydia? What does this have to do with *Lydia?*'

'Long story,' Harriet pushed him towards the door. 'I'll tell you in the car.'

As they pulled up outside the grocery store, the flatbed tow truck Dakota had sent was backing up in front of Kiran's car. There was no sign of Lydia, or any of her team, but that didn't mean she wasn't on her way. Sam went to talk to the driver. Harriet bent down and groped around the wheel arch until she found the little box with the key.

Opening the boot, she found a large plastic crate full of assorted rubbish, a kit bag of crumpled clothes, and a green plastic bag with a logo that matched the store they were standing outside. Inside that was a squashed pasty, some fruit, a bottle of water and a newspaper. Harriet dumped it all into the back of Sam's car, although she had to do two trips before she could hand over the key to the truck driver.

He was loading Kiran's car when a familiar black BMW screeched up beside them and Lydia jumped out, not quite as cool as usual. Sam, the coward, ducked down the other side of the truck, while the driver carried on with his work, oblivious.

Lydia strode straight up to Harriet. '*Why* are you seizing that car?'

'Hi, Lydia. Good to see you again. Is there a problem?'

'The *car?*'

'Oh, yes, the car. Sorry. The tax has expired.'

'The *tax?*' Lydia spat each word out.

'The car does have a valid MOT but we're also concerned that it's not roadworthy.'

'Are you *serious?*'

'I'm afraid I don't understand. Is there a problem?'

'Where's your boss?'

'DI Taylor? Not sure. I think he went to speak with an informant.'

That was definitely the wrong thing to have said, because Lydia's green eyes immediately narrowed. 'You do know whose car this is?'

'Yes, it's Kiran McKenzie's. I don't know if you remember, but she's a person of interest in the Amita Kaal murder.'

'Where *is* Kiran McKenzie?'

'I haven't got a clue.' Harriet knew Kiran was with Ben, but Ben hadn't shared their location when he'd called. She knew where they were *likely* to be in about twenty minutes, but that wasn't the question Lydia had asked.

More fool her.

Lydia switched her attention to the car being loaded onto the truck. 'Did you find anything inside the car?'

'I checked the front and the back,' Harriet said, carefully not mentioning the boot.

Lydia didn't notice. 'Has DI Taylor arranged for the usual forensic tests?'

'I don't think so.' From what Harriet remembered of their conversation, Ben hadn't seemed much interested in the car, just Kiran's personal belongings.

Lydia seemed pleased. 'I can do that for him.'

'You're very kind.'

For that, Harriet received another narrow-eyed look before Lydia stalked away.

She slumped against the side of Sam's car and watched Lydia drive off.

'All done,' Sam announced. '*Was* there anything in the car?'

'Just Kiran McKenzie's personal belongings, which we're about to hand right back to her.'

Sam was silent for a moment and then, 'The DI is a good

bloke. You know that. If he thinks Milla – I mean, Kiran – is innocent—'

'Don't say it. Just *don't*.'

They drove to Ben's house in silence and parked on the drive. Sam carried the crate to the front door; Harriet was left with the kit bag and the grocery bag. She carefully stacked everything against the door, beneath the little porch. It wouldn't save them from getting wet if it rained, but hopefully Ben would be home soon.

'Shouldn't we wait for the boss?' Sam asked, as Harriet stalked back to the car.

'No. I don't think I can face him at the moment. I'm too angry.'

He was silent for a moment, and then said, 'You can't continue to work for DI Taylor if you have no confidence in him.'

Why didn't she tell Sam the truth? They'd been friends since they were five.

'I was thinking of applying for the MIT. Apparently there are going to be vacancies for two detective inspectors.'

'Nothing to stop you,' he said. 'You'd make a great DI.'

'What will you do? Stay in CID?'

'I go where you go. You know that. I only joined the police because of you.'

She laughed. 'Don't say things like that! People will think we're more than just good friends.'

'Have I ever given any indication that I care about what people think?'

'That's exactly what Ben said and look how *that* turned out.'

Sam sighed. 'And we're back to talking about *him* again...'

'It's pretty much all I can think of at the moment. His behaviour... it's so *frustrating*! It's almost as though he's deter-mined to get himself fired.'

Sam muttered something unintelligible beneath his breath

as they got back into the car, but she'd already zoned out. *Was she obsessing about Ben?* He was her boss, nothing more, and she'd only known him for five months, but she liked him, and the way he'd allowed himself to become so involved with Kiran felt like betrayal. They were supposed to be working together as a team. How could she ever trust him again?

And if she didn't trust him...

* * *

Ben had left his car halfway up the lane, hidden behind outbuildings. As they drove back to his home, he played Billie Holiday to de-stress. This time Milla made no comment, staring out of the window and watching the forest pass in a green blur.

He had thought Harriet would be waiting on his doorstep but there was no sign of her. Instead, one very large plastic crate, a slightly smaller kit bag and a carrier bag of groceries had been plonked carelessly in the porch. Milla fell on them in delight.

Good old Harriet. He owed her a serious number of favours.

'I'll be happy to take you wherever you need to go,' he told Milla. 'But you do need to go. You know that, right?'

'I suppose it's for the best – until things quieten down.'

'Where would you like me to take you?'

'*Now?*'

'Yes, now!'

She picked up the kit bag and the groceries. 'The train station?'

He looked at the crate.

'Do you think you can hold onto it, until it's safe for me to return?'

'Certainly,' he said. At least he'd have the opportunity to search it first. Not that he was likely to find anything interesting, or she would never have considered leaving it with him.

'You have my phone number.' How many times had he said that? 'If you get into any kind of trouble, call me.'

Please don't.

She beamed. 'Of course I will.'

Great.

He locked the crate inside his house, loaded the rest of her things into his car and drove her to the nearest railway station which, coincidentally, was just outside Calahurst. He bought her a one-way ticket to Southampton and escorted her onto the correct platform.

Instead of thanking him, she frowned. 'Why Southampton?'

Because it's far, far, far away from Raven's Edge.

'You have family there, don't you?'

'The Kaals?' She gave a short laugh. 'Like they're going to be pleased to see me.'

'Perhaps you'll be surprised.'

'Not half as surprised as they will!'

Even though he knew he was wasting his time, he waited until the train arrived and watched her get on it. She immediately turned around and got off again.

He was getting very close to losing his temper. 'What now?'

'Why were you there?'

He stalled. 'Where?'

'Rosemary's cottage.'

If he answered that, she'd never leave.

The door tried to whoosh shut but he blocked it with his hand and it automatically opened again. 'Get on the train, Milla.'

'Only if you answer the question!'

He'd really had enough. Picking her up, he dumped her back on the train and then stood directly in front of her so she couldn't get off.

When she opened her mouth to protest, he said, 'The

cottage is in the name of Kiran McKenzie. Rosemary Graham left it to her in her will.'

Which struck her dumb long enough for the doors to slide shut. There was a shrill whistle from somewhere down the platform and the train began to move away. He stepped back, watching her rattle the door and then bang her fist on the window demanding to be let out, and he grinned. Any more of that and she'd be in trouble with the British Transport Police but what the hell, at least she was no longer *his* problem.

For a couple of hours at least.

He watched the train slide off into the forest and out of sight but knew he hadn't seen the last of Milla Graham.

Later, sipping coffee back at his desk, Ben flipped through the photographs he'd taken on his phone. Snapped at high speed, some were blurred and out of focus, others all too worryingly clear. The silver-framed photographs, lined up on Rosemary's chest of drawers; her jewellery, mostly bought from high-street stores and still in their original boxes; the magazine, from the month of her death. Everything was immaculate and dust-free, as though she'd only walked out that morning.

Someone was taking care of Rose Cottage.

Or living there.

Milla? Was she spinning him another of her stories? Had she returned, even now?

Yet her shock and pleasure when she'd seen the photograph of her cousins would have been hard to fake.

Dermot Graham? He knew of the house and had been there with Lydia, although Ben had seen no sign of a second vehicle. Had the two of them arrived together, or was Dermot the one in residence? But why, when he owned a dozen far more luxurious houses?

The biggest mystery was that the property was in the name

of Kiran McKenzie. Had Milla really no idea she owned Rose Cottage? It was completely implausible.

The last photograph came into focus. The garment bag he'd unzipped in Rosemary's closet. The extravagant evening gown of pale silk tulle, the petals of the voluminous skirt dipped in dark pearls and rhinestones to stunning effect. He'd recognised it immediately. He'd seen it before in one of Sophie's books of fairy tales.

The gown Amita had been found in had been vintage Dior. It had once belonged to Brianna Graham, and Rosemary had used it in an illustration of *Sleeping Beauty*. If he'd had time to unzip more garment bags, would he have found more of Brianna's gowns? And why were the gowns stored at Rose Cottage instead of somewhere more appropriate, or even in a museum? Brianna had told his team she'd given the gowns away, years ago. Had she been lying? If so, who was she protecting?

Is this where Amita's murderer had found the gown he'd dressed her in?

Was this the incontrovertible evidence linking Amita's death with Rosemary Graham, indicating the same person was responsible? It was enough to obtain a warrant and perform an official search. Regrettably, the evidence irrefutably linked Milla to Amita's murder. Something he couldn't believe – didn't *want* to believe.

His attraction to her was having a serious effect on his judgement and his ability to do his job.

He had a decision to make, and he had to make it very soon. Tell DCI Cameron what he'd discovered, which would likely result in Milla's arrest and his suspension. Or keep quiet, continue to gather evidence, and hope the murderer didn't strike again.

Reluctantly he reached for the internal phone and dialled Cameron's number.

He was listening to it ringing when there was a soft click and the door to his office opened.

Harriet backed in, carrying a pile of files.

Ben dropped the phone back into its cradle. 'Ah, Harriet,' he began, well aware of how awkward he sounded. 'Thank you for... earlier.'

Harriet didn't even look at him. 'You're supposed to be giving an interview to the press in ten minutes,' she said, noisily dumping the files on his desk. 'Had you forgotten? *I'm* certainly not doing it. I've brought you the statements. Sam's already in the conference room, setting up. DCI Cameron *was* on his way in, but got caught by the Super who's now bending his ear on budgets and manpower.'

Damn. It was going to be hard enough admitting to DCI Cameron what he'd done, without the prospective audience of Harriet and the rest of his team, and the media.

'No sign of DI Cavill though, thank goodness.' Harriet's attention was caught by his mobile phone still lying on the desk, and the close-up of the sparkling rhinestones. 'Ooh, pretty!' she said, turning her head sideways to get a better look. 'What is that? Some kind of party dress? Is it going to be a present for Sophie?'

Ben casually closed his fingers over his phone, slid it across the desk and into his pocket.

'Something like that,' he said. 'Let's go.'

By the time the Hatter reached the downstairs hall a dark ribbon of smoke was already curling around the top of the staircase. The house had a Georgian façade, concealing a far older building of stone and wood. Perfect fuel for a hungry fire. He should keep walking, out into the sweet night air and onto his new life. And yet...

And yet.

When he opened the kitchen door the boy was waiting for him, his pale eyes as hot as the fire raging above, a frying pan held grimly before him as a weapon. Of the girl there was no sign.

The Hatter yanked the frying pan from the boy's hands and tossed it away. 'Stupid boy. You kicked over the candles and now the house is on fire.'

The boy's eyes flickered towards the ceiling, his panic clear. 'I must go—'

The Hatter held out his hand in a time-old gesture of friendship. 'It's too late for them. Come with me and save yourself.'

THIRTY

Raven's Edge didn't have its own train station, only an unmanned platform, but it did have security cameras. When Milla got off the train she was tempted to give one a cheery little wave but maybe it would be better if she didn't break the habit of a lifetime and draw attention to herself. She kept her head down and blended with the tourists heading towards The Crooked Broomstick and Practically Magic until she was well away from the station, and then she took the first path leading into the woods.

She had played here so often as a child she had assumed she'd immediately recognise her surroundings but, apart from the sinister silhouette of Rosemary's Tower, the landscape had changed considerably.

There was no sign of the extensive gardens that had once surrounded King's Rest. Now they were as one with the forest. Occasionally she would stumble over a lump of masonry or fallen statue but there was nothing she remembered. It was an unsettling feeling, as though her entire childhood had been a dream.

Being snatched from that fairy-tale world of wealth and

privilege had changed her. Six-year-old Milla, who had believed in handsome princes and happy ever afters, would never have grown up to seduce another woman's Prince Charming purely to prove he had the heart of a troll. But, as usual, Milla had been so determined to prove she was right, she'd broken Amita's heart in the most brutal way possible.

Then there was her motivation for returning to Raven's Edge. Did it matter who had killed Rosemary? Discovering the truth wouldn't bring her back to life. Was Ben right? Was she turning this crusade for justice into something personal? Was she really making it all about her?

The trees grew so closely together the path was in permanent shade. Despite the heat the air was cooler, almost chilly, and it was so very, very quiet.

Maybe this wasn't the time to remember every ghost story ever associated with the place now known locally as the Grim House.

Milla heaved her satchel higher over her shoulder and walked faster, recalling all those horror movies where the gullible and stupid were picked off one by one until only the star name was left. Well, no one would be picking *her* off, that was for sure. She had a nice sharp knife in her satchel, ostensibly to peel fruit, but she could think of plenty of other uses it could be put to, starting with any creep who tried to do a number on her.

She had been walking for so long that when the blackened, broken stones of King's Rest peeled away from the shadows it came as an unpleasant surprise. Her fingers curled tighter around the strap of her satchel and she remembered the photo of Amita glaring out from the front page of *The Calahurst Echo*. Did she *really* want to do this? OK, so she'd have a roof over her head and no one would think of looking for her here, but wasn't this taking stupidity to a new level?

'*Drive as far away from here as possible,*' Ben had said. If she did that, she'd never discover who killed Rosemary and why. And she needed to know. She really, *really* needed to know.

A need enough to die for?

Shaking off *that* thought, Milla ducked beneath the branches of a rhododendron and found the path leading around to the back of the house. The kitchen entrance had been newly boarded up but there was a tiny window level with the ground, unnoticeable to anyone who didn't know where to look. She took the knife from her satchel and slid it along the catch, although the weeds had to be cleared away before it would open. After that, it was easy to push her satchel through the gap and slither in after it.

She landed on her feet in a vast, empty, underground room, which she recognised as the cellar she and Mal had once pretended was a dungeon. With the comfort of knowing the knife was still in her hand, she closed the window and followed a twisting stone staircase up into the kitchen.

Despite the heat outside, the interior was cold and smelt unpleasantly of damp and decay. She avoided the family bedrooms on the first floor, walking straight up to the staff quarters above. The vandals had not reached this far and, eerily, the rooms still had their furnishings. The staff must have fled their beds the night of the fire and never returned to claim their possessions. Bed linen and curtains were black with mould, and everything else was covered in a thick layer of ash and soot.

As Milla began to despair of finding a habitable room in which to camp out for the night, she finally found one at the very end of the corridor. It had originally been a nursery but there were no toys here now, nor any trace of the bars that had once been set in the window. She sat on the sill to eat the pasty she'd originally bought for her lunch. From here she could see Rosemary's Tower stark above the trees, as well as a streak of sliver glinting in the far distance that was probably the sea.

It was growing dark, and on the other side of the forest, in the direction of Hartfell House, lights were beginning to pop on. Was Dermot back in residence? What would he think if he knew she was so close? Had Mal told him the truth about her departure? And Brianna, would she be sorry Milla had left – or glad to see the back of her?

Unexpectedly lonely, Milla tried phoning Patrick to update him on her progress but her call went straight to a recorded message. She was tempted to call Ben, just to have someone to talk to. How sad was that?

She watched the sun sink slowly behind the trees and realised there was nothing to do but get some sleep. She burrowed into her sleeping bag, feeling thoroughly miserable, trying to ignore the sinister creaking from the floors below.

And fell asleep within seconds.

Despite the thunder rumbling distantly along the coast.

Despite the wind rattling loose the tiles on the roof, sending them crashing through three floors to shatter on the billiard table.

Despite the floorboards of the great staircase creaking every time Dermot Graham trod on them.

Dermot found the woman calling herself Milla Graham curled up like a child in the room that had been his old nursery. A room used by generations of children, until Rosemary McKenzie married his brother and declared that no child of hers was going to be banished from sight and raised by strangers.

How supremely ironic that turned out to be.

He sat on the dusty floor, leaned back against the wall and watched over Milla until dawn.

And then phoned the police and told them where to find her.

* * *

Milla woke up to the sensation she was being watched.

She was used to waking up in strange beds and unfamiliar surroundings, and immediately recognised where she was and how she'd got there.

Which was more than she could say for the person standing over her.

'Hello, Kiran,' Lydia said. 'Sleep well?'

Damn.

It had never occurred to Milla that she'd be found so quickly. Had Dermot placed trackers amongst her belongings as well as her car? Or had she walked past some police guard last night without even noticing? At least Lydia appeared to be alone. She was perched on the windowsill in much the same way as Milla last night, meaning the route to the door was clear.

'Good morning, Lydia,' Milla said cheerfully, pushing the sleeping bag free of her legs for a quick getaway. 'How lovely to see you again. Would you like a coffee?'

Lydia didn't bother to hide her shudder, stretching out her foot to delicately kick at Milla's camping stove. 'Is this honestly how you live?'

'I had a really nice apartment up until a couple of days ago.'

'Could it really have been termed "yours" when you never paid the rent?'

'Tiny administrative oversight,' Milla said, all the while calculating in her head, *ten paces to the door, twenty paces to the stairs.*

With any luck, she'd be up and out of here before Lydia could put one elegantly shod foot in front of the other. Would she also have time to grab her satchel, with her laptop, phone and money? At least she'd had the foresight to sleep in her clothes. Her Docs, however, had been neatly placed by the window. Right next to Lydia.

To think, she'd been more worried about ghosts.

'Time to pack up and go, little Kiran,' Lydia told her. 'It's over.'

'Milla,' she said automatically.

'It's so sad, the way you persist with that.'

'With what?' Milla asked, even though she knew she should let it go. Why was she still arguing anyway? If she made a run for it, Lydia would never be able to catch her.

If only she could grab her satchel.

'I understand why you do. After all, who would want to be Kiran McKenzie when they could be Camilla Graham?'

'I have *no* idea what you're talking about.' Slowly, carefully, Milla curled her legs beneath her, shifting into a position from which she could launch herself through the door in one fluid movement.

'Your hard-done-by Nancy Drew act might work on Ben Taylor but I know you, Kiran. I've known you since you were a child.'

Milla grit her teeth and determinedly didn't say anything. If she could somehow close the gap between her and Lydia, she'd be able to grab both her boots and her satchel from beneath the other woman's nose.

She'd have to be very lucky though.

'There's no point in running,' Lydia said, as though reading her mind. 'We have your car, despite the best efforts of DI Taylor. You won't be able to rely on him anymore. He's about to be suspended from duty. How does it feel, knowing you've single-handedly destroyed a man's career?'

Milla's gut twisted in guilt and she itched to wipe that smug look from Lydia's face, preferably with a hefty punch. Lydia was lying, she *must* be lying. Ben couldn't be suspended for just that one thing.

Except it wasn't one thing, was it? He'd followed her into Dermot's cottage and helped her search it – basically breaking and entering. Despite Ben wiping away their fingerprints, they must have left all kinds of forensic evidence behind.

Bitch.

She couldn't react. Lydia was watching her too carefully.

'We know you're in contact with Patrick Graham,' Lydia added. 'We have all your meetings caught on camera. Are you that desperate for a father? The man murdered his own children, for heaven's sake! How could you even want to be associated with such a monster?'

'Have you ever considered he might be innocent?'

'Is that what he's telling you? Forensic evidence doesn't lie, Kiran.'

'Evidence can be compromised, twisted and even faked if you're determined enough, if you're rich enough and certainly if you're powerful enough. Someone like Dermot Graham could make the Pope look guilty.'

Lydia shook her head. 'I can see I'm wasting my time talking to you. You're as cracked as Patrick.' She extracted something metallic from her pocket and Milla braced herself, assuming Lydia was about to bring out a pair of cuffs. But it appeared Lydia let her monkeys do her dirty work, for the metallic object turned out to be her phone.

Panicked, Milla rose to her feet, determined to keep Lydia talking, determined to stop her calling for backup. 'Are you sleeping with him?'

'*What?*' Lydia was evidently startled enough to almost drop her phone. 'Who—'

'Are you hoping to become the next Mrs Dermot Graham? Is that why you're working for him? Is that why you'll do anything to please him, even risk your job?'

'Now listen to me, you *stupid* girl—'

'*I'm* stupid? Did you know Dermot and Rosemary were having an affair? That's why Dermot killed her – because she wouldn't give up her children to run away with him.'

'I suppose Patrick told you that? And *you* believed him, without any proof, without any evidence? You poor, deluded *idiot*. The man is a murderer. How many times do I have to warn you about this? He'll murder you too if it suits his purpose and he won't care whose daughter you are.'

Milla took a step forward, putting herself within grabbing distance of both her satchel and boots, but rather too close to Lydia. Now she could see the faint lines of tiredness beneath Lydia's eyes, even see the swirl of grey against green that gave them that curious sea-glass colour.

'Have you ever been in any of those rooms at Rose Cottage?' Milla demanded. 'Have you seen Rosemary's bedroom with her clothes, her jewellery, everything she ever owned, just as she left it, like some freaky shrine? Rosemary might be dead, but Dermot's still obsessed with her. You have *no* chance. He'll never marry you.'

Lydia regarded her with pity. 'Now I *know* you're as unhinged as Patrick and it will be my absolute *pleasure* to charge you with accessory to murder and ensure the pair of you are locked up where you'll never be able to hurt anyone ever again.'

'You and whose army?' Milla snapped, happily envisaging her next move as snatching Lydia's phone and shoving it down her elegant white throat.

Lydia held up her hand. 'Listen carefully and you'll be able to hear the delicately stomping boots of the county constabulary heading this way right now.'

She was right! The sound was distant but it was there. Maybe the flying monkeys had only reached as far as the first floor but how *could* she have been so stupid as to assume Lydia was alone?

How long had she got? Minutes?

Seconds, if Lydia gave one good yell.

Assuming she had that opportunity.

Lydia was tall and slender with the kind of lean muscled body that implied she worked out regularly. How far would she go to make her precious arrest? Would she fight? Undoubtedly. But would she fight dirty?

Maybe it wouldn't come to that.

Because Lydia was still balanced on that windowsill, over-confident and completely at ease, with nothing behind her but the chill air of an English summer morning. In one hand she held her phone; the other was only lightly curled around the wooden sill. Her legs were stretched out in front of her, elegantly crossed at the ankle as she flaunted the distinctive red soles of her impractical shoes.

In short, she seemed blithely unaware how precarious her position was.

Really, all it would take was one big shove and...

THIRTY-ONE

For the second time in a matter of days Ben opened his front door to find Harriet on the other side, wearing her favourite pale grey suit accessorised with glittery pink wellingtons.

He sighed. 'Don't tell me; I'm going to need boots.'

'Wear what the hell you like,' Harriet said and stalked off.

He supposed he deserved that, but he grabbed his Hunters and followed Harriet to her car, dropping them into the back and sliding into the passenger seat. 'Where are we going?'

'King's Rest. Another body's been found.'

Milla?

As he drew enough breath to ask the question, Harriet added, 'DI Cavill was found dead early this morning. I can't believe it. One of our own!' She reversed at high speed into his driveway, screeched to a halt barely more than a centimetre from his hired car and then shot forward onto the road, hardly bothering to check for oncoming traffic.

Thank goodness he'd put his seatbelt on. 'Are we sure?'

Harriet gave him that look again, the one which plainly said she thought him an idiot. 'What? That it's Lydia or that she's dead?'

'I meant *how*?'

Had he and Milla been the last to see Lydia alive?

Harriet jammed her foot on the accelerator to overtake a coach, flattening him back against the seat. 'Isn't that *your* job?'

'Harriet,' he began, the note of warning clear in his voice.

She didn't let him finish. 'I'm putting in a request to join the new Murder Investigation Team as soon as possible. You might not care about your career but I'm not having you drag me down with you.'

'Fair enough,' he said. 'Your prerogative. Until then, could you cut the snark and brief me on what happened to DI Cavill?'

For a moment he thought she wouldn't reply and then, 'I don't know. The call only came through twenty minutes ago.'

'What was Lydia doing in Raven's Edge? Or, more specifically, King's Rest?'

'Her sergeant says they were called out early this morning. She told him they were responding to a tip-off. She must have taken the call personally because there's no record of one being patched through to her or of any message being taken. They separated to search the house and the next thing anyone knew, Lydia was dead. And yes, they do suspect foul play.'

Milla. This *had* to be connected to Milla. It made perfect sense. He'd put Milla on the train at Calahurst and she'd promptly got off at Raven's Edge, making her way here. But why? Was the answer as simple as her wanting to find a bed for the night, or had she planned to meet up with Patrick Graham? If that were the case, where were the pair of them now?

Harriet took another glance in his direction. Sideways. Expecting him to say more. That he was sorry Lydia was dead? Well, he *was* sorry Lydia was dead, in the same way he'd be sorry anyone he worked with was dead. He'd liked her and no one could deny she was a bloody good officer.

Harriet seemed to have read his mind. 'Lydia might have

come across as a cold-hearted b... well, whatever, at least she was working all hours to try and solve Amita's murder.'

'It wasn't her case.'

'Who *cares* whose case it is, whose patch it is? Amita Kaal has been dead for a week and, as far as I can tell, we're no closer to knowing who killed her than we were then. Now we have another body and all you're bothered about is chasing some tart—'

'Harriet.'

'It's the truth!'

'It's the truth but not in the way you're choosing to see it!'

'Then tell me! Tell me what the bloody hell is going on and how I can help – how I can do my job, Ben! I'm supposed to be your sergeant. We're supposed to be a team; you don't tell me anything, and you keep going off without me!'

Ben rubbed at his temples, trying to soothe the headache that had been coming on ever since he'd woken up that morning. 'How can I, when I'm not even sure where to start?'

'At the beginning,' was her sharp reply. 'Once upon a bloody time—' and then she must have seen something in his expression because she quickly shut up.

'I need to see Lydia's body,' he said. 'I need to see where she died and how she died, and all the forensic evidence gathered to date. You know how this works. It's all about the painstakingly slow collecting and filtering of information. It all takes time – weeks, months. We can't arrest someone on a hunch.'

'We haven't *got* time. We have two murders in the same place in the space of a week. One of whom is a police officer. The media are going to take this and run with it. We'll look like idiots.'

'I do *know* this, Harriet, but it's got to be done right. Milla Graham is the link between Amita's murder and that of Rosemary Graham and her children. I don't know how and I don't know why but Milla's not the murderer. I know that much.'

'Because of a *hunch*?'

'Because of a hunch,' he agreed, 'and ten years of experience.'

Harriet turned left at the junction for Raven's Edge, hardly slowing to negotiate the bend. Ben surreptitiously grabbed at the door handle to keep himself upright. The car swung briefly onto the other side of the road, before Harriet jerked the steering wheel back to compensate.

'Lydia was found by one of her team,' Harriet said, 'but they didn't see anything. They didn't see anything, they didn't hear anything, they don't know anything. Useless, the lot of them. Apparently not even capable of a single thought process without her.'

'I'm assuming they're capable of following procedure?'

'That, at least. They've cordoned off the scene, called everyone on their list, and now they're waiting for direction from the investigating officer.'

'OK.'

Harriet stuck the knife in. 'DCI Cameron.'

Cameron was taking over? Had no one thought to tell him? Perhaps Harriet wouldn't need to put in for her transfer. Perhaps she could have his job.

The gates to King's Rest had been unlocked, unbolted and wedged open with police cones. A uniformed officer was standing guard beside them, along with a fleet of police and other emergency vehicles – and an outside broadcast unit from the local TV company. No doubt the first of many. The murder of a serving police officer would be headline news. They'd need to deploy more officers to keep a check on the perimeter but how could a cordon be placed around an entire forest? The crime-scene photos would go viral before he'd even got halfway up the drive.

Ben pulled on his wellington boots feeling a distinct sense

of déjà vu, not helped by recognising the officer on the gate as the same man from last time. There was more barrier tape at the end of the drive, giving an incongruous impression that the entire house had been gift-wrapped. They gave their names, signed themselves in, donned the usual forensic suits and joined the huge team of people required to investigate a crime scene.

Lydia's body lay to the side of the house – the mostly intact west wing. The undergrowth had been flattened by the CSIs, taking photos and searching for forensic detail. No stylised crime scene here. Her body was bloody and broken, as though it had hit something with great force – or fallen from a great height. Instinctively Ben looked up. The windows on the ground floor and the one above had been boarded up, but the one above that was open to the elements.

Poor Lydia.

He headed back around to the entrance of the house. Here he found another officer, who lifted the tape and allowed him into the house. CSIs were moving up and down the stairs carrying equipment. He didn't need to ask what they'd found. Once he'd reached the room Lydia had fallen from, a CSI approached him, holding a clear plastic bag with something inside, something that glinted silver. He recognised it immediately.

She held it out to him. 'Dropped recently, sir.'

He couldn't take it. He just couldn't. He stepped around her to peer into the room, leaving Harriet to cover for his rudeness. When she saw what was inside the bag – a miniature silver hat, no bigger than a fingernail – she whistled.

'This is gorgeous! Is it some kind of a charm? From a bracelet?'

Ben feigned disinterest. 'It looks as though it came from a Monopoly set.'

There it was again. The look that said he was an idiot. 'It's *jewellery*, Ben. Solid silver. Look at the detail; it even has a little ribbon around the crown.'

The ribbon would have a ticket tucked into it, a ticket that said 10/6, but he said nothing, letting his gaze sweep around the room, taking in every sign that signalled someone had been living here very recently. A sleeping bag, a camping stove, a carrier bag of groceries...

'The sleeping bag has been well-used but it's of good quality,' the CSI said, realising what had caught his attention. 'The same for the camping stove.'

'Someone camping rather than sleeping rough,' said Harriet. 'A woman, used to the finer things in life.' She squinted again at the little silver hat. 'It's a strange thing to have on a charm bracelet. I think there's an inscription, but it's too small for me to read.'

'"In this style 10/6",' said the CSI, too helpfully. She grinned at Ben. 'Magnifying glass? Comes as standard kit.'

Harriet turned it over in her hand. 'I wonder what it means?'

He could have told her. He could have told her about the other charms too: a potion bottle labelled 'drink me', a little toadstool with a tiny caterpillar on top, a pocket watch and a teapot. He could have told her of *Alice's Adventures in Wonderland* and the girl who featured in every illustration, but he didn't. He felt as though he'd walked into a surreal fairy tale of his own.

Had Milla been stupid enough to have returned here, only to leave all her belongings behind? Everything that would identify her as guilty? Everything she owned in the entire world?

No, not his Milla. She wouldn't have done it. She was too smart for that.

Unless she'd been running away from someone.

Or something.

Or something she'd done.

Harriet began asking the questions that should have been his. 'What else have you found?'

'There's a kit bag, with spare clothes and toiletries,' the CSI said. 'They're all from the more expensive end of the high street. And look,' – she held out a newspaper – 'it's dated yesterday.'

Ben kept his hands in his pockets; Harriet took the newspaper instead.

She whistled again. 'Have you seen what's on the cover?'

As she was holding it right in front of his face, he could hardly avoid it.

Sleeping Beauty Murder at Grim House.

He also saw the exact moment when the penny dropped.

The kitbag, the groceries – Harriet had seen them all before.

'Is it hers?' Harriet demanded. 'Does this belong to Kiran, or Camilla, or whatever she's calling herself today?'

The CSI wisely made herself scarce.

'Well?'

All he had to do was shake his head and deny it, or be vague and say he wasn't sure. He could even evade the question completely. He was becoming a little bit too good at that. Whatever he did, Harriet would know he was lying, and he couldn't keep lying to protect a murderer.

He couldn't. He just couldn't. It went against everything that was right, everything he believed in, but he wanted to. How had he fallen into this mess? How could he have fallen in so far?

'You can't keep protecting her,' Harriet was telling him. 'I understand why you want to. You think you can save her but you can't. It's too late. She's gone too far this time.'

Still, he said nothing. He couldn't find the words to explain why nothing had changed. That despite all this evidence to the contrary, he *knew* Milla was innocent.

So he kept silent.

Fortunately, Harriet had already decided a reply wasn't necessary, for she pulled out her phone and called DCI Cameron, telling him what they'd found and suggesting a warrant be issued for Milla's arrest on suspicion of two counts of murder: Amita Kaal and Lydia Cavill.

And there wasn't a damned thing Ben could do about it.

The boy shoved the Hatter away. Hatred lit up those pale grey eyes and for a moment he looked just like Rosemary.

'No! I won't leave them!'

The Hatter shrugged. 'Suit yourself,' he said and turned away – just as the boy launched himself at him, a ball of flying fists and primeval fury.

It was the work of a moment to clip him across the jaw and render him unconscious.

The Hatter slung the boy over his shoulder and took one last look around the kitchen. Apart from the messy remains of Camilla's birthday cake, the staff had left it immaculate. Everything was neatly tidied away, leaving no place for even the smallest child to hide.

Except, perhaps...

One.

The Hatter smiled.

And switched on the oven.

THIRTY-TWO

As they drove the short distance back to the station the humidity was overpowering, making it hard to breathe, harder to even think. Harriet still had her car roof down, although it didn't make much of a difference. Maybe she should have kept it up and switched the aircon on. Meanwhile, Ben's headache appeared to be fast developing into a full-blown migraine.

Taking one look at his white face, she took her left hand from the steering wheel, groped in the footwell for her bag and dumped it on his lap.

'Paracetamol, second pocket,' she said, 'and you'll find an unopened bottle of water in the middle to wash it down, so no excuses. Tablets work quicker if you take them with a drink.'

He looked a wreck. The bruises were still evident as dark smudges along his jawline, not entirely hidden by his beard. He'd failed to solve Amita's murder and had contributed towards Lydia's death by withholding evidence and consorting with a suspect.

He should resign now and be done with it.

By the time they arrived in the village, the clouds were so

dark and heavy they appeared to almost touch the church steeple.

Harriet bumped her car down the lane beside the police station and into the car park at the back. Ben helped her yank the roof back up over her car as fat raindrops fell lethargically onto the hot dry tarmac, and they made a sprint for the station, practically falling inside as the door slid open at a swipe from her warrant card.

Sam, walking past with a tray of coffees, was almost startled into dropping them. 'Wet out there, eh?' he said, as they shook off the rainwater.

'Something like that.' She didn't need to count the cardboard cups to realise Sam was about to become the bearer of bad news. 'What's happened?'

'DCI Cameron is on his way, due to arrive any moment.'

With Ben looking like death warmed up? Terrific.

Sam was obviously thinking the same thing, turning to Ben and saying, 'He's... er... taken over your office.'

Ben shrugged. 'Fair enough.'

'Permanently.' When Ben failed to comment, Sam added, 'The boss asked me to clear out your things. I've left them on Georgia's old desk. It's the one by the window.'

'Thank you, Sam,' Harriet said, as Ben showed no indication that he was going to reply or had even heard. Instead, he was staring longingly at the back door – and freedom, presumably.

Well, they'd all had days like *that*. The trick was to just get on with it.

'Come along, sir,' she said out loud. 'I'll make us a nice cup of coffee and...'

Everything will be all right?

Sam raised an eyebrow sympathetically. Even he knew that this was one time when a cup of coffee *wasn't* going to make everything all right.

What else could they do? They had to solve Lydia's murder and Kiran McKenzie was the most likely suspect. There was no getting around it – or out of it, she realised, watching Ben flip up his collar and head towards the door, which obligingly slid open again. The rain, now falling sideways, soaked the entrance mat within seconds.

She put her arm out in front of him, effectively blocking his escape. 'Where are you going?'

He pushed her arm away. 'There's not a lot of point in me being here.'

He was going to walk out and leave them to it? Was he *serious*?

'DCI Cameron will be expecting you to give the briefing.'

His laugh was derisive. 'I'm no longer in charge but I still get to MC?'

'Don't be a child.'

'You don't need me. You're more than capable of giving the briefing by yourself. You'd probably do a better job.'

'I know I would, but that isn't the point. You're paid to do a job, not wimp out at the first sign of adversity.'

'Wimp out?' he repeated, pure ice.

She met his glare full on. 'Isn't that what you're doing?'

Sam muttered something about the coffee growing cold and escaped up the stairs.

'No, it's *not*,' Ben said. 'I need to find Milla. She might be in trouble.'

'There's no "might" about it. She's killed one of our own and half the Force is out looking for her. What good can *you* do?'

'I have contacts—'

'Your cousin, Drew Elliott? You'd trust that lowlife pond scum over your own team?'

That got his attention.

'How did you know Drew's my—'

'You may have un-barrelled your surname, but everyone knows your father was one of the notorious Elliott brothers.'

'No one *said* anything!'

'We liked you! In spite of your dodgy relatives, you seemed like a decent guy. Someone we could rely on. Someone who would work hard to get the job done. You know what happened to the last guy who had your job? He went for a walk in the woods and never came back. Now you seem intent on committing career suicide for a credit-card thief and murderer.'

'Milla is not a thief or a murderer. She came here to find out who killed her mother and instead—'

'Is she *still* telling everyone she's Camilla Graham? That woman really is delusional!'

'Perhaps, but it doesn't alter the fact that Milla is a vulnerable woman on her own. Someone has tapped into her eccentricities and created the perfect mark to take this fall. You said half the Force is out looking for her? All it needs is some rookie PC with an itchy trigger finger and it'll be Milla's face on the front cover of *The Calahurst Echo* tomorrow, and the real murderer will get away. I've got to find her, Harriet. Can't you understand? I'm not needed here. It's my fault she's in this mess. I didn't take her seriously. I didn't believe her story and now—'

'How is any of this possibly *your* fault? Honestly, Ben! *You can't save everyone!* If you walk out now, you'll be put on a discipline, you know you will. Ask yourself this, is she worth it?'

'A woman's life against my career?' He threw out his hands. 'How can you even ask the question?'

'*Ben!*'

'I'm done,' he said, and turned to walk out the door.

Only to realise DCI Cameron was already standing there.

Now it was Harriet who wished she could make a quick exit.

Cameron shrugged off his raincoat and hung it carefully on

the rack by the door. 'If you could kindly spare me a couple more minutes of your time, Benedict?'

'Sir?'

'I need you to explain why you think this woman is worth losing your job over and then you can tell me why I shouldn't fire you.'

* * *

Ben followed Cameron up to the first floor, where his boss swiped one of the coffees from Sam's tray and said to Ben, 'Come into my office,' without the slightest trace of irony.

Before Ben had the chance to close the door on her, Harriet slipped through the gap and dropped into the nearest chair. Cameron made no comment and took the chair which had once been his, leaving Ben leaning against the bookcase again, as though that had been his intention all along.

The King's Rest files were still boxed up against one wall but his personal belongings had gone, along with the contents of the bookcase. Although technically the bookcase was his too. Not that there had been much to move out; he'd barely had time to move in. Even his pot plants still had the price tickets on.

Cameron took a fat cardboard file from his briefcase and, flipping it open, held up a familiar photograph of Milla. The one of her on the beach at Weston-super-Mare with Patrick Graham.

'Are you having sex with her?' Cameron asked.

'*What?* No!' The unexpectedness of the question ensured a realistic denial, even as a voice in his head mocked, *But you wanted to...*

Cameron shrugged, apparently satisfied, and dropped the photo back into the file. 'I had to ask. You seem so protective of the woman. Where were you tearing off to in such a hurry? Do you know where she is?'

'No, I don't. I thought if I could find her, I could reason with her; perhaps get her to give herself up. I don't want to see her panicked into doing something stupid.'

'None of us do,' Cameron said smoothly, 'but you're aware your officers no longer have confidence in you?'

Ben glanced in Harriet's direction, but her expression remained carefully blank as she stared dead ahead. How much of their conversation had Cameron overheard?

'Yes,' he said. There seemed little point in denying it.

'I could move you sideways to some obscure research department and forget about you?'

Great.

'Or fire you for gross misconduct.'

The silence stretched out.

'Lydia is dead,' Cameron said at length. 'She was a fine officer. I thought very highly of her.' Pause. 'I used to think very highly of you.' He picked up his coffee, appeared unimpressed by the cardboard cup it had been served in, and returned it to the desk. 'You're going to face a discipline. I can't stop that. But if you can give me a credible reason for your appalling conduct, I'll put in a good word for you.'

'Sir?'

'You said Kiran McKenzie was not involved with Lydia's death. That implies you have a theory?'

'Yes, sir.'

'So, convince me.'

Where to start?

Opposite, he saw Harriet sarcastically mouth the words, 'Once upon a time...'

It wasn't such a bad idea.

He reached down, flipped the lid off the nearest box of King's Rest case files and there it was, right where he had left it: Milla's copy of *Alice's Adventures in Wonderland*.

He dropped it onto the desk, in front of Cameron, and turned the pages until he came to the first chapter.

It was time to go down the rabbit hole.

THIRTY-THREE

Ben watched the rain thud against the window at Rose Cottage, blurring the beautiful garden until it was nothing more than a smudge of green. The roses had been completely destroyed by the storm and their scarlet petals now covered the lawn like a sea of blood.

He hoped it wasn't symbolic.

Milla was out there somewhere. As much as he told himself she'd be fine, that she'd bounce back in her usual irritating way and was probably making some other poor bastard's life hell right at this very minute, he couldn't help but worry. Did she know who had killed Lydia? Had she witnessed it? Why hadn't she come forward? Self-preservation? Or was she protecting someone? Patrick perhaps? What motivation would he have to kill Lydia?

Behind him, someone switched on the light. The garden vanished and all he could see was a reflection of himself slumped against the side of the window, his hands shoved into his pockets. Around him was chaos as the contents of Rose-mary's bedroom was carefully catalogued and packed into crates, while his team grew more excited with every new discovery.

Although they were hardly his team any longer.

Ironically, DCI Cameron had been dismissive when he'd shown him the photos of Rose Cottage.

'You want me to raid the home of one of the wealthiest, most powerful men in the country?' he'd drawled. 'You really do have a death wish, Benedict.'

'It's not his house,' Ben persisted, knowing he had little to lose. 'Legally it belonged to Rosemary Graham before her marriage and in her will she left it to her niece, Kiran McKenzie.'

That had got Cameron's attention. 'You think the woman might be hiding there?'

'Milla wasn't even aware she owned the property until yesterday. It was held in trust by the Graham family until her twenty-first birthday.' Which was long gone, admittedly.

Cameron had merely looked at him.

'Although I concede Milla may have lied about that.' After all, she lied about everything else. 'But the house is furnished like some kind of shrine to Rosemary, and look...' He'd scrolled down until he found the photographs he'd taken in Rosemary's closet. The row of decades-old evening gowns, hung in identical garment bags. The one he'd unfastened, with its petals of pale silk tulle dipped in pearls and rhinestones, and a hand-stitched label that clearly said:

Dior

Cameron, after a moment's silence, had said, 'That's good enough for me.'

Now here they were, reducing the life of Rosemary McKenzie Graham to half a dozen crates of family photographs, worthless costume jewellery – and a fabulous collection of designer gowns.

A collection of gowns that had never been hers.

He was an *idiot*...

Ben turned away from the window. 'We're being played.'

The nearest officer glanced up briefly but no one else took any notice. It wasn't surprising. He was no longer the one in charge. In fact, he wasn't exactly sure what he was anymore, or even what he was doing here. Cameron had demanded he came along, ostensibly to advise but more likely to keep an eye on him. Now he was going to get the benefit of that advice, whether he wanted it or not.

Cameron was standing by the open door of the closet, watching intently as Harriet and Sam reverently brought out each gown. Harriet couldn't resist opening each garment bag, just a centimetre or two, to glimpse the gowns inside.

'These are *fabulous!*' she was enthusing, to Sam's obvious amusement. 'But they really shouldn't have been stored like this. I mean, they're in muslin bags but they're on hangers. They should have been stored flat. The weight of all the beading will pull the fabric out of shape. It's criminal. They really ought to be properly preserved in a museum.'

Ben hid his smile and leaned over her shoulder to say, 'So why aren't they?'

She didn't even jump. 'Oh. Hi, Ben,' she said, in a voice that really meant, 'Why are *you* still here?'

'Remember when we first saw Amita lying on that four-poster bed? I said something like, "I've seen this gown before" and Lydia said it was unlikely because—'

'"It's vintage Dior, worth thousands,"' Harriet rattled off. She paused, staring down at the gown in her arms. 'Even damaged, collectively these gowns are worth more than the house. Why are they here? The Graham family must know how much they're worth. Were they included in Kiran's inheritance?'

'I thought Rosemary used them in her illustrations?' Cameron looked to Ben for confirmation. 'Wasn't that what we agreed?'

'Yes, but Rosemary didn't work from here.' Ben turned to Harriet. 'Have you found any art materials, any sketch books?'

She shook her head. 'No, nothing like that.'

Cameron frowned. 'So where *did* Rosemary work from?'

'No idea.' Ben watched Sam hang the gown he was carrying into an upright packing case and tried not to grin as Harriet winced. 'How many gowns are there?'

'Twenty,' said Harriet.

Ben indicated the packing case. 'Did you check what each one contained before you packed it?'

'A preliminary check, yes, but that kind of thing really ought to be done by a CSI and—' She broke off as Ben strode into the closet and began running his hands over each garment bag. 'What are you doing? Be careful!'

He ignored her, patting down each bag until he found the one he was seeking. The one which, when compared to the others, appeared almost empty.

'Bingo,' he said softly, lifting it from the rail. 'Who wants to be the one to open it?'

'Not you.' Cameron beckoned over one of the CSIs and pointed to the garment bag. 'If you would do the honours, James?'

The CSI took the bag from Ben and, laying it flat on the bed, unfastened it.

There was a dress inside, but it certainly wasn't Dior. Although fifties-inspired, it was pale blue with a pattern of pink cabbage roses, and the label clearly said,

Zara

Cameron whistled softly, 'I'll be damned,' and Ben knew exactly what he was thinking. 'What was Amita wearing the day she went missing?'

Harriet had not taken her eyes off the dress. 'A pale-blue summer dress with a design of pale pink roses. Scooped neck, full skirt, petticoats. Blue ballerina-style shoes, a wide blue belt. Pale pink nail varnish, jewellery from the Kaal collection—'

Cameron cut her off. 'Are the accessories and jewellery there too?'

As one of his colleagues took photographs, James unfastened the bag from end to end and carefully separated the fabric. Lying casually at the bottom was a curled-up belt and a pair of ballet shoes. The ballet shoes still had mud and grass stuck along the side of the heels, and when James tipped one of them up over his gloved hand, jewellery fell out.

'Which rules out robbery,' Cameron said.

Robbery? With effort, Ben remained silent.

'Who else has access to this house?'

'Dermot Graham,' Harriet told him. 'The house is in Kiran's name but all the utility bills are paid by Graham Media.'

'So, any of the Graham family, basically?'

'Dermot has been paying a private detective to follow Milla for the past eighteen years,' Ben said.

For a man seeing his entire case unravel before his eyes, Cameron was taking it surprisingly well. 'Did we get the wrong man? I can't believe it. If we did, why would Dermot Graham kill Amita? Where's his motivation?'

'Perhaps he mistook her for Milla,' Ben said. 'They were of similar age, they were related and they looked alike.'

'Why would he want to kill Mil—' He frowned. 'Now you have me doing it. I meant to say *Kiran.*'

'If Milla can prove she's Camilla Graham, she's entitled to an automatic seat on the board and a share of the Graham billions.'

'And Lydia?'

'Because she found out the truth?'

'It's plausible, I suppose...' but Cameron obviously wasn't happy.

'Plus, he can achieve his objective of removing Milla by framing her for the murders?' Harriet added.

'No,' Ben said. 'Although Patrick was removed from the board of directors when he went to prison, he kept his trust fund.'

'You think this is about control of Graham Media rather than money?' Cameron said.

Ben stared at the pretty summer dress on the bed and thought of the woman who'd once worn it, the woman he'd last seen lying as though sleeping on a four-poster bed in that monstrous heap known as the Grim House.

'I don't think it's that simple. It fits together too perfectly. We're missing something.'

'Why worry?' Harriet sighed. 'If it gets your girlfriend off the hook?'

He really wished she hadn't said that because predictably Cameron's eyes narrowed.

'Kiran could be working with our murderer,' Cameron said.

This had already occurred to Ben but he kept his mouth shut.

Unfortunately, Harriet didn't. 'What now, sir?'

'The warrant for Kiran McKenzie's arrest still stands,' Cameron said, 'and we need to bring Dermot Graham in as soon as possible.'

'You're going to arrest him?' Harriet couldn't keep the note of surprise from her voice.

'I think so.' Cameron looked around Rosemary's bedroom; at the garment bags already squashed into the packing cases and those still hanging in the closet. 'We certainly have evidence.'

Did they? Would it hold up in court? Ben watched as the

CSI re-fastened the garment bag. No doubt they'd find evidence Dermot had been here, had even been living here. Ben had witnessed it and Graham Media was responsible for the bills. Would that be enough? He doubted it. When he opened his mouth to say so, Cameron turned his attention on him.

'You, take a couple of weeks off. Spend some time with that child of yours. You're best off out of it.'

'*You*'? What had happened to the more personal, albeit overly formal 'Benedict'?

'No, thank you. I'd rather be—'

Cameron raised an eyebrow. 'I'm sure you would but it's not optional.'

'You're suspending me?'

'I'm suggesting you take a few weeks off. If you want to make more of it, that's up to you. Think very carefully unless you're planning the next word out of your mouth to be anything other than "Goodbye".'

Ben thought carefully.

'Goodbye,' he said.

And walked out of the door.

Ben had brought the hire car with him but one of the CSI vans had blocked him in and it took a while before he could get on his way. While he waited, he phoned Caroline to cancel Sophie's visit. Annoyingly, he got Caroline's answering service, which meant she'd already left for Raven's Edge.

Perfect.

He wasn't in the best of tempers when he reached Port Rell, abandoning his car outside the sailing club and taking the stairs to Drake's office two at a time.

He didn't allow Drake's secretary to get one word out, just shoved open the door marked *Kieran Drake* with, 'I'll see myself in.'

If Drake was rattled to see him, he didn't show it.

'Lovely to see you, Detective Inspector,' he said, not looking up from his laptop. 'Now go away.'

Ben closed the door behind him. 'I need your help.'

Drake gave an extravagant sigh and snapped the lid of the laptop shut, spinning round on his chair to face him. 'I can't keep helping the police. It'll ruin my reputation.'

Ben kept walking, right up to Drake's desk, before leaning down to grab him by the T-shirt and hauling him to his feet. 'If you don't help me, it will be even worse for your reputation.'

He was prepared for Drake to retaliate with some kind of defensive move. What he hadn't expected was the outright attack of Drake head-butting him, kneeing him in the groin and then kicking him as he went down.

As Ben rolled over, curling himself into a defensive ball while stars exploded around his head, he was vaguely aware Drake was still talking.

'Impressive ability to switch to the dark side, mate. Kind of lacking in conviction but still, nice try.'

It was a good few minutes before Ben could even see past the pain to form the words, 'What if I offered to pay you?'

'You have my complete and undivided attention.'

By the time Ben found the strength to push himself up into a sitting position, Drake was back in his chair, fingers tapping on the desk, green eyes alight with amusement.

'How much?' Ben sighed.

'It depends on what you want?'

'I need to find someone.'

Drake's angular face curved into a sly grin. 'I'm sure we can come to a mutually agreeable arrangement.'

That's what worried him. 'I'd rather pay cash.'

'It's not about what *you* want is it, petal?' Drake spun around in the chair and swung one foot onto his desk with a heavy clunk, showering the already grubby surface with dried mud. He slid his laptop off the desk and onto his lap and flipped it back open. His fingers flew so quickly over the keypad they seemed to blur. 'No sightings so far. Your girl is *good...*'

Ben didn't bother to ask how Drake knew who he was looking for, but just staggered to the nearest chair and lowered himself into it. Very, very carefully. 'Do you have a permanent tail on Milla, or a huge network of spies?'

'You think I'd tell you? And don't get comfy. Just because I've agreed to help you doesn't mean we're friends.'

Ben closed his eyes and daydreamed about shoving Drake out the window, but he really did need the man's help. It was incredibly lowering. How the hell had it come to this?

'I'll put the word out,' he heard Drake say, more business-like. 'As soon as I find out anything, I'll be in touch. Don't call me. I really don't want to see you again or we're going to seriously fall out – influential relatives or not.'

It was the best he was going to get. Ben pushed himself up out of the seat, took his business card from his pocket and let it fall onto the desk.

'Better contact me on my personal phone though,' he said.

Drake's grin turned into a definite smirk. 'Like that, is it?'

Feeling as though he'd debased himself enough for one day, Ben turned away without replying.

'You know, you could try retracing your steps?' Drake called after him. 'Check out the last place you saw her, that kind of thing.'

'King's Rest?' Ben shook his head. 'Unlikely. No matter how desperate she was, I can't believe she'd be *that* stupid.'

Drake laughed. 'I guess you know her better than me, but with that woman, "unlikely" is the first place I'd look.'

When Mal woke, the world was upside down and swaying.

A few seconds more and he realised the emerald-green wool beneath his cheek was the coat on the back of that increasingly mad Hatter, and the swirling grey fog surrounding them was smoke.

It smelt foul.

Fire.

The house was on fire.

He tried to wriggle free but the Hatter gripped him tighter.

So he reverted to that good old standby, 'I'm going to be sick!' and added a theatrical groan for good measure.

He was unceremoniously dumped on the floor. By the time he'd worked out which way was up, the smoke had cleared enough for him to look up at the man who had killed his mother.

And saw double.

Two men wearing the same green coat and cartoon-sized top hat.

Father and uncle.

Hero and villain.

But which was which?

THIRTY-FOUR

Considering Ben Taylor was a police detective, Milla thought, the security on his cottage was terrible. He obviously wasn't in. There was no car on the drive and every window was shut. There was a huge walnut tree on the left side of the house, scraping against the brickwork and weaving itself into the thatch. She could climb it and gain entrance through one of the upstairs windows but really didn't feel like exerting the effort. The shiny brass letter box on the front door was wide and located far too close to the door handle. It would be astonishingly simple for someone with slim hands and wrists (not unlike herself) to unlatch the door from the inside. Although maybe a little too easily spotted by anyone passing by?

She splashed through the puddles to the back garden, where both flowers and vegetables had been grown in incredibly neat rows and everything had been labelled with lollypop sticks marked in a childish scrawl. Either Ben had appallingly bad handwriting or they'd been written by his daughter. There was a rabbit hutch too, currently unoccupied, and a tiny, unlatched window beside the back door, presumably leading to a downstairs cloakroom. *Seriously?* He wasn't even *trying* to make this difficult.

The rain was unrelenting. It had soaked through her clothes and she was doing her best to ignore the way it constantly trickled down the back of her neck. She needed to find a way into Ben's house as quickly and easily as possible, and she needed to stop being quite so picky about it.

The cat flap was far too small, so she backtracked to a window she'd already passed and bent to peer inside. Bookcases, files, desk, laptop – this must be Ben's study. She swiped one of the lollypop sticks from the vegetable patch, slid it between the window and the frame, and knocked up the latch. Tossing the stick over her shoulder, she swung herself over the windowsill, landing with a distinct splat on the other side.

Ben's study was dark and cool; the surrounding woodland and tiny medieval windows ensured there was very little light. Milla left a trail of wet muddy footprints to the door, and did feel a little guilty about that, but what else could she do? The door took her into a short passageway. To the left was the back door, so she headed right until she reached the front door, with the open-plan sitting room and the kitchen directly opposite – and a large black cat watching her from the bottom step of the staircase.

'Hi, erm... Jinx?'

Could cats roll their eyes?

'Binx! Sorry, your name is Binx, right?'

The cat slowly blinked, then jumped from the bottom step and trotted into the kitchen, pausing only to check she was following.

'Some guard cat you are. Don't tell me: despite your automatic cat feeder, which appears to be working just fine, you've not had a bite to eat for three days?'

'Meow,' Binx said pitifully.

'Really?' Milla laughed and bent to rub his head. 'Here's a

tip for you. Don't try to con a con artist.' Her stomach rumbled and she checked her watch. It was barely 10.00 am. Assuming Ben worked a nine-to-five shift, he wouldn't be home for hours yet. In which case...

She grinned.

She might as well make use of the facilities.

* * *

By the time Ben arrived home that evening he was shattered. He'd toured around all the neighbouring villages, even returning to King's Rest, but found it swarming with police. There was no way Milla would have returned there. She was reckless and irresponsible but not entirely senseless. He checked the boarded-up lodge beside the massive gateway and although there were signs someone had been sleeping rough, the way they'd relieved themselves against an interior wall implied the occupant had most likely been male.

He checked the cafés and the grocery stores – she'd have to eat sometime – but considering the amount of time she'd spent in the area, no one recognised her photo. He even returned to the station to wheedle an update on the case out of Sam King but there was nothing Ben didn't already know. Milla had vanished. The police had searched Hartfell and found nothing incriminating. Brianna Graham had been questioned about her collection of couture gowns but had apparently given DCI Cameron complete hell and threatened to set the Chief Constable on him.

Two-nil to Brianna Graham.

Grinning at that thought, Ben parked the hired car on his driveway and followed the little stone path to the front door. He was so tired he barely had time to register the downstairs lights were on, and that someone appeared to be cooking dinner in his kitchen, before a woman threw herself into his arms (almost knocking him off balance) and hugged him hard. Beside her, his traitorous cat was purring loudly.

'You're here!' Milla squealed, taking the words right out of his mouth. 'I was so worried about you!'

That was the very next thing he'd intended to say – to her.

'Where have you *been*?' she added.

Yes, that too.

Then she slid one hand behind his neck, yanked him down until he was at her level and kissed him right on the mouth.

* * *

He didn't kiss her back.

Milla opened her eyes to see Ben's cool green eyes staring directly at her, slightly bemused. What was wrong with him? Didn't he find her attractive? Impossible.

'I think you can do better than *that*,' she said. As he opened his mouth, presumably to snap something sarcastic back, she kissed him again.

This time he joined in, his arms wrapping themselves around her body, crushing her against him until she could hardly breathe; she certainly couldn't think. But she could feel, and there was far too much fabric between them. She remembered the last time she'd seen him naked and wanted to see him that way again. Now.

He was wearing his beloved suit and she managed to yank his jacket from his shoulders without too much trouble. When she tugged out his shirt and slipped her hands beneath to touch his skin, he broke away, grabbing her around the waist, hauling her up and plonking her on top of the kitchen counter.

'Sorry,' he muttered, kissing her again. 'Crick in the neck.'

The buttons on his shirt were directly in front of her, so she busied herself undoing each one. As her fingers slid over the smooth warm skin of his chest, she heard his breathing become heavier and more rapid, and felt his own fingers slide beneath the tie that held her towelling robe together, following it around to the front and tugging on the end.

She broke the kiss. 'You'll have to undo the knot,' she said helpfully.

Nothing happened.

She should have done it for him. As his face swum back into focus, she realised he was still holding the end of one tie with a quizzical expression. Had he never been in the Boy Scouts?

'This looks familiar,' he said, looking down at her.

'That's because it's yours,' she admitted.

'Oh.'

'Would you like me to take it off?'

He ducked his head down again, pressing open-mouthed kisses against her cheek and along her jawline to her neck, tantalisingly brief kisses, down and down until she felt his warm fingers edge her robe apart, off one shoulder, enough for him to dip his head and kiss her there, his stubbly beard scraping against her skin.

She'd never been kissed by a man with a beard. She had no idea it could be so...

But as all kinds of wicked possibilities began occurring to her, he stopped.

'You've had a shower,' he said.

Why was he still talking? 'It was raining. I got soaked—'

'With my shower gel?'

'Um, yes, sorry.'

'Disturbing,' he muttered.

'In a good way?'

'You smell like me.'

She wrapped her arms around his neck, pulling him closer, tangling her fingers into his blond hair.

He reached up and pulled her hands down, placing each one on either side of her, firmly holding her in place. When she thought it was about to get *very* interesting, he leaned forward, rested his forehead against hers and said,

'We can't have sex, Milla. We don't know each other well enough.'

What?

That one kiss had started a deliciously warm flicker of desire beginning all the way down in her toes, leaving her fit to explode at any moment. Now he was turning her *down?*

This was why she preferred bad boys. They weren't interested in the finer details, such as whether they'd known you for six days or six hours. They weren't interested in details at all, only mind-blowing sex – which is what she'd quite like now, if she could persuade bloody Prince Charming to get over himself and get over her instead.

'What would you like to know, Ben?'

He stepped away.

Well away.

'Did you kill Lydia?' he asked.

Lydia?

What?

What had he said?

'Lydia is dead,' he said, slightly more gently. Perhaps the stunned shock she was feeling was evident on her face. 'Her body was found at King's Rest this morning. Someone pushed her out of a third-storey window.'

The kitchen was warm but now she was shivering, goosebumps on her bare thighs. She smoothed down the robe, hiding the faint silvery-pink scaring on her knees, still visible after eighteen years.

Ben hadn't even noticed.

'You think I did it,' she said.

'Yes – no – Of course I don't!' He shoved one hand through his hair until it was practically standing on end. 'I don't know what to believe. It all seems so incredible, like something out of a fairy—' He broke off, frowning. 'If you did kill Lydia, where is your motive?'

'Motive?' she repeated dully. 'I don't have one, other than I hated her.'

'For goodness' sake, don't tell anyone else that!'

She was too vulnerable perched up here. She shuffled forward, intending to slide down to the floor, but he must have got it into his head that she intended to run, because he was back in front of her in a second, leaning on the counter, effectively blocking any escape route.

'Were you there?' he demanded. 'When I told you to leave the area, and I put you on that train, did you head to King's Rest?'

There wasn't much point in lying. 'Yes,' she said, hearing him curse in return.

'Did you see Lydia?'

'She was there when I woke up this morning. We talked; or rather, she goaded me about how she was going to ruin my life. She was so busy doing the whole monologue thing, I escaped. She was alive when I left her, I promise you.'

Lydia certainly *had* been alive; her screams and curses had echoed around King's Rest as Milla had fled down the servants' staircase. Now she was dead? It didn't seem possible.

'You tell so many lies, how can I believe you?'

He sounded so weary, so defeated, it took a moment for his words to sink in.

'I wouldn't lie about something as important as this.'

'You lie about everything. Sometimes I think you lie for the fun of it. Even when you have every opportunity to tell the truth, even when a lie's no longer necessary, you can't seem to stop yourself.'

Where had *that* come from? 'Sure I can!'

'Milla, you're a pathological liar!'

And she'd thought he was different. More fool her.

'Don't judge me! *Everybody* lies, including you.'

His eyes darkened. 'No, I don't—'

'You lie to your daughter.'

'I would never—'

'Father Christmas? The Tooth Fairy? The Easter Bunny? Parents lie to their children every day.'

'That's not the same!'

He stepped back, effectively releasing her. Milla slid down from the counter, checking the robe was wrapped firmly around her, without even an inch of flesh showing from her chin to her toes. Behind him, the washer dryer had stopped turning and she could see her clothes flattened against the door. They'd be creased but honestly, she was long past caring.

She stepped around him, careful to keep out of grabbing distance, but he did nothing; only watched as she released the door on the machine, bent down and scooped out her clothes.

'What are you doing?' he asked.

'I would have thought that was obvious.' She spun around to face him, keeping her chin high and her expression blank. 'Thank you for your hospitality. I'll dress and then I'll go. You'll never have to see me again.'

'You can't go.'

'Try and stop me!' she snapped back, kicking the door of the washing machine shut.

'You misunderstand,' he said. 'There's a warrant out for your arrest.'

'Yes, I know. Credit-card fraud and non-payment of rent, am I right?'

'Murder. Two counts.'

She laughed. 'No one's going to believe that!'

'They already do. Listen to me, Milla. I'll say it again. There's a warrant out for your arrest, for the murders of Amita Kaal and Lydia Cavill.'

'I didn't do it!'

'You must understand how important this is? You can't leave this house. The entire Force is out looking for you. They think you've killed one of their own and they want your blood. If they suspect you have a weapon, you might be shot. The police never shoot to wound or as any kind of warning. They only shoot to kill.'

'Don't be ridiculous.' Even to herself, her voice sounded nervous. 'The police don't carry guns in this country.'

'They do if they think the person they're hunting is dangerous.'

'I'm not dangerous...' To her horror, she felt a tear roll down her cheek. It was too late to blink. She lifted her arm and rubbed her face against the towelling sleeve of the robe. 'I only came to Raven's Edge because I wanted to find out who killed my mother. I suppose your lot are going to blame me for that next? Even though I was only six years old! Bloody police, I hate the lot of you!'

She heard him curse and the pile of clothes was taken out of her hands and dumped on the counter, and she was back in his arms and he was stroking the back of her head and muttering something she couldn't quite hear.

'Come on,' he said, leading her towards the stairs. 'To bed. We're both tired and stressed and not thinking clearly.'

That shook her. Maybe he wasn't so much the hero after all.

'With *you*?' After everything he'd said? Accusing her of being a liar and a murderer, and everything else?

He laughed, albeit with very little humour. 'No, you can have my bed. I'll sleep on the sofa. Tomorrow we'll talk and work out what we're going to do about this. Everything will seem better in the morning.'

She tried very hard not to roll her eyes. *Sure* it would...

Why did she have the feeling he was trying to reassure himself as much as her?

THIRTY-FIVE

Milla woke to find the bed empty yet a definite sense someone was watching her. She could hear a rumble of voices echoing up from the sitting room and recognised Ben's clipped accent, and the deep voices of at least two other men... and a woman. Were they friendly or hostile? It was hard to tell through solid oak floorboards but who came calling this early in the morning?

If Ben was downstairs, who was in the room beside her?

She kept her eyes closed and let her other senses do the work. Her side of the mattress had dipped, as though someone was kneeling beside the bed and leaning against it. They were so close she could feel the faint movement of their breath on her cheek and smell...

She breathed in slowly.

Nothing.

Possibly faint traces of vanilla?

A woman?

Ben's friend, the fast-running, fast-talking blonde?

Or someone else entirely?

Allowing her eyelids to flicker, she caught a brief glimpse of green fabric. A dress or a T-shirt? It wasn't a suit, that was for sure.

She had decided to mimic the movements of waking up when a hand clamped down on the bare skin of her shoulder and shook her roughly. Fortunately, she registered how small and light that hand was before she swung her own out from beneath the duvet, clenched in a fist.

A small girl aged about six or seven was regarding her dubiously.

'You're naked,' the girl said, with obvious disapproval.

Milla tried not to laugh. There was no mistaking the serious expression and clear green eyes behind wire-rimmed glasses, although the girl had presumably inherited her dark hair from her mother.

'You must be Sophie?'

The girl scowled, placing her finger against Milla's lips. 'Shh! If you keep quiet, the police won't know you're here.'

'*Police!*' Milla sat bolt upright, clutching the sheets to her chest. 'How many police?'

'Well, there's Auntie Harriet and Uncle Doug.'

'Two? That's not so bad.'

'Uncle Ash and Auntie Dakota are waiting on the front path, and I saw Uncle Sam leaning on the wall outside the back door.'

'Bloody *hell*.' Her favourite escape route. How well they knew her.

'Oh, and there's one I don't know, sitting out front in the car...'

Milla had the idea the child was enjoying being the dispenser of bad news a little too much. 'OK, kid, I get it!'

The scowl came back. 'My *name* is Sophie.'

It was like meeting herself, eighteen years ago.

'I'm Milla, nice to meet you.' Still clutching the bedsheet, she swung her legs out from beneath the duvet and looked around for something to wear, hoping she wouldn't have to improvise, but her clothes from yesterday had been left neatly folded on a chair. Her Docs had been cleaned and polished and were beside the door.

Ben... Who else could it have been? She *so* didn't deserve him. He was too kind, too honest, too good... Yes, he was definitely too good for her and didn't deserve someone like her rotting up his life. Look how much damage she'd done to his career in the short time she'd known him. He was teetering on the edge of dismissal and he had a daughter to support.

It was going to be hard to leave him behind; to let him think the worst of her when she ran out on him again, as she always ran out on everyone.

'When did you arrive?' she asked Sophie, pulling on her clothes as quickly as possible.

'This morning. Mum's gone to a conference in Norchester, so I'm here for the weekend.' She looked Milla up and down, slightly disparagingly. 'Are you Dad's new girlfriend?'

'Yes... er, no. Um, it's complicated.'

Presumably having heard that one before, Sophie rolled her eyes.

Milla pulled on her Docs. 'What's the plan?'

'Dad said you'll know what to do.'

'He did?'

Sophie nodded. 'Uh huh, follow me.' She ran lightly over the slanting floorboards and into the passage beyond, without making the slightest sound.

The girl was more mouse than small child. Milla, remembering how loudly the ancient floorboards creaked, followed as quickly as she dared, slipping into the gloomy narrow corridor that ran the length of the house in time to see Sophie vanish into her bedroom at the end.

Now what was the girl doing?

When Milla had last seen Sophie's bedroom it had been in

darkness. With the curtains drawn back and the sunlight streaming in, it was revealed in all its fairy-tale glory. She remembered the bed, where each post had been beautifully carved into a tree with branches, leaves and even tiny acorns. Although a small leather valise had been dumped on top of the old-fashioned quilt, the bed didn't appear to have been slept in. The walls had been painted with forest scenes, and garlands of silk leaves looped around the ceiling, dripping with tiny white lights. A veritable fairy bower and perfect for the pretty dark-haired imp currently hanging out of one of the small windows...

'Bloody hell, kid!' Milla grabbed the belt around Sophie's jeans and yanked her back. 'Be careful!'

Sophie blinked owlishly. 'I'm perfectly fine!' She pointed through the window. 'Look!'

Incredibly, no more than a couple of feet below was a walkway completely enclosed by wooden panels, creating a bridge between the cottage and a tree house in the walnut tree. She must have stepped directly beneath it the day before and not noticed a thing.

'That's fantastic!'

Sophie beamed. 'I know.'

She realised Sophie was regarding her expectantly. 'What?'

'Dad told me there are two things you're really good at. The first one is climbing in and out of windows.'

Milla winced. 'How kind of him to say so.' She had a pretty good idea on the second one too but asked anyway.

You're a pathological liar...

'Improvising,' Sophie said, pointing to the window.

Milla leaned through the window and had another look at the walkway. It seemed sturdy enough, leading through the thick leaves of the walnut tree into a little house built where the branches met in a fork. The tree house looked older than the bridge. Had it been built for Ben? Had he lived in this cottage as a child?

'Are you sure it'll bear my weight?'

Sophie eyed her up and down, considering the question. 'You're not that fat.'

Fat!

'Oh, I nearly forgot!' Sophie dug into the pocket of her jeans and pulled out a handful of crumpled twenty-pound notes. She shoved them at Milla. 'This is for you. Dad said...' – She closed her eyes with the effort of remembering – 'This time, make sure you go a whole lot further than bloody Raven's Edge.'

So much for her noble intentions; it seemed Ben was equally as keen to get rid of her. For a detective inspector, someone with her dubious past would hardly make suitable girlfriend material.

'What job does your mother do?' she asked Sophie, not really wanting to know the answer.

'She's a police pathologist,' Sophie replied, a little too cheerfully. 'That means she cuts up dead people to see how they died and find out who killed them.'

Which proved her point: what did she and Ben have in common?

Thoroughly dispirited, Milla clambered through the window and onto the bridge. It was a tight squeeze; the window was only slightly wider than her shoulders. She let one foot rest on the bridge, put more weight on it—

'Hurry *up!*'

A small fist hit her between the shoulder blades. If she hadn't still been holding onto the top of the window frame, she'd have landed heavily (probably face first) onto the bridge. Despite the large bolts she could see securing it, she wasn't under any illusion that they'd hold under that kind of pressure. The bridge had been built for a child, possibly a small adult, but as to jumping up and down...

'OK,' she muttered, 'I'm going.' Letting both feet rest on the bridge, she released her grip on the window.

It was fortunate she did so, for at that moment Sophie squeaked, 'They're coming!' and abruptly closed the window and snapped back the curtains.

She was on her own.

Milla risked another glance towards the garden below. It wasn't that far; she could easily lower herself to the ground. But anyone walking around the corner of the cottage would see her before she saw them.

She continued across the bridge to the tree house, careful to duck beneath the branches, trying to ignore the way the bridge bounced alarmingly beneath her feet.

The tree house was sturdily built but rustically simple. Not much more than four walls and a floor through which the occasional branch protruded, thatched to mimic the cottage beside it. She was too tall to stand upright and had to crawl to the trap door set in the floor. Directly beneath, a knotted length of rope and several slats of wood nailed into the tree trunk created a rudimentary ladder. Despite sticking her head down as far as she dared visibility wasn't great; she could only see a few metres in either direction. But she couldn't stay here forever.

OK, she could, but if Ben's police buddies got it into their heads to search his house, they'd want to search the garden and any outbuildings too. That would include the tree house.

Milla reversed her position and stuck her feet through the gap, feeling for the steps as she went. There seemed to be nothing for her hands to hold onto and she ended up swinging from the rope like Tarzan before landing inelegantly on her bottom.

It was a miracle no one saw her. Police cars were parked along the road and she could hear voices in the front garden. She ran around to the back, hoping to find a way into the woods behind, only to turn the corner and walk smack into a man in a suit leaning against the back wall.

Unfortunately, this time it wasn't anyone she knew.

For a moment they stared at each other, and then he raised his finger to his lips before pointing across the garden to a small gate half-hidden in the hedge.

'Thank you,' she mouthed, backing away.

'You're welcome,' he mouthed back, then grinned.

On the other side of the gate was a corn field but not the kind one could hide in. Keeping close to the hedge, she ran alongside the road until she reached a five-bar gate beside another cottage. This led into a muddy lane and back onto the road, to where a bus had stopped to let a little old lady get off.

Before the doors could slide shut, Milla jumped on board and slapped one of the notes Sophie had given her down on the counter.

The bus driver looked at the twenty-pound note and then at the sign beside him that said: *Correct Change Only*. And then he looked back at her.

She gave him her most winning smile, hoping there were no leaves or twigs in her hair to ruin the effect.

He regarded her steadily for a few moments more before scooping up the money. 'Where to?'

'Raven's Edge, please.'

It was well past the time to stop running.

Two men, dressed identically.

Only one had clown-like make-up smeared over his handsome face.

Only one Hatter was mad.

'Where are the children, Patrick?'

'At this time of night? Sleeping, of course.'

'The house is on fire. We have to get everyone out.'

Patrick frowned and shook his head. 'We can't wake them.'

Mal scrambled eagerly to his feet. 'I'll get them, Uncle Dermot!'

Dermot hauled him back by the scruff of the neck. 'No! Get out of the house and wait in the garden! Now!'

But Malcolm had been caught like that before. In a second he'd ducked his head and pulled away and Dermot was left standing in the hall holding a T-shirt, while Malcolm sprinted up the staircase and straight into the billowing black smoke.

THIRTY-SIX

Ben stayed in his sitting room while his former colleagues took their time searching his house. And they did take their time, for the house was so tiny it should only have taken minutes. He made himself coffee and settled down in his favourite armchair. He'd thought about switching the television on but that might be overdoing it. He didn't offer to make anyone else coffee, which definitely was overdoing it, but it was his house. He could do whatever he liked.

Sophie, after giving Milla the early warning, had staggered downstairs with her largest, heaviest book of fairy tales and had settled down to read in front of the unlit fire. At least she hadn't chosen *Alice's Adventures in Wonderland*, although it hadn't stopped her from giving him an extremely unsubtle wink. Fortunately, the only person who saw her do it was Harriet, who merely gave him her 'Seriously?' look.

It was hard not to keep glancing at his watch and guess how far Milla had got. He could hear voices overhead, as they gathered in his bedroom to discuss tactics, plainly unaware he could hear every word they said – if he could be bothered to listen. Through the window he could see DC Dakota Lawrence outside, talking to someone on her phone. He caught her eye, but she determinedly looked away before placing her phone back in her pocket and coming inside.

Without even glancing in his direction, she went up the stairs.

Something was up.

Sure enough, after more conferring, DCI Cameron came back down the stairs followed by his team.

'We've got her,' he announced to Harriet. 'Let's go.'

A cold fist seemed to clench inside his stomach.

Harriet glanced in Ben's direction and then nodded, leading the way outside.

Who? Who had they got? Milla?

It was all he could do to keep his expression neutral.

Cameron, the last to leave, stepped in front of him. 'Find someone to look after Sophie. You're coming with us.'

'I thought I was on gardening leave?'

'Kiran McKenzie's just walked into Raven's Edge Police Station, as cool as you like, demanding coffee.'

Ben closed his eyes in despair. Was the woman a complete idiot? After everything he'd done to keep her safe, even risking his career. What the *hell* was she thinking?

'Why?' he said at length, opening his eyes to find Cameron still watching him. 'Why do you need me?'

'You're the detective. I'm sure you can work it out.'

Because Cameron wanted to see how the two of them reacted to each other, how they behaved around each other, and to confirm what he already suspected: Ben was helping her and they were having an affair.

'Fine,' he said, pushing himself up out of the chair. 'I'll take Sophie around to Mrs Lancaster and follow on.'

'Take your time. Kiran's not going anywhere. We can wait for you.'

Brilliant.

It seemed he was about to find out how good a liar Milla really was.

* * *

With an increasing lack of patience, Milla waited in the tiny room she'd overheard someone call the interview room. It was hardly hi-tech, and nothing like what she'd seen on TV. There was one window overlooking a car park but no bars of any kind. She had the feeling the police hadn't even bothered to lock the door. They were hardly trying. It was almost offensive.

She wandered to the window and peered out. It had a lock, which would take her seconds to break through, but it seemed a bit pointless when she'd walked through the front door and given herself up. Even then the guy behind the front desk hadn't appeared to know who she was or what to do with her. Despite what Ben had implied, she wasn't exactly public enemy number one.

What else had he been wrong about?

As though her thoughts had conjured him up, the door opened and in he walked, wearing his usual charcoal grey suit and carrying a tray of coffee. Behind him was another detective, very smartly dressed, who'd paused to talk to someone in the corridor. Presumably he was the one in charge?

She returned to the table and sat down, as Ben placed the tray in front of her. Excellent. It might be the last chance she got to speak with him alone.

Unfortunately, he beat her to it. 'Didn't I tell you to go as far away from here as possible?'

Since when had she ever done what she'd been told?

She pretended he hadn't spoken, picking up one of the coffees and peering into it. 'I'd rather have a flat white – and do you have any Danish?'

'Tough, it's out of a machine,' he said, as the detective behind him finally came into the room and closed the door. 'The choice is black, white, or tea.' As he placed each cup onto the table, he appeared to deliberately spill one. When he leaned forward to mop it up, she distinctly heard him say, 'What do you think you're *doing*?'

'Saving your career.'

'You pick *now* to start telling the truth?'

'Thank you *very* much!'

The guy in charge dropped a pile of files onto the desk and sat opposite her, looking remarkably cheerful, as well he might. It meant any more conversation with Ben was impossible. It didn't stop him from glaring at her though.

There was no pleasing some people.

'OK, Kiran,' the other guy began.

'Milla,' she grumbled.

'I beg your pardon?'

'My *name* is Milla Graham.'

'Yes... right... OK. Now, before we start, I notice you've declined legal representation?'

'I have nothing to hide.'

Ben rolled his eyes.

'I'm Detective Chief Inspector Douglas Cameron and this is Detective Inspector Benedict Taylor-Elliott, although I believe you've already met?'

The DCI's cheerful expression now turned shark-like. Evidently he thought her a pushover.

'In passing.'

'I'm going to ask you a few questions and I'll be recording your answers. Let's get started, shall we?'

'Absolutely,' she said, unable to stop herself mimicking his educated accent.

Beside him, Ben slumped further into his chair.

DCI Cameron cautioned her, and then she proceeded to tell them everything. About why she'd come to Raven's Edge, about meeting Patrick, and about her search for any evidence that would convict Dermot for the murder of her family.

And every word she spoke was the truth.

Mostly.

* * *

Ben listened to Milla weaving her tale like a bedtime story. How much was true? If he were to guess, pretty much all of it. It certainly seemed to tally with what she'd already told him, and what he'd managed to find out himself.

She chattered away to Cameron as though they were old friends, telling him all about the night she'd spent at King's Rest, how Lydia had found her sleeping rough and how she'd run away before Lydia had the chance to catch her. The usually sharp-as-a-blade Cameron silently absorbed every word. Did he believe her?

It helped that before they'd come in for the interview one of Lydia's team had confessed he'd heard Lydia shouting for help *after* he'd seen Milla sprint off through the woods, effectively giving her a rather neat alibi.

That left them back at square one. Who had killed Lydia?

Patrick, Dermot – or someone else entirely?

His head began throbbing again and when Cameron asked Milla how she'd spent yesterday and last night, he was caught out.

Milla smiled. 'With a friend.'

Guilty heat burned his cheeks.

Busted...

Now it was Cameron's turn to roll his eyes. 'Maybe we should take a break?'

Sam was waiting outside the interview room. He didn't look happy.

Ben forgot he was no longer in charge. 'Spit it out.'

'Dermot Graham? Pete and Freddie were bringing him in for questioning; they stopped at some roadworks outside the village and he stepped out of the car, as cool as you please, and disappeared into the woods.'

Cameron crashed the side of his fist against the wall. It was the first time Ben had seen him lose his cool.

'Did nobody think to lock the bloody doors?'

'It wasn't a marked police vehicle, sir. And there seems to be some misunderstanding about whether Mr Graham was being arrested or coming in on an informal basis.'

'Give me *strength*. And what the *hell* is that racket?'

There was an increasingly loud disturbance coming from the front reception area. Raised voices and a steady thump, thump, thump, which sounded exactly like someone's fist making contact with the front counter.

'That would be Mr Graham, sir,' said Sam.

'I thought—'

'Mr *Patrick* Graham.'

'*Here?* In Raven's Edge? He actually has the audacity to—'

'He says he's come to collect his daughter.'

'What daughter?'

'He says he's here for Camilla Graham.'

* * *

When the door to the interview room opened, Milla had expected to see DCI Cameron again, along with Ben, or even his blonde sidekick. Instead, the man she'd last seen leaning against the back door in Ben's garden came in and told her she was free to go.

Thoroughly confused – was it some kind of trick? – she

followed him along the warren of narrow passageways back to the front of the police station and, to her complete amazement, saw Patrick waiting there. Even more so, when he flung out his arms and said,

'Darling, the cavalry is here!' as theatrically as ever.

She walked into his embrace. There was nowhere else to go. The room was full of men in suits. Some were police but she had a horrible feeling the others were Patrick's solicitors. After all, why have one when you could have three?

'Hello, Patrick,' she said, well aware he was expecting her to call him 'Dad' but somehow finding she couldn't. 'That's very kind of you but actually I don't need rescuing.'

And you're eighteen years too late.

Everyone's attention was on her, especially the police. She could no longer see Ben. Where had he gone? Did he no longer care what happened to her?

Despite choosing to come here, suddenly she wanted out.

It didn't help that Patrick picked that moment to hug her, almost squeezing the breath right out of her.

'I've come to take you home,' he said.

'To Somerset? Won't Charlotte mind?'

'Charlotte will *love* you,' he said. 'You won't need to worry about that! For tonight, we're heading to Hartfell. Everyone is desperate to see you. My mother, in particular, is very worried. You made quite an impression there.'

She frequently did, Milla thought abstractedly – although not necessarily a good one.

Milla felt the warmth of Patrick's hand stroke down the back of her head, following the line of her plait, even curling his fingers around the end and tugging gently, and she resisted the impulse to jerk away.

'What about Dermot?' she asked him.

'What about him?'

'Hartfell is his house!'

'No, darling, Hartfell has never been a family home. It belongs to Graham Media. I thought you knew that? When the news of Dermot's arrest hits the media, it could wipe millions off the company. The trustees have asked me to take over in the interim.'

'That was quick work.' It came out before she could stop it.

'I have to do what's best for the company. I can't let the shareholders down.'

'The shareholders?' What about his family?

'Running the business is not really my thing,' Patrick said. 'I admit I made such a hash of it last time. Luckily, Dermot has an excellent MD in place, so I'm sure everything will be fine.'

Did he mean Mal?

Any moment now and Patrick was going to start talking about roses and kittens, or maybe rainbows and bluebirds, but this wasn't the place to contradict him. Was it?

Again, she scanned the room, checking for Ben, but saw only hostile faces.

Where was he?

Pausing only to shake the DCI's hand and thank him for his help, Patrick gathered his solicitors around him like bodyguards and swept out through the entrance.

Elvis has left *the building.*

Milla trailed awkwardly behind. It wasn't as though she had anywhere else to go. She didn't dare look back, although she could have sworn she heard the DCI mutter, 'Bloody *hell!*'

A long sleek car, complete with uniformed driver, was parked on the double yellow lines outside the police station. It was attracting a lot of attention.

As the driver held the door open, Milla quickly slid onto the back seat beside Patrick. She glanced back at the police station, hoping to see Ben one last time, but the only officer to follow her outside was his blonde sidekick, carrying a small cardboard box tucked beneath one arm.

Milla raised her hand to politely wave goodbye but when the other woman didn't even crack a smile, she turned it into a sarcastic salute instead.

Without any discernible reaction, the woman walked back into the station, still carrying the cardboard box.

THIRTY-SEVEN

Ben threw the last box of his possessions into the boot of his hired car and slammed the door, only to find Harriet standing beside him holding another one.

'Don't forget about this,' she said, thrusting the box at him.

Instinctively he caught it. 'This isn't mine,' he said, holding it out for her to take back.

She was already walking away. 'It is now.'

Oh, bloody hell! What had she given him? He juggled the weight into his left arm, flipped open the box and found a motley collection that could have been cleared out from the Lost & Found. A tatty leather satchel, a wallet, a cheap mobile phone, a heavily scratched MP3 player...

'What the hell is this?'

Harriet, halfway across the station car park, paused to regard him disdainfully. 'Don't you recognise any of it?'

'Obviously not!'

'It's what Milla had on her when she was arrested. Logged, boxed up, signed for – and then she left without any of it. Don't you think that's odd?'

'As her father's just hired the UK's top legal team, I should imagine her possessions are now disposable.'

'Including her purse and credit cards?'

'They probably weren't hers to start with.'

Harriet's blue-eyed gaze narrowed. 'Coming from you, that's low.'

She turned her back on him and headed into the station.

Guilt whacked him right in the stomach. It *was* low. Watching Milla leave with her father, without saying goodbye, without even acknowledging how he'd helped her, had left him feeling bitter and bad-tempered. Milla drove him crazy, but he still cared about what happened to her. Overlooking the fact he'd put his job on the line for her, he thought they'd had... a connection?

What did it *matter*? She didn't care about him. Now she'd gone to live with her rich and powerful relatives, he'd never see her again. She no longer needed help. She certainly didn't need saving. Not that she'd needed 'saving' in the first place. All he'd done was try to keep up with her and avoid being out-manoeuvred, but it had been...

Fun?

He grinned, remembering how she'd broken into Rose Cottage right in front of him, wriggling up and over that windowsill as though she'd done it a hundred times before.

She probably had.

He was going to miss her.

She wouldn't miss him in the slightest.

But she might miss her belongings.

He checked the box again, frowning as he recognised her laptop and a surprisingly small make-up bag. He unzipped it with his free hand and found eyeliner, mascara and some kind of chubby pencil he assumed was lip-colour, although he'd never seen her wearing any.

He dropped the make-up bag back into the box, feeling

uneasy. Harriet was right to be suspicious. This was *everything* Milla owned: the contents of that precious satchel she never let out of her sight. He still held the crate of her clothes, books and music, hidden away in his garage. Her kitbag, with the sleeping bag and camping stove, had been seized as evidence in Lydia's murder. Why had she left this behind?

Even if she no longer wanted it, it didn't make sense. Once she'd been officially released from police custody, there would have been the formality of signing them back into her possession. It was standard procedure.

Unless the oversight had been deliberate?

Was DCI Cameron up to something? Had he intended this to be a ready excuse for Ben to maintain contact with the Graham family? If so, why had it become Ben's problem?

Because he was officially on leave.

Making him officially *unofficial*.

And Cameron knew Milla trusted him.

Feeling as though he were playing lucky dip with Milla's life, he jiggled the box to see what else was in there. Half-hidden beneath the laptop was the photograph Milla had taken from Rose Cottage, now with a large spidery crack fracturing one corner of the glass. A photograph of five children, standing on a jetty, laughing.

He picked it up, shaking the broken glass free, remembering how pleased Milla had been when she'd found it. How she'd refused to leave it behind at Rose Cottage. And now she'd left it here?

'I remember when this photo was taken,' she had said. 'We'd been on the boat, right out to sea. Mal caught a fish, a sea bass. He was so proud. I fell in, one of the twins lost a bucket and poor Kiran was sick. So, so sick! We could have done with the extra bucket!'

Sure enough, there was Mal holding the fish. Beside him was the girl Milla had identified as Kiran, wearing a pretty summer frock and looking as though she might burst into tears at any moment. At the front were the twins, forlornly holding one bucket between the two of them. And at the back, in scruffy shorts and T-shirt, her hair hanging in rats' tails around her shoulders (but with the hugest grin on her face), was Milla.

And then it hit him.

Four brown-skinned children with the pale grey eyes of their parents, Patrick and Rosemary.

One brown-skinned child with dark eyes.

The girl who had been 'Alice'.

The girl who had died in the fire.

The girl who lay buried in the churchyard at Raven's Edge.

Kiran.

So why had all those adults lied?

* * *

Milla sat on the back seat of the car, watching the last of the quaint thatched cottages blur into the forest and her old life slide into the past. There would be no more Kiran, no more Milla. She was *Camilla* and everything she had dreamed of for the past eighteen years was about to come true. Her life was finally on the right track.

Why did it feel so wrong?

She was alone in the car with Patrick and his driver. The lawyers, travelling in their own car, were presumably on their way back to their own homes; there was no sign of any other car on this stretch of road and it was the weekend, traditionally the time to spend with one's family. Now she had a family too – Mal, Brianna... Patrick.

He was reclining in the seat beside her with his eyes closed. Was he asleep or trying to avoid conversation? In the short time she'd known him he'd never been big on the emotional stuff, unless it was about himself. Ben had said she was all 'Maximum volume, maximum drama'; it could as easily be applied to Patrick.

Funny how she still thought of him as 'Patrick' rather than 'Dad'.

More time passed, with only the muffled swish of the tyres on the tarmac to break the silence.

She *hated* silence. She liked conversation, jokes, laughter and loud, loud music. Anything to help her feel as though she wasn't alone. Why wouldn't he talk to her? They had a lot to catch up on and there must be *something* they had in common? He hadn't even thanked her for helping him prove his innocence. Although, technically, the police appeared to have done most of that.

She fidgeted around in her seat. She was so short the seatbelt was threatening to strangle her. There was an entertainment console directly opposite. Would Patrick mind if she switched on the TV or maybe the radio? Right now she'd even suffer that golden oldie stuff Ben loved. What kind of music did Patrick like? Did he even *like* music?

She pulled the seatbelt away from her neck and leaned forward to examine the console. There was a dazzling array of lights and buttons but it did have a dock for an MP3. Too late, she remembered she'd left her own back at the police station, along with her laptop, phone and purse.

Would Patrick kick up a fuss if they turned around and headed back to Raven's Edge?

Probably, but she'd have the chance to see Ben again. To talk properly this time.

About what, exactly? Their relationship? They didn't *have* a relationship. To Ben she'd been a damsel in distress. Once she'd proved she didn't need rescuing, his interest in her would have disappeared. They had nothing in common either, particularly with her dubious past, and there was his daughter to consider.

What did she know about children? *Nothing*. She'd make the worst stepmother ever.

Why was she even thinking of being a mother to Ben's daughter, when all they'd done was share one kiss?

One perfect kiss.

Oh, *hell*.

It was hopeless, especially now she knew how this was all going to pan out.

She'd still like her stuff back though.

There was a window of clear glass separating her from the driver. Was she supposed to knock on it? Press a call button? She couldn't even catch his eye in the rear-view mirror. And Patrick? Bloody Patrick was still pretending to be asleep.

Milla slumped back against the seat. By now the police must have tipped everything she owned into the bin. She'd miss the laptop though. It had all her original festival interviews, all her photos, her music – her entire life.

Her old life.

The one she really wanted back.

She blinked. It must be the bright sunshine, finally breaking through the clouds and flooding the car, which was making her eyes water. It was later than she'd thought, for the sun was now very low, turning the underbellies of the clouds pink. As the road dipped down a hill, the coastline finally came into view: a bleak line of rocks, mud and seaweed.

She'd rather have gone to Somerset.

She could have met Patrick's wife, Charlotte, and her new baby half-sister, Sasha.

The *other* Camilla.

Would they have liked her? Sasha was little more than a baby, so she'd like anyone who was kind to her.

Like the twins.

Blinking no longer worked. Milla rubbed her eyes with the back of her hand, grateful Patrick couldn't see her. What was the matter with her? She couldn't lose control, not now she was so close to getting what she wanted.

Was this journey *ever* going to end?

As though on cue, the car began to slow before indicating and turning left. The huge black gates of Hartfell automatically swung open and there, in the distance, she saw its glass façade flashing fire as it caught the first rays of the sunset.

The Ice King's palace. Now it was to be her home. She'd see Mal in a matter of minutes. How would he react when he saw her, when he learned she really was his sister? Maybe she'd better not mention she'd been responsible for getting his beloved Uncle Dermot arrested, even if it was for the best. Knowing Brianna, she would take everything in her stride, even the return of Patrick. Mal, however...

Mal would not be pleased.

She glanced sideways. Patrick's eyes were *still* closed. As his lips were quirked in a smile she doubted he was asleep. OK, she got it. He didn't want to talk; fair enough. Why couldn't he say so? Why couldn't he ever be honest with her? It was almost as though he didn't trust her.

Coming from *him*, that was insulting.

At this close proximity she could see the scattering of freckles across his pale skin, his sandy eyelashes and the streaks of grey in his blond hair. There was little resemblance between them, in personality or in looks (apart from their shared love of the dramatic), but he *was* her father. Like all the best fairy stories, it might have taken him eighteen years but he had come for her in the end. She had the opportunity to live happily ever after, as she'd always dreamed.

Except now she knew there never would be a happy ending. Not for her.

Dermot sprinted up the stairs with Patrick in pursuit.

Any delusion Dermot might have had that Patrick had followed to help disappeared the moment Patrick spun him around and his fist connected with his jaw.

Dermot staggered back, faintly surprised. His brother was older and taller, but he had always been broader and tougher.

'What?' Patrick goaded. 'You didn't think I had it in me?' He followed up with a punch to the gut, which Dermot managed to deflect – but not as easily as he'd anticipated.

'Why are you fighting me at all? Your house is on fire, your family are in danger—'

'What family?'

'Rosemary, the children—'

'You think I want Rosemary after you've had her?'

So that was what this was about?

Another punch, which he was too slow to avoid, connected with his ribs.

'Can we talk about this some other—'

A one-two to the other side; Dermot doubled over in pain.

Patrick laughed. 'For you to play the hero and live happily ever after with my wife and children? Except, as it turns out they're not all mine, are they?'

'I don't—' He stumbled back as Patrick landed another blow in his gut.

'You're not sure which one is the cuckoo?'

'Damn, Patrick! I don't have time for this!'

He turned away, only to be yanked back.

Patrick was laughing, the madness clear in his eyes. 'Too late,' Patrick crowed. 'The love of your life is dead. All your little bastards are dead. Now you can rot in hell, knowing they died because you had to take what was mine.'

Before Dermot could make any move to stop him, Patrick tilted back his head, flung out his arms in some grotesque parody *of sacrifice, and stepped backwards – crashing through the broken bannister and disappearing into the thick smoke below.*

THIRTY-EIGHT

Ben arrived home to find the downstairs lights on but the upper storey in darkness.

No surprise there. It was well past Sophie's bedtime but she probably had poor Mrs Lancaster reading her fairy story after fairy story. He pushed open the door, careful to hide his grin with what he hoped was a suitable look of apology – that died the moment he saw a man sitting in his favourite armchair, giving every appearance that he'd stepped out of a book himself.

He wore the clothes of a Victorian gentleman – cravat, waistcoat and all. Except his frock coat was the emerald green of a cartoon character, and his face had been smeared with greasepaint.

Dermot Graham.

In one hand was a familiar-looking copy of *Alice's Adventures in Wonderland.*

The other held Sophie in a tight embrace.

Ben was going to kill him.

Instinctively clenching his hands into fists, he strode into the room. 'Get the *hell* away from—'

And stopped.

For Dermot had casually pulled aside his coat, revealing the knife tucked into his pocket. A long, slender knife with a wickedly sharp edge, lavishly decorated with pink-red stones that might have been rubies. It looked old; it looked valuable; but Ben didn't care. It was a knife and Dermot Graham had possession of it – less than five centimetres from Sophie's heart.

Ben stopped dead. His heart stopped, his thought process stopped, and everything in his life at that exact moment was brought down to three cold facts.

Dermot.

Sophie.

Knife.

How still she was. Eyes closed, long dark lashes feathering pale cheeks; too pale, too still. Was she breathing? Had he killed her? *Bast—*

He would have surged forward but Dermot raised one hand as he bent his head to whisper, very softly, into Sophie's ear, 'My dear, your Daddy's home.'

Sophie raised her head, blinking sleepily against the overhead light. 'Is he?'

The hammering in Ben's chest eased fractionally. She had been asleep, just asleep.

'Sweetheart?' he croaked. 'Are you all right?'

She yawned widely, without bothering to put her hand in front of her mouth. 'Why wouldn't I be?'

He forced images of blood and death from his head and tried to sound calm, *normal...*

'Where's Mrs Lancaster?'

'Oh, *her*.' Sophie rolled her eyes. 'Uncle Dermot sent her home.'

Uncle? His nails dug into his palms, sharpening his concentration.

'Don't be cross,' she added quickly, perhaps glimpsing something of the white-hot rage threatening to consume him. 'Mrs Lancaster told me Uncle Dermot's mother is her greatest friend.'

It explained why Mrs Lancaster had so blithely deserted her post. He supposed he should be grateful he wasn't about to find the woman dead in the kitchen, but right now all he could think about, all he could care about, was Sophie. Thankfully, Binx appeared to have made himself scarce.

'Uncle Dermot is *so* much better at reading stories,' Sophie said, sounding more awake by the minute. 'He does the voices and everything. Show him, Uncle Dermot. Do the Caterpillar one again.'

'I'm afraid it's well past your bedtime, Sophie,' Dermot said. 'Your father is not pleased with me for allowing you to stay up so late.'

'Pah! Only kids go to bed before 10.00 pm.'

Dermot laughed and ruffled Sophie's dark curls.

It took every bit of Ben's control not to rip his head off.

Instead, he held his hand out to Sophie and said, 'Come to me, sweetheart.'

As she tried to scramble from Dermot's lap, the bastard held her back.

'Wait,' he said. He slid that wicked knife from his pocket, turning it over in his hand, apparently enjoying the way the light sparked off the silver...

Before slipping the knife between the pages of the book and closing it, leaving the long, jewelled hilt protruding from the top. 'Could you give that to your father for me, Sophie?'

She took hold of the book with both hands, transfixed by the glittering knife. 'What a strange thing to use as a bookmark...'

'You should meet my Uncle Fergal, darling. He loves to read and uses all kinds of objects for bookmarks. Bus tickets, pressed flowers, even a slice of his breakfast bacon once.'

Sophie's eyes were huge. 'Didn't it spoil the book?'

'Oh yes, and the smell as it rotted nearly drove my poor mother mad. It took her days to discover where it was coming from.'

Sophie laughed and turned away to give the book to Ben.

Before she could hand it over he snatched it away, throwing it carelessly onto the sofa.

Swinging her up into his arms, he held her tightly against him and backed towards the door, without taking his eyes from Dermot.

'Aren't you going to ask me what I want?' Dermot enquired.

Ben yanked open the door. 'I don't *care* what you want. Get out of my house!'

Dermot didn't move from his seat. 'I need your help.'

'After this stunt?'

'I need to explain something—'

'*Go!*'

'Daddy!' Sophie's little fist crashed against his chest. 'Why are you being so mean?'

Mean? It was only her presence stopping him from doing what he really wanted to do.

Killing him.

'If you put your daughter to bed,' Dermot said, as though it were a perfectly reasonable request, 'we could discuss this matter in more depth.'

Ben gripped Sophie tighter, hard enough for her to squeak indignantly, 'Daddy! You're hurting me!'

Ignoring her, he flipped out his phone and hit speed dial. 'Oh you're going to talk all right – just not to me. Harriet!' he bellowed, as the call was answered. 'Dermot Graham is in my house. I need assistance. He has a knife. Yes, my daughter is here with me.'

'Well, that's unfair,' Dermot said, as Ben disconnected. 'I gave *you* the knife.'

'Now I'll give you a chance. You have less than ten minutes before my colleagues arrive. Start running.'

And he walked out the door.

THIRTY-NINE

Milla realised Patrick's driver had opened the car door and had been waiting for her to get out for some time. She stepped onto the driveway, instinctively reaching back into the car for her satchel, only to remember she didn't have it anymore. She smiled her apology up at the driver but received a very blank look in return.

As the car drove away, scattering tiny white pebbles in its wake, another drew up in its place. The lawyers, she realised, as three men in dark suits emerged practically simultaneously. They hadn't returned to London after all.

Patrick, already on the footbridge crossing the lake, had uncharacteristically waited for her. 'Darling, are you quite all right? You look dreadfully pale.'

That would be the guilt. The guilt that she'd made a terrible mistake and was about to make it worse.

She forced a smile. 'I'm fine,' she said, only to stagger as the ground seemed to slip sideways.

Famous last words.

He was there within seconds, taking hold of her arm.

'Although I do feel a bit strange.'

'I'm not surprised.' He slipped his arm around her waist to support her weight. 'You've had a long day, suffered a terrible ordeal. I bet you haven't eaten anything?'

She hadn't eaten anything at all, not since yesterday evening at Ben's house. The only thing she'd had to drink had been that foul coffee at the police station. The caffeine and sugar had undoubtedly kept her going this long; now she was crashing.

Their little party crossed the bridge in silence, towards the main entrance to Hartfell, which remained resolutely shut.

Patrick didn't seem perturbed, and as he reached out to punch a code into an electronic panel set into the wall, the door opened.

Instead of the butler it was Mal who stood there, one hand on the door as though he'd like nothing more than to slam it shut again. Dark smudges emphasised those strange pale eyes.

Her eyes.

Dermot's eyes.

How could she have been so stupid?

Patrick didn't appear particularly pleased to see him either. 'Where's Hodges?'

Mal shrugged carelessly. 'How should I know?'

'You live here!'

'Do I?' Mal glanced past, at the lawyers coming across the bridge. 'It's reassuring to know I'm not about to become unexpectedly homeless.'

'Hardly homeless.' Patrick pushed past him, heading into the hall. 'You're my son.'

Milla thought she heard Mal mutter, 'Lucky me,' but then his languid gaze fell on her and sharpened. 'Why is *she* here?'

'Because Camilla is going to live here too, Malcolm.' When Mal didn't move, 'Stop being such an arse and let her in!'

Slowly, insolently, Mal moved aside. 'Welcome, *sister*.'

She was tempted to snap a sarcastic comeback but something in his expression made her think better of it. Something dark and...

Frightening.

He leaned down to kiss her cheek and she felt his lips, cool against her skin, as he murmured, 'Traitor.'

She drew back, stung.

Patrick hadn't noticed. 'Are the rest of the staff still on site?'

'I assume so,' Mal said. 'I haven't actually felt the need to check.'

'Presumably you'd notice if your dinner failed to arrive?'

Mal lifted one shoulder in another insolent shrug. Milla could almost hear Patrick grind his teeth from right across the hall.

'Well, check! I need refreshments for my guests and food for your sister, who looks dead on her feet.'

She really wished he'd used some other simile.

Mal's unsettling scrutiny fell upon her once again and she resisted the instinct to clench her hands into fists. Why didn't he come right out and say he hated her if he felt it so strongly? Tell her he blamed her for his beloved Dermot's arrest and that he still refused to believe she was Camilla. That he'd *never* believe she was Camilla.

Because if he did, he was likely to find himself immediately cut off from his millions? At least she would have respected him more.

'I'll see if I can winkle out our housekeeper,' he said. 'Although I wouldn't be surprised if the woman has walked out. She did have the most enormous crush on Dermot.'

'You do that,' Patrick said, opening the door to Dermot's study, indicating the lawyers should enter first.

Milla waited for the door to close, for them to be left alone in the hallway, so she could ask Mal why he was deliberately baiting Patrick, even though she knew the answer, but he'd already turned away.

She ran after him. 'Where's Brianna?'

'Staying with an old friend.' Mal didn't even slow his pace.

'And Hodges?'

'Why should you care about Hodges?'

'He's loyal to Dermot, isn't he?'

'Aren't we all?'

Had he said that? Had he actually said *that*?

He stopped on the threshold of the library, looked her up and down and said, 'Or maybe not.'

Before Milla could formulate an answer, he'd entered the library, closing the door with a decided clunk, in case she really hadn't got the message.

She almost kicked the door out of frustration.

Patrick reappeared in the hall. 'Has Malcolm relayed my instructions to the housekeeper?'

'Yes.'

'What's keeping her?'

'I have no idea—'

'Then go and check, darling!'

Darling.

She found her fists clenching again. In all the weeks that had passed since she'd met him, he'd never called her 'Milla'. Or 'Camilla', or 'Kiran', or any name at all. Just 'darling', as though she was anyone.

As though she was no one.

It should have been a bit of a clue.

Why had she never picked up on it before?

Because she'd been *so* desperate for that happy ending.

Stupid.

The kitchen wasn't hard to find, although in reality it was a massive suite of rooms at the back of the house, dedicated to serving the masters of Hartfell like some kind of twenty-first-century *Downton Abbey*.

It was completely deserted.

Another clue.

Evidently the staff had no trouble identifying where their loyalties lay.

They had left the place immaculate, with every surface gleaming. While waiting for the kettle to boil, Milla made a sandwich and ate it, and then, as an afterthought, slid the knife she'd used to cut it into her boot.

It wasn't like she'd seen in the movies. The moment she took a step forward the knife moved, pressing against her foot with fortunately only the blunt side. So she took it out, removed her boot and made a small incision in the lining, sliding the knife into that instead. Far more effective.

Feeling like a domesticated Lara Croft, she busied herself making pots of tea and coffee, and placed them on a tray with the plate of homemade cakes and biscuits she'd found in the larder. Then she took the whole lot into Dermot's study without troubling herself to knock first.

And yes, it would always be *Dermot's* study.

Not that Patrick was particularly grateful. He fell silent the moment she went in and didn't resume talking until she'd left and closed the door after her. In the intervening time he didn't say a word of thanks. She told herself she didn't care and took the opportunity to search the house.

It was much as she suspected: the three of them were alone, save for the lawyers. Most interesting of all, the bedrooms upstairs were incredibly neat, with no personal possessions. As though the occupants had been forewarned what was about to happen and had moved out.

Or had never lived here at all.

Why was Mal still here?

The last room along the corridor was the one that had been

her own. It was much as she'd left it: immaculate, like the others, and empty save for a carafe of water on the bedside table.

She touched her hand to the side of the glass, feeling how cold it was, despite the fact there were no staff. The aircon had gone some way to keeping it cool but this water had been here for less than an hour – and hadn't been left by any member of staff. Crystal clear water; how perfectly tempting on a warm summer's evening – to anyone other than her. Patrick could have labelled it 'drink me' and it couldn't have been more obvious.

She had to leave.

Now.

Then she saw what lay beside the carafe.

A bracelet with silver charms. A teapot, a hand of playing cards, a little key...

She knew she'd not left *that* behind.

It had been on her wrist the last time she'd seen Lydia.

The last time she'd seen Lydia *alive*.

Two charms were missing, the top hat and the heart, but there was no obvious damage. The little silver links hadn't even been broken. It was almost as though they'd been removed deliberately – but by whom?

Dermot? He'd been arrested. Mal? Patrick...

She didn't touch it. She couldn't touch it. The bracelet had been her most treasured possession, a birthday gift from her father. But seeing it here, in this place... and knowing...

Patrick wasn't her father at all.

Milla took a step back, before her resolve broke. All her life she'd had a plan. Find the man who had killed her mother. Get revenge. It was going to be simple.

Stupid.

She scooped up the phone and tried to get an outside line. It was dead. She let it fall through her fingers and ran to the door.

She had to find Ben and tell him everything. That Dermot was...

How *could* she have made such a terrible mistake?

Dermot was...

Innocent.

Smoke billowed around the gallery. Dermot couldn't even see the staircase, let alone know if it was alight. He abandoned Patrick to whatever fate he'd chosen for himself and ran in the direction of the east wing. Rosemary, the children; he had to find them, he had to—

He stumbled and, on reaching down to discover why, touched something soft and warm.

It was Malcolm, curled up on his side, unconscious.

Had he been going into the fire, or coming out?

Dermot stepped over him, running towards the twins' bedroom. He couldn't see a thing through the smoke, only feel the unrelenting heat.

'Rosemary!' and he felt his throat scorch as soon as he opened his mouth.

Someone grabbed his arm, tugging at him, and he swung around, ready to punch.

It was only Mal, his poor little face smeared with soot. 'I couldn't wake them up,' he sobbed. 'I couldn't wake them up.'

Dermot didn't reply. He couldn't reply. He had to force down every emotion threatening to overwhelm him and focus on getting them out of here, so at least one of Rosemary's children might live. After the way he'd carelessly destroyed her happiness, it was the least he could do.

He reached down and swung Mal over his shoulder, turning back towards the staircase as the floor shuddered and the twins' room collapsed behind him.

FORTY

The police cars sped past Ben as he stumbled along the grass verge in the dark, but they didn't stop. As this stretch of road had no street lamps, they probably hadn't even seen him. If they had, they'd have mistaken him for a drunk staggering back from the pub. The elderly Mrs Lancaster was his nearest 'neighbour', and she lived a good ten minutes' walk away in a cottage that looked much the same as his own. Thankfully the lights were still on, although she opened the door in a bright pink housecoat and fluffy slippers. And then he had to explain exactly what he was doing knocking on her door at this late hour, and why he needed her to keep Sophie overnight.

'The poor little mite hasn't even got her pyjamas on!' she said, giving him the kind of look he'd seen far too much of since becoming a divorced parent. 'And what about her toothbrush?'

'We left in a bit of a hurry,' he admitted, reluctant to go into the finer details with a fascinated and very wide-awake Sophie listening to every word.

Mrs Lancaster frowned. 'I heard the sirens. Is everything all right?'

'Absolutely fine,' he lied, 'but if I could leave Sophie with you until morning that would be brilliant.'

Her eyes narrowed. 'Is it connected to that Milla woman? Sophie told me all about *her*.'

Oh dear... Had she?

Everything?

Unfortunately, not replying immediately meant Mrs Lancaster had the opportunity to build up a full head of steam. 'You can't save them all, my lad. You're in the wrong job for a start. You should be arresting women like that, not giving them a bed for the night.'

He winced, sincerely hoping Sophie hadn't told Mrs Lancaster exactly which bed he'd given Milla for the night.

'If your grandmother hadn't been one of my oldest friends, God rest her soul...'

As Brianna Graham had also been her 'oldest friend'?

Tempting as it was to inform her how she'd glibly delivered Sophie into the hands of a murderer, it would hardly be kind or constructive. Not when he badly needed this favour. He deposited Sophie on the doorstep, gave her a little shove over the threshold and thanked Mrs Lancaster effusively, effectively cutting her off.

'You are an absolute treasure, Mrs Lancaster,' he added, bending to give Sophie a kiss on the cheek. 'Be a good girl, Sophie. I'll see you in the morning.'

'You'd better,' Mrs Lancaster grumbled, firmly shutting the door in his face.

He took his time heading home but arrived to find three patrol cars parked haphazardly outside the front gate, red and blue lights flashing, and his front door open to all.

Inside, Harriet had Dermot's face pressed against the wall and one arm twisted behind his back, as she read him his rights. Despite Harriet being tougher than her angelic blonde curls suggested, Ben was under no illusion that if Dermot hadn't wanted to be in that position, or had at least been resigned to it, Harriet would have been the one with her arm twisted behind her back.

What the hell was he playing at?

DCI Cameron, perched on the sofa and plainly aggrieved, had apparently come to the same conclusion. More of their team, including Sam and Ash, were hanging around and trying not to clunk their heads on the low overhead beams, and Binx was back on the windowsill, licking his paws as though this were a perfectly normal evening.

DCI Cameron saw Ben first. 'Ah, Benedict,' came the familiar sardonic voice. 'How kind of you to return. Perhaps you would like to explain to us exactly what's going on?'

Ben flicked a thumb in Dermot's direction. 'Hasn't he told you?'

Cameron's scowl deepened. 'He refuses to speak with anyone but you.'

Ben strode across the room, hardly giving Harriet enough time to scoot out of the way, before he hauled Dermot around and punched him so hard he fell back into the armchair.

'That's for threatening my daughter!'

Sam grabbed him before he could yank Dermot up and repeat the exercise.

Dermot wiped his bloody nose on the sleeve of the jacket. 'You must love your daughter very much.'

Ben let loose a stream of curses that had even Harriet wincing. He attempted to wrench himself away from Sam, but the other man had too firm a grip on him.

'I also love my daughter very much,' he heard Dermot say, 'which is why I came to you instead of going directly to the police. I thought you cared for her? Evidently, I made a mistake,' he added, indicating the crowded room.

'Daughter?' Harriet repeated, frowning. 'I didn't know you had a daughter.'

Dermot's eyes met his. The strange grey eyes that were so familiar.

He smiled. 'Yes, I have a daughter. You know her quite well, I think?'

Ben felt very, very cold. He was an *idiot*.

'Milla is your daughter.'

Dermot reached into his pocket, sending every armed officer reaching for his gun.

He paused. 'May I?' he enquired icily. 'You've already searched me. Thoroughly. I think you would have noticed if I had a weapon?'

Cameron nodded. 'Proceed.'

Dermot took something from his pocket and handed it to Harriet, who was nearest.

She unfurled her fingers and gasped. Lying directly in the centre of her palm was a little silver heart.

Ben recognised it immediately. It was one of the charms from Milla's bracelet.

He cursed again, shaking himself free from Sam. 'Where the hell did you get that?'

'The last event I recall with any clarity is returning to Hartfell and finding my brother waiting for me. Then I wake up at King's Rest an hour ago, lying in the same room where you found Amita, and I'm dressed like this. On the bed beside me is that book, the knife and a top hat.'

'That's ridiculous,' Harriet said. 'King's Rest is a crime scene. There's at least one officer on duty, twenty-four seven—'

'Two, actually,' Dermot said. 'Unfortunately, when I saw them they'd both been killed, probably with that knife. I suspect the culprit was my brother.'

Killed? Was that *possible?* His team exchanged horrified glances.

DCI Cameron nodded to Ash, who immediately took out his phone and retreated into a quiet corner to make a call.

Dermot looked up at Ben. 'Patrick has her, doesn't he? You idiots released Milla into his custody and now he has her.'

'Why come here?' Cameron persisted. 'Why not call us?'

Dermot raised his eyes heavenwards. 'With what? I have no phone, no money, nothing but the clothes on my back. The police officers had neither phones nor radios – Patrick must have taken them. I had the choice between waiting for my brother to return to King's Rest with Milla – and he will return, I'm sure of that – or calling into the police station looking like the bloody Joker.' He indicated his costume with disdain. 'Or finding someone who I thought might believe me.'

'But I don't believe you,' Ben said. 'I don't believe a word you're saying. I overheard your conversation with DI Cavill. You've done everything you possibly could to get Milla locked up. That's not the action of a loving father.'

'To keep her out of his way! Everything I've ever done has been to keep her away from *him*. He can hardly kill her if she's in police custody!'

'You'd do that?' Harriet interrupted. 'Risk your own daughter ending up in jail?'

'That's why you paid Drake to plant the stolen necklace in her apartment,' Ben said, ignoring the way his boss suddenly said,

'*Necklace?*'

Dermot inclined his head. 'It was only meant to be a temporary solution.'

'You're rich,' Ben said. 'You could have hidden her anywhere in the world or given her bodyguards. There's no guarantee she would have been safe in police custody. If she'd ended up in prison, Patrick could have paid someone to take her out. All your effort would have been wasted.'

'You know Milla,' Dermot sighed. 'Do you think she'd allow herself to be hidden away in some ivory tower because it would keep her "safe"? She'd as likely go and confront the bastard.'

Ben remembered how desperate Milla had been to find her mother's killer – and of the photograph he'd seen of her looking so happy with Patrick. Happy to have finally found her father? Or happy because she'd found her mother's murderer?

'You should have told her the truth,' he said, 'and let her decide for herself.'

'I needed time to sort everything out—'

'Yes, and see how well that turned out! Two women are now dead because you needed time to manipulate the situation. I assume Patrick killed Amita?'

'I suppose so, although I have no idea why. He can't have mistaken her for Milla. He'd already met Milla. He knew what she looked like.'

'But why go to all the trouble of setting a scene?'

'It could have been meant as a message to me,' Dermot said. 'Perhaps he wanted me to assume Milla had died in the same way he'd killed her mother. Now he really does have her. Call out an armed response team. Send them to King's Rest. Please!'

DCI Cameron glanced over at Ash, who was replacing his phone in his pocket.

'There's no response from King's Rest, sir. Would you like me to arrange for a patrol car to check it out?'

'Send them straight into a possible trap?' Cameron snapped. 'I don't think so! But contact the Tactical Firearms Team, get them on standby while we sort this out.' He picked up the book with the knife which Ben had thrown onto the sofa. 'Is this the weapon that was used to kill Rosemary Graham?'

'I have no idea. It resembles an antique Patrick once bought for Rosemary to cut paper, but she never liked it and never used it. She said it gave her the creeps. Why are you wasting time, asking stupid questions?'

'Because they're *relevant*. Answer them to my satisfaction and perhaps I will send a car to rescue your precious daughter.'

Ben shifted, uncomfortable with his boss's attitude and the

time being wasted. Dermot obviously believed Milla was in immediate danger, and there had been no reply from the officers stationed at the house, so...

'Sir, perhaps we should—'

'Later, Benedict.' Cameron dropped the book back on the sofa and got up. 'Why did Patrick kill Rosemary?'

'He learnt Milla was mine. I believe he intended to kill everyone that night, including himself, but Mal and Milla caught him in the act and were able to escape.'

'You happily adopted Mal but sent Milla away to be brought up by her maternal grandmother, Parminder McKenzie?'

'Patrick hasn't realised that Mal's my son. I thought Milla would be safe if she disappeared. I never dreamed she'd remember her previous life and want it back! She started writing to Patrick in prison. The man who killed her family! Who could have foreseen that? He learnt she was still alive and now I'm certain he's planning to kill her the same way he killed Amita – and the same way he killed Rosemary.' He indicated his costume. 'Why else would he go to so much trouble framing me?'

For a moment Cameron stared at him. And then he said, 'I've never heard such utter rubbish in all my life. You're insane!'

'Completely,' agreed Dermot. 'And absolutely desperate.' Before any of them could react, he reached forward, grabbed the knife and then grabbed Harriet, holding the blade to her throat. 'Now, are you gentlemen going to help me or not?'

Within seconds, Harriet had caught hold of his wrist, ducked beneath his arm, and twisted it behind him so that he was forced to release the knife. It clanged onto the floor. She kicked it towards Ben.

'How about we talk through this, one more time?' she said.

FORTY-ONE

The hall appeared much the same as when Milla had left it, except the door to Dermot's study was now open and the room was in darkness. The lawyers had gone. Where was Patrick? She didn't care. All she wanted was out and there was the exit in front of her. Moving as silently as she could in flat-heeled boots, she took hold of the door handle, wrenched it around and yanked hard. It didn't move. She rattled the handle again. Nothing.

Damn!

Think clearly, don't panic. There had been an electronic panel on the outside, maybe there was one on the inside...

And there it was, easy for even her to reach and right next to the door. Except instead of a single release button there was a keypad and she had no idea of the code.

Dermot and his bloody futuristic house! What if there had been a fire? Hadn't he learnt *anything* from the past?

There had to be more than one door and, failing that, there were a lot of glass windows. If it came to it, she could smash her way out. She surveyed the gloomy hallway. It stretched all the way through the house, past the enormous stairway to the kitchens at the back. She hadn't remembered seeing a rear entrance; presumably that would be locked too.

OK, a window it was.

Behind her was the salon where Brianna had held court at the piano, and the next door along was that starkly Gothic dining room. On the *other* side of the hall was the library, with a whole row of glass doors opening onto the stone walkway surrounding the house.

It was Mal's favourite room, although she'd never seen him read a book. Was he still there? She could see a light beneath the door but it was very dim. Not bothering to knock – why should she? – Milla shoved open the door.

The light came from a lamp set on a desk by the window where Mal usually liked to sit. Except Mal was now face down on the floor, surrounded by broken glass. She knelt beside him, pulling at his shoulder until he rolled onto his back. When he failed to respond, she slapped his face, non-too gently.

'Get lost, Camilla.'

The words were slurred but distinct enough.

She sat back on her heels. 'You called me "Camilla"!'

'It's your name, isn't it?' His eyelids flickered open before closing again and he flopped one arm over his face, shielding the light from his eyes. 'Or are you calling yourself something new this week?'

'How long have you known?' She punched his shoulder. That wasn't gentle either.

'Since I met you at the pub.'

'Bastard,' she said mildly.

'That makes two of us.'

'Why did you lie?'

'To protect you. Why did you come back? You were safe. Now you've started him off again.'

No need to ask who 'he' was.

'Maybe if you'd been honest with me from the start —'

She broke off as he rolled over onto his knees, stuck two fingers down his throat and began retching.

'What the hell are you *doing*?'

'Making myself sick.'

'I can see that but—'

'A sedative,' he muttered. 'In the water... Same reaction last time... Got to make myself... sick...'

He did.

'Are you OK?'

'Not really.' Mal wiped his hand across his mouth. 'The one night I thought I'd stay sober. Talk about sod's law. Oh hell...' He groaned, and threw up again.

'How could you be so stupid? That water carafe practically had "drink me" written all over it.'

He leant back against the chair, skin as grey as the flagstone beneath him, his eyes closed. 'Your gentle words of sympathy are much appreciated.'

'You don't need sympathy. You need a doctor. Give me your phone.'

'You seriously think he's left me my phone?'

'Has he?'

'No.'

'Damn.'

'My sentiments exactly.' He opened one bloodshot eye to glare at her. 'Why *did* you come back? You were safe!'

'Safe?' she echoed bitterly. 'Living a half-life?'

'Better than no life at all!'

He had a point.

Back to plan 'A'. 'We need to get out of here.'

Mal made no effort to move at all. 'No kidding.'

'If Patrick wants to recreate the night of my birthday party, he'll set fire to the house next.'

'You've seen too many movies.' Taking a firm grip on the chair, Mal hauled himself up, swaying slightly. 'Firstly, *I* set fire to the old house. I knocked over a candle. Secondly, if there's one thing Dermot is really keen on, it's alarms and sprinklers. A fire wouldn't last five seconds.'

'Brilliant! Let's set off the alarm—'

'I already did. Can you hear bells?'

'Then we light a fire!' Scrambling to her feet, she grabbed an armful of books from the nearest shelf and dumped them on the floor. 'Have you got any matches?'

He rolled his eyes. 'You are *such* a drama queen! No, we don't light a fire. We get the hell out of here.' He grabbed her hand and dragged her over to the French windows.

They were locked but he merely raised one foot and kicked them open; glass and wood shattering immediately. That would get Patrick's attention, thought Milla, suddenly glad she had her big brother here with her. Now there were two of them against one of Patrick. She squeezed Mal's hand and felt him squeeze hers back.

They ran into the dark.

Mal knew his way better than she did, leading her around the uneven walls of the house, past potted trees and water features, until she saw the bridge silhouetted in front of them. By the time they were halfway across, Mal was flagging.

'Leave me,' he said, stopping to lean heavily against the balustrade. 'It's you he wants. Escape while you can.'

'For him to kill you instead? No.'

'You're sweet,' he said, planting a wet kiss on her forehead, 'but stupid. Make a lot of noise and with any luck he'll follow you not me.'

'Er... What?'

'I'll double back to the house and try to reconnect the alarm. Trust me.'

Did she have a choice?

'Which direction should I go? Is there a security office where I can find help or a garage where you keep your cars?'

'Everyone loyal to Dermot has left. The garage will be locked up, and even if it wasn't the keys would be. Head into the garden. There's more cover and if you make it to the woods, you can follow the main path to the village and the police station.'

'I know it.'

'I should hope so. We played there often enough.'

But not in the dark.

Patrick's silhouette appeared on the balcony.

'He's here,' Mal whispered, ducking out of view. 'Go!'

Milla waited until Mal had vanished into the garden, before sprinting towards the rear of the house, following the edge of the lake. She didn't have to create noise: her Docs on the shingle drive did that for her. She heard Patrick shout, then the sound of his feet clattering over the bridge. He'd taken the bait.

If only the bait wasn't her!

The moon was full and clear, and she found her way through the gap in the hedge easily enough. Once she reached the lane she had to slow to walking pace. The mud had dried into hard tracks and wide potholes. It would be easy to stumble or turn her ankle.

The woods, as usual, were supernaturally silent. Her footsteps echoed back to her, along with her laboured breathing, yet there was no indication Patrick was behind her. Had he given up? Or had he found Mal instead?

She limped to a halt, feeling dizzy and sick. The lights of Raven's Edge were tantalisingly close. A few hundred metres. All she had to do was keep going and she'd make it.

What would Ben say when he saw her again. 'I told you so'? She'd let him have his moment. She was glad to be out of that house.

Would the police station be open? Who cared? In the village there'd be people willing to help her and that was all she needed.

Only a few more metres.

She could do this.

She tried running again but the muscles in her legs had cramped and the soles of her feet burned. She should never have stopped. One step in front of another. That's all she had to do. Follow the lights. Concentrate. One step in front of—

Something slammed into her with the force of a wrecking ball. The ground came up, knocking the breath from her body. She was yanked over and rolled onto her back, and there was Patrick, his long fingers curling around her throat and tightening...

As her world grew black around the edges, narrowing until there was only him, he leant forward and said,

'You should have drunk the water.'

FORTY-TWO

For the second time in a matter of days, Milla woke up in a strange bed – a genuine four-poster, far older than Sophie's. As she sat up the springs creaked, raising a cloud of dust and she forced back a sneeze knowing that now, of all times, it was not good to be making any kind of a sound.

She was back at King's Rest. No surprise there. This must be one of the guest bedrooms. It might have been the one where Amita had been found. She hoped not.

She rather thought it was.

Beside her on the bed was a hat: a full-sized version of the one on her charm bracelet. It even had a ticket tucked into the band that said: *In this style 10/6.*

'Come here my little White Rabbit. Don't be afraid.'

If she'd been the faint-hearted type she could have gone into a decline right there, but she was Milla Graham and she *would be damned* if any creepy, low-life, murdering pig was going to get the better of *her*.

She slid off the bed and ran to the window, her boots clomping softly over the bare, dusty floorboards. Like the nursery above, there was no glass in the window and the wooden frame had rotted clear away. She stuck her head into the cool night air and found she was on the first floor, but too high to jump. There were no balconies or drainpipes, or even clumps of soft undergrowth to cushion a fall. Directly beneath was a small strip of tarmac; perhaps part of what had once been the drive.

No escape that way.

She turned back to survey the room. It was empty save for the bed, and the candles arranged in a wide circle around the walls. They were fat and white, the kind found in a church or at Christmas, providing a dull and flickering light. Should she head for the main staircase, and risk bumping into Patrick? Or maybe the servants' staircase? But before she could move in either direction, she heard a soft creak from the corridor outside and all hope died.

She checked the inside of her boot for the knife and for one terrible moment thought it had gone. She wriggled her fingers further into the lining and found it had slipped sideways. Ripping the lining, she thrust her fingers into the gap, nicking herself in the process.

She pressed her thumb to her mouth to stop the bleeding, hearing his footsteps pause outside the room. Instead of walking in as she'd anticipated, he gently pushed the door wider. Apparently, he'd realised she was no longer on the bed.

Before she lost the element of surprise she slammed the door into him, knocking him off balance. By the time he'd recovered she was standing in front of him, holding the knife with the point set against his throat.

'You evil bastard,' she said, pleased she sounded more confident than she actually felt.

Patrick regarded her with something close to admiration. 'You really have grown into an incredible woman. Rosemary would have been very proud.'

She did *not* want to talk about her mother.

'*You* killed her. All these years of protesting your innocence...'

Now she had a knife at his throat, she wasn't sure she could follow through. Did she really have it in her to kill a man in cold blood? A man she had grown up to believe was her father? What was the alternative? Let him go? Patrick Graham really wasn't the kind of man to turn your back on. She tried recapturing her rage, but it was already slipping away.

Patrick reached up, taking hold of the blade between his finger and thumb, and moving it to one side. 'Always best to aim for the jugular, darling. It implies you are serious.'

She refused to let him unnerve her. 'I'd hate for you to die too quickly...'

There was a creak and a rush of cooler air as the door opened wider, but she didn't look up. She couldn't allow herself to be distracted.

Besides, she knew who was there.

'Hello, Ben,' she said. 'Didn't I tell you I'm not the kind of woman who ever needs rescuing?'

'You did,' he agreed, and at the sound of his familiar, calm voice she wanted to weep. 'I see you have everything under control but I can take it from here. Please?'

'For this pig to go back to jail? So he can plead insanity, *again*, so he can get away scot-free, *again*?' Realising her hand was shaking, she took hold of the hilt with both hands, manoeuvring herself directly in front of Patrick and staring directly into those flat, emotionless eyes. She would be the last thing he saw before she killed him.

'Not this time, Milla,' Ben said. 'I promise you'll have justice for your mother, for all of them.' He walked into the room, holding out his hand. 'Please give me the knife.'

'No.' She pressed the tip further into Patrick's skin.

Then the knife was snatched from her hand and it was

Patrick pressing it against her throat, backing her across the room and away from Ben.

'Quick tip,' Patrick told her. 'If you're going to kill someone, do it. Don't stand around talking about it.'

She stumbled against one of the bedposts, inadvertently smacking her head. Maybe it would knock some sense into her. She should have killed him when she had the chance. Now he was going to kill her and there was nothing Ben would be able to do about it.

Patrick hauled her up, holding her against him. 'My, what beautiful big eyes you have,' he laughed. 'My brother's eyes, watching me.'

'*Bastard!*'

Ben had crashed forward, momentarily distracting him, but Patrick whirled her around, using her as a shield between them as he backed towards the window.

'Go ahead,' he taunted Ben. 'Shoot me. I'll kill her before you've had the chance to pull the trigger. Or shall I throw her out of the window, as I did with poor besotted Lydia?'

'No!' Ben jerked to a stop, his face ashen. He bent to place a small handgun on the floor. She hadn't even been aware he had one. Then he raised both hands in the air. 'See, I'm unarmed. Don't hurt her.'

He would make a terrible poker player. Despite his best efforts to keep his emotions in check, they were plain on his face for anyone to see.

He cared about her.

Idiot.

He was going to get them both killed.

Well, *she* wasn't going without a fight.

She couldn't slam her head back as she was too short to do any damage. Instead, she stamped down on Patrick's foot, as hard as she could, her booted heel to his toe. It should have been excruciating. He tensed, she felt that, but he didn't thrust her away from him, didn't step back, didn't move his foot or react in any way.

'Do that again,' he murmured against her ear, 'and I *will* kill you.'

She shivered, furious. How could she have ever believed this man was her father?

'Please don't hurt her,' Ben was saying, holding up his hands as he took another step closer. 'Do you want to spend the rest of your life in prison?'

Patrick took another step towards the window. 'You're assuming I want to live.'

Milla began to struggle, desperately. She should have killed him when she had the chance. Why hadn't she? To prove she was the nobler person? Well, she wasn't. She didn't care whether she was his daughter or not, she *hated* him and she wanted him dead, *now*.

He struggled to get a grip on her, to hold her tighter in his arms. They were jammed right up against the window. Would he push her out too? Maybe fighting wasn't the best way to resist him. She allowed herself to go limp in his arms and felt him relax.

'Good girl,' he said. 'You see, it does neither of us any good when you fight. And it upsets your boyfriend. Look at his face.'

Milla would rather not. If she were going to die, she'd much prefer Ben not to see it. She knew the guilt would consume him.

'Tell her,' Patrick said. 'Tell her if she moves again, I'm killing her.'

Why hadn't Patrick done so already?

Because he wanted to drag it out.

Maximum drama.

'Milla, sweetheart...'

She closed her eyes as Ben was forced to beg for her life. He'd called her 'sweetheart', as though he'd meant it.

Patrick chuckled and she was tempted to stamp on his other

foot, but even as the thought crossed her mind she heard Ben speak again; coolly, and quite calmly.

'Milla, look at me.'

He was standing there, so brave, so noble, like the prince out of a fairy tale, and she wanted to cry with the hopelessness of it all. What was it she had told him?

I don't need rescuing.

I don't need a hero.

She certainly needed one now.

'Milla,' he said again. 'Whatever you do, *don't move.*'

Did he think she was *that* stupid?

He blinked. Or rather his eyes flickered, almost as though he'd glanced down and up again. And although his hands were still in the air, the fingers were no longer splayed, but curling into his palm, one by one, almost as though it was...

A countdown.

'Trust me,' he said.

Milla closed her eyes and allowed her legs to give out from under her. She slipped through Patrick's hold, taking him by surprise. But as he cursed and lurched forward, making a grab for her, he seemed to tense and then topple over, crashing down on top of her, slamming her hard against the ground, his knife clattering harmlessly to one side.

The breath was knocked right out of her. She struggled to regain it, the panic beginning to overwhelm her. Patrick was shoved to one side as Ben dragged her out from under him, enfolding her in his arms and muttering over and over again,

'It's all right. You're safe. He can't hurt you.'

Dermot stumbled out of the house, one child in his arms, the other clinging onto his hand as though he would never let go. The emergency services had already arrived, and a fire officer rushed over to him, saying over and over again, as though he couldn't understand plain English,

'Is there anyone else inside?'

'Not alive,' he said, and kept on walking. A paramedic took Malcolm, who went away quite happily to be checked over, but the girl wound her arms tighter around his neck and refused to let go.

An elderly Indian woman was waiting for them beneath the trees, winding a scarf between her fingers, pulling the delicate silver threads to pieces. 'Where's Rosemary?' she demanded.

'Dead.'

Flattened by his own grief, it came out far more brutally than he intended.

'Kiran? The twins?'

He shook his head, unable to say any words of comfort except, 'I'm sorry. So, so sorry...'

The woman pressed the scarf to her face, rocking back and forth. 'Rosemary, my beautiful Rosemary...'

Helpless, he watched two more paramedics run past. On the stretcher between them lay Patrick, his eyes closed.

He hadn't a mark on him. The bastard was completely unscathed. After everything he'd done, he was the one who had survived.

It wasn't over.

It would never be over.

The girl in his arms snuggled closer. It would kill him to let her go.

'I need you to stay strong,' and his words were for himself as much as the woman who'd also seen her entire world destroyed. 'If not for me, then for... Kiran.'

The elderly woman blinked at him. 'Kiran? But you said—'

Dermot handed the girl over to her, silently shaking his head.

'Take Kiran. Get her away from this horrible place. I'll come and see you tomorrow, explain everything. But right now, you need to get her away.'

They watched as Patrick was transferred into an ambulance, waited until the door slammed and there was no possible way they could be overheard.

'If Patrick knows Camilla's alive, he will kill her. He knows she's mine, but he doesn't know about Malcolm.'

The woman inclined her head and carefully set the girl on the floor, before taking hold of her hand.

'Come along, Kiran,' she said loudly, ignoring the way the girl tried to pull away, to run back to Dermot. 'We need to get those burns seen to.'

As they disappeared into the dark and the smoke and the chaos, Dermot could hear the girl protesting at the top of her little voice, 'I'm not Kiran, I'm not! I'm Milla, Milla...'

He leant back against a tree and wept.

FORTY-THREE

The End.

It didn't happen in quite the way Milla had imagined.

She got what she wanted. Eventually. The man who had murdered her mother was dead, shot by a police sniper the moment Ben had given the signal. And her real father had come for her too, snatching her out of Ben's arms and hugging her so tightly she felt she might snap. She'd listened as words of love and regret poured from him until she couldn't distinguish one word from another, until they were no more than the sound of the wind whispering through the surrounding trees.

Because now she was the one who was frozen.

Reality came back in stages.

First, the sunshine, warm against her skin. The intoxicating scent of roses on a summer's day. But it was music which finally broke through her consciousness; her favourite track, the one which made her want to dance and sing; she felt her lips begin to move as she spoke the lyrics, heard her own voice, croaky from lack of use. Finally, she opened her eyes.

She was in a garden.

She was lying on a huge rattan sunbed that had been set on a little stone terrace and surrounded by pots overflowing with flowers. On a table beside her, completely out of place in that very rustic environment, was a laptop, a pile of fashion magazines and a can of cola. Stretching out before her was a long expanse of lawn, and a river in the distance with an old wooden jetty.

Rose Cottage.

How was that even possible?

She pushed herself up, wincing as the earphones she'd not realised she was wearing yanked at her head, pulling at her hair, which was loose around her shoulders and not bound back in its usual plait. Strange...

She pulled off the headphones, following the lead until she found the MP3 player they were connected to. Her own MP3 player – battered and scratched, so definitely hers – the one she'd last seen in a box at the police station. How had it got here? How had *she* got here?

She scooped it up, dropping it onto the table, and got up, turning towards the house, determined to find out some answers, when she saw him.

Dermot Graham.

He was dressed more casually than she'd ever seen him, in scruffy jeans and a black T-shirt, and was carrying a tray containing a cafetière and two mugs. For a moment he paused in the doorway, regarding her warily. And then he smiled.

'You're back.'

She didn't need to ask him from where. She knew where. The place she'd retreated to when she'd seen her father – the man she had *thought* to be her father – killed in front of her. When all those walls she had created over the years, as protection against the outside world, had collapsed inward, burying her.

Instead, she asked, 'How did I get here?'

He set the tray on the table and poured out the coffee, perhaps rehearsing in his head the words he intended to say before risking speaking them out loud. Because he'd changed. He was no longer that brittle, sardonic man she'd met by the lake at Hartfell. He still looked terrible: pale, gaunt, and every bit of his fifty-odd years, but he also looked... at peace.

'I brought you here, to rest. You can leave at any time,' he added quickly. 'You're not a prisoner. Here.' He ducked back into the cottage and emerged with her satchel, something else she thought she'd never see again. 'Your phone is here, your wallet, money... and look, I've got you this...'

From his pocket he pulled out a little blue jewellers' box marked *Vanders*. When she opened it, nestling on the velvet inside was her charm bracelet.

'I had it repaired for you,' he said.

She shrank back, unable to even bring herself to touch it. Once the bracelet had been her most treasured possession, but now, knowing *he* had bought it for her, the father who hadn't been at all, all she felt was revulsion.

Misunderstanding her reluctance, Dermot lifted it out, letting it dangle from his fingers.

'The workmanship is incredible. You can't even see where it was broken.'

How could she explain how much she hated it and everything it represented?

A lie.

He undid the catch and held it out to her.

Still, she didn't move.

His dark brows drew together. 'Does it have bad memories for you?'

A convenient excuse. Let him believe that.

'I understand.' He let it slide between his fingers, stroking against each charm in the exact same way she used to do. The little pocket watch, the toadstool, the tiny teapot... 'When Rosemary told me how obsessed you were with *Alice in Wonderland*, I had it made for you,' he said. 'I even designed each little charm myself. Me, who can barely draw a stickman. And yet somehow the jeweller created this magic from nothing.'

Out of love.

'Mum gave it to me on the day of my party. She told me it was a present from my father.'

His eyes darkened. 'You assumed—'

'Of course I did! I was six!'

He flinched, curling his fingers over the bracelet and taking a step back. 'You're not a prisoner,' he repeated. 'You can do anything you want, go anywhere you like. It's completely your choice.'

Was he trying to get rid of her? Already?

Or perhaps, like many other families before them, they still hadn't learned to communicate.

'What would *you* like me to do?' she asked, careful to keep her voice neutral, unaware the emotion in her eyes was sending another message altogether.

He smiled. 'Stay.'

Was this what it felt like, to be wanted, to be loved? Warm and fuzzy, inside and out?

She held out her hand for the bracelet, and when he was about to drop it into her palm, said, 'Would you fasten it for me?' and watched as he did as she asked, his fingers shaking slightly. Although she couldn't resist adding, 'Of course, this is *my* house,' purely to tease him.

'I'm afraid it isn't.'

'My mother left it to me in her will.'

'She left it to Kiran,' he said, 'because you were due to inherit a million-pound fortune and Kiran had nothing. Now

Kiran is officially dead, the house has passed to her next-of-kin, Robbie McKenzie.'

The mysterious uncle she'd never even met. Wasn't that ironic?

'Damn,' she said out loud. And it wasn't because she'd thought she finally had a place of her own; she *liked* this house. It felt like home. It reminded her of her mother.

'I'm sure Robbie will sell it to you, if you wish. You are now extremely rich.'

'Did he know who I was all the time? Is that why he never contacted me?'

'To be fair, Robbie was in the army for years. Contact would have been difficult for him, if not impossible. Perhaps he thought it would confuse you to have two fathers when the truth finally came out?'

'What was *your* reason? You had me followed all these years. You knew who I was and where I was. Why did you never tell me the truth? Why this elaborate charade?'

'I wanted to protect you. From him. If he thought you were dead, he wouldn't come after you.'

She wanted to believe him, but, 'Mal is your child too. Don't deny it. Anyone can see the resemblance.'

'He is.'

'You adopted *him*. You hid me!'

'Patrick knew you were mine, but he had no idea Mal was too. He was safe. Well, as safe as any child of Patrick's could be. My brother was completely insane, you know.'

'Because no sane man would kill his own child?' She'd been so thrilled when Patrick had answered her letters and began a correspondence with her, and when he agreed to meet her. And all the time...

The beautiful garden blurred in front of her. 'Don't you *dare* make excuses for him. He was sane enough. He knew what he'd done was evil.'

Dermot made a movement beside her, as though about to take her in his arms and smooth away the hurt. But he didn't. Because he felt he didn't know her well enough. And that made her want to cry too. They had so much to catch up on. All those years they'd spent apart. What an utter, utter waste.

She remembered the tower in the woods and Rosemary's drawings arranged around the walls. The ones not meant for publication. The ones of Rapunzel, growing old as another prince fell to his death from her tower. Suddenly they made a lot of sense.

'You didn't love her.'

'No, I didn't.' At least he had the decency not to lie. 'Not at first. What can I say? I was young and stupid. Rosemary was the most beautiful woman I had ever seen. And supremely talented. I was the one who hired her to do the illustrations for the fairy tales collection. I fell madly in lust – but not love, not until much, much later, when it was far too late. By then she wouldn't believe me. She thought I was spinning another one of my "tales", as she called them. She told me she was going to stay with Patrick, for the sake of her children. Not "our" children; "*her*" children. She chose security and safety – and his love – over me. I called her all manner of names, none of them pleasant, and I left, like the immature bastard she knew me to be. I wish I'd stayed. I wish to—' but his voice choked, leaving him unable to finish.

Hardly realising what she was doing, she reached across to touch his shoulder, to reassure him. 'Was it the night of my birthday party? The night she gave me this bracelet?'

Immediately his hand gripped hers, holding her tightly, as though it gave him the strength to say, 'The night I lost her forever.'

She felt it then, a ridge of skin beneath her fingers, and she lifted his hand and turned it over, stared at the scars on his palm. The same scars she had on her own hands. The same ones she'd seen on Mal.

'You came back,' she said, tracing her finger across his palm. 'Even after she told you to leave, you came back. It was you who saved me from the fire. You came back.'

She wrapped her arms around him in a hug.

'Yes,' he said, and this time he returned her smile. 'I did.'

FORTY-FOUR

Ben knocked on the door to Rose Cottage. He waited, knocked again, but no one answered. He followed the path around to the back of the house, thinking that if he were Milla, he'd have climbed in through the window by now. Unsure of his reception, it would be more diplomatic to try conventional methods first.

To the rear of the house was a stone terrace where almost every square inch was crammed with some kind of shrub or plant in a tub, and real grapes tumbled from a trellis overhead. Dermot Graham was sitting at a little round table reading a newspaper the old-fashioned way, his spectacles sliding off his nose.

'DI Taylor,' he said, without glancing away from the article he was reading. 'I did wonder when you would turn up.'

Ben ignored the barb. 'Is she OK?'

'Yes, but missing you, I think.'

Despite the dappled shade from the vines overhead, Ben could see the bruises from where he'd hit him.

'Still slightly painful when I wear my spectacles,' Dermot said.

'I'm not sorry,' Ben said. The night Dermot had turned up in his home and threatened Sophie would be good for a few more nightmares yet.

'I deserved it.' Dermot rose from his seat, folding the newspaper and tucking it beneath his arm. 'She's down by the river,' he added, moving towards the house. 'I'm sure I don't need to tell you that if you hurt her in any way, I shall be the one punching *you*.'

There was no path to the river, only a wide expanse of lawn sloping down to the water's edge and the same wooden jetty where Rosemary and her children had been photographed all those years ago. It was a glorious sunny afternoon and the river was busy with all kinds of sailing boats. Milla was sitting right on the very end of the jetty, wearing a pale pink T-shirt and faded jeans, her feet dangling in the water.

She'd heard his approach and was watching him warily. Why did she think he was here? To arrest her? He'd forgotten that when she looked at him all she'd see was 'police'.

Milla hated the police.

He remembered the last time he'd seen her, when she'd been covered with the dirt and grime of King's Rest. Did she hold him responsible for Patrick's death? For her entire life she had believed he was her father – and Ben had been the one to give the order to shoot.

'If you were planning on sneaking up on me, you've totally failed,' she said.

He should turn back now. Wish her well and return to his safe, comfortable life. The safe, comfortable life he'd had before he'd met her. The safe, comfortable, *boring* life.

She'd tipped her head back to get a good look at him, shielding the sun from her eyes with her hand. Her hair fell over her shoulders in silky black waves, almost to the jetty. He wanted to run his fingers through that hair. He wanted to—

Her face creased into a smile. 'You brought me flowers!'

Something inside of him melted.

Possibly his last honourable intentions.

'For you,' he said, handing them over with a flourish.

She laughed, taking hold of the flowers with both hands.

'No one's ever given me flowers before.'

His heart almost broke right there. 'Never?'

She ran her fingernail over the brown seeds at the centre. 'Sunflowers?'

'I thought they were cheerful and sunny.'

She grinned. 'But most of all, not roses?'

'I thought you might have had enough of those.' He sat down beside her, peering into the water below. The current swirled around the wooden posts, stirring up the silt and making the water look murky. The river was tidal and it wasn't that far from the sea.

'If you're going to paddle, you need to take off your trainers,' she told him, 'or it's going to end really, really badly.'

'You think I should?'

'Yes.'

He did as she requested, sliding off his trainers and socks and rolling up his jeans. The water was deceptively icy and he couldn't help cursing, but at least he made her laugh. She needed to laugh more.

'Do you realise, I've never seen you in anything other than a suit,' she said. And then, mischievously, 'Apart from that one time I saw you naked.'

'Naked? When was that?'

He wasn't sure he wanted to hear the answer.

'The night we met, I came into your room for your wallet.'

He remembered waking to the sensation someone had been there, to the faint scent of lemons.

He smiled ruefully. 'I sleep naked.'

'I noticed. You looked so beautiful, I couldn't help kissing your forehead before I left. Well, I kissed my fingertip and then...' She mimed the action.

'Our first kiss and I slept through it?'

'Uh huh.'

'I'm awake now,' he said.

She tilted her head on one side, considering, and then she crooked her finger. 'You need to come down a bit. You're too tall.'

He leaned forward until they were less than a breath apart. Until he could see the darker rings of charcoal around those beautiful grey eyes, the tiny flecks of blue that warmed them, the—

She kissed him. Gently and far too briefly. Her lips were warm and sweet, and tasted faintly of cola.

When she was about to pull back, he murmured, 'I think you can do better than *that*,' and slid his hand behind her head, tangling his fingers into that glorious silky black hair while he kissed her back.

'I've missed you,' he said, when they finally broke apart.

Her lips quirked in smug satisfaction. 'Good!'

'Did you miss me?'

'Maybe...'

'Truthfully?'

'I always tell the truth when it matters.'

'This matters. If we're going to have any kind of relationship—'

'Relationship?' Now her smile had become an outright grin.

When she looked at him in that way, he couldn't resist her. He placed his fingertip against her lips and tried to sound serious. 'No more lies, Milla. I mean it.'

The smile was gone in an instant. 'You want me to promise to tell you the truth, the whole truth and nothing but the truth, as long as we both shall live?'

He hesitated. Was that *really* what he wanted? If she

agreed, she wouldn't be Milla anymore and he certainly didn't want her to be anyone else.

Before he could say this, she burst out laughing.

'Are you *crazy*? Where would the fun be in that?'

'You're right,' he said, bending to kiss her again. Could the jetty be seen from the cottage? He couldn't remember. Because he wanted to—

He groaned, forcing himself to pull away.

'You are definitely right,' he said.

She fixed him with one of her typically 'Milla' looks.

'Of course I am,' she said. 'Trust me.'

A LETTER FROM THE AUTHOR

Dear reader,

Thank you so much for reading this book. I hope you have enjoyed Ben and Milla's story. I have lots more mysteries planned for Ben, Harriet and the new Murder Investigation Team at Raven's Edge to solve. If you'd like to be the first to hear about new releases and bonus content, you can click on the link below to sign up. Don't miss out!

www.stormpublishing.co/louise-marley

If you have enjoyed this book and could spare a few moments to leave a review that would be hugely appreciated. Even a short review can make all the difference in encouraging a reader to discover my books for the first time. Thank you so much!

Writing a book is like baking a cake. There's not just the one idea (ingredient) but several coming together to create the story. I had the original idea for this story, many years ago, when the image of a beautiful girl popped into my head. She was dressed in a ballgown and lying on a four-poster bed in a derelict mansion, and I had no idea why!

I've always loved fairy stories, particularly those with a darker edge, although I prefer them to have a traditional happy ending! I blame my grandparents, who bought me two huge books of fairy stories when I was about six years old. I also owned the Ladybird versions, particularly *Cinderella*, which I loved because she got to go to the ball three times in a succession of spectacular dresses. Yes, I know, I'm shallow: what can I say?

The third ingredient, the location, presented itself during one of my walks through the Welsh countryside, where I stumbled upon a ruined Palladian mansion, covered in ivy, with trees growing up through the rooms. It really did look as though it had come straight out of *Sleeping Beauty*!

Other influences include the Katharine Hepburn/Cary Grant film *Bringing up Baby*, and Lewis Carroll's *Alice's Adventures in Wonderland* – although you probably spotted that last one yourself! Mixed together, these elements became the book you have just read. I had such fun writing it. I do hope you've enjoyed reading it!

Thank you for being part of this journey with me. Do you want to know how Ben got that scar on his forehead? Why he doesn't get on with his family? What Harriet's father did to be called a hero? Do stay in touch. I have so many new stories planned!

You can contact me at louise@louisemarley.co.uk. I'd love to hear from you!

Louise x

louisemarley.co.uk

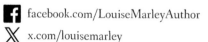

facebook.com/LouiseMarleyAuthor

x.com/louisemarley

instagram.com/louisemarleywrites

threads.net/@louisemarleywrites

ACKNOWLEDGEMENTS

Huge thanks to Kathryn Taussig for her belief in my work and being such a wonderful editor. Her insight helped me to polish this story into its very best version and breathe life into the village of Raven's Edge. Also, to Oliver Rhodes and the fabulous team at Storm for all the hard work that goes on behind the scenes. I'm very fortunate to work with some of the loveliest people in publishing!

Lots of love to my family for putting up with me. It is *very* difficult living with a writer, especially a writer with a deadline. I'm also sorry for the spoilers during movie night, the burnt/late/forgotten-to-cook dinners, and for leaving cold cups of coffee all around the house.

Big thanks to my writing buddies, Novelistas Ink, who are always there for me. I don't know what I'd do without their unwavering support. Special mention to Trisha Ashley and Juliet Greenwood for the caffeine-fuelled, brain-storming sessions at various cafés and garden centres throughout North Wales, and to Lottie Cardew, for her kind, supportive messages during some dark times, and introducing me to the fabulous Gladstone's Library!

Last but definitely not least, a big hug to my lovely readers for all your support, the shares on social media, the kind-hearted messages, and the wonderful reviews. You never fail to brighten my day!

Printed in Great Britain
by Amazon

46699619R00219